Just Relations

RODNEY HALL

Just Relations

THE VIKING PRESS   NEW YORK

C.1

LIBRARY OF CONGRESS CATALOGING IN PUBLICATION DATA
Hall, Rodney, 1935—
  Just relations.
  I. Title.
PR9619.3.H285J87   1983   823   82-40369
ISBN 0-670-41114-0

Printed in the United States of America
Set in Cloister

To the future: my darling daughters, Imogen, Delia and Cressida.

Acknowledgments

During the six years I worked on this novel I was most generously supported by the Literature Board of the Australia Council. I am grateful to the Board and glad to acknowledge their help.

The first person to read the complete manuscript was Iain McCalman. His enthusiasm and his advice on historical matters were of the greatest importance to me.

I was educated into the ways of the extremely aged by the late Mr Freddie Bowker, my grandmother Mrs Edith Buckland, and my godmother Mrs Vera Bridgstock-Choat; I am in debt to them all.

My wife and family – and friends too numerous to list here – helped influence the book and my views to be found in it.

Above all, I must thank Humphrey McQueen. His detailed editorial suggestions and challenging criticisms were an incalculable benefit. Without him, the novel would not have been provoked into being as it is.

Contents

The Mountain Road

```
Former gold mining town in Australia
fights to keep it's small town identity
in the face of progress.
```

<u>One</u>

If it's the day of the letters we're talking about, Miss Felicia Brinsmead was in top form.

And to think they once had a Chinese joss-house right on this plot my child, she said, standing in her shop expecting customers.

Only for a year or two, the shop objected.

My goodness you are a grumpy wreck of a thing, she laughed. Considering you're younger than I am.

Miserable, miserable, whispered the shop.

I've no patience with property anyway, she sniffed and gave her attention to the first of the letters which she held open in her hand, not yet sent. So she read it back to its author, her brother, that venerable man forever standing idle, his days spent observing the exchange of money and goods. His copperplate handwriting invested this letter with the authority of a legal document.

Dear Sir,

Thank you for your correspondence. We would wish you to convey back to the Australian Aesthetic and Historical Resources Commission the following information.

We residents of Whitey's Fall are aware that, as you point out, our 'historic township is falling into disrepair and ruin'. The fact is that we ourselves grow old. We do not wish you to spend a single dollar of your money on restoration here. The buildings have been used. They have done well enough for us. But we shall soon be dead; so let the place also fall into ruin.

We prefer not to enter into debate on the subject of our own lives; rather, we would ask you to extend us the courtesy of considering the matter closed.

Faithfully Yours, &c., on behalf of the residents of Whitey's Fall, I am,

S. Brinsmead, Esq.

Miss Brinsmead folded it along the creases, tweaked it with fingers already pink from handling things, and popped it in the envelope.

– You surpass yourself Sebastian, she declared. Wait till they get this. I entirely approve. Put so succinctly, there can be no excuse for misunderstanding us now.

He smiled but did not step forward to retrieve the letter. Smiled at it from a dream of Corfu, across sacks of potatoes and an insurrection of groceries, through waves of earthy scents he smiled, too pleased with her response to look her in the eye. The shop muttered, disgruntled, the cracks in its timber walls opening wider so that more convolvulus vines burst in from outside and cast garlands of vulgar flowers among the bins of sugar where they trembled, listening, purple with concentration.

– I shall post your letter when I take my outing, Miss Brinsmead promised.

Miserable, miserable, whispered the shop.

Next moment, the second letter arrived. It happened this way: The door opened and an unknown young woman stepped in. She hesitated, lost, while her eyes grew accustomed to the dim interior. Objects of glass and tin glinted messages, biscuit packets blinked exhausted cellophane eyes, spirit kettles sat with their spouts raised and trouser-presses lounged against the wall as if who cared? The young woman stood where she was at the entrance. For a moment, only the three human beings were inanimate. Who are you? grunted the hanging flitch of bacon so that its flies were disturbed and buzzed around irritably. A chorus of sou'wester-clad seamen sang from sardine tins their surprised North Sea chanties, powdered bananas from the Abdul Gonzalez Company of Manila leaked colonies of pollen, frozen chickens held their breath (lampooned by a shelf of corsets), rubber gloves gently and hopelessly cradled one another's sorrows. Glass cases showed the stranger herself as a ghost. All the tons of goods long since sold and eaten mourned from the shelves *requiem aeternam*.

While ladies' frocks clustered on their rack to gossip about her, the visitor stared amazed at the comprehensive range of items on sale. This was the only shop in a remote settlement; something foreign to her. Stacked round the counter stood twelve towers of newspapers, the bottom ones mouldy and kicked ragged, the top ones for sale but never sold; the dispensable murders of the past beneath the dispensable rapes of the day before yesterday, the fall of Singapore under the rise of valium; and all standardized in broadsheet and tabloid; millions of dollars' worth of truth-gathering squandered in the effort to persuade the citizens of Whitey's Fall that things are so. On one shelf new mousetraps were heaped among used traps with the mice still in them. A cat warming the sugared eucalyptus drops lay waiting to hypnotize a customer. And the whole place reeking of termite industry.

If I had brought you here, I would have taken you into this shop expecting to surprise you.

Miss Brinsmead behind the counter was made up of pillows, so large, so soft and white. But the instant you spoke to her she reacted with energy, her body colliding noiselessly with the fridge and the till; her eyes twinkling, blue irises outlined as crisply as a child's; her aged hands immediately on what she wanted; the *oof* of satisfaction as she reached up for your request, and her silk dress stretching in diagonal quivers across her back. The thing everybody noticed first was her hair. Like a hideous grey scab, she kept it as a matted lump crammed into a net, hanging down stiff and crackly against her back, an enormous bag which reached almost to her waist.

So, when that unknown woman came into the shop, this was the place as she found it and this was the person who stood ready to serve her.

The customer clasped her hands preparing for the indiscretion of delight. Were the Brinsmeads once again to be discovered, taken up, admired and found quaint? They knew the type. Miss Brinsmead adopted her most uncompromising manner and made ready to deny she stocked any of the young woman's desires.

– Excuse me, the stranger whispered.

Miss Brinsmead said nothing.

– I meant excuse me because I didn't mean to stare. It's all so solid. So ... well ... sensible.

At that one word, Miss Brinsmead fell in love with her.

– You see, the young woman explained. I'd hoped it would be like this. Though it's better, richer. Oh do *please* excuse me. I'm making myself ridiculous. I have a letter here. I'm looking for a Mr Sebastian Brinsmead. Could you tell me ...

– I'll take it, Miss Brinsmead offered tenderly. I'll take it for him. So she took it, opening it right there and then without explaining who she was or what right she had. She read the letter out loud, embellishing it with comments as she went. *Dear Seb,* my goodness who's it from? Sebastian, the letter's from Anne McTaggart: Annie Lang! a letter from the dead. How delightful. How interesting. *If you have not forgotten an old acquaintance,* she says, *you will surely do me a favour,* one wonders what possessed her to use a word like acquaintance, though.

Emerging from the loom of his musings, concealing reluctance with mildness, the old man detached himself from the wall to witness the letter in person. A full white beard clothed his massive chest with wisdom and softened the buttoned-up Boer War tunic he had inherited from his father.

– This is my brother Mr Sebastian Brinsmead, Miss Brinsmead explained politely. *A favour,* mark you, she goes on, *I dare say you are well in command of Whitey's Fall by now, you have had sixty years to make it since I saw you last, all said and done!* there's a touch of bitter truth in that, my dear. Annie always was a sharp one wasn't she? *this letter is being brought by a dear young woman who is buying the house off me.* Well now that is surprising. That is the first genuinely surprising thing to have happened here for goodness knows how long. Buying the house! Let me take a look at you, Miss Brinsmead suggested, and proceeded to do so. Where were we? ... *is buying the house off me. It's no use to me now, after all.* Why not, one wonders? But then we know nothing whatsoever about her life since she left. *Please be sure she manages alright, I am certain that I may depend upon you of all people,* there's a little bouquet for you Sebastian. *Give my love to all my friends and most of my blood relations.* Ha ha ya har. Good old Annie, she still hasn't forgotten or forgiven apparently. *Ever yours,* she signs herself. What a very peculiar thing to put. *Ever yours, may the good Lord bless and keep you,* oh dear that's a bit provoking. Signed *Anne McTaggart.* So! what are we to think? This is an event. And why do you have an English accent?

– Because I'm English, the woman answered rather primly, beginning to feel some distaste for this lady's bluntness. And my name, she added with intentional testiness, is Vivien.

– You think I'm taking liberties with you, the quick Miss

7

Brinsmead observed. But why should we behave like strangers if you're to live here Vivien? You may call me Miss Brinsmead. We're very casual in Whitey's Fall.

Sebastian Brinsmead took the letter and read it through for himself.

– This is singularly precious, he explained. I am grateful to you for bringing it. You see, Annie Lang, or Mrs McTaggart as she became, was a missing thread. It's very satisfying to feel we have connections, continuity, in the face of death, in the face of a heathen dependence on the self.

– Sebastian you're shocking her, Miss Brinsmead warned. You are making her wonder what sort of town she's come to. We don't want to frighten anybody away. That's the last thing.

– Thank you, Vivien said smiling especially for him. I understand exactly what you mean. I really do hope there's a place for me here. The first thing to do is to find the house and then lay in some supplies.

Miss Brinsmead offered to arrange everything. She went round plumping against the shelves, filling a box with essentials and calling from the door to a Young Tony who, she assured the new arrival, would happily drive her up to the house with her provisions and her luggage (was that her luggage outside, those two suitcases and nothing more?), her bright eyes returning again and again to this new object of love, her scab of hair swinging so it creaked. And a giant youth called into being at the door, grinning, cracking his knuckles and going to pieces entirely on being introduced to an unknown female. Miss Brinsmead supervising, Tony tucked one heavy case under his arm, picked up the other with that same hand and then cradled the box of groceries on his free arm.

– Why must you walk up to the house, the old lady demanded dismayed, when you could easily get a vehicle and drive her up?

But that's how they went, the wind chasing them with fragments of advice and instructions to call down any time. So Felicia Brinsmead returned to her place behind the counter with a new grip on life. The day's newspaper felt her palm on it, the sweet dark of time suppressed, the Prime Minister on page one kissed her hand. Fat lot Miss Brinsmead cared for him! She thought only of Vivien with her English voice and her delicious coldness.

– I shall introduce her to Remembering, she promised the shop.

Who had the right if she hadn't, being leader and discoverer? People ought to be grateful. It was evident from the day of her birth that she would found a religion, considering she could remember being born. Even details. Conception occurred on 22 January 1901 at the exact moment Queen Victoria died. This was, in the purest sense, coincidence. Nine months later promptly she was born. She remembered it this way: as a sensation of intolerable speed, falling, she was travelling above moon craters upside down and weightless, feet first, head first, outerspace flying past her, black with a high wind noise. She hurtled headlong, recklessly towards the creation of light, rocked red by an earthquake. Some calamity impending. In the grasp of forces beyond her will. And then the earthquake settled into a repetitious thudding. Pulsations kneaded her flesh, hugging, pushing, rejecting. She suffered anguished reminders of that familiar life of pure feeling when it was she whose body pulsed like this, she herself who created the shape of pain. The rush of her coming lessened, she existed only as a pit of nausea. Her tremendous fear blazed scarlet. The rushing wind stopped. She was the sole ark to be spewed up by the flood. The panic which seized her was the clamouring of last survivors: her skin full of beasts with fangs and spines, wings unfolding, scaly coils flexing, the desperate working of gills, a menagerie of coupling forms. There came a particular moment (as the sun rises) when her round shell began to edge out of its horizon. The pan of her skull the sun, a flaring circle on the crown gradually lipping down. The terrifying brightness in that head already illuminating her world. By the sensation of streaming hair and crawling scalp, of watery joints and shivering, she knew she had been through this before. The fiery eyes, hot behind their lids, slid up beyond the rim of earth. Air itself exploded into her, shimmering. Her nose fluttered. Her mouth was free: she spoke her first word.

What happened after this was the sound of her mother's screaming. The laying on of violent hands ...

Now look at me! Felicia Brinsmead thought, as she arranged herself to receive customers, giving her lump of hair a good shake, and drumming with her soft fat fingers on the dead newspapers.

– I shall introduce Vivien to Remembering, she said.

Her brother heard but chose not to comment. He, too, was perhaps a little in love with this young woman who had encouraged him to believe she understood about continuity. Might she be another Christian at last? Was it so very unlikely? Why should he argue with Felicia? He had told her his views on this heresy of hers, she knew perfectly well and in detail. Often enough he had reiterated his opinion that Remembering was a satanic game to be lumped with The Night Watch, Parsifal and Anna Karenina. She'd fly into a temper and cosset him as if dealing with an imbecile, she'd spoil lunch taking the trouble to din in that her religion was religious whereas art was a heap of agreeable baubles of an altogether lower order. Felicia enjoyed condescending to art, having inspected a good deal. There's altogether too much art in the world, was one of her sayings. And what would be the point of his counter-attacking or citing her weakness for the art of conversation as evidence? Small comfort, the truth. In conversation her taste ran to the rococo.

– How old are you Sebastian?

– Eighty-two.

– Strange number don't you think? In a sense a warning to one.

They were proud of their style, their subjunctives, their rigorously adjectival thats, their whoms and third person impersonals.

– Oh no it's a benevolent number Felicia.

– Well most certainly it's not like seventy-three.

– Were you to ask my opinion I'd call seventy-three positively forbidding.

– You see! you do understand, you're not wholly insensitive to the finer things, my dear. Forbidding is seventy-three to a T. I feel it.

– I shall have to laugh perhaps.

– What a child you are Sebastian. When I was your age I'd have been perfectly serious about such a question.

– Ignorance is armour of a kind, I dare say.

– Just because I'm seventy-three doesn't mean I've never been eighty-two. Where's the logic in that, I should like to be told.

For the sake of style she would sometimes pursue the issue at irritating length. If challenged to defend the odd proposition, she instantly did so at such a pitch of fervour there was no stopping her, you simply had to ride out her glittering torrent of words. And all the time she'd nod her head agreeing with herself, the bundle of hair loyally bouncing, her hands describing solid weights in the air, her tongue flicking out to keep her lips shiny as she liked them, her bosom heaving and her lungs gasping for a break. Enough to daunt a braver man. So Mr Sebastian Brinsmead, author of that stern letter to the Australian Aesthetic and Historical Resources Commission, retired to his place against the wall to contemplate the gentle feelings he associated with the woman Vivien, whose surname, he was now aware, remained unknown.

Having seen the new arrival safely escorted to her house by that halfwit Tony McTaggart, Felicia Brinsmead settled behind the counter. And there she stayed for a week. Vivien called in every so often for milk, bread, meat, this and that, a good morning and a chat, and accepted the choicest apples without suspecting how lovingly they'd been set aside, but occasionally being unpleasantly surprised to find treats in her basket when she got home, unwanted tokens of favour which she promptly took back. But at the end of the week Miss Brinsmead had calmed down. The likelihood that if she wasn't careful she'd be made to suffer once more persuaded her to pull her horns in. The ache of being rebuffed was something she could do without at any age. And what for? In return for generosity? Was she to be slighted by a young chit of no more than thirty or forty when she herself had nothing to gain by her kindnesses? Decidedly not.

– Decidedly not, Felicia Brinsmead announced one morning as the door opened.

11

The usual subtle change happened. Because a customer had come in, the contents of the shop displayed themselves, rustling and primping. The sagging timbers mocked his arrival.

– Miserable, miserable, the shop muttered.

The double doors on their springs clashed-to behind him, batting at the invasion of flies attempting to follow him in. He didn't look round at the doors, so you knew he wasn't surprised, you could tell he was used to the racket, hadn't noticed the play of light on those gilded glass scrolls PROVISIONS PATENT MEDICINES (on one door), HABERDASHERY BOOTS & SHOES (on the other). He was a young man in jeans and a blue singlet, his bare arms warming the whole shop, his laceless boots flopping open like a couple of faithful dogs at ankle. No sooner was this customer inside than he began speaking to the appearance of Felicia Brinsmead floating behind the counter, brown air veiling her with secrets. She grew more substantial in company because of this talent she had for drawing off people's ideas and pumping herself up with them. One hand flat on the day's date, she waited to be spoken to. The man cleared his throat with the first word.

– Half a dozen sticks of gelignite please Miss Brinsmead, he said as he advanced keeping his eyes down but his voice making him sound quite the man of the world. Plus a fuse, he added when no reaction came. About twenty feet of that please. And some detonators too.

The shop trapped him in an interrogation of silence. He inspected his broken fingernails.

– Or dynamite would do instead, he suggested helpfully. There's a job to be done. He now looked directly at her, his eyes defiant and dark with innocence.

The woman moved. So large and soft she was, she filled him with wonder. When she coughed she coughed in a high girlish voice that surprised people. But now she was not put out enough to cough. She was amused. Her lips moved in sympathy with his, shaping the young man's words before he could get them out, helping him with the difficult job of making such a conspicuous

12

request, her moony face already animated, she could hardly wait to speak her own words.

– When is it needed? she asked.

You couldn't help noticing her eyes snap alert and blue so that he was afraid she knew his secret, even though this was impossible. She nodded encouragingly. The thump of grey hair knocked at her back. So she faced the customer with her question about when he needed his gelignite. Attentive, she anticipated his reply, her lips ready with the syllables while he admitted them. But he was used to her and her ways. He had shopped here all his life. He knew her face, the fifteen expressions none of which could be trusted, also her famous hair. Legend had it that her hair had never been cut since the day she was born. Perhaps because mothers will do anything to keep their children as they were when manageable and therefore lovable. Or might there have been some superstition in the family? Isn't it common knowledge that after death the one thing the virtuous take with them to the next world is their hair? Wasn't this why, seventy years ago, a wild lad named Kel McAloon dug up his dead cousin a fortnight from the burial to snip off a pinch of bristle from the chin, and later turned savage and a government agent as a result? Who could explain how Felicia Brinsmead's hair had, at the bottom of its sack, a protruding wisp of gold, one curl of child's hair which some miracle kept young and delicate?

Using the simple expedient of asking her for an article on the shelf behind her, I might have shown you this hair long enough for you never to forget.

– Right away I need it, the customer eventually answered in his assertive young voice. I needed it yesterday.

At this the military uniform in the corner shook with cultured laughter and wagged its white beard: yesterday, how could you need explosives yesterday! It was the sort of nonsense he delighted in, frail whiskers catching on the buttons of his tunic, and whiskers wandering free behind his ears. The customer greeted him with the politeness left over from childhood.

– I'll see for you, Miss Brinsmead promised. She made it her business to drift about, bouncing off the furniture, parting the veils of bacon smells, as if the stock of lethal weapons might be in among chocolate creams or washing soaps. But who knows what was going on beneath her shopkeeper's decorum? Perhaps she wasn't really paying attention to the present, perhaps she was reliving the time she had run through London, her long skirts heavy with rain, dodging hansom cabs and dogs, looking for somewhere to shelter, the steam rising from her woollen jacket mildly obnoxious and altogether too personal. Miss Brinsmead confronted the customer with kindly despair.

– No luck, Billy. I shall check outside if you wish. Offering this much hope, and why not, she backed through a curtainway to the house behind the shop.

The young man was left with the helplessness of those not reconciled to waiting. Unemployed at the counter, he glanced about as if observant. Jesus, he thought, this shop's a bloody junk heap. Those old dresses hanging as thick with dust as a lot of thin women in a fog.

– Nice drop of rain, he said to Mr Brinsmead who smiled.

Take those gumboots up there, must be perished by now. You don't see anything like this when you shop in Yalgoona. Mind you Yalgoona stocks one hundred percent garbage, whereas here at Whitey's you can still get things that'll last, even if they are worn out when you buy them.

– Bit of a cold snap this morning though Mr Brinsmead. It shut the damn frogs up, he went on conversationally. Just getting a go on, they were, when bang, cold snap hits them. Bit of humour in the bush, he explained as he turned away from the smiling lunatic.

Considered however you like, the Brinsmeads, brother and sister, were mysterious in their ways. For one thing, they had left Whitey's Fall twenty-three times and always returned to be the people's link with what was happening out there, telling the sort of thing the radio or television kept back. They understood that a person would want to know the condition of the soul in Los Angeles, how much the land was loved in Portugal, who first spoke the word Zaire, and if there were snowcapped mountains

14

on the equator did the people grow shorter and fatter the higher up the slopes they lived? They brought back tidings of the different rhythms of the Pacific and the Atlantic, the progress of butterfly migrations.

Billy, for a moment of wonder, knew how it was to be Sebastian Brinsmead, brother of the bat with her mind-reading. What else would you do but stand with your back to the wall tuning in to another world and occasionally leaking a bit of an overflow of laughter? You couldn't help sympathizing.

Miss Brinsmead returned and took up her station at the counter where it was still warm, placing her hand over the indiscretion of today. She made her announcement.

– We have none in stock so it is to be supposed we can't do a thing about it until another order comes in, Billy. She was a heap of cauliflowers.

The customer slapped the counter with annoyance. The sardine-can choristers sang joyfully. He bought an ounce of tobacco and some cigarette papers which his father had challenged him not to forget, and then left without another word. The worst fears of the frozen chickens were confirmed. The veteran nodded his halo knowingly. The promises on the double-doors shuddered. The cat lay among the eucalyptus drops, licking aromatic sugar from its paws, feeling through its skin those mouse corpses further along the shelf, breathing dry papery air, reducing the recent intruder to a mere slit in its eye.

– Time for lunch Sebastian. Time to close the shop. Sebastian would you please close the shop? Miss Brinsmead was ordering her brother about as usual.

– So it's time for luncheon? Very well, but you know what this means? He tottered away from his supporting wall and clutched the door.

– I know what everything means, that's a fact you've never understood about me. Saying this, she removed her hand from today's date, leaving it at large, challenging the world to cope as best it may, inviting a generation's barbarities to slip out in search of new contexts.

– Latch is loose. Bolt getting too stiff. Must oil it, the dummy

15

commented. Himself hinged and folded double now, becoming desperate as thin evils of greed plastered themselves against the glass, seeking the crack he struggled to close.

– You're ageing with use, there lies the ruin.

– What would you. Suppose. Felicia. That young fellow. Might want. Gelignite for? He grunted as the bolt gave under his huge strength and rasped home. He pulled down the rattling blinds with the air of a man who has done the right thing.

– How should I know about science, with *him* in the house? she whispered. But what a very agreeable girl we're to have among us, she said loudly. Fancy her buying that place with not much of it fit to live in. So it's lunchtime at last. Let's go through, I'm quite peckish.

– After you my dear.

– Thank you my dear.

He looked down at her filthy lump of hair as she walked in front of him, acknowledging that she had at least this to show for her life's work.

– Shall I call him to the kitchen, Felicia?

– Not yet. I'll make the tea, then he will have no excuse.

Mr Brinsmead caught his sister shooting him one of those side-long glances.

– Ahh, it's a relief to sit. My goodness I've a fine hunger in me.

– I cannot imagine why you stand all day against the wall like some beastly martyr. At your age. You put the customers off.

– I never sit in there, he insisted.

– That's just what I said.

Felicia watched him fondly. What a decorative old buffer he'd made of himself. And the conversation pleased her. She attended to kitchen matters, waiting for him to say something else, knowing what it would be before he could speak the words.

– Did you see the startled way that young fellow reacted when I laughed Felicia? His surprise took me aback considering he has known me all his life. And so on.

– Who's this?

– Our customer, young whatshisname. How could you forget

16

already. It's those things you eat, brown rice and wild plants, they affect your memory.

– I heard you laughing and I thought, he doesn't know what he's doing laughing at someone else. I feel bound as a sister to tell you frankly Sebastian you have become a very strange man, and there's no end in it.

Weary of this ancient and self-perpetuating folly, he reverted to the other topic of the morning.

– One wonders what that young woman might think of Annie's place.

– You mean will she settle?

– Oh she won't stay, Sebastian decided promptly, sadly.

– I believe you're wrong. Well dear, I'm ready. Time for Fido, the tea is waiting, and anyway he'll take ten minutes to cross the corridor. And this is the age of jet propulsion they say. I shall laugh soon myself.

– Fido, Fido! you are required for lunch, called the old man raising his massive head and setting frail whiskers aflutter. Please come now old chap. Can you hear me? He never answers. It's those liberal ideas about free upbringing that make him so rude.

– I can remember, I can remember ... the same thing being said to me before. I remember Julius, you see Sebastian, Julius Caesar, the Italian one you know, leaping out of bed one morning. When I put my hand across to his side, to where he had been sleeping, it was not only warm but damp. What on earth would you make of that?

– What did you make of it is more to the point.

– I don't recall. It was a long time ago. And perhaps it didn't strike me as irregular.

– Was it a hot night?

– Oh the weather! she dismissed the weather as too trivial for the grandeur of her history.

– I'm trying to be helpful, being well aware how aggravating it is not to know the reasons for something.

– Reasons reasons. You're still victim to the French and their timid obsession with proof. Why else do you think laboratories are boiling harmless animals to observe whether it kills them?

17

– I don't see what that has to do with the French I really don't. Nor with Julius Caesar for that matter Felicia. He touched her hand affectionately; really she was one of the wonders.

– We never had anything peculiar happen did we, you and I? Not in our bed. Nothing. For years. Do stop that awful neighing. You're so sudden. It stands my hair on end.

– My hair has stood on end any number of times, he said artlessly.

– Why doesn't Fido answer. He knows it distresses me.

– Fido! Please forget your modern disposition old chap. The tea is in the cup, I warn you. I do believe he's coming at last. Such condescension.

– It's doubtful that the night could have been particularly hot because we were up at Gessoriacum on the edge of the empire. There you are Fido, at long last. The tea's in the cup. One must learn manners if one is to be liked by this hateful world. No Sebastian, you can't conceive how I suffer because I'm not free of what everybody else has been. Stop slurping Fido, I can't bear the noise.

– A story, her brother replied inconsequentially, is the autobiography of an imagination. He turned kindly to Fido. I want you to remember that, as we begin your education.

Two

Whitey's Fall perches halfway up a mountainside, the mountain the people created. Year by year they accumulated the knowledge, the experience. They have the words so they know how to live with it. By their toughness they survived to heap up its bluffs, by scepticism they etched its creekbeds. They've lived and spoken every part of this mountain, they've dreamed it and cursed it, looked to it for salvation and penance. Its outcrops of granite are the very ones the people named, quarried and picnicked on before you could say there really was a mountain in this place at all. And the forest covering tells of its secrecy.

So the mountain came to be there and indifferent to the people, those clinging whittlers in mud burrows. The mountain stood up, hunched and massive, shouldering into the rain, drenched and indistinct; just as it sprawled in the sun drifting with spirits of steam and giving out birdsong from grateful pores; so it crackled with frost and early morning, yellow robins with twiggy legs hopping among the crystals, spiderwebs drooping under the weight of clear beads; so it hissed softly when dust storms swirled round it, deceived into becoming a grainy sepia photograph of itself. All the while, whatever the season, the mountain was busy. The life of the mountain had to go on. Water wavered in trickles of hair down to the gullies, runnels joined together with a sparkling clash. Soil broke apart to re-form itself as grass, grasstrees, fern and treefern, vines and huge eucalypts for the vines to hang from. Rock strata at the mountain's heart, with inconceivable slowness, tilted themselves, turning in millennial sleep, the seams of quartz fracturing brittle as glass, clay compacting to stone, fissures appearing and closing, soil falling away to reveal cliffs and cliffs crashing one by one down the mountainside in a flurry of gold dust. And the mountain created a wind appropriate to its shape, so the wind set and that's how it remained.

In those times the Aborigines of the region, the Koories, had no knowledge of any such mountain. Neither did they know nor care about gold. And but for gold, who would have stayed here at all? The people were families of diggers. Never mind that later they turned their hand to dairy farming and making cheese.

Whitey's Fall is also a religious centre. Meetings are held in the public bar of the Mountain Hotel every day except Sunday. It's a religion of remembering, observed over pots of beer. A stranger coming in during this remembering could be excused for failing to notice anything unusual. Except perhaps the age of the drinkers who are mostly between eighty and one hundred-and-fourteen. The lack of conversation isn't so very remarkable either. True, the people drink in silence because they need to concentrate, but even here on this remote mountainside in New South Wales among ridges of virgin rainforest and at the end of a screwing dirt road, a television flickers above the publican's head. The set leaks a humdrum of commentary on the *coup d'état* in Ethiopia, the Luxemburg hot-air balloon championships, and the exhibits of a now paralysed actress who has provoked more fantasies throughout the Western World (this part of which lies in the Far East) than any other female in its entire history. So the television drones on, leaving the entranced drinkers to live again their memories of other times; thoughts primitive enough for the enemies of Babylon, those nocturnal marauders in their dogskin nightshoes.

Such visitors as there are, in any case, don't like to stare. After all, death in its grotesque forms awaits us, every. one. And they do find themselves among people exhibiting a gallery of the least-desired aspects of age: figures of arthritic gnomes and of huge dislocated ruins, here a mutilated neck, there a cast eye, hands appearing hand-made, fat noses and sticking-out ears, skin grown part vegetable, hair in the wrong places. And they find the women in such respects oddly difficult to distinguish from the men. What's more, most of these ancient ugly folk resemble each other to a disconcerting degree, even the bloated village idiot with his babyish forehead, his puffy eyelids and thick dry lips bears clear traces of family.

The Mountain Hotel is the obvious place for intellectual pursuits, having the right atmosphere, the patrons the appropriate introspective tone. Here piety can be free from ostentation, it is possible to be committed to an idea. The pub is the last place where people can afford to be collectively serious; and in the case of Whitey's Fall this is a privilege available to the whole town, the population being forty-nine and the bar-room moderately large.

I speak in the present tense, which is not quite accurate, things have changed lately. The description I've given you of Whitey's Fall would be hotly denied now, especially in official quarters. But in a country where there are no great buildings, where there has never been the will to conceive of great buildings (which is to say, great and permanent functions) history is always in the present. It is ridiculous to postulate the past as something separate. Why, men are still getting drunk here who drove bullock wagons up the range into the backcountry; McAloon and Whitey, discoverers of the McAloon-Whitey nugget, eleventh largest hunk of gold ever unearthed, died only last year and the year before, respectively. We have a woman here who attended the creation of Australia as a nation state, and to the present day holds in her head a living image of the Duke of York performing the ceremony of Federation, the great leap forward or as Miss Felicia Brinsmead commented, that pompous ritualizing of small-minded fears and back-biting compromise ... as though she could remember.

Three

Look once more at the street outside Brinsmeads' general store. Bill Swan, the customer who wanted gelignite, stood in the spring sunshine, not quite decided what to do next but aware he would never grow tall. Whether to go on waiting here or wait elsewhere was the question while he became as passive as the earth underneath his own feet. He felt he could experience himself as a deadweight on two heels. Also the weight of his trunk on his pelvis, yes bearing down, and his neck carrying the weight of his head full of rebellions. The weight of arms hung from his shoulders. He opened and clenched the hand in his pocket; lumps of muscle rose along his forearm and at the back of his upper arm when he pushed his fist against his thigh, which he now did. The muscles also could be felt by their own weight. This might have puzzled him had he been in a thinking rather than a feeling mood.

What he did think a few moments later was the short, dreadful sentence: I'm nineteen. Yes, with that blank future ahead too. This is what he thought while waiting for Tony McTaggart to come blinking out of the iron shed where he worked, head stuck forward like a snake from a dark cave, expectant and defensive at the same time. Billy Swan rocked on his heels, watching.

I'm nineteen, he told himself against all possibility of being understood, perhaps to forget that he had openly tried to buy gel-ignite, gambling everything on being casual, and for no result. I won't grow any taller now, he thought, being in the habit of casting the stone of his shortness at himself till he might one day become numb to the fact and not notice any longer: as he had once practised swallowing tadpoles. An old wound re-opened obligingly. I used to be only an inch shorter than Tony a couple of years back.

If Tony, that timid giant with his fuzz of fair hairs, were to stand beside Billy this moment you'd find it hard to credit. Harder for Bill to acknowledge there had been any change, the recent past of childhood seeming closer to the natural order than the uncertain present. And hard for him to suffer the gently protective behaviour of his friend. He thinks he's bloody somebody, Billy objected savagely, wishing Tony would hurry, hoping nothing had gone wrong, and thinking contemptuously: if I could be his size I would be somebody. Yet Billy's shortness was not so immediately noticeable as his face with its bold features; nose large and fine and, from under thick eyebrows, brilliant dark eyes that challenged a world of too few experiences.

Outside in the sun, with his back to the shop, Bill Swan brooded on how Miss Brinsmead had refused to sell him the gel-ignite he needed. Of course she had some hidden away. The reason she wouldn't sell it was that she didn't know what it was for. Her claim to know everything brought her power in the community. Who gives a stuff for her, he thought now his real worry loomed to the surface like a stingray from unplumbed depths: the plan, the risk, the explosion; and he must face the townsfolk afterwards.

He scuffed the dust, waiting. He balled his fist trying hidden tests of strength against himself. Why the hell couldn't Tony be on time: he had nothing else to do but put down his tools and step out of the shed. Then they could have a pie and a beer at the pub and things mightn't seem so complicated.

The little township sagged and sighed around him, an ever-present wind prising the trellis from the porch of Whitey's Fall School of Arts. Bill stood, the sole figure in that pointillist dust, among flaked and peeling walls, buildings insubstantial and camouflaged. Belonging imprinted itself on every aspect of his body's language; the way he wasn't looking about him, the bored shoulders, the one hitched-up hip bearing his whole weight. He hated waiting. To express his exasperation he faced up the hill, watching a single chicken emerge from under a fence and make her enquiring way along the middle of the street. Now at his left shoulder stood the monument to the unforgotten Fallen of a forgotten war (a symbolic granite column broken short halfway) beside which he'd propped his motorcycle. Behind it drooped the façade of Brinsmeads', two tiers of verandahs exhaustedly grappled to the wall, overhung by boulders pointing up to the vast forested slopes of the mountain beyond. Bill Swan was at the lower end of the main street of his hometown Whitey's Fall. To his right, the ornate drinking fountain awaited hot lips in front of the welder's shed where Tony McTaggart was still working five minutes late. The bellchimes of a heavy hammer must be Tony, old man Ping no longer had the strength surely?

Underfoot the dust shifted. Before him, that single street of goldrush buildings wound grittily up the mountain. You had only to turn off between any two buildings to be instantly in the countryside, confronted by paddocks tipped crazily on edge and gymnastic cattle walking their tightrope trails or standing still with their eyes shut to recover from vertigo. The forested peaks and ridges beyond the town were, he knew, pocked with abandoned mineshafts. As for the hinterland, it was uninhabited and commonly believed to be dangerous with the forces of Aboriginal spirits: little mountain men, the hairy men, gunjes and the like. This territory stretched a hundred miles to the west, a thousand miles to the south, and three thousand miles north where it was said islands like stepping stones connected it with the secret tribal grounds of New Guinea headhunters.

Jesus a man could hate this place, Bill Swan thought as he began automatically whistling a few notes. Jesus he could too. Once more he swung on his heel, for the sake of change. That one awful looming thought of what he must do, kept down by a succession of trivial occupations. He busied himself with an unseeing examination of Brinsmeads'. After two more minutes he'd leave; wouldn't wait longer if it was the Governor-bloody-General. Spread away to his left, the plain far below finally merged in a blurred line with the east coast and the sea. Just as the crest of Whitey's Fall hill butted straight into the foot of the mountain peak, so the bottom of the hill dropped away another thousand feet to the valley floor. The waterfall a short walk from where Billy stood tumbled so far that it ended as a snailslick down the rockface. This was where boys of his father's generation habitually whipped each other to such daredevilry that D'Arcy Collins had the privilege of throwing himself off for the sake of the mountain, and after bouncing twice into the cliff his body was never seen again on earth.

To fill in time Billy read the painted curlicues on the shop doors, which he'd known all his life without suspecting they actually meant something. HABERDASHERY... what in the hell? PROVISIONS ... memories of arithmetic? and the rest. Then old man Brinsmead was there, leaning against the doors to shut them and force the bolts home, his face going pink. After this he straightened, reaching tall, filling the space, began to draw down the holland blinds while Bill stared at him.

Very slow and shaky he is too, must be a couple of hundred years old, and all made of porcelain. Weird bloody place. Imagine being a stranger. What would you see? Little grotty houses too small to stand up in probably. How do people live like this? What do they do? How does time pass; knitting, watching themselves in the mirror, poking at cobwebs, still fiddling with crystal radios and cats' whiskers? Ought to shout in a loud voice, foreign accent, see what happens: suspicious face in every window, portraits in frames, doors being shut by unseen hands, chains slipped from three-legged dogs. Ought to go up and try the bubbler which failed to work the day it was declared open and ever since. They'd lynch me. Never done. Dirty. Stink I suppose.

So Billy Swan had the idea: to put lips to the drinking fountain and turn the tap on, the putrifying gases of disappointed generations would sigh up into his mouth and poison his brain. He thought of it with his back to it. A voice spoke loudly into his ear, but it was not Tony.

– Look out for me gammy leg, the voice said gaily. Or I'll dong ya with me walkin stick.

– Goodday Uncle. Billy turned to find Uncle there sure enough and beaming.

– I said to old dog Bertha I said I haven't seen Bill these three days. Course me dog took no notice a what I said, no more'n me wife did, time I was with her. He chewed on his gums before adding in the lilting telegramese peculiar to the mountain – Dog's much of a muchness with wife: one word a command from me and she'd do whatever pleased erself. Winning form!

Uncle was no taller than Billy, indeed he was the same build though going to fat with extreme wear. Standing there together smiling at each other for no particular reason, you'd immediately pick the family resemblance, that stubborn squareness, two blocks of seasoned wood, equal pieces in a chess game. Yet their tough brown faces were welcoming, their broad hands describing friendly gestures.

– Was you on yer way to the house a consolation then?

– Only waiting for Tony, Uncle.

– In that case we'll wait together.

Despite his crusty manner, the old man was too courteous to suggest they cross the road and call for Tony: if Bill hadn't done so already, there must be a reason. He settled himself to wait, leaning on his two walkingsticks.

– Never get married son, that's my advice. Speakin as your only survivin grandfather, I've got one piece of advice worth givin from a long life of doin. Never get married and never be first with a girl. Uncle thrust out his head, his humorous eyes watchful, seeing if this sagacity had sunk in.

– You're a fine one to talk of not marrying! his grandson returned tolerantly.

– I shouldn't wonder if churches was the invention of women in the first place.

– You wouldn't want to let my father hear you say it to me.

– That no-hoper! Uncle spat. Tell yer what, son, if you turn out like him I shan't go on lettin you buy me a beer. Him. He'd shear a sheep's face he's that greedy. Ay? Speak up. I can't catch your words.

– Didn't say a thing, Billy replied ready to laugh.

– More fool you. If you can't see your father's worth a pinch a pigshit and not a penny more how'll you ever learn to judge strangers? How'll you discriminate? Tell me that now.

They were conspirators, the bond strong. The buildings hunching closer projected sharp shadows on the dazzling dust.

– He's at me to marry, you know.

Uncle cast his eyes up in despair, opening his pale mouth and slapping the gums shut again. There could have been a tear in his eye.

– What's in it for him anyway? Did you find that out?

– Fair go! How can I ask a thing like that?

– It's how you can't that has me beat. Simple. You grab a hold a him and say look here you bastard what's in this marriage crap for you? Simple. You got a tongue I suppose? You got brains? An if he hits you, yer hit im back. Pinch a pigshit, though it hurts me to say so. And I should know, I sired him, all said and done. Time you woke up to yourself. Hop in for your cut.

Uncle shifted his weight from his wrists and scratched in the dust with the rubbers of his walkingsticks. Himself the biggest mug kissing a youthful Bertha McAloon and her busy locking him up with her skinny fingers. A new idea struck him.

– Oy, what're we loafin about here for? There's good cold beer to be drunk up the road.

– I told you. We're waitin for young Tony, said Bill slipping into the old man's rhythm and tone of voice.

– Who? Uncle's massive head swung on its gristly neck to catch the scoundrel creeping up on him.

– Tony. Young Tony.

– E's no younger than you I dare say. And twice your size. Solid as a stud bull that bloke. Dare say you wouldn't mind bein built like him instead of bein a runt like all us Swans?

– Runt yourself, grunted Billy, blood fluttering momentarily across his vision.

– Oh yes, right enough I'm a runt, Uncle agreed cheerfully. And had ninety year to get accustomed. Bein a runt's better than kickin shit, so long as you can say to yourself I'm a runt so what the hell.

– Well I won't.

Mr Swan Senior glared, denying that this lad meant the world to him, trampling flowers underfoot, his tough face calculating, judging. He clashed his sticks together in frustration.

– You can't, more like, he bellowed, his fears confirmed. Runs in the family. That was the beginnin of your father's trouble. He was going good till the point came when he couldn't face bein what he was, a runt like you Billy.

– I'm sick of preachers. One of these days I might give you a friendly thump just to shut you up.

– Knock the sticks out from under me, would you? cried the old man excitedly.

– Why not?

Uncle's gust of anger turned to amusement.

– Can't say I blame you. Listenin to advice never was my style and I don't see why it should be yours neether. Winnin form! Talkin of yer grandmother, he went on, I blame Ireland for a lot of her troubles, she's got it on the brain. Poor Ireland, with Saint Patrick fool enough to rob the country of snakes. Where does that leave the spirit of the soil, I should like to know? Typical religious Johnny, full a business and never knowin what's what.

The wandering street was a rough rivercourse of sunshine flowing down to envelop them. The wind had eased and shifted a couple of degrees south so that the lowing of a distressed cow reached them distantly, a baritone edging up the scale. Or at least Bill heard it.

– What're ya lookin at? Don't keep the world a secret. One thing more botherin than another about the deafness is you miss out on why everybody's goin where.

– Only a cow. Mrs Ping's Alice by the sound of her, having trouble calving.

– Not surprisin with the weight she had on her. By Christ she put up a fight last time too. I like the beast with spirit. And Mrs Ping'll be doin whatever has to be done, you can bet on that. Uncle waved his stick at the School of Arts, a humble structure, its weatherboards brown and grey as a fungus grown on the spot and dying. See that heart painted up by the roof? I haven't showed you that before have I? Up above the vent thing. God struth, my eyes is better than yours. A heart, see, big as your belly. That brown-lookin paint was red one time.

– Be buggered!

– No one taught you how to look. That's your story. I knew, a course, seein I was the fella who painted it up there.

Shoulder by shoulder they gazed, with all the time in the world, at the peak of the building, above which two thrusting clouds parted momentarily to reveal a feathered shape of space, blue wings suspended over that memorial to love. Neither man noticed, their concentration being of a purely historical and personal kind.

– Long ladder.

– No way! Regular monkey I was then. Shinned up the verandah posts at the side. Over the back roof and up the gutterin. What should happen but the blasted pipe came loose in me hand. Near cost me somethin I shouldn't mention. Your age I was, and mad, in love, that is. On to the top roof I went. I didn't crawl neether. I stood up there and put back me stupid head and bellowed like a dumb animal. Talk of that cow. A bloke could do that sort a thing in them days. You didn't have to worry what other people thought. Most of all you didn't have to trouble what you'd think of yourself. You just got up and did it. So I went skippin along the roof ridge till I got to this end. Laid down and leaned over riskin me silly neck to paint that heart, upside down from where I was so's it'd come out right from the street. Plus the usual initials in it.

– A.S. . . . A.L. Who's A.L.?

– Annie Lang, old donkey. Dead now, I suppose, but as sweet a darlin lump as you'd ever come across. Though she was clever I'll say. And all the world's troubles on her shoulders. By cripes

29

she was still smilin too. Never spared erself. Even to marryin Joey McTaggart. There was a public service for you. That couldn't of been love, with him weak and skinny as somethin out a the Bible. Funny about them McTaggarts, eether they're as big as a bull or as weak as piss.

Uncle contemplated the faint heart, his eyes balls of lead.

– First time I kissed Annie she near knocked me down she gave me such a whack. Next time I whacked her first, and then kissed her. She never held grudges. Winnin form, she had.

– Why didn't you marry her?

– Didn't need to, did I? his rough voice caressed the mountain lilt. If she'd have wanted it, she'd have had it. I don't say I was much of a catch, no way. Off drivin me bullocks three parts of every week. Plus bein ugly as a toad into the bargain. Four inches shorter than her. And never able to keep a quid longer than two hours at a stretch. No wonder. Serves me right. Mind you, if I had of married her I'd be dead by now.

Billy laughed with pleasure.

– Why's that Uncle?

– She'd of made me soft. Livin with er I'd of got so comfortable and that-there, I'd just of laid down and said come and get me God.

They squinted at that trace of a heart till the initials began peeling away. A crow flew past.

– Bad luck, declared Uncle. He's on his way to help pick skins clean along Jamie Collins's fence, I dare say.

– Or dad's place.

They stood nodding at ghosts.

– Jesus but a man could hate this dump, Billy shouted to be sure Uncle would hear.

– Your dad! That crow'll poison himself if he don't watch out. Oy, he said projecting his huge voice in the direction of the general store. What's young Felissy Brindle doin leerin out at me through the window? Goodday you bag. How's your hair? She's had her lot. And very good luck to her I say. Good morning. How do you do? Her and your grandmother used to fight like foxes. Of course my wife was what you'd call an acquired taste, not to put too fine a point on it, that I will admit. On top of which, so was Felissy.

Again Billy laughed. Whenever he spoke to his grandfather he felt like laughing, he felt as young as he was, it made you want to jump. That was the effect Uncle had.

– Goodday Uncle, said Tony McTaggart approaching respectfully, modestly, but not from the shed where he worked. He came down the track at the side of the shop from the direction of Annie Lang's old place, looking flushed and pleased with himself.

– Where have you been? Billy demanded, meaning two questions.

– Have you been waiting? Tony resorted to evasion.

– What's up young McTaggart? You and my grandson here on the slops, is that it? Allowin him to lead yous astray? Saying this, Uncle let go of Billy's arm creating a gap to emphasize his mock disapproval.

– I haven't got there meself yet, Bill confessed. Though I'm working at it.

Uncle flapped his walkingstick wings to indicate that he joined the angels in renouncing moral responsibility for sinners.

– You'll get there, he promised. You'll go astray alright. Me eyes is open and me wits is buzzin, which is more than some can say.

The trio set off up the hill toward the famous Mountain Hotel.

– You walk a step or two behind us Mr McTaggart, the old man ordered. So's that'll bring yer mouth down about level with me ear, then I shan't miss yer pearls a wisdom.

Tony obediently fell back a pace, his arms still cradling the memory of a young woman's luggage. But they didn't talk. Poor old cove, he was thinking, must be ninety and you can't last for ever, especially burning himself out to keep up his reputation. And what's got into Bill? He won't talk like he used to. You can't please him. So Tony observed a forested mountain ridge sprouting from Billy's head.

Bill Swan had other things to think of than finer feelings. His discovery had to be kept secret. Gold all over again. And with the trouble this led to, it was enough to occupy a better head than his. To cap everything Miss bloody Brinsmead refused to sell him gelignite though he was positive she had some. So now the dangerous word was spoken. Gossip was bound to follow. Oh shit. But it had to be done. He tried diverting himself with other concerns: if Mr Ping didn't finish fixing Dad's tractor soon the new paddock mightn't be done before the rain set in; you could hear Alice bellowing along the wind, so she might die this time leaving someone else in need; the whole town wearing poorer and poorer; Tony kept wanting something and you couldn't tell what.

– A course, Uncle volunteered as they trooped into the musty porch of the Mountain. She was a world beauty once, Felissy was, even them people up from Melbourne'd just stop and stare. She was alright, but. That is, till her pa died and Sebbie kept takin er tourin round the Empire like she was queen erself. About twelve thirteen year ago, they went and when they come home of a sudden she showed as somebody you never knew was there under the skin.

– Jesus himself could easy hate this place, Billy growled.

– True enough, Uncle agreed placidly as he poked a stick at the door to the public bar.

– True, Tony echoed lamely, holding the door open for them.

At this moment, when there was no one in the street to hear, a faint voice deep inside the general store called Fido, Fido! you're wanted for lunch ...

Four

Sebastian Brinsmead, I said to myself, your duty is to wait for what will be known when it happens. Have faith, I said. Life is God's tapestry, nothing more, and nearly complete by the look of it today. Just one corner here to finish. Every detail my understanding of Him. Yet haven't I helped with this tapestry in some way? Isn't it mine too? And repentance in each imperfection? Precious repentance because it's a way to Him. Have I the right to claim? The work of God being the comprehension of the world. The vastness itself a design. Even the wicked, the ugly. Is there anything else to happen, Lord? If I can only stand still enough to keep the tapestry in focus ... still ... to see it whole and equally. The tapestry of eternity and so forth. That was young Bill Swan in the shop a moment ago. And my poor parents thought they had the testament of Jesus for the permanence of profit!

– He gave me a photograph once you know Felicia.

The tapestry in all its detail is the work of ... As the weft too could be a symbol ... The glorious radiance of it rich with detail, colour and ...

– I heard you Sebastian. But a photograph must be of something to be a photograph. What was this a photograph of?

33

– That dead president of the United States, the Kennedy boy we met once in Boston, I clearly recall the occasion, visiting a school among flowering trees. He must have been no more than twelve years old and he stuck his tongue out at you.

– President Kennedy, Miss Felicia Brinsmead observed, was of course pure fantasy. He was a religious fantasy. He only seemed to be there running America because Americans wanted to believe they had someone like that.

Last time she explained this in public there was a priest visiting who chuckled, charmed, worldly to his fingertips; repartee he recognized as readily as unsaved souls, though the good lady seemed not to notice how beautifully he was following her nonsense.

– What there was instead, she cried warmly, was another person who for the sake of convenience shall remain unnamed, by no means a man of the same appearance as the supposed President Kennedy because this unnamed one had nothing to do with appearances, he was a ruthless cold-minded political tactician who had Winston Churchill and the betrayal of the Greeks on the brain; or Jenghiz Khan and all those horses.

– See-see-ha-ya-wa-ya-haa, the priest had sniggered, discreetly appreciative, though she had not yet finished.

– He was a man in his element with confrontations against great nations abroad and also in deceiving great minorities ... (for a moment the phrase clanged doubtfully, but she allowed it to stand) ... at home.

– But, protested the witness of God's tapestry remaining paralysed under his halo of white hair, Kennedy was the only humane intelligent president to lead the Americans since Independence; that is why I have made a point of remembering him.

– Nonsense! No president ever led the United States of America, she patted the side of one of her newspaper towers as if encouraging a horse, swaying ahead of a polite but incredulous hunting party, seeming now to look back at them and smile.

– So Bill Swan was here again Felicia with a peculiar request, the dummy added in that infuriating way of relatives who change the subject to neutralize your best insights on some celestial score card.

– You heard what he wanted? she asked.

– Yes but not why. He's out there in the street with a friend. Friends are a good sign.

Indulging his fatuousness, she made no comment. True, Sebastian was the one person to whom she had consciously and systematically bared her inner life. Yes, to strengthen her own grasp on it, she'd invited him to share what mattered. But he hadn't the foggiest idea what she was on about, being slave to his own inner truths, truths she understood all too well, with their obsessive rights and wrongs. He could hallucinate moral conundrums regardless of what was going on around him. So he couldn't quite tell whether the answer he actually gave her was what he'd just said or what he now thought: countless generations have bequeathed this to us, the kings and queens of England have served us; we are casting off the tapestry; only a few more stitches left to be double-tied, slipped free. Without a doubt it's the Lord's work. The shape of life. I'm laughing perhaps. Waiting for the moment when I shall know the truth I have believed in; the piercing burning fire darting into my legs chest neck cheek stomach. Laughing gently. And I think quietly laughing. So be it.

– Don't ogle me! I'm not in on your comfortable joke, cried Miss Brinsmead stoutly. I won't let you save me.

Not only was Miss Brinsmead's hair a feature of the landscape; not only was she still indiscreet in love, as shown by her reaction to the young woman bringing a message from the dead; but in that same household lived the author of a secret document with SECRET actually printed on the cover, a diary of entries pencilled first and then inked in later.

Nobody has remembered my birthday. I'm twelve and I might as well be nothing. I used to promise this is when they would let me free. If I escape, it won't count.

Fido's room at the back of the shop had only one window; high up on the west wall, really more of a fanlight, perpetually filled with the mountain minus all foreground. He began by seeing the mountain as an outline, an ink drawing that invited one of several colour tints (topaz as the mist lifted, jade in the winter morning sun, amethyst in autumn rain) waiting for a foreground, waiting for somebody to come, something to happen. Only the mountain knew what he did all day, saw him read the piles of newspapers and hide the sticks of gelignite he stole from the shop before his mother was up. What the mountain could not be expected to know was Fido's genius. The mountain had no idea it was nodding in through that narrow rectangle at a prodigy who understood all he read and observed: for example, when Fido saw it as a coloured drawing in a frame he could have made another, identical, drawing if he had wanted to. He could even have invented a neat little town to tuck in front, architect-impressions, verandahs, windows, and the roadway dotted with horses pulling buggies, white and black horses, legs kicked forward in the style of champion trotters, plus a sky dabbed on in washes. Or else no buildings, but the smooth flanks of the mountain parched brown above a belt of skeletal trees rising among dry rather pernickety shapes suggesting dust more than cloud.

Fido folded away the news of 1933, British troops dealing with religious riots in Alawar; he completely suppressed the fighting between Hindus and Moslems occasioned by a theft of camels, to write in his diary *Nobody has remembered my birthday*. One day of course he would win the VC and then he would be able to withstand anything.

As the mountain watched him, so he watched the mountain grow lush with detail, every treetop equal in its particulars, saw it become a structure heaped up solely to support trees, a display stand for the world's biggest exhibition of leaves, also a freak of light picking out one treefern with unnatural clarity and loving prominence, the whole picture no longer a record of alienation but a celebration of the exotic. He wrote in his diary *I'm twelve and I might as well be nothing*.

He sat on the chest where the gelignite was hidden and calculated how long it would be before he had sufficient. And wrote in his diary *I used to promise this is when they would set me free*.

– Fido dear there's no call to bolt your food. (He's rather lovely, though hateful.)

– Better? (When are you going to die?)

– This modernist education, Felicia, is beyond me. Not to mention the pernicious influence of television. (At times he looks so exactly ... it's positively painful.)

– But Uncle Sebastian I don't think I've had any education at all. (Uncle, Uncle.)

– Let us at least converse about something more refined than definitions. We were not born to this dismal shop.

– Very well Felicia, you begin.

Both her brother and her son could see how she thought her face sweetly expectant as she placed her spoon and fork on the plate the better to concentrate.

– Public hangings, she said hopefully.

– Is that not rather a dinnertime topic? Saint Sebastian objected. A trifle too responsible for lunch?

– Umm, she agreed. Or Fido could choose.

– Alright, said Fido promptly. Why don't we sell the dismal shop?

– The next child I have will be a ringtailed possum! she clapped her hands over her ears. Why should she listen to such things? It was her mother, not Felicia, who tried to push the baby back as it was being born. Fido was spared that humiliation. Fido was a love child.

– All those games of Monopoly he plays against himself. You've got property deals on the brain I suppose, old fellow? You see, Fido, the problem of life is not whether to swap Fenchurch Street Station for the Water Works. Sebastian found himself measuring the boy anew, an act of praise. God be thanked for so perfect and complex a child, yes for this deviousness that spiced the intelligence they already knew.

– Or we could burn the place down and live on the insurance, Fido offered obligingly. (Did you hear me? hinting?)

– Sir Edgar Ross was a favourite with the Princess, said the aged Felicia. He piled stooks of straw round the kitchen because he said he couldn't bear another day of English cooking. He was thought a great eccentric. He'd been living at Versailles where the food was always halfway cold. He said the hot food in his own house burnt his palate. Yes, so he swore to heat it up properly if the cooks couldn't do as they were instructed. And set fire to the straw. I remember it clearly, the flames ran round under stooks like frightened fowls.

– Really Felicia your conversation has degenerated to a mixture of iced weddingcake and boiled turnip.

– Did they cook him cold pancakes then Mother?

– No they just cooked. He had to escape in a hurry. The house burnt down entirely. Nothing standing but two walls with a cluster of chimneys built in 1585. He was a fifty-year-old child, doing everything for the first time. So many were killed. Servants that is.

– Why didn't they call the fire-brigade?

She sighed. People nowadays have no sense of history. The three mouths opened and their blunt primitive teeth dug into red lumps of corned beef. A fly circumnavigated the room once and then clung despairingly to the window.

– He was not a wicked man in the eyes of his peers the peers. Far from it, she was answering unspoken accusations. They thought him quite the hero for nearly frying to death rescuing the horses.

This was not a fresh conversation. Something was said every day at lunchtime, they felt driven to observe the sociability of exchanging words. To protect the silence. They cast the sentences as dice for the jackpot of a companionable ease. For the same reason Felicia obliged herself each day to share a portion of what her son and brother ate.

Outside the window which hadn't been opened for ten years or sixteen, the steep road doubled about and wriggled down the mountainside. Half a century ago, it had seemed a miracle when the last twenty yard stretch was hacked out with pickaxes, the rubble shovelled off the lip of the ridge and the road first opened. For three weeks the children had to lead horses and cattle over it, backwards and forwards to trample it hard. Right at this moment, the road presented the unusual sight of a visitor, yes, a car toiling up towards the town, jerking through gear changes, dragging its parachute of dust. Fido saw it crawling round bends overhung by bulbous lumps of rock, passing the damp coiling flanks of some prehistoric amphibian. What Felicia saw were globular blue shadows lapping over the vehicle, one giant jellyfish after another ... she couldn't count the number of times she'd been to sea and associated jellyfish with freedom and failure. Sebastian saw a bobbin drawing the golden thread closer to his hand.

– Why shouldn't I go for a walk down the hill? asked Fido choosing his weapon.

– Because you don't understand, the old man explained gently. We don't understand the wickedness of the world.

– Because the policeman would drive here all the way from Yalgoona to get you and shut you away in a cell, that's why, Felicia mumbled as she chewed the salty meat wishing for something more like real food.

– I wouldn't care if he did. Because I'm shut away anyhow, aren't I? I'd like it. Yes I'd like to go to jail for a change and talk to the policeman.

They all stared hopelessly at the dusty picture of freedom offered by the window.

– I might do that myself I dare say, the boy's mother replied irritably. But who would cook the dinner or clean up or serve in the shop?

– Why not me?

– Why not you when it comes to behaving yourself and doing what you are told and being some comfort to your mother?

It was stiflingly familiar, these incompatible personalities distressed into a dance of love, their most characteristic shapes offending each other's sense of decorum, ugly when most rhapsodic, their suppressed injuries crying out to be revenged, discordant bells in the night.

– False teeth, said Sebastian pronouncing the words in the powerful distinct voice of a strategist.

– I knew we could rely on you for a topic my dear. Does the tea want freshing up? she asked right away to leave herself free for the pleasures of conversation.

– False teeth is a subject genteel enough for the Queen Mother's garden party.

– I'm sick of that bloody mountain looking in, Fido whined as he stole a glance at the sideboard mirror, afraid he might have been blushing, his mind filled with flames and the delicious screams of harmless victims suffering the fate of the harmless, also animal hoofs lashing out at Sir Edgar trying to save the poor stupid dangerous things, the smoke massing, smothering the scene, blank as that dusty view of escape down an unreachable mountain road.

– Why hasn't there been more gold found in the world? Fido asked.

– If there were more gold than there is, said his mother promptly, all our societies would collapse, great nations would be in ruins. Something has to be precious. Too much gold is a plague. Ruin.

– What if we had so much here in Whitey's Fall that we could use it to destroy the world?

– What if you ate up your corned beef!

– What if the whole mountain was really solid gold inside, Fido shouted. Would that ruin them? Would it, Mother? Would it change everything? Uncle Sebastian, would it be enough, a whole mountain of gold?

– I'm sure I don't know, replied the saint giving the matter his earnest attention.

– Somebody must know.

– Perhaps it would, Miss Brinsmead decided past the obstruction of an unswallowable boulder of meat.

– Then I hope it is gold right through, that's what I hope.

– At last, the saint mused contentedly, they make teeth you can eat with. It's a triumph of technology that one no longer need slip them out at mealtimes. You bite on them and they stay firm.

– My first false teeth, said his sister dislodging the boulder with a gulp of tea, were made of whalebone you know. Or was it hippopotamus? They clipped on to the ones that belonged. Oddly enough I have the impression they enhanced my beauty. Was I beautiful, Sebastian?

– Appalling.

– I thought so, she primped endearingly.

– But that didn't compensate you for never being happy I'd suppose?

– Happy! she shrieked.

A hen nodded into the room from the backyard, advancing with nervous stateliness, paused, listening, sizing up any possible risk, stabbed at a flake of breadcrust on the lino. She flapped away fussily discommoded when the old man nudged her with his shoe. But Felicia so loved a compliment she could forgive her brother his moralizing.

– You must have been going to say something about teeth yourself, she suggested obligingly.

– Only that I once knew a man who carried his wealth in his mouth for safety, everywhere he went. A digger, he was, no sooner had he got enough gold than he was off to have it fashioned into teeth. He ended up with a whole pound of solid gold in his mouth made up as a full double plate faced with bone.

– Just imagine, Sebastian, imagine those teeth discovered a thousand years from now by an archaeologist. She'd call it religious, she'd be on her knees. They'd be precious as Tutankh-Amun's chamberpot. Do you know, an acquaintance of mine once stole Louis XIV's chamberpot, solid silver he said it was.

– You understand as well as I do Felicia that there will be no such thing as a thousand years from now, at least not for this civilization or anything like it.

The sister recoiled as if hit in the face. Her lump of hair patted her on the back. She glared reproachfully, so the offender felt bound to mumble an apology.

– I should be sorry, I dare say. And I am.

– I believe in it, she replied with dignity. I've always believed in our ways. We might be miserable, greedy people but the one thing we hold to is the present. That's why it's worth reliving the past. I've never stopped hating our ways because I've never stopped believing in them. They're the seed of the future. And we do stick together, you mustn't despise that. If we're wicked let's admit it and live with it. I've always said wickedness is full of life if nothing else. At least you can't accuse me of saintliness.

– You cannot.

– What if I ran outside and called for help, Fido suggested getting up and going to the door to put to the test this taste for wickedness.

– And be seen? Sebastian challenged him in alarm.

– Let him do as he wishes, cooed Felicia with composure. Who are we to bother if the policeman comes to get him? Master Wilful Will-do brings it on his own head, he'll have no one but himself to thank.

An indecisive silence followed. Then Fido could be heard tiptoeing to his den. It was a mystery what he did in there, but that was the arrangement; nobody intruded on his sanctuary, poor boy.

Five

Only that morning there had been no tensing for a crisis. The wind blew a bright warm sky over the town. And Vivien sang. She sang in English, in German, in mock-Italian and in near-Russian. She enjoyed playing with her voice and pulling faces like an opera singer. Her singing was the marvel of three small children who crawled through the long grass on their bellies to be close enough to hear. She hammered and painted, swept, scrubbed and repaired, while pouring out *Nun beut die Flur das frische Grün dem Auge zur Ergötzung dar. Den anmutsvollen Blick erhöht der Blumen . . . something . . . Schmuck.* The children gazed into each other's astonished, delighted eyes.

– Schmuck, whispered one of them. The dirty word a talisman. The blooming schmuck.

– *Kräuter Balsam aus, hier . . . something . . . Wunden Heil . . .*

The children crouched closer to the ground as she looked up, unseeing, in their direction. Of course she saw them: bright eyes through the rotting pickets, busy fingers among the kangaroo grass and blackberries. The delicacy of them, the charm of their conspiracy. So she carried her morning tea out on to the porch, together with a heap of chocolate biscuits, for her campaign had been planned. She smiled as her teeth snapped the first biscuit through. She laughed to herself and hummed while she poured the tea. She breathed the scent of the hillside, the wild raspberry, the cattle. Quarter of a mile away she sent crows clustering along her neighbour's fence, picking at the line of raw sheepskins hung there to dry.

– You're welcome, she applied her invitation to the crows and the children. A slim black snake edged out of the rockery, so that she was a little unnerved by her power. Close at hand some person's cow again began bellowing with pain, as it had through the night. Then Vivien stood. She walked firmly down the path straight for the picket fence. They were caught: no hiding now, no escape and not seen.

– Fee Fi Fo Fum, she called so that the three small heads bobbed up to their different heights. I smell biscuit-watchers, she fixed them to the spot with unreal guilt. Biscuit-watchers, she said now quite close. Who are you? she pointed to the tallest one.

– . . .

– I see. And you? she pointed.

– . . .

– Hm. And you? she pointed.

– Fred.

– Fred. I once had a goldfish called Fred and he lived to be a hundred.

– How do you know? croaked Fred in panic.

– Because he was ninety-nine when I bought him. Here . . . she offered the plate of biscuits. One each, if you promise to answer three questions.

Fred held back, but the girl reached out and accepted a biscuit.

– I'm Susie, she said. I'm oldest.

– How about the others? said Vivien.

The middle one sidled towards the plate, fatalistically accepting the world's corruption.

– Merv.

The bellowing cow caught a sobbing breath.

– That Alice! Susie complained in exasperation.

– Fred, said Fred, he and Merv each taking a biscuit in turn.

– Question number one, Vivien began. Who am I?

– Dunno, said Merv.

– 'no, agreed Fred.

– The lady in the haunted house, Susie burst out with maniac laughter.

– Alright, how do you know the house is haunted?

– Because, said Fred his teeth flashing.

– Because nobody has lived in it, said Susie.

– ... since the beginning, Fred added to make everything clear.

– Because, said Merv slowly so that the others looked at him with envy. Because I've been in there when it was dark and I heard him creeping about and I ran all the way down the hill home and only just slammed the door at our place before he got me.

Vivien turned toward her house disbelievingly.

– Liar, Susie accused him.

– I did so too.

– He did so too, said Fred and thought of something. That's why his eyes went a different colour.

Merv squinted so they shouldn't see. But you couldn't help noticing the blue and the brown.

– Third question, Vivien put in hastily. Why doesn't anyone come and call on me?

– Because you don't call on them! Susie declared.

– On us neether. Easy! said Fred. You could, our mum's always home when she's not down at the dairy. Milking down there, he added helpfully pointing out the dairy.

– Another thing, Vivien asked ...

– Three questions! shrieked Susie. You've asked all three.

– The wind'll change, said Fred so that they licked their fingers and held them up, turning them, sensitive to the airflow, in the direction of that cow's hopeless repeated monotone. Much as they hoped, it never did.

– What's schmuck? Merv demanded sending the others into convulsions of suppressed laughter.

– Schmuck? Who said Schmuck?

– You did Miss. You sang it.

His sister and brother writhed about at this display of boldness.

– It's German, she answered which made them suspicious. German, you know, the language.

An all-white cloud wheeled solidly along the skyline.

– People in Australia speak English and so do people in England. People in Germany speak German.

Plainly they did not believe.

– It's another language, a foreign language.

– Schmuck, said Merv rudely. But this time his young audience was frightened.

– It means jewellery, ornament.

– No, Susie was quite definite about this feminine branch of knowledge. No.

– Yes it does Susie, I assure you it does.

But the girl shook her dark hair. It wasn't right. Deep down you knew it wasn't. The taste of chocolate biscuits lay poisonously gluey in their mouths.

– Please can we go now, Fred begged.

– I'm sorry, Vivien replied. I spoiled your game. But come up any time. I'm always here.

Fred ran away, cavorting downhill among granite boulders. His brother and sister walked slowly after. They couldn't have any German-sayer thinking they were scared.

– What are you going to do? hissed Susie when she was sure she couldn't be overheard.

– Tell somebody.

– Who?

– I dunno. Somebody, he threatened.

– But, Susie protested. She was nice to us.

– Boo! yelled Fred hurtling out from behind a rock and making them both jump.

– I'll get you for that, snarled Merv. He grabbed at him and missed. And bounded after him down the slope with suicidal abandon.

– Schmuck, said Susie safely alone for a moment. Schmuck.

One golden hair hung on the fence. Vivien picked it off and ran it through her fingers, astonished at its brilliance in the sunlight. That was Fred, it had to be his. The hair glittered in her hand now seeming silver.

– What a fool I've been, she explained.

She walked back to the house with her biscuit-plate, not pleased at having frightened away some rare species of native fauna.

– The chance was there, she grumbled to herself.

The tail of the black snake still hung from its hole in the rockery. She stamped her foot, but it didn't move. Mentally she kicked at him, but in fact she had no wish to do so. He'll keep the mice down, Vivien thought, exercising her new Australian knowledge.

Her house, like all the houses of Whitey's Fall, was built on a steep hillside. It stood apart from the town under the mountain's shadow. From her front door she could look across the rooftops of the general store, the pub and the butter factory to farms on the northerly horizon. Three miles away, off the road, the ruins of another settlement, Wit's End, showed among cypress trees. Compared with the fortress-like cluster of Whitey's Fall, Wit's End could have been a sacred grove. Vivien stood on the steps, shading her eyes. She no longer felt like singing. She felt like, yes, action. Three small figures emerged below on to the dirt track. Now, I shall not let them out of my sight; when I know where they live I shall pay a call. At the main street they crossed to a path leading down the side of the welder's shed. There's only one place that could go to, Vivien told herself, gazing across to where the paddocks tipped on end tilting at a wild incline down to the valley: the small house by the creek there. Why wait? Who knows what stories the children might tell? Would they say she had bribed them with biscuits, that she'd asked questions, demanded to know why no one had called on her, that she sang in German? None of it looked good. Best to act immediately. She went inside, tugged a comb through her short hair, inspected her work clothes and decided they would have to do. So Vivien set off down the hill at a brisk walk into the future.

The children were nowhere to be seen around the house in the valley when she arrived, she had lost the expected introduction then. But she wasn't the kind to lose heart. She walked unhesitatingly to the door and rang the bell.

– Come in, called a female voice. Come in Elaine, the voice called again as she stepped into the hallway.

– It's not Elaine, she apologized.

– Well come in anyhow, the older voice had a smile in it. Vivien walked through to the kitchen which to her surprise was large and filled with women. She stood, vulnerable, for the hostess to protect her. There were six women at the table smoking and sustaining the various gestures of a few moments ago, another stood at the sink, another supervised a kettle on the stove.

– So you've come at last! cried a broad elderly person, her brilliant blue eyes welcoming, her white hair standing up in anarchic tufts. I had the feeling somebody was travelling.

– Couldn't you find us?

– You only had to stand still and listen, you'd have heard us. We're real cacklers.

The broad lady, still seated, held up her hand to be shaken. Vivien took it, a comfortable, capable hand.

– Mrs Collins, said the lady. And Mrs Collins warmed her. Vivien smiled in return. Her hostess had a wide prominent jaw that thrust her lower teeth out in front of the upper set, but far from looking aggressive, her mouth rose generously at the corners and the deep creases blossomed up into high colourful cheeks. When she opened her mouth to laugh she showed a wide flat tongue of clear pink. Creekbeds wandered in towards her eyes where the unfathomed water shone with sunlight. Single tufts of white grass flourished here and there on her cheek, her chin, at the side of her nose. This nose, bold but not firmly shaped, was expressive and would adapt to her mood.

– How you've kept us guessing, a little round woman admonished. We began to think you'd never come. A whole week since you arrived and not a peep out of you.

– We thought, the one with the kettle began to explain.

– Aren't we ever to have that fresh cup a tea? a crone snapped to establish her originality.

– This is Miss McAloon, the hostess wheezed in a froggy

voice. Mrs Buddall, Mrs Swan, Mrs Buddall (Mrs Mary Buddall), Mrs McTaggart and Mrs Collins (another Collins, like myself, by marriage), and Mrs McAloon (Mrs Jessie).

The ladies nodded and made mutters and sighs of delight.

– I'll never remember, Vivien apologized.

– Now you tell us your name.

– Viv, said Vivien. And that's simple enough.

– I knew she'd be alright, little Mrs Buddall decided waggling her head which bristled with hair-curlers like some rather fearsome creature that had forgotten what it was going to do. I saw her buying at Brinsmeads' and I told you all along.

The younger ladies reintroduced themselves by their first names.

– Dolly.

– Mary.

An animated conversation then began while they explained that this house, close to the shop but away from the men, was where they usually gathered of a morning, besides you wouldn't dare go anywhere but Mum Collins's. They advised her not to jump to conclusions and think the town was peculiar, on the contrary she'd find good folks here. And not to get too confused by the different names of the family.

The two matriarchs Collins sat proudly together.

– We're all more or less related by marriage.

– And so am I, said Vivien. My last name's Lang.

This provoked an astonished hush. Mum's huge nose took on the fine arched shape of having known all along.

– From Annie Lang who became a McTaggart?

– I told you something, declared the other Mrs Collins.

– Mrs McTaggart is my great-aunt, said Vivien not knowing how this information might be received.

– So you got her house. It all fits. A young lady living in Annie Lang's house and really one of us then.

– Tell us about it Viv. They sat forward, ready for the business of fitting the world's chaos to their model. This was a treat. A great deal of laughter and a terrific sense of energy filled that room. These women knew something: they had spared themselves from wasting effort on useless things. It was hard to imagine any of them afraid or vain or at a loose end. Even old Miss McAloon who kept sounding a sour note had this vigour, tolerating the jokes of her sisters and cousins and nieces. The newcomer was struck by how extraordinary it was for there to be such gaiety in Whitey's Fall, such a concentration of noise in that silent township. She had assumed the gnomic brooding of Brinsmeads' Store and the speechless drinkers at the public bar of the Mountain were the soul of the place. Here, the assumption blew apart in gales of merriment, the bright cheeks working, the shy easy eyes, the stout hands placed gently on that lino-covered table.

– My great-aunt Annie is still alive.

This was greeted with gasps and cries (some of which she did not recognize as dismay). In the flattering excitement, the tea stood forgotten.

– Yes, she lives in England at a little place in the country.

– So she's gone to live in the new world. Tell her when you write that we're still here safe and sound in the old one. Tell her we think of her.

– Auntie's just about an invalid these days, not ill though.

– She must be ninety, Annie must.

– Well her brother . . .

– He knew us older ones, the rascal, the piping Mrs Collins contributed.

– . . . was at sea most of the time.

– Fancy Archie a seaman.

They sat dreamily, the life of sixty years ago fresh in mind, so that slight changes came over them and they grew younger.

– He sailed the world. Vivien suspected for an instant they were mocking her with extravagant attention, but went on, I can just remember him telling stories of foreign places. He was my grandfather. He died a good while ago.

They let out a concert of breath. Archy's grand-daughter large as life, so that suddenly the family likeness was obvious. The good and the bad were remembered about these lost Langs.

– My father's dead too, but I always knew where we came from because of Aunt Annie.

– Did your grandfather die rich?

– He made enough to be comfortable. In my turn, she changed tack as they inhaled the word comfortable, I've saved to buy my house and move out here where I want to be. I'm not rich any more than Grandpa was. But my father didn't do well in life.

– Did he tell you stories about us?

– Bedtime stories of the giant grasshoppers and murders on the goldfield.

The curlers pinched Mrs Buddall's scalp deliciously.

– So you came home to your auntie's house, Mum Collins put the question as a statement.

– She was delighted I think.

– Of course she was.

– Because if she ever feels up to it, she'll come over and visit.

But perhaps they no longer believed in Mrs Annie McTaggart as a person continuing to survive nobody knew where or how.

– Well, you're one of us, one of the Whitey's Fallers.

– Whitey's Fallen as I call it! Mum covered her mouth with her hand for fear of the omen she'd spoken.

– Yes and I'm very glad, said Vivien so that both Mrs Collinses reached out to touch and claim her.

– Fancy Annie, one of them repeated confounded.

They recreated her with amazement. Mum Collins felt distinctly insecure at the idea: Annie and all the intimate things she stood for, the darling difficult managing person, quick to flare up and no mistake, slow to forgive too. Though for the underdog she'd do anything. You could never tire her out, not Annie, not if anyone was suffering or in need (which was enough of itself to put independent persons off). An untidy housekeeper and no cook, good Lord no. In fact you couldn't really, for the life of you, see what men went after in her. But they did go after her, that's certain. And she was loyalty in person. She left the town when she was thirty; pfutt like dying, only not so familiar and without the same goodbyes. But to suppose she must now be someone who'd lived what you might call a whole life ... this was a difficulty. And smaller than she was, age does make smaller, shrinking a body in a manner of speaking. Thinner or fatter it was equally strange. She might be crippled with arthritis, who could tell, after sixty years' living as a stranger. Maybe a chronic sufferer from indigestion: and we know what that means, habitual chewer of Rennies. Well, yes. Deaf possibly. Senile, not knowing what she's doing and not being able to hold herself in. Embarrassing as it always is. And day-to-day though. Corns on her feet. Swollen ankles. Rich was she? A wallowing pig in jewels and wicked money she never did a hand's turn to earn for herself? Or an ageless busybody organizing charities and playing golf? Hard to imagine. A nuisance to think of. Because nobody else had ever done anything like that. No, nor sent a substitute back to remind you and make you think.

– I've never been anywhere, Vivien began again feeling a stranger among these plump ruddy smiling faces. Which felt so much like home.

– It is home.

– Make no mistake, we've got our share of problems though.

– I remember a time when scarce two families were on speaking terms, Mum Collins agreed. It was dreadful. You wouldn't read about it. Open slather. The Miles McTaggarts blamed the Joe McTaggarts for their bad season with the crops, the two branches of Swans having a shot at one another, somebody forever getting stoushed. Jessie and Bertha McAloon gave us no rest from their wranglings, that'd be right Bertha wouldn't it? You see. The Buddalls got stuck into the Collinses and split. And Eggie Schramm went bush rather than share the pub with his brother. Look at Jasper now; winners never get over it. Worst thing that can happen to you is to win an argument of the blood. It was a time to forget. You'd only need a milkchurn to go missing for half the people to be at the other half's necks. Supposing a cow strayed, there'd be holy war to follow. Thank the Lord it's past and mostly mouldy.

The room became a bustle of elbows and hips and vigorous practised movements while they cleared dishes and cups, sluicing them in washing-up water. No doubt about the problems. The ladies touched Vivien, reaching her with a wonderful tenderness in their clumsy fingers. Teatowels were a flurry of work and cupboard doors flapped open for the glittering crockery. The house alive, a cat leapt out of the window in protest.

– The question is, Miss McAloon persisted, sounding a sour note as if Vivien wasn't there to hear. Will this Lang girl stay? Will she stick it out?

– Will she ever! wheezed Mum and tucked Vivien under her arm, a new possession to be kept warm. We know what we know, she announced. And now Viv you've got to call me Mum like everybody does, because I won't answer to anything but. Her jaw jutted and her nose bulged a contented shape.

The doorbell rang, suburban and out of place, immediately followed by a voice calling.

– Hullo, is Mary there Mum?

– That's Elaine now, several people said. And Mrs McTaggart went out to the front. As the chatter died down they heard Elaine's voice on a note of alarm.

– Scared me to death! She talks dirty words in German and gives them chocolate biscuits. I told them never never...

The speaker surfaced into the kitchen and realized instantly who was standing among her safe neighbours and aunts. She halted at the doorway, pushing the stray hair back from her forehead with one hand, damp and shaky, the word *never* a solid object holding her lips apart, the hair aggravating her difficulties, anger brightening her eyes and colouring her cheeks; a thin worrying woman of forty, bitter at what her plain dress now showed about her.

– Elaine this is Viv, she came to pay us a call and would you believe it she's one of the Langs. Do you remember? The old Langs and their Roman bones.

– I was speaking to your children I think, said Vivien tackling the problem head-on and bravely.

– They told me.

– Fred, she explained lamely. And Susie. And Merv.

– They're mine, said the mother, meaning whatever she meant to mean.

– Merv ... someone sniffed affectionately for the brown eye and the blue.

– They said, said Elaine confirming it.

– I was so glad they called, Vivien explained. Really.

– Really?

The younger women cast their eyes down with embarrassment, because it could be them, after all, with the worries. But Mum Collins, cheeks ripe in kindliness, ignored Elaine's sarcasm and guided their visitor to the door, leading her by the arm.

– Call in again tomorrow, she invited. If I could get my rotten flesh up that hill of yours I'd come to visit, I would. And I go out any time of day, mind you, except of an evening. Of an evening I'm usually pooped. But not up that hill of yours, no way, not even when I'm at my best. Otherwise I'd be there like a shot to talk over old times of me and your grandfather and your Auntie Annie and to see how you was going with putting the place in order, getting it swept and that. Terrible lot of dust always, she called by way of goodbye.

– Viv, she murmured softly. Viv Lang. Caressingly she said it, wondering what might be going on in that young head bobbing up and down. Watched her manner of walking, the tall rather heavy frame, broad back, stepping out purposefully so that you wanted to smile. The short curly hair. Smile. Thirty perhaps? And every inch a Lang now you came to look. Mum returned indoors on her fat padded feet. She continued to smile, filled with the anguish of loss when her friend, her impossible Annie, the one she loved most, had gone with the troops to the Somme.

– What the hell's all this babble about? she demanded borrowing a tone from her late husband as she reappeared in the kitchen, an outbreak of strife on her hands.

Six

The town's workmen gathered by custom for their lunchtime meeting at the bar of the Mountain, their traditional two-hour break. Seeing each other gave them a firmer grip on the present, which had a disconcerting habit of slipping away. Among them, the three who met outside Brinsmeads', Billy Swan, Uncle and the giant Tony. The bar, smoky and uncomfortable, was once the seat of mayoral deliberations before Whitey's Fall ceased officially to be a town. Its mirrors held strange sights yellowed at the edges.

– Goodday Jasper me boy! Uncle hailed the publican.

– Hruh, said Jasper polishing a cloudy glass with a greasy cloth.

– 'Jas, Tony greeted him, still spinning with thoughts of the new lady whose bags he carried on one arm last week and whose house he had just been spying at in the hope of a glimpse.

The publican kept his head down, hiding his face. He stuck the glass under a beer-tap. The sparkling beer flowed. Two more cloudy glasses, still wet, were filled. He favoured Uncle with the dried glass; then placed his lifeless hand on the counter for payment. Tony hastily produced some silver.

– My shout, he said, slapping the money down beside the hand.

– Alright young fellamelad, Uncle conceded. Most probably it is about time you shouted too.

The cool beer stung their throats deliciously.

– So how's business Jasper?

– Hruh. The money was scooped off the bar and some spilt beer along with it.

– Well that's right, you never see the place empty. And what with so much sunny weather and that-there. Uncle waved his glass to greet the eight men already in the bar, one of whom signalled back. The others stood, glazed, watching neither Uncle nor the flicker on the television screen; men absorbed by inner visions.

– 'Ian, Uncle politely acknowledged the contact.

They drank. Tony studied his mate. Why was he hoping for a friendly sign? But Bill's eyes were shiny transfers stuck on his face, behind them something dense and obstructive. Reassuring himself he couldn't be the cause, Tony wisely ignored it as a mood coming on. Uncle was speaking again.

– How's that tractor Tony?

– Not ready yet Uncle. Mr Ping's putting the finishing touches to it today. Bit of neatening. Bit of welding and that. It'll be good as new.

– Finishin touches! Christ if you ask me young Pingaling must be smeltin the bloody iron hisself to take all this time.

– You should have seen it.

– What's more, Uncle considered the case more objectively. Ping's the kind of bloke'll stop at nothin short of perfection. That's his trouble. Could have made a fortune and bought hisself a sheep station by now, Ping could have, if he wasn't so damn particular. That's the Chinese in him I suppose. You can't help bein what you are.

Ten minutes ago Billy had been the earth under his own feet, feeling his weight, the weight of his body, his arms, his head. Now he was communicating silence to the others while they drank.

– Rrssturmminipromburtilistioning, muttered Jasper with sudden expressive gestures directed somewhat to one side of his customers. No one noticed.

– Groomahumpresnotisma, he shrugged and lifted his head so that his face could be fully seen for the first time, the conclusion he had come to being evidently uncomplimentary to the world. Lassisquorpalkinnyra, he grimaced. His damp clay features crumpled and winced, the tiny eyes half-blinded by disillusion and drink, gummed up with a mucous excretion. He took a bottle of whisky from the shelf, turned his back to save others having to acknowledge seeing, and tossed off a generous draught. An announcer appeared on the television to read the news: emotional scenes at Parliament House over the country's financial crisis.

Uncle laughed outright.

– You interested in politics Tony?

– Not much.

Tony relaxed, he knew what was happening to his friend Bill now. They all knew and no one would risk interfering.

– Dad's keen to see the back of this lot, that's all I know.

– Maybe, Uncle allowed. But who's keen to see front of the others? That's the joke. You get rid of one Prime Minister, you've got to put up with another. And he's always worse for some reason. One of the marvels, that. You can't tell me nothin about politics. They don't care. We might as well stop existin. You try fronting up to them you'll find out. The next one'll be worse than anythin we've known so far, mark my words. Stands to reason.

– We don't exist, Tony nodded agreeably as he had nothing more to contribute and it was his policy to agree with the old man. He looked up to Uncle because Billy looked up to Uncle.

– Durrmumprowgerostiment, Jasper growled ferociously.

Billy's throat began swelling and working. (He lay against a stony bank, his head below the crest of grasses, he was panting. The time had come, the test. Messengers dispersed all over the country with news that the Romans had defeated the Gaulish clans and planned to attack the White Land itself. Their boats were just out there, they had arrived. Trembling with energy, he could hear the enemy forming up in the dawn twilight. He was ready to fight. Listen. Yes you could tell there were a lot of them and you could hear their comical clothing, hide skirts with discs and knobs, you could imagine their legs how they were said to be, tied up with leather thongs as if the muscles would fall off otherwise, you could hear metal clinking, the creak of foot coverings, even a hoarse whisper in their stiff language, but on this side of the embankment an awesome silence, marshmen as far as the woods in one direction and reaching to the swamp in the other, women too, flat against the ground. The sky dissolved to liquid light, washing out the last stars. As the witch had said, you are the deadly plants of the soil. The outlanders whispering now so close, and not knowing. At first sight of them, your hair bristling. A single gold eagle rigid as a dead bird rose above the grass from the slope below, death glittering on a pole in the sky, next a row of horsehair tufts jerking into view. White and red tufts: the sign foretold. The terrible unbelievers the Goddess had cursed. He was on his feet and so were all his kin, the marshmen, a scream curdling in their throats, echoes immediately yelping back from the surrounding hills. Screaming and flailing, arms jerking, stones and spears hurtling among the invaders, thudding into flesh or ringing against strange metal. He was running right in through the enemy ranks as all his folk were, among hot stinking bodies. He glimpsed their leader, the dreaded Yulius Kyser being carried ashore on a platform to command the battle, the man who had spoken of us as if we were small boys without science or art and too stupid to see the benefits of slavery. The nameless power of what he knew was with him. The enemy who all looked the same, not really men, who must be killed for the Goddess; life depended on this. To be conquered would be impossible. It was known. He ran and leapt, shrieking into their caged faces, he and his brothers, limbs smeared with muttonfat, throats raw. Fighting against a man now whose very appearance filled him with horror, a man with dark skin dark all over, brown like a corpse, his hair black as a demon and black eyes that saw right into you. He struck at the dark man with all the strength of his fear, his knife. Bright blood fountained surprisingly from the brown neck. The enemy dropped his sword and clutched the wound as if to stuff the blood back in. The Goddess had chosen this moment as a gift to him so he had time to scrabble, terrified, for that weapon, he had the sword. He experienced its strange unaccountable weight. Yet it lived in the hand, gave power to the arm. He swung it and it sang so that he was invincible. The Roman soldier, still clutching his neck, blood squirting out between his knuckles, stood in the frontline unarmed, displaying his incredulity, absorbed by the need to keep himself from dying. But the dreadful thing could be seen in his eyes, it was as if watching his killer he saw some dirty dangerous scavenging dog who swung the sword like an idiot, amazed at its harmless whistle. The dead man fell simply as a tree. You have to leap back so the corpse won't contaminate you with death. You suddenly understand about weight, a falling man is so much heavier than he was when alive, the shape of a man is seen to be to do with the life of a man not his death, the body suddenly lumpish and ridiculously helpless, its weight a measure of weakness. The dead thing rolls slightly in the dust where it falls so that you hate it and stamp on it and waste your energy kicking at it, horrible, you don't want to look but you have to because you have to be sure. So with this man who fell simply as a tree, while countless duplicate legionaries clambered up the ridge into view to take his place. And the dreaded Kyser set his foot on the White Land. Hei-e-e-eigh! sang the defending marsh people and the strength of earth was in them though they were losing.)

Billy groaned, his restraint breaking.

– Next round's on me, said Uncle distinctly. Another beer Bill?

Billy nodded, gazing at the television announcer who was explaining the market price of carrots.

– Carrots, he can talk! commented Uncle scornfully. He doesn't know a thing about it you can see that. Someone else writes it all out for him, I'll be bound. He wouldn't know a carrot if he had one for a dick. Winnin form!

Jasper gathered the glasses, swilled them out and refilled them. Uncle raised his new beer the moment it was set in front of him.

– Here's to Remembering, ay Bill? the old man was the only one able to refer openly to religion without offence.

– To Remembering, Uncle.
– Was it clear?
– Clear.

Jasper presented his back. He swigged some more whisky.

– I've never had a Remembering, Tony admitted, and as he bent his head, Billy noticed the unscarred neck, smooth and thick as a young tree. Though I've tried.

Seven

A little truck wheezed and spat its way off the upper track into the main street, where it proceeded with extreme care along the exact centre before pulling slightly to one side and stopping far enough from the kerb to seem abandoned. Having twice checked that the handbrake was fully applied, a woman climbed out, a tiny, principled person who thought before she acted and therefore had the manner of someone who knows precisely what she wants. As for her black bun, her sober cardigan, her darned stockings and the shoes she herself had so often repaired, these she gave attention only as they were due for it. Once ready they were forgotten. She would no more have reassured herself (with a hand patting her hair) that the bun was still in position, than she would have glanced critically at her shoes when out of the house. She also left her truck without a backward glance. As years ago she put behind her the dragons of wisdom. She walked into the twilight of the welder's workshop.

– Mr Ping, the Chinese woman called. You know I don't come here for nothing. She peered into the corrugated dimness, in among chapels of metallic symbols: crosses and crooks, moons, crescents and mandalas, to where the crucibles of black oil and the faint acidity of labelled bottles were ranged on a workbench.

61

Finally she discerned the man-shape she was looking for. He knelt at the far end of the place in a crude apse; he was beneath a tractor elevated on the hoist, an altar supported by its gleaming silver column. She felt respectful in this place even though she never intended to. The man turned his torso in answer to her voice, a dying shower of sparks falling from his hand. A wisp of smoke. One glove still held the blue-tongued torch angled away from him in that practised gesture, the flame menacing with a will of its own. His head, a square steel mask, canted stiffly up to observe the intruder through black glass.

– Mr Ping, she said again.

Mr Ping didn't answer, but the mask was attentive.

– You must do something for the sake of Alice, she needs a vet. This is all I came to say. You know my misfortunes, she added. And I ask for nothing. Not for my rights, because of what has been. Only for Alice. For help.

Mr Ping's mask waited. Concentration itself taut enough to snap at a touch, or ring like a harp-string. The place accumulated mysterious hints of large shapes. The tractor loomed above her, she had advanced right into the sanctuary. Any minute, perhaps, it could roll on top of the welder now his attention was diverted. But the longer she had to wait the more she grew able to use the infiltration of light, so that those sacred symbols defined themselves as the functional, the greasy adjuncts of his trade: wheels brackets vices struts and crosstrees.

– Mr Ping? Her neat black head compelled attention. Suddenly she thought it couldn't be him she was talking to. Too small for the boy, she thought, it's a complete stranger! No, but the boy's in the shadow perhaps and it's not proper to bring out my troubles in front of the boy.

– Is he here then? she asked.

The mask said no silently.

– Well? she demanded, I'm waiting for you. The touch of annoyance being her pride showing. She was embarrassed for him that he could descend to demeaning them both, so she spoke again to cover up for him.

– There's nothing more I can do, the truck would never make

the journey to fetch the vet from Yalgoona, not down the mountain nor up. And everybody has their own troubles, you can't telephone him today because it's Thursday.

Silence congealed round the two people breathing that tank of oily dim air. Tiny sounds from outside embedded themselves in the space: a paperbag bowling along in the dust, a swirl of wind through the peppertree, a distant dog barking and, even more remote, the airborne bellow of a cow in pain.

– You know this, Mr Ping, she continued with gentle determination. You know how hard things have been. I've had poor Alice a long time. She's only just finished with that lazy Iris's calf; Alice being the last milker I've got left, it fell to her to suckle it. And I reared Alice from the bucket when she lost her mother. Well the calf died and now she's to have her own it won't come. She keeps lying down but there's nothing to help the pain. You can hear that if you listen, even from here. I'm down low myself, last month I had to put Iris to the market, not that it gave me more than a minute's regret once the calf had died, but the country is dead, there's no living in it any more. And that's a fact we're all aware of. Not with housecows at any rate. Iris went under the hammer for sixteen-thirty. Sixteen dollars and thirty cents, that is, for a whole healthy fat beast, lazy and inhuman as she was, but she had such a bloom on her, you had to love that bloom, you could eat her as she was, no cow could have looked better. And with steak in the shops between one and two dollars a pound. But by the time they'd taken their auction fees all I had was my cheque for nine dollars twenty-five. I could have cried. I did cry too. I'd have used more than that in shoe leather just running about after the animal, one way and another. I could have made more if I'd butchered her and minced her all up and sold her as dogmeat, I'd have cleared more than nine twenty-five. Couldn't have been less. And don't say it's no use crying over it now, I've got to live since the school shut down.

She inspected the mask for a sign of comprehension.

– I'm asking nothing for me, she said. Only for Alice who's been good to you too across the years.

The answer clear as a shot rang in her head. Nothing could

be done to save him exposing his mean spirit. It disgraced her to have him like that. Abruptly she hurried to the door, escaping. A vessel of helpless misery, propelling herself into the sunlight. And thus she was observed by a woman she had never met who stood outside the shop opposite.

The woman, prisoner of neutrality, watched a Chinese lady rush from the welder's, her eyes big with tears. Her hands, belying the composure of her hair, groped blindly for the door of her ancient truck.

Mrs Ping had no choice. Really it was madness to attempt the mountain road. Being a disciple of reason, she knew this.

Come on, the mountain urged her. This way.

Her truck already in motion, how could she resist, and somebody ran out to cheer her along. Alice knew help was on the way; no use saying Alice was a simple brute. The hot sickening milk, far from being her gift, the one thing the cow longed to be rid of; if it didn't whine a hymn among the clanging pails Alice could not care what happened to it. Mrs Ping was the one to understand this.

Downhill all the way, said the mountain.

– It is, Mrs Ping conceded, letting the clutch ratchet in.

Also, motion soothes the troubled spirit. She had no choice, the impossible mission entrusted to her.

What can go wrong? asked the mountain.

Leaving the morning tea at Mum Collins's with qualms to brood on, Vivien had arrived back at the main street in time to notice several events: three men walking up to the hotel in single file including the blond lad who had carried her bags the day she arrived; and secondly the small truck parked like a lifesize toy, a crazy vehicle with rolled tin mudguards and an upright windscreen. But she had matters on her mind. Abstractedly, Vivien recalled herself as a child in the woods with a man who exposed himself to her so she ran away in horror of the hair growing round it. She was definitely on Elaine's side; a mother scared for her kids. She ought to have invited her for a cup of tea, because Elaine was the first person in Whitey's Fall Vivien had injured. That gave them a kind of intimacy. Ordinary routines threatened to claim her again. Yes, she gazed out over the valley. On a clear day you could see the ocean, she knew this. But not today, thanks to the dust haze. Now her attention was claimed by something moving down in the valley. A blue car a long way off, crawling up the road, climbing the first cluster of hairpin bends. She watched it weaving in and out of sight. The power of the climb inexorable. Unexpectedly she was witnessing a drama the very next minute. A Chinese lady running out of that big shed, every movement expressing tragedy, scrambling into her truck. The motor ticked like a frantic clock. Vivien looked away politely, not to stare at the driver's mouth set tense as a learner being examined, her eyes staring at a road of tears. The handbrake released, the crazy rattletrap of flat plates and gill-vents lurched into motion. Though she juggled the wheel, she gave the impression of remaining desperately immobile. A wave of dust flowed over Vivien who flapped one hand in front of her nose. From the upper ridge that damned cow began bellowing again, enough to send anyone mad. Then she was part of the drama: she had noticed something wrong.

– Hey, she shouted. Look out. Stop. Your tyre's flat at the back. Stop! And now the observer herself ran across the road, just in time to slap the sideboard of the moving vehicle, dislodging from the timber a puff of termite dust. Yet the Chinese woman did not stop, gave no sign of noticing her, steering the hobbling lorry out along the road and swinging its blunt nose quivering down the hill.

– O God, Vivien whispered. She looked about wildly. Who might help? Miss Brinsmead of course. She blundered into the doorway of the shop and just as she was about to hammer on the door, one of the holland blinds was pulled aside a crack, enough for the child who held it to contemplate her with steady, knowing eyes.

– She'll kill herself, Vivien screamed.

Fido recognized the woman his mother loved. He knew his mother loved her the moment she poked her nose into the shop bringing that letter a week ago.

She stood panting and shocked. The child disappeared, dropping the blind back into place. Vivien banged at the door. She shouted help, emergency! already losing hope. But then, thankfully, there were footsteps inside. The blind was pulled back a second time and the rescuer, the perpetual Miss Brinsmead, confronted her.

– Closed for luncheon, the shopkeeper's voice hooted, muffled by the locked door.

– It's urgent. Miss Brinsmead, there's a woman ... Vivien began frantically. Accident! A truck! she shouted at the stupid creature.

– No thank you all the same, Miss Brinsmead declined remotely and let the blind drop again.

The bloody fool of a woman.

There was nothing Vivien could do. Out on the road once more, suspended in dust, watching the truck wobble into the first bend. Snap out of it. She ran to the welder's workshop.

– Who's here? she shrieked into the spitting darkness, peered at a pool of electric light underneath a tractor. That lady will kill herself you know, she explained shakily. It's miles to the bottom of the range.

The oxy torch threw off a constellation of sparks. No reply.

– Please, she cried. Please.

The welder snapped back his mask and brandished the hissing flame still alive in his hand. His aged Chinese face nestled in sparse white hair.

– What is it then? he spoke slowly in an Australian accent at the furthest extreme of nasality.

– We've got to help, she wept at the responsibility.

He said nothing to this.

– Someone has to do something, she pleaded. She's got a flat tyre but she didn't notice.

– How do you know she didn't? Mr Ping drawled raising questions you'd never think of. Vivien saw again the woman's tear-heavy eyes, her carelessness of who might be watching, and not a hair out of place to betray her weakness.

– There can't be any reason on earth for not helping, she retorted in a burst of anger.

Mr Ping sighed perhaps. Or whispered incomprehensible syllables to himself. The mask snapped shut, the flame made contact with metal and assumed its intended meaning. Outside, the wind freshened and that cow could be heard clearly now, launching its succession of single hoarse yells into the valley and across the mountainside.

Had he meant suicide? What sort of place was this after all? His voice had filled her with horror; it was . . . yes . . . not interested in what she said. Vivien ran up the hill. Her only hope, the Mountain Hotel and the giant halfwit.

Mrs Ping fought the wheel. Her truck slewed down through the gravel, skidding round corners, the brakes useless. She wrenched the gearstick, her leg pumping at the clutch. The truck went faster. She had to, she would, she must force it, must, had got to force it out of third. The wheels whined into the next curve inches from the precipice. Ahead on the coiling road below, Mrs Ping saw the impossible: an approaching car.

Felicia Brinsmead stood in the dim shop after she let fall the blind, robbed of motion. Naturally she had been upset at young Vivien's agitation and had heard the word accident too. Her affections made her yearn to help, but she needed the way of least pain. She struggled against love which tempted her to rush out and involve herself in futile suffering. The accident would happen. Her mind worked at it, she murmured the name Mercy Ping; what more could she afford to do, love being a complication too appalling? And who was she to care so much about Mercy Ping of all people? She sighed for lost opportunities.

– I know I know, she told the shop irritably. You don't have to comment on the obvious.

The sardine fishermen in their sou'westers mimicked her O O. The frozen chickens persisted with that silly drama of holding their breath. The convolvulus flowers eavesdropped, but she understood too much for them. Back in the kitchen, Felicia explained to her brother what was happening.

– The poor good woman! he cried, and he raised himself from the chair to see out of the window, his nimbus of hair trembling to its roots, his saint's face disarranged.

– Yes, Felicia declared. On the road.

She watched with him as the small truck swept down out of sight, still safe enough till obscured by the bushes and vines that ran riot in their back garden.

– Poor Mercy, he prayed. So little has gone right for her through the years though it's difficult to think how she deserved such a miserable lot.

– There you go with your moral nothings, as if we deserve anything, good or bad.

– Cause and effect, he explained still watching the road.

– It's all causes, she retorted. It's never effects, till everything's wound up. The big bang.

– Day of Judgment.

– Certainly not. The idea of a Day of Judgment, even if one were so simple-minded as to believe it, would be no more than another cause; bliss or damnation, mindlessness or torment. Fido! she went on without a break or change of tone. You haven't finished your meal. Fido.

– Poor Mercy, the unselfish woman.

– Fido never answers. Never.

– Well you would insist on bringing him up with your modernistic system. What else could you expect? Had it been left to me he'd have begun with ancient Greek and *The Lives of the Saints.*

– My modernistic ideas! You miserable good foolish creature. I don't have ideas, I accept myself as I am.

– The problem with rationality, he replied mildly, is that its consequences are unpredictable, thinking of his Wolfgang Amadeus Fido, his loved-of-God.

– Who wants to predict? I'm sure I don't. It's all inevitable, so therefore futile. So much for reason, mere tampering with fate. I hope I've never been guilty of inventing an idea in my life. I certainly didn't think up any system of education for Fido, I can assure you of that for a start. Why am I imprisoned to suffer your endless purity? You are a monster, Sebastian, did you know that? An unnatural monster, simple like a saint is simple: passing the poison with an open hand, so to speak. Smiling as if death weren't breathing down your collar. Which it is. Oh my goodness, you callous man, how you make me suffer, keeping my mind in check as you do.

Miss Brinsmead picked up Rastus the cat and carried him cradled in her hands as she had once borne sacred reliquaries, back into the peace of the shop. From its paddock in the high neck of the valley, that cow gave one shocking bellow which silenced the birds. Everything listened for a minute to the stillness of what had happened.

Eight

In the pub, the smoked mirrors caught and sealed that gathering of ancient heads, presenting them as a gallery lovingly softened by the haze, and among them the two young men as unlikely missionaries carrying news nobody understood. The place was quiet and the drinkers immobile. Bubbles rose gently in the beer.

– I once heard a voice, said Uncle picking up the thread of Billy's unspoken thoughts. Singing in the middle of the night, it was. Coming from miles away. My dog Bertha gave one bark and then sat down. Unaccountable that. You'd think she was listenin. A man's voice. It sang and sang as if there was no endin and nothin else to do. Never heard anythin in all my days so beautiful. In the still of night, he said. Not even Annie's violin. I was sober too, he added to combat their disbelief. I was sittin up as wide awake as I am now. You don't believe me. It wasn't no dream and it wasn't no Remembering. Wasn't the radio. It was right here somewhere in our district. Up home I was, and all of a sweat though it was a cold night clearin to a touch of the frost.

Bill and Tony shook their heads so it might be thought they were sceptical about the unknown singer.

– An I thought I knew everythin, Uncle chuckled derisively. Wouldn't have been much more than a month back. If you wasn't so damn lazy, your generation, you might of heard it too. He took out a crumpled handkerchief, pulling the stuck creases apart. When he was ready he plunged his nose in and blew violently. Satisfied, he tucked the stiff handkerchief away again. Well, he said to their silence. Well, I might go and treat myself to a leak if you'll look after the beer. He waded through air heavy with Rememberings and plunged out the door and round the back to the lavatory outhouse.

The cow uttered her one penetrating hoot and at last fell silent.

– Bronumburnringunderruminyum, muttered Jasper behind the bar savagely controlling some latent outburst.

– A man could easy hate this place, Billy repeated himself.

– True enough, Tony agreed with a grateful smile.

The door slammed open and there stood a woman luminous with desperation. Jasper made use of the diversion to steal another tot of whisky from himself.

– What is it? Billy asked.

– This is the new person at Lang's, Tony introduced her being so pleased Bill had covered for him about the singing; also pleased in a more unexpected way which scarcely bore analysis.

Gasping for breath, Vivien told what she had seen, the Chinese woman, the truck with its flat tyre, the car climbing up the pass.

– Mercy Ping, Jasper declared in a normal voice.

Billy Swan caught hold of the woman's arm and propelled her back out into the street demanding to know if she was a nurse, forced her to a trot, made her run with him, run hard, the two of them belting down towards Brinsmeads'.

– No. But I've. Done some. First aid.

– Good enough let's hope, he found words to reassure her, then raced ahead. By the time she caught up he was already on a battered motorcycle kicking the engine into life. Vivien knew what he expected and climbed on, just as the surprised enquiring face of Elaine McTaggart, young Fred's mother, appeared round the corner of the welder's shed. The face filled with complex assessments. Elaine leaving the wives' tea-meeting had walked up in the nick of time to catch that woman running, no less, to climb on behind the Swan boy as if she had a right. Billy let in the clutch

71

and they roared away, an unexplained gap remaining where they had been, Vivien having to hug him round the waist to save herself being jolted off. She knew what he expected; not just concerning her pillion-riding. As he swung the bike into the first curve she tightened her hold on him, her palms flat against his flat, hard stomach. And he felt her envelop him. His head diamond-sharp with purpose, driving them both beyond safety, his body already heavy with its own designs. The bike swayed elegantly as a sailing-boat; Vivien was abandoned to it, let herself go, this was so easy, the roaring seemed to come from the rocks above, or now from inside herself she vibrated so strongly. Or else she and he were the silent rushing core of life, the axis of unmeaning matter. What purpose could be greater than theirs as rescuers? Once he turned his head as if he might shout something to her, but didn't. She responded with a slight pressure of her hands. So they roared on, abandoned to intimacy. Though she felt guilty in the emergency, her fingers crept about with tiny trespassings. The machine blared inappropriate appetites for all to hear. Cliff faces folded back at their approach, turning aside ridges, aeons, simple as pages. Far below, pictures of a farmhouse could be glimpsed, a small triangular dam, a clump of trees, half a dozen sheep, a black bull trotting across a paddock, a crow planing the ground. They bounced and rattled along the dirt road, they banked round a long curve which seemed to lead them burrowing right into the mountain ... and suddenly clear to where a man stood on the road ahead, outlined against the midday sky. Parked as far to one side as safety would allow, a car cooled, with a dog's head stuck out of the window. They drew up, scattering pebbles, the rich tune of the cycle throttled back.

– You bloody hooligan, yelled the man. At that speed ...

Billy swung his machine expertly on to the gravel verge and parked it in against the rockface.

– Where? Vivien asked the man, a gap eating her insides.

– You bloody fool, the man swore and she realized he was near weeping.

They saw the missing guidepost. The stranger in his city suit turned his back on them and went across, peering down. At a couple of bounds Billy was there too. In her mind Vivien relived the sight of that Chinese face lined by the compassion of years, her feverish concentration on the rutted track, tiny hands at work wrestling with the steering wheel as if it were a beast with contrary intentions. She was looking straight down the cliff at a wide ledge, perhaps one hundred feet below, where the upside-down chassis of the truck lay, one of its wheels still turning obediently.

– I saw her face, the city man confessed, speaking as if hypnotized. Then collected his nerves and controlled himself. He succeeded in putting on a public manner to shut off their intrusion.

The wrecked truck had the character of completeness, nothing to do with motion or happening. Only that one wheel offered a clue to any continuity. Otherwise this utterly alien thing (the never-seen, mud-caked, sunlit underside of a chassis) lay rectangular and final: the immobile past-tense flat on a shelf which had once been a bullock track hewn out of the mountainside by hand. Not even any dust hanging in the air. Simply a fixed object, in the present but already finished. And you knew it without thinking. The wheel thought for you; signalled messages raw and forbidden. Too late for pain.

– Was there a collision? Billy asked feeling the question itself dignified and a formality. But he didn't wait for an answer, the emptiness too much to bear. In fact he was following Vivien who lowered herself against the cliff, already below the lip of the roadway, groping for footholds, her shoe working this way and that, selecting, testing. She was reassuring herself too, the chunkiness of the rock more secure than she might have feared, the broken granite surface. Bill was beside her now, a little reckless in his determination not to let his sex down, not to be outdone in such a physical matter as rock-climbing. And asking himself who would act like this? How did she know what to do? She could climb, you saw that straight off.

– Should I come too? asked the man above with a display of indecision.

– No trouble, she called back angrily between breaths.

Billy glanced at her face, her concentration on the need to

climb well, she wasn't wasting time looking down, nothing less than complete control needed, he admired her then for feeling nervous and not showing it. He moved easily on the rockface of his country, accustomed to the feel. But, much as he wished to guide her, some important rule of tact told him not to. Together and in silence they crawled down towards the truck. For the duration, the world comprised handholds and footholds, cracks, grit, the occasional bush treacherously easy to grasp. There was a sense in which they wrestled with the land ... and in doing so, with each other. Vivien wished she had taken her cardigan off, but it was too late. She acknowledged that her knees were grazed though no pain could be felt in them. The rockface grew above them till the watcher was hidden from view. Trickles of water issued from seams. Periodically he or she dislodged a lump of rock, hearing it rattle and thud down; once quite a heavy one definitely clunked against the truck body (so that they glanced at each other with a shameful intimacy). Then they came to a diagonal ledge wide enough to sit on. Vivien's legs were shaking and she recalled that she'd been tired already before the emergency, having walked down to Mum Collins's and halfway back up the hill. They rested briefly, squatting at the rim of vast spaces. She forgot to control her breathing and let it come in grateful gulps. Billy watched her covertly, unexpectedly aware that she and Tony knew each other, that this was the woman Tony avoided talking about.

– You don't know who I am, said Billy with a lopsided smile, as inappropriate as it was strained.

– Do you mean? How can I trust you? Do you mean? What if you? Tried to push me off? she flung her furious mirthless joke at him.

– Yes, he replied to her astonishment. That's what I mean. His lopsided smile grew more pronounced, leaving one side of his face painfully serious.

– I've no breath. For rubbish like that. Acutely disappointed in him, she stood, ready to go on. She could see the man above them again and waved with a perfunctory flap of the hand.

– Careful ... a voice came drifting down.

But the worst was over. They completed the rest of the climb in less than half the time, antagonism between them. Billy who was ashamed of himself and puzzled, scrambled on ahead and leapt the final part. He ran to the truck. The cab was completely flattened. No one could be in there. He looked around, believing Mrs Ping must have been thrown clear. No sign of the body. But how far could she be thrown? Distance, he knew, being inexplicable in a motor accident. Or, for one mad lapse of hope, he believed she must be alive. He looked back up the cliff, expecting her to be clinging there. Then he was watching Vivien raking at the dirt where the door might have been, a waste of time. He was hearing her choked cry. He was beside her in fact. In a clump of grass lay a woman's hand chopped off at the wrist, where it issued a tiny blot of blood.

– Mrs Ping Mrs Ping, shouted Billy, the anguish suddenly clear and inescapable, wildly heaving at the dead vehicle, rocking it on its uncertain axis, his lungs thick with death in the stink of spilled petrol: that shimmering spirit hovering above the metal. Wait a minute, he gasped, the effort taking away his voice as he got his shoulder under the edge of the tailboard, just managing to ease the weight of the little truck and tip it slightly sideways.

– No use, Vivien wailed.

– Can't you see?

– No use! she shouted hysterically. Let it go.

– But if I ... crouch down this way ... oh.

He could no longer hold the weight and lowered the truck to its resting position. Rubbed his shoulder, foolish with his *Oh*, foolish and flat.

– Poor lady Mrs Ping, Vivien breathed the words in horror at what she'd glimpsed. They squatted in the dust together, childlike, companionable at last. Till with a hacking cough Bill was surprised to find his stomach knotting, himself leaning forward retching. Covered his face with his hands. Yet it was she, this unknown woman, who had seen what was there, who would carry for the rest of her life the knowledge of that smashed body, the grotesque random attachment of an arm and a leg to the pulp of bloody meat.

– Mrs Ping, she whispered through her tears, learning the name as if the name might of itself rescue some dignity.

– Can I help ..., came the faint contemptible voice above. It drew the two of them closer.

– But no one like this, Bill said not making sense as he reached out and picked up the hand. In his rough fingers it appeared icy and so frail. She used to hold my hand, he explained. Hers was bigger than mine then, I remember that.

Vivien watched fascinated because she caught him stroking the fingers lightly. You couldn't hope to divine his real thoughts. You wouldn't want to.

– She must have been opening the door, Vivien spoke quickly to prevent herself daring to look again at what he was doing.

– Is it the blood? he asked, examining the crushed wrist and then replacing Mrs Ping's hand where it now belonged among the grass. We don't understand do we?

– Not much.

– Everyone knew Mrs Ping. And then he nodded as if he'd been asked to reaffirm the fact.

– Listen, she said.

There was nothing. Billy felt the ache in his shoulder and contemplated the truck, hardly able to believe he had found strength to tilt it even so little. The stench made him ill. Then a single blowfly came circling in, droning, homing on blood.

– Her cow was dying, he said. They listened to the silence and the fly some more. The blowfly settled and they could hear the voice above talking syllables, incidental to the new void.

Vivien felt desperately thirsty, the air swayed heavy with petrol fumes. Her grazed knees began paining. Billy the priest was without the right phrase: somehow his ignorance had escaped detection so far. And even now the dignity of his bearing protected him, even God awaited his voice, the correct formula, before accepting the dead woman's soul. But he had not learnt: the secret never given him apparently. Yet today? So he pronounced his benediction haltingly as if hearing the words for the first time as he spoke them, as his lips recognized them by their shape.

– Our news, stay, queer then it, in no mean, a damn, any, down the face, wreck, we ... um ... (He was carrying some terrible burden for the inarticulate of earth.) Being, he sang. Addict us (achieving the gesture of reverence he'd never been taught). Queer vanity, he sang. Not many, too many, do not eyes? (and he saw the truck). Wreck! we aim simply, turn home. Billy took Vivien's arm as he had at the hotel and continued in his ordinary voice.

– Her cow was Alice. She loved Alice. Each of her cows, and his intonation rose almost to singing again. Dies Iris dies Alice, he began to explain. So the vet ... but lost any sense of vocation. He slapped the pockets of his leather jacket in a gesture of emptiness and she forgave him what he had done on the cliff face. They were mourners who paid their respects in their different ways.

Then they began creeping back up under the weight of knowledge, to report what they knew.

– You'd better come with me, the car driver decided, meaning except Billy, meaning Vivien, and shut her in.

Billy shrugged, slighted, and roared away ahead. Who was it had done all that could be done anyway? He was angry with the woman, whatever her name was, angry with her particularly. Was she too stuck up to go back on the bike? Hadn't she come with him? Hadn't he been good enough then? Hadn't he felt her hands on him? His front tyre reeled the road in, pulling the town towards him.

– I'll bet, I'll bet, he was muttering between clenched teeth, furiously kicking the bike through the gears. He watched them in his round mirror; the blue Ford nosing up into the curves, impersonal and closed. Who could know what was being said in there or how that fellow might be smiling at her, serious and confidential, shaken and smiling with fright? Bill Swan cut a semicircle in the dirt outside Brinsmeads', parked his bike as usual by the war memorial. He stood, slightly stiff in the legs, perhaps even trembling if he'd admitted it. Let the foreigner do the talking. He watched the two of them step out of their privacy.

Felicia Brinsmead was already at the door.

– Yes, she said when all three had gathered on the footpath

but before they'd had a chance to speak. It's a sad day. Mercy Ping dead under her lorry.

Vivien looked sharply at her, for how could she have known? Then noted that Billy didn't appear surprised.

– We do still have the telephone I suppose? Miss Brinsmead waved the stranger into the shop and the house without mirrors beyond. My brother will show you, but once you reach the police on the line it takes them an hour to get here as a rule. She shook her head till the bundle of hair swung heavily. Well Billy, she continued. You'll have some memories of Mrs Ping?

He looked away, nodding.

– The bad part, she concentrated. Was the hand. The door did shut on it. Still she'll have been pleased all in all, considering. The way it happened.

– What way did it happen? Billy confronted her savagely.

– I mean she didn't smash into him, her face assuming the eighth of its fifteen expressions, the exact middle, the neutral one.

– It was almost like, Vivien said. It was almost as if she ...

– Yes, Miss Brinsmead interrupted, having no patience with gentility. I'd surmise, my dear, she steered over the edge on purpose. To save involving him, him in there. Isn't that it? Mercy Ping saw things that way all her life, avoiding collisions, taking the easy way if it could be thought of as virtuous.

This filled Billy with helpless rage; it sounded so convincing. And Miss Brinsmead fixed him with her lively stare, eyes snapping alert, as clear as saying *Now if I can know all this without being told, can it be supposed I do not know why you were here this morning asking for gelignite?* He faced up to her but with no lie ready. His breath came quickly. His secret. As long as she didn't guess his secret. The simple need to swallow grew intense; it might look like a gulp and be interpreted. Out of the question. The old lady pursued her line:

– Mrs Ping made a necessity of virtue! Neither of them smiled at this repartee, few people bother to retain the least command of elegant wit, as can be demonstrated any day of the week. Doubtless, she added, this was thought advantageous to her profession.

– What was she then? asked Vivien at last, saving Billy from scrutiny, her eyes swimming in tears.

– The schoolmistress, dear. She taught all our children until the school closed down. And then most of the young men went away. Why? you ask. Because otherwise they'd never be free to run their own lives, their fathers wouldn't let them, fathers being what they generally are. You see Vivien, we're pretty tough in these parts, the old ones live a long time and keep a tight rein on their farms. But sons want to inherit while they're still able to make the most of the work. There's the problem for you. Last year for instance a couple of brothers inherited their place after working for their father all their lives.

– How old were they then?

– Eighty-one and seventy-nine as I recall.

Footsteps could be heard creaking across the shop floor and the voice of the car driver, who emerged accompanied by the patriarch Brinsmead.

– ... and I should be most interested to hear them.

– Felicia my dear, may I introduce to you the Honourable Frank Halloran, Senator Frank Halloran ... my sister, Miss Brinsmead.

– How do you do.

– I'm good for another seventy years of wickedness, thank you.

– This is Miss Vivien who has recently come to join us and reside in our dying township. Also Mr Swan one of our young residents.

The senator shook hands with Vivien only, though he did bestow on Felicia Brinsmead a sweet lingering smile such as men gratify themselves giving out willynilly to ladies old enough not to misunderstand. However, this particular lady adopted an unexpectedly ironic tone.

– Senator Halloran. How could we forget? The gentleman whose committee wants us to find a use for its surplus paint. Stormtroopers in the battle against rot. Next you'll be trying to save yourself going to sleep at night. Death is coming, Senator, despite the dear committee. She chuckled, careless of his feelings.

– I have already reaffirmed that we wish the matter dropped, Sebastian explained to his sister reprovingly.

The visitor mutely supported this rebuke.

– Well thank you, Felicia crooned. The country is lucky to be so rich.

– I assure you madam … the senator attempted.

– Don't bother with *me*, she cut him short. I have the freedom to say what I please, I'm well fed, I have a house to live in. Bother about the rest. Now, she demanded denying him any chance to reply, what of the police? Did you get through to Constable Pope? Is he on his way and what did he say? Are there any clues as to why Mercy did it, poor Mercy?

– He'll be here in about an hour, the senator addressed Vivien Lang who replied by speaking generally to the whole party:

– If you'd like to walk up to my house while we're waiting I'll make a pot of tea. She was pulling herself together, to use her father's phrase, wonderfully. She avoided the senator's eyes, not wishing anybody to think she meant him especially, aware of how out of place his carefully casual clothes looked, his clipped much-combed hair, his polished fingernails. She was critical of how his head tilted back, the way he clasped his hands behind him, even of his black dog who strutted about the car inspecting its wheels with the air of one who knows.

Billy glared at her, though by what right of possession you couldn't be sure. Watching his behaviour it would have been difficult to guess at their relationship, he was so tentative and then so impulsive, distanced yet passionate. At any rate, he appeared to have very little control of his expressions. So Vivien turned to him coldly, forbidding any presumption, explicitly awaiting a reply to her invitation. Which he was now weak enough to give.

– My grandfather's expecting me back at the pub.

And Vivien caught herself avoiding his furious impotent eyes, to inspect his shoes, judging him by them. She observed how one toe had been dented and dulled, though she didn't know enough to connect this with the motorcycle. It was the senator who replied to her invitation; of course he would come and delighted.

Having excused herself for a moment and promised she

wouldn't be long, Vivien crossed the road and into the welder's workshop, determined he wouldn't get away with it. The masked man engrossed in cutting a sheet of steel, sparks splashing round his feet, put aside the oxy torch and pushed up the mask when he sensed an intruder. He listened, politely serious. Was this what he had expected?

– I just wish you'd seen what I saw, it choked her to say.

– Was there a fall first?

She was swaying on the motorcycle, delirious with submission, breathing petrol fumes as Mrs Ping gave up her spirit, she was kneeling into the knives of the cliff, then her feet sticking in puddles of blood, her eyes a casket still heavy with the sight of a living head of hair plastered to a blob of meat.

– I saw her face when she came out of here, Vivien squawked.

– Who gave you the right, Mr Ping asked. To teach me about my own wife? And the two pieces of steel he'd cut he now clamped in a vice.

– Your wife! You could have tried. You might have saved her.

– From what? Mr Ping struck a match and relit his oxy torch indicating that the simplest questions are those you can seldom answer. He adjusted the flame to a faintly feathering blue tip and tugged the mask over his face. His accuser meant nothing to him. Mr Ping, absorbed into the rituals of the metal heating, red then white, stared through his tinted window as the point of juncture turned liquid. He applied a drop of soft steel creating a brilliant globe. An act of respect. The liquid now dazzled, a tiny sun. He kept it like that, meditating, a disc of no meaning, this symbol beyond human care or blemish was the sun. And in Mr Ping's head his creation pulsed and shone, imprinted at the back of the eye. Silence surrounded him as he stood absorbed in this mystical event, unaware his visitor had left. The shed was certainly empty by the time the metal cooled and the weld set and something now became possible. He lifted the joined steel carefully and examined it by daylight. Yes, he and Mercy had once been happy.

– Who can say? he said, replying to some question of his own. And when he went to the door to squint at the world, Felicia Brinsmead was alone outside her shop watching him.

Nine

I don't believe, Felicia thought, I've got a soul. So I'm not in hell. When I was born my mother shouted *Go away,* but I was older than her (and she sensed it) and felt sorry for her too. Nothing could be worse for a parent than the child feeling pity. But she's had her revenge if ever she wanted it, darling Mamma, kiss kiss, she'd already bred her avenging angel, her painted saint rocking my pram, a nine-year-old wonder in an isolated community where a child of any kind but mine is gold, both in value and heartbreak, the old house at Wit's End gone, a few stumps among the grass, dead with its cruel memories of the darling and the dear, but the saint hurt them before he hurt me, Sebastian found them out, oh yes, that evening I'll never forget, no one expected it, he came home late, face caked with dirt, jacket torn, legs shaky I saw them I saw, made his announcement, he had found a new lead, would stake a claim, a skin of gold between the strata, and the darlings went white with fear, the Golden Fleece I'll call it because I've been reading the classics, sigh smirk, him not among the rabble of illiterates. Who have you told, who knows? they whispered, God in their voices. No one, nor shall. Right, and all four of us crept about like criminals, creep, pad, ssh, pulling down blinds and huddling round the kitchen table to divide the spoils, Papa offering the special favour of going down to check it out for him and already heaving his coat on, like dead wings the coat, no, the saint speaking upright, no thank you, so calm and strong, beginning to behave like a man under authority as the Bible has it, and Mamma's hair starting out round her head, she bristled, she demanded, oh it was worth it, she moaned, she begged, dear Mamma who wanted to push me back inside her when she knew what I knew, the Golden Fleece and she grovelled and pretended to have a fit, eyes rolling white, and Papa sitting numb at the table in his heavy coat grinding his hands till the fact sank in, weighing his dignity against his greed, the poison, dead to all intents, the Golden Fleece killed him though he dragged out his drunken life another month, and Sebastian never did tell, saint's word as good as his deed, straight and narrow, but he took my hand like a lover, spoke gently, you come, ah, we walked out into the cold night on the crisping grass round the mountain to sleep an hour by someone's haystack, then riding on a bullock wagon past Whitey's Fall and down the track, lurching to the edge laughing into space, right down and over the plain to the port, oh saint you gave her her revenge, and I was sixteen already too soon, then sailing up the coast, him being tender yet never touching, stroke of the feather, next day in Sydney, the cliffs like cathedrals in the rain, who never thought of rain in Sydney from the pictures, and the hills suffocated with houses so close you could never know anybody, tramcars, stalls selling deadly-coloured fruits, must be touched up, thousands of office people so I whispered whoever makes all their shoes, and we lodged our claim, joint names, the registrar questioning us, had we this and did we that and sign here here here here here and here, so that we came out side by side glad of the rain and splashing feathers of water round our ankles, like a bride and groom.

When it first happened I kept my eyes down because I couldn't tell what they might show.

Until I found my powers I thought this was the end, well it was the end, admit the fact Felicia Brinsmead, it was the end and has been ever since for fifty-eight years, when we left the house, left that woman's hate and that drunken hopeless man remembering his dignities, it was Uncle the young bullock driver took us down to the port and never said a word to anybody about us running away, must be loyal, ask after his health.

She placed the cat in the open box of eucalyptus drops and stood a moment looking at him. She patted her wad of hair allowing her hand to linger on that crusty lump heavy against her neck and shoulders, reaffirming its uniqueness.

– What about me! she cried. She went cold all over. Knowledge bound her icily in its windings. That a Chinese youth with a godlike carriage of the back should come to her from the east, was all she guessed out of the chaos at the time. She despaired of rising even when she suspected that by now she must be rising.

– When shall I breathe again, she pleaded.

The cat purred from its bed of lollies.

Ten

The faithful Tony McTaggart remained in the Mountain bar waiting for Billy to return. And now came Billy, giving out a black mood.

– Another beer? Tony offered by way of asking if there was anything he could do.

– Where's Uncle?

– Went out a while ago.

Billy thought this over. Just his luck when he wanted the old bloke. But why had he gone? It was unexpected. He watched Jasper for some clue in that clay complexion.

– You met her then? Tony asked with reluctance, thinking but saying nothing of his first meeting with her, the companionship of walking up the hill, himself in her service, almost reverently.

– Yes. Another Lang. Miss Lang, Bill's tone of voice told everything his friend could not bear to believe, even to the exasperation.

So it's to be them is it! Tony cried in his mind. His voice took charge:

– One beer Jas, just the one, me mate's on the wagon.

This slight dig caused Bill to sigh with annoyance. Why must they all demand so much of him, what was he failing to do this time? Jasper, when bringing the beer, dropped a few words like small change on the counter.

– Your grandpa's been fetched Bill, he wheezed. By Elaine McTaggart. His troublesome head wagged fitfully and let fall a few more dull coins. Gone down that way.

The news had a perplexing ring. Something to do with Mrs McTaggart he'd seen only recently, a corner of his mind where he had tucked some information about her. Were the twins found out? The kids in strife: Fred, Susie? The unease persisted.

– Well, said Bill. I'm staying here with my mate. He'll know where to find me.

Which caused Tony to smile gratefully. For a flutter of light he was in touch with those moments when he submitted to Billy's teeth flashing at him, when a waterfall drowned out the blood in his ears, when he felt Billy's hand creating his shoulder, shaping its draught-horse muscles; and squabbling magpies flickered black and white puzzles on the green paddock.

– Mercy Ping got killed then? the publican asked in a mumble.

– Mrs Ping! Tony shouted, astonished because Mrs Ping was part of his life so she couldn't die without warning.

– She was the last schoolie of Whitey's Fall, announced one person in the bar. And this was the cue for everyone to have his say.

– There'll be no more now.

– A good little worker Mercy was, God rest her.

– She didn't half give my youngsters a belting once.

– It was me gave her away at her wedding, her father being dead before then. She never had no children of her own, that's the wonder.

– There's a warning in it.

– Could've sworn I heard her slaughtering her cow a while back.

– Never did take to Chinese myself I've got to say in all honesty, but she was another case and one of the best, more like us if you know what I mean.

– I used to say why don't you get yourself a new vehicle

Merce? Or get your bloody husband to patch it up, he's the expert.

As a child, Billy Swan had been eager to learn. Things came to him with singular clarity when they came at all. So he learnt about the seven-year cycle of the cicada grub, also the difference between solar and lunar months. No trouble at all. He understood immediately that sand or sugar running from a hole in the bottom of a bucket would run at the same speed whether the bucket was full or half-empty, he knew that a cow he'd seen in the bush three days ago had been loose for too long and needed stripping out, that the first notes of a whipbird's cry are made by the female bird and the whip-sound by the male, that you can find your way anywhere on earth by close enough observation, that there was once a poet called William Shakespeare who wrote the most famous history of England, that if you chew the flowers of a selected gumtree you feel dizzy, that for more reasons than the obvious you can't breathe underwater, that the whirlpool of hair is on the left side of a boy's head and the right side of a girl's, that *amo* means I love in a dead language, that there are people in the world who would think him rich even if they could see how he lived. These things he knew without effort, but had great difficulty anticipating what he might come to know next. He was modest about his knowledge because he knew it went no further than that: it was just things he knew, and he was glad to know them but they were the kind of things anybody could know. And generally speaking everybody did. For this reason he was slow to offer advice. Except to Tony who didn't qualify.

More of Billy's knowledge had been learnt from his grandfather than from Mrs Ping though. It was his grandfather who pointed out the whistling eagle's nest in August and the death adder's nest in May; who made him an expert with the bowline, the sheepshank and the blackwall hitch; who brought him home some squid from the coast and demonstrated how to select the vein, slit the fine membrane and peel off the skin at a single flip of the wrist; who else could have taught him to tell the time of year as well as the time of day by observing the mountain's shadow? Also to forecast the migration of birds? He owed it to his grandfather that each morning he was in the habit of watching ants as well as aircurrents to know the weather. And thanks to the same source of knowledge Billy had learnt to laugh at his first failures with women.

– Benedictus qui venit in nomine Dominus, Jasper intoned in the trembling voice of his childhood.

– She's part of our religion now, someone said.

– She is too ... she's dead, a surprised voice agreed.

– She could tell a tale or two after today.

– She'll have us to remember when she learns how.

Jasper held up his glass of illicit whisky and led a general toast to Mercy Ping. Afterwards the silence congealed, but the only person aware of it as such was the one who remained outside it, Tony McTaggart who couldn't learn how to lose himself. The rest had slipped back where they had been before. He waited, a respectful unbeliever.

– It's all over then Rupie. Miss Felicia Brinsmead's words prevented Mr Ping from ducking back inside. Even so he did not reply, knowing better than to make that mistake. Indeed what was there about Felicia he did not know?

– All over for both of you, Miss Brinsmead added significantly. And she advanced on him as he stood theatrically in the dark doorway.

– Yes, yes, she said commenting on his thoughts. I'm quite well aware what a nuisance I am. Times have changed. And it's no good pretending everything's alright or that Mercy would have wanted it to happen quickly now she was tired of living. She was tired of you and tired of her loyalty to you. No more than that. And worn out by the long years of work, days as numerous as dogs in Lhasa, howling days, slinking hungry days, hungry for you. Very well Rupie, so you suggest I'd better be mindful of my part in her unhappiness. I am. But I have unhappinesses of my own, we Brinsmeads do have. You'd never understand. What? It's no use trying to present me with a blank mind. You can't keep it up, no one can. After all I'd like to help. You were so beautiful once. Goodness what an ugly little possum you've turned into since you gave up trying with Mercy. You were like the sun when I fell in love with that hairless skin, those eyes, that shining charm, and your body so small, so strong. You were a surprise to me, something exotic. At last I was surprised. I was surprised once by Julius Caesar. And you surprised me again. I took a long time to forgive Mercy, but one does forgive. Especially when it's Mercy. There was a strange thing, you're the only one who ever had difficulty forgiving Mercy. You didn't forgive her did you? What had she done Rupie, you're going blank again. And don't think such things about me. It's just that I know what I know.

They stood talking in the sunshine, two old friends: he sad and silent, the bereaved husband; she animated but observing the propriety of a respectful demeanour and restrained tone. Mr Ping suffered her examination, a blank lack of expression on his face, but rocking agitatedly from the ball of his foot to the heel.

– It's to do with your vanity Rupie. Somehow she was killing you and you thought: soon it'll be a case of her or me. Now aren't I telling the truth? You don't mind her dying, because you're alive. And inside that pair of overalls you think you're still young and handsome. O my God what a fool the person is. You're a wrinkled wreck and no more likely to tempt the world into giving you pleasure than I am. So there. Goodness, you must think I've lost my mirror. I'm just waiting for the time I can slough off this hideous hulk and start afresh. But things won't be rushed, they take their own time. You never did join our Rememberings. Were you afraid of me and what I knew? I don't blame you, I used to be very, very angry with you. Jealous as well, I'll admit it. That was so long ago though, fifty-five years I suppose. Look at you now, it's enough to make a cat laugh.

The elderly Chinese composed his hands in front of him, eyes set in a spiderweb of meaningless wrinkles; and the fat lady, her moony face filled with gentle unconcern, her definite gestures, her bag of dead hair with one wisp at the bottom escaping as a child's golden curl.

– The cow died, Miss Brinsmead commented. Why does that make you jump? Alice died. She what? Mercy went because of Alice? To save her?

For the first time the man opened his mouth and spoke.

– What if I smashed your bloody head in with this spanner?

– Of course you're upset, she cooed imperturbably. And we all offer you our sincerest condolences Mr Ping. This is a sad day. The people are gathering at the Mountain, I should be there by rights. Don't forget me if there's anything I can do.

She turned her back and ambled home.

In the turmoil of his conscience, Rupert Ping knew there was a lot he could be accused of, and far more that folk would try pinning on him. He wished at this moment he might be an artist like Miss Bertha McAloon and have some means of creating a statement that he could give the town as a gift, summing up his long martyrdom to Mercy and the Whitey's Fall school.

Was I frightened? Fido wrote in his diary marked SECRET. He had gone to the door believing for a moment it was a birthday cake delivery.

He recognized the mountain now as an obstacle. Yes he painted it with dark resentful impasto and yet in a sense carelessly. He asked himself was he frightened? But it was only that mad lady at the door yelling for help when there was nothing but a revelation of yellow street, which he felt as physical joy. He had pulled up the blind on a glaring sea of saffron dust from which her shoes and her legs grew mauve shadows. He let her look at him, on purpose, because of this gift. And if news got round, so what? Was it any worse than the goldrush?

Also, when he looked out of the kitchen window at the familiar swirling shapes, the bleached snake of road being eaten by green frogs, hadn't he seen her with the man called Bill Swan going fast downhill leaning the motorbike as they went round corners? Bill Swan who came asking for gelignite, the very gelignite he needed himself and had hidden away? Fido enlarged the diary entry:

Her face twisted up like a lot of big freckles. Gruesome. Is it always like that? Her neck was red with tiny green goose-bumps. I could have bitten it. Inside her jumper she was all shaky and mumpty. She has got big teeth that look strong. I don't like them. Stones.

The overlapping weatherboards of the School of Arts behind her advanced busily as grey breakers in a windy sea. He brought the brown of her hair forward with pink confetti. As for the sky, Fido took brave risks with the sky, this being a more familiar tradition, even to leaving bits out altogether. Which pleased him.

Tea being served on the verandah amid the smells of paint and disinfectant. Senator Halloran insisted he found it delightful and didn't object to any smell. This was true enough while he angrily recollected Mr Sebastian Brinsmead's lecture: Australia is a continent on which you cannot build anything acceptable both to the land and to permanent habitation. The old fogey dialled the police: it isn't a country for buildings, the natives never had any, and if we'd been more sensitive to where we were neither would we in all probability. What we do put up can't possibly stand as part of the country, either it will remain an imposition or else it'll rot, hello, Constable Pope? Constable . . .? No, the senator wasn't in the least troubled by any paint smell, thank you. He received his cup of tea with gratitude and began to explain how slowly and with what habitual care he had been driving up the mountain. But even while he talked, his attention was employed in closely observing his hostess. Of course he was agitated and suffering a nervous reaction himself, nevertheless he remained collected enough to find her positively pleasing: the warm swell of her breasts a reassurance, her quick eyes lovely, her decisive movements comforting. In all, she was energetic yet feminine. So capable but vulnerable, yes, this he felt to be true, and hadn't he witnessed her prompt courage out there on the road? Then as she answered him and changed the topic he admired her for diverting him from treacherous confessions. Yes he admired her. He knew now he had been admiring her all along. And especially the discreet signals of a sense of humour, which might blossom on a more appropriate occasion. He commented on the view, the splendid prospect of the entire region.

– Miss Lang, he observed. You at least appear to have no aversion to painting and repairing your property.

– Ought I to have?

– Well Whitey's Fall as a whole has ... or I've been led to believe so. A definite preference for a state of collapse.

– If the condition of the buildings ... she partially acquiesced.

– And they've told me to mind my own business. Though I'm on the Aesthetic and Historical Resources Commission. You see, we have a plan for the area, including monuments which we'd like to keep untouched, he explained, his breath coming in short bursts.

– Picturesque, Vivien supplied with a hint so faint it was missed.

– I came hoping to hear other views than those put by Mr Brinsmead in his letter, so I'm very pleased to have met you. But tell me, what does a woman of education do in a backwater like this?

– Please don't quote me as having any opinion, Vivien said hastily. I'm quite new here and still feeling my way. Mr Brinsmead is a genuine identity, not to mention his sister.

The senator gazed at the future, displeased. Had he been wrong? She was violating his image of her already. As if wilfully punishing himself, he reverted to the subject of the accident and his own part in it.

– The strange thing was, I knew we were headed for trouble. I did see the truck on one of the bends higher up, only for a couple of seconds, but enough to notice something the matter with it.

– She was driving with a flat tyre.

– The truck was wobbling, quite definitely I saw it wobble. That's why I think it couldn't have been avoided.

– I was a witness. I shall certainly tell the police the truck was out of control.

Vivien looked away hurriedly towards the garden to protect her distress as she remembered. Her lips trembled on the verge of tears. She could not face him, little expecting the whole new situation awaiting her.

– Hullo! she said in quite another tone. A visitor.

An elderly man edged his way up the track towards her gate, pushed along on two walkingsticks. He paused, cleared his throat and spat discreetly to one side.

– The pace things happen here, complained the senator. The shock reaction prepared to set in.

Vivien made her way down the steps, unaware of how closely Senator Halloran observed her movements, though a certain look in his eye had already astonished her. The visitor waited a polite few yards from the gate allowing her to reach it first. He was nodding agreeably to the tea party.

– Beautiful day, Vivien greeted him, realizing in retrospect that in some way she had caught the senator out.

– Could do with a drop more rain though, replied Uncle smiling in all his hundred wrinkles. Bessie Collins told me you was here. Are you comfortable in the old place, like? He moved to the gate and rested his arms there.

– I love it.

– By jiminy you're ...

They stood close but not shaking hands, his face telling her something forgotten, sweet and precious. Uncle could not speak, a painful happiness beat in his chest and choked him. The perfume of grass tugged and nudged them, the wind rushing to get past.

– Annie, he croaked finally. His eyes in their slack lids filled with the youthful shining sky. She had nothing to say, understanding what she wasn't able to put a name to.

Uncle had walked this way countless times. He knew every bend in the track. The turning leading to her gate he had cut with his own mattock, so shouldn't he know it? Through a private mist he saw Annie walking down to meet him with that loping dignified walk just suppressing a dance in the step, her large limbs, her manner giving her away, the pride of being sensible. So he'd tease her with his wicked suggestions until the blush spread from her cheeks to her neck and down across her bosom. He also knew her quick anger when she thought her independence was challenged. There had once been a gold digger went mad, shooting at random, stumbling up the track in a frenzy and Uncle, scared as he was, went out on that verandah just up there to chase the bloke off and protect Annie, but Annie had followed and she it was who'd said poor man, has nobody bathed your cut head? Here hold still, you can't imagine how it's been wounded, and I'll see to it, come along in. It was Annie who'd pushed aside the shotgun like an irrelevance and led the madman into her house to feed and bandage him and later explain to the new doctor the stresses of a lonely life prospecting; so the man went back to the main street and apologized to everyone, shamefaced and polite, before driving away in the ostentatious luxury of the doctor's American car, down to the coast where he could catch a steamer home to Sydney. And weren't the four cypress pines, each guarding a corner of the house, the very saplings he had planted for her seventy years ago, wanting to say: my love will grow and last as long as these, but instead saying: make sure you water the bloody things or they'll die on you, so that she laughed and kissed him. And wasn't the verandah itself the one he'd built singing as he hammered and sawed, swearing it would be solid enough for a clan of Scotchmen to go dancing the strathspey. And when he came home from a trek, the bullocks a-lather and storekeepers bullying to be first off with their orders, men weeping over their mail and women handling the heavy bales of fabric, dogs setting up such a racket the bullocks would jingle their yokes and kick out sideways from fear . . . wasn't it always the way, he'd look for her and she'd be among the women not making anything special of it, smiling at her work and heaving solid bolts of cloth or crates of bottles, and Walter Schramm who'd opened the Mountain Hotel with a German band concert, giving her a pat on the bottom like the cheerful Rhinelander he was, so she swung round and clouted him a beauty, and the nightflares had flickered and smoked right through till the early hours on these great occasions while diggers drank and danced and sang and did their best with their lives, while the shopkeepers slaved the whole night unpacking goods, tallying the stuff and its condition, marking the delivery slips and invoices, spiking each one completed, then loading their counters and shelves with temptations. But most of all wasn't his mind full of Annie's violin, that lonely, close, strident, wistful sound? Sweet, clumsy Annie perched on the edge of a kitchen chair, fiddle jammed under her chin, eyes closed to help her remember, and fingers a-flutter while the bow sawed; the music

94

of reels and jigs, sad airs and keening, old songs and new waltzes, she gave them all. Sometimes of an evening you'd hear her from as far as the School of Arts, you could stand under the trellis out of sight and think what you chose (it had been done) while the distant melodies threaded their way down to you with the occasional help of night birds and treefrogs. Every step of the track Uncle knew. The slope of it, the sideways cant, still caused him to suck at his lips with resignation; he'd meant it to be perfect but he wasn't the best with a mattock nor the most patient. That perfume of grass made his silly head sing. He slapped one hand on the gatepost.

– Annie Lang, he said. You always said you'd get me in the end. Here I am at ninety year and no more sense than I had at twenty.

Vivien watched the visions moving in his eyes, the ancient hand like a weatherworn glove, the quivering chin, cruel comprehension breaking down his smile into a grimace of disillusionment. He consulted her eyes shyly, pleadingly: one stranger to another.

– Well, she said. I'm Annie's kin. She's my great-aunt. I look like her, don't I? She's told me about you, if you're Uncle. She calls you Arthur.

What he needed was comfort, you couldn't mistake that. It gave her a power which she found gratifying.

– My aunt told me she'd been a fool to throw her life away on anybody else but you.

He didn't bother to conceal the spasm of pain. This resolved a question of sixty years' standing. He had not been wrong.

– She's still alive and she said to give you a warning, those were her words. Any old buck from you and your noisy mates, Auntie said, and she'll be here with the big stick to sort you out. That was exactly how she put it.

Uncle's joy was urgent, he clasped her across the gate, no words in him for what he knew. Tears ran down the side of his nose because his face was cocked at an angle, for as well as being taller, she stood higher on the slope. He had to reach up to hug her. So, with the awkward gate between, they swayed in an unequal embrace. His heart sang its unbearable pulsing, his face alive with the rich years. Vivien returned the gesture. Sick though she felt with the knowledge of Mrs Ping's death, she answered his hands with hers. She was learning. She had not known people other than Auntie could behave like this. And Auntie wasn't the same, being a relative. Vivien's upbringing had been polite and urbane in most respects: for as long as childhood lasted she sat at table with her elbows tucked in the way her father wished to see them, or hands in her lap, always knocked at closed doors, never lounged crosslegged. Necessity had made her compliant. Her father was a widower and he relied on her cooperation so that a decent home would be possible. He used to say: If I have to wear myself out teaching you the basic things, how are we going to have time left for fun? Not that they were ever known to have fun or anything like it, even though she satisfied his least whim in this matter. She came to be in charge of the practical things, that was her reward; cooking, sewing and washing since she was seven. But there'd always been some necessity for not having it seem so. Half her energy (it was her own energy the relationship exhausted, not his) was wasted on appearing to be good when she felt wild, appearing to be helpless and decorative when she was practical and bossy. The only time she had ever disgraced herself in his company was once in church. It was an ancient church, perhaps the one at Peterborough because they did visit Peterborough, right in the middle of a solemn silence, somebody in a nearby pew broke wind; she doubled up, cramped her stomach to stop herself laughing and shaming Daddy, but the culprit ruined everything by saying in an elderly apologetic and perfectly audible voice, pardon! This finally was too much and her obscene bubble of laughter caused an entire family in front to half-turn disgustedly in her direction, and a deaconess behind leaned forward to scorch her with a hiss. Daddy was mortified, which you could understand, especially on this particular Sunday because some important person with him was apparently impressed by his piety. And Daddy knew hardly any people of the assistant manager class.

Taken as a whole, Vivien had enjoyed a happy childhood, but one so needlessly taxing that she could not now understand her father's motives. Nor those of any of his circle, the visitors who came and joined them for dinner occasionally, or more often for ersatz coffee after dinner, who stayed till late to make up a four for whist or a three for darts or a pair for draughts. She (who now struggled again for the control to accustom herself to the thought of Mrs Ping's pulped flesh underneath the truck, the stench of bile) had been encouraged by her sole parent to appreciate nature, harmless things like primroses and catkins and brooks, but not vipers or nettles or caves; to be kind to animals, which involved putting oneself in the animal's position – How would you like to be a beetle trodden on by some mountain like you? She learnt to express profound respect for Queen Elizabeth, Henry VIII's daughter, Henry himself being another honoured if naughty person, Sir Francis Drake, Boadicea, Lord Nelson, King Alfred and many more. She thought affectionately of Scottish heather which she'd never seen, of the Orchard of England, the snowcapped mountains of Wales and the Welsh coalmines with their dead canaries as well, the goodness of Sir Humphry Davy's heart, she thought affectionately about the Houses of Lancaster and York, the red rose and the white, wool and cotton, about Stonehenge and the Potteries, the Fens and the Backbone of England which was a Watershed. She knew why Mary Queen of Scots had been in the wrong and Cromwell too, for different if similar reasons. Hitler was anathema to her and so were the Japanese. She remembered Heligoland and the Bikini Atoll, knew the hums of Pooh and had herself treasured a teddybear until she was thirteen. Lord Tennyson was the poet she most admired though she'd scarcely read more than 'The Lady of Shalott'. Yet through her childhood of adult impositions and strictures, she remained adventurous. She never hesitated to be first into a boat, or across a railway line when the signals said all-clear for the train, or up a ladder, or into the Haunted House. Her friends had squealed with alarm, but she plunged her hands into the beehive to lift out the frame of honeycomb crawling with its dangerous creators, she it was who'd mixed the bad-egg gas for the geography teacher's desk, and though it wasn't she who actually put it there she accepted the blame. And who was it had torn a map of the stars from the public library's *Encyclopaedia Britannica* to use that night in a successful bid to identify Orion? Most of all, she it was who had loved and loved Aunt Annie when everybody else laughed at the mad old lady, and it was to her that Aunt Annie had given her violin, that eccentric instrument with its powerful tone. Vivien's talent for music had disconcerted her father even in the comb-and-paper days. So she realized her hands, surprisingly, knew what to do. They untied knots when others failed, cleaned fish, painted portraits that shocked Miss Mountcastle, mastered the fiddle, kneaded bread. And now they knew how to cope as a leathery old man clutched them, praised them with his gentleness, adored them with his lack of restraint. She was embarrassed to have him behave like this in front of an outsider who would certainly be weighing every move over the rim of his teacup, but her embarrassment was more on his behalf than her own so he didn't feel it. The sick nausea that had been with her for some reason (surely?) was no longer a trouble.

– Please come in Uncle, I'm not alone but never mind.

– Your husband is it? Keepin you under his thumb? He raised his voice to be heard from the house. Ah well, take me arm and he won't suspect a thing.

– He's just a visitor, she whispered. A stranger who'll soon be going and then you can tell me everything.

What a morning it had been: the children at the fence; her visit to Mum's tea meeting; conflict with the children's mother; the crazy truck; her run to get help; the haunting face of a pale child at the Brinsmeads' door; the motorbike ride; that young man with demanding eyes; the dead body in the truck; meeting with a senator; and now Uncle bringing a reminder of poor Auntie and the prospect of loneliness. She unlatched the gate.

– That still works then, he observed.

– I'm Vivien, she introduced herself as they walked up the path together studying one another's shoes. Vivien Lang.

– So you're a Lang. Her brother's ...

– ... son was my father. Yes.

– And where's he now?

– Dead. In England. Even Auntie is in England you know. Though she's not dead. Anything but.

– Go along with you! I can't seem to see Annie over in England. How did she come by the money?

– Now, Senator Halloran this is Mr Swan who was nearly my great-uncle.

The guest on the verandah offered formal greetings.

– What're ya doin here then? Uncle demanded. Try the other ear, that one's gone on me again.

– Waiting for the police.

– Fine place to pick, considerin they haven't got a station for thirty-five mile and too damn close at that. Uncle scrutinized him. You must be city-bred then are you? He shook his head, pleased and amazed, confirmed in his knowledge of the world. Police out here at Whitey's . . . Shall I tell you a story? asked Uncle crashing into the shaky clutches of a wicker chair.

– Please go ahead, the senator replied testily.

– Well there was this fellow walkin along a riverbank, see? He come on a lump a string. Simple ordinary string. So he kicked it out a his way. You can understand that. No use to him. But he got his foot caught in a bit of a tangle. And when he pulled at it he found one end led into the river. What does he do but pull on it, gentle fisherman's touch, you see. Pulled in the wet string till it got a bit heavier and he found the end of the string tied to a piece of wire. You with me? Well this fella said it was a mystery, so he pulled on the wire till he found the end of that tied to a chain. He couldn't stop now could he? A course he pulled the chain, you'd do the same, and up with the wet chain came the end of a bloody great cable. The cable was so heavy he could only just lift it but he pulled all the same. The cable was as heavy as he was. They pulled at each other, stuck like that and him on the river bank, a toss up whether he'd get it out or it'd pull him in the water.

Pause.

– Then what? the senator prompted, airing the virtue of patience.

– Then nothin a course. That's it. What more do yer want to

be told? Sorrow welled up in Uncle. Hadn't he seen with his own eyes the letter Annie wrote to Sebbie Brinso in her unmistakable writing while there was no letter for him? He took hold of himself.

– A friend of mine collects folk stories, the politician volunteered.

Vivien solved the enigma of that sick feeling in her stomach.

– Have you heard the news Uncle? The dead woman in the truck?

– Mrs Mercy Ping, Senator Statistician recited.

– Mercy Ping dead? the old man reached out his hand helplessly, bewildered by life.

Think of Uncle's hand already bearing the signs of decay, stretched, like a blindman seeking direction. Yes. And now see it with Vivien Lang's eyes, because she touched it and recoiled. Yet she had held his hand down by the gate. Was she reminded of some fear? The hand of the man who exposed himself to her. The flaking painted hand of God in an Italian fresco. Mum Collins's hand that morning when she covered her mouth at the omen of calling her relations the Whitey's Fallen. Miss Brinsmead's hand on the newspapers making a secret of the day. Or was it that hand in the grass, the severed wrist issuing a small blot of blood, the hand still there, halfway down the mountainside?

BOOK TWO

The Golden Fleece

One

The goldmining operations are twofold. First there is the main ridge settlement, a cluster of canvas dwellings, a jostle of tents like whitecrested waves, among which rough-hewn public buildings float their ungainly timber barges. The waterdiviner appears incongruous then, as he drifts about with his split rod quivering and a penny on his tongue to tell if it's salt or fresh. Smoke rises from all quarters of the settlement and hangs perpetually in the treetops so that everything smells of it. Dogs and children riot unchecked. And at all times during daylight the mountainside issues a sound of lakewater breaking on pebble beaches as hundreds of fossickers rock their cradles, stone chippings racketing against the wooden rims and slapping backwards and forwards in the trays, till their eyes jump with strain and they disbelieve their failure. People whistle, pickaxes clink randomly. The creek water swirls down from the mountain clear and sweet till it reaches a network of channels, the races, cut in geometrical shapes, where miners squat in lines with their puddling tubs. The water is then scooped up and given back yellow, liquid clay washed clean of gold, so that it flows on slower, salted with the sweat of men. The unity of the place is in the frenzy of work. Main Ridge is hand-work personified, a chaos of rivalry, the individual as king. Every man is your enemy; if you miss a nugget today your neighbour will be sure to stumble across it tomorrow. Only newcomers on the field are able to work levelly, with sober patience, without emotion beyond a general expectancy. Older hands are either feverishly elated or else downcast, energetic with success or hopeless with lack of it (nothing can tire the former, everything exhausts the latter). Men jump claims and fight, they arm themselves, in gangs they assault each other, they beat up the licence inspectors who suspend the claims pegged by this one and that. Pits the size of manholes are dug and gold winkled out, little one-person mines with nostalgic names: For the Love of Irene, Stanford-Dingley, The Holy Mary Mother of God Goldmine, The Red Flag of Liberty Mine. People are in the holes working. People are working around them, along the creeks and inside the hill slopes. Men and women, they are all hectically alive, murderously joyously alive. Such is Main Ridge settlement with its shanties selling rum, its stooks of bark drying ready for making roofs, its washing hung up and its countless open fires where pots simmer, its self-appointed experts and officials, pimps and informers, quacks and spruikers, its drunks, no-hopers and cheerful layabouts, its hubbub of small-scale activity.

Away on the northern horizon are the timber towers of the other kind of goldmining operation, the mines at the New Reef. Here huge forest trees lie felled and left to rot at odd angles on the ground, here wooden rail tracks weave their bumpy erratic course from minehead to crushing mill, impressive steam engines mounted on rubble huff and sizzle, driving moving-parts deep in the pits and tunnels, water can be heard perpetually splashing over the vanes of a pair of paddlewheels set up for the only electric generator ever seen in the district. The New Reef is the preserve of companies. Individual diggers have no place here. The crushing-mill stamps and thunders all day, horses whinny as they lug huge loads and drive windlasses round and around. The whim-boys in charge of these blinkered beasts grow dizzy with power. People are shouting orders, something seldom heard across the valley at the ridge. Here the rains wash mad rivers of stones and mud down the mountainside, setting the fallen trees rocking and groaning. In general the men work cheerfully and may be seen on occasion in large groups drinking tea from panni-kins, but just as their security is greater so their excitement and energy are less. They might rarely be penniless but they'll never be rich either; and riches are what it's all about. Their gold is the company's. Small wonder the Main Ridge people hold them in contempt.

During cold winter mists, the frames at New Reef, like medi-eval siege-machines, float in air so that when the buckets are wound up they emerge from cloud; the fur frost eats through old boots and grows into feet as mould; shouted instructions bounce among the rocks like wooden balls; and during the all-obliterating act of copulation steam creeps out of lovers' hair as their breaths come short, explosive, regular, timed to the sigh of pistons. Water freezes on the paddlewheels, the generator whines to immobility, modern civilization weakens and fades. The ancient god of slavery is invoked, till human pride survives only by frequent derisory excursions to Main Ridge to laugh at the mud-puddlers and the clay-caked ratlife popping indignantly out of slimy bur-rows. They are saved by the onslaught of spring. Spring hits the mountain with a deluge of rain followed by a blast of sunny days when cliffs crack and landslides gather force, when countless birds swoop down to scavenge among the diggers' pantries, lizards as long as a mineshaft terrorize the dogs, butterflies grow strong enough to carry off the beads of gold, and a conspiracy of grasses covers the cleared soil overnight obscuring all trace of where gold might be discovered.

Spring at Main Ridge is quite a different season, powdering the hills with wildflowers, washing away the hopeless dust of win-ter pickings, laying bare new shiny pellets of the precious metal, herding succulent mobs of wallabies to within easy shot, raising spirits and gilding the skin of young families, scattering new roofs on old shanties and patching the canvas city, bursting from the earth as lusty cabbage seedlings and potatoes, bearing the scent of new bread like triumphal banners among the trees, and gather-ing people in laughing crowds for the full rigour of the coming summer. The butcher might be seen on any Sunday afternoon, standing on his step in the sun, scissors in hand, clipping the hairs on his chest so the young women will still find him attractive; the publican's wife ties gay ribbons to the scroll of her fiddle and the patrons dance till they're struck down by drunkenness. And over at the Germans' Camp a glee club, sick with sentiment, beefs out folksongs about hunting in the Black Forest and shipwreck on the River Rhine.

Summer is the season of brawls and disputed claims at Main Ridge, wives are unfaithful to husbands, as are husbands to their wives, because of the weather; there are even husbands and husbands, wives and wives, who take revenge making covert gestures together in the small hours high up at the furthest edge of the goldfield. Illness strikes: first the people are half-blinded by sandy-blight and then they fall victim to dysentery. The only relief for the bowels is Mother McAloon's Miracle Medicine (bring your own clean bottle) compounded of chalk and brandy with a dash of opium. Summer. Leaves hang limp and vertical in the sun. The ground turns to iron at the touch of a pickaxe. This is the time for poisonous snakes to pay their annual visit and for the water supply to turn brackish, for suspected foot-and-mouth disease to break out among the small herds of dairy cattle, for the bullock team to labour up from the plain so slowly all the goods come out spoilt and shrivelled, rotten and fermenting by the time they're unloaded. Granny Collins declares ruffianism is rife. But it's summer after all, season of excesses. Summer at Main Ridge is the time for white ants to bring down the shop buildings and chew church floorboards to lace, it descends on the settlement so that you breathe dust and speak clods of hard dirt, it is a magnet lifting scales of paint from rockinghorses, drawing the colours from washed clothes to disperse them on the glittering wind.

For the New Reef mining companies, summer marks an annual record production, the eroded landscape left in the wake of spring now falls apart at the touch of organized labour, the mountain begins changing shape and yielding its secrets, in cool mineshafts the workmen sing to set the mountain itself murmuring of the new Jerusalem from tiny orifices, trucks squeal and bounce along the rails, the uprooted trees season into building timber and carpenters hunt out the tallow-woods for flooring, new windlasses reach higher than the old, packhorse tracks are widened into roads, a crusher is installed for the quartz reef, heaps of rivetted iron pipes arrive for a grandiose plan of tunnelling through the mountain for more water, long evenings gather up the sound of banjos and magnify them till the bush is alive with music. What could matter more than music in summer! The dancers are dancing, so that the moralists also flourish. And to cap it all a notable worker for the Good Templars Lodge assembles a choir to sing in the Wesleyan chapel. These are the quartz miners, the crushers, cock of the walk, stiff with braggadocio wearing their company's colours as a sash or a hatband. Owned men, sold out and proud of it, disdainful of the clay-footed puddling sluicers down at Main Ridge.

But when autumn comes the New Reef is re-named Dead Reef, which tells its own story. The spider-towers lean, abandoned. The relentless din of the crushers dwindles, stammers and is hushed. The rutted earth lies naked in its wounds. The wheels won't turn. The steam engine rusts, with a stagnant pool of water oily as poison in its belly. The two churches each have the one bell they possess rung incessantly to ward off thunderstorms that might ruin the harvest. Harvest! This is the end. And fire breaks out, the first wild whisperings of flame scurrying among the grass. Foremen shout for bucket lines to form and squads of the last remaining workers equip themselves with beating bags. The sleepy army troops off into the early afternoon, heavy with bad food and nervous of danger. Where is the fire? they grumble. Where the hell is the fire? they call, sarcastic with relief. What bloody fire? Their hearts are not in it because why should they care, employees of the companies? And the autumn wind swoops blustering up the gullies to reply. Flames, tearing at the ground, ripping the vegetation apart, wrapped ragged around treetrunks, utter an answering blanket of smoke. Before anyone is prepared, fire comes jumping, snickering its dazzle of weapons on every side. The ears are filled with crackling, smoke piles cottonwool inside the lungs. The first treetops flare alight as giant flowers.

The crown has caught, there's nothing any man can do to stop it now. Smoke shoots up in an appalling rush, the sky turns copper, the workmen are on the run. Managers and foremen are running. The shareholders on the other side of the world know nothing of this and will never understand. Flames glorify the crushing mill and dance among the high trees, covering the forest in great leaps. Wallabies in the scrub are roasted and kangaroos topple as burning stumps. Lives are in danger. But God's hand (it must surely be God) thwarts the catastrophe; a new wind sweeps in from the north-east and drives the fire back on itself, up the mountain and away from camp. The people of Gomorrah flee, they stuff their pilferings, their old survivals of identity, into socks and canvas pouches and by nightfall they've unharnessed their horses, packed the wagons; then their trembling lanterns may be seen forming a luminous, spotted caterpillar creeping down the mountain track, frightened by how long they'd stayed, how far they'd forgotten themselves, beaten by the greed for gold; the plunderers who leave behind nothing they have made but the ravages of machines in the choked valleys and their nightmare hummocks of salt. And they hear, as they pass, the residents of rival Main Ridge out in full force hacking firebreaks through the bush, clearing tracks and felling trees just in case the bushfire changes direction again, the women dragging buckets of their precious water to key points of the fire-watch, children raking the ground with branches to clear it of dead leaves, livestock protesting at being moved from their home paddocks down to the dam.

By dawn the Main Ridge folk are ready; though the work of felling goes on, they're sitting grimly in groups, not speaking, watching the smoke-line advance towards them. Then someone spots the first flames to cross the lower creek. They slough off tiredness, their rivalries forgotten. This, as they will later see, is the moment when a town is born, at this point they commit themselves to stay, without each other they could not survive, they are brothers and sisters in knowledge. The upper creek will seal their fate, being the centrepiece of their firebreak. A teenage girl foams at the mouth and threshes on the ground in a fit brought on by the tension, but young Mr Whitey takes her gently in his mutilated hands and says it is a good omen. A treacherous wind swings about the compass chasing clumps of smoke. Now the sky is brown, driving in one solid push to blind the defenders. And at that moment of blindness the fire leaps over the trees and among them, raging along the far bank, burning right down to the waterline. The fire has reached the upper creek. An ancient ironbark tree stands decked with ribbons of flame remembering the spinning maypole, black leaves float through the air. Burning twigs and grasses come bowling murderously across the gap, hopping clear over the water, nestling in the ready undergrowth. Men and women beat and beat these crackling colonies, calling for help or soaking more sacks for flails; the children squat behind keeping a lookout for fresh emergencies, tense with responsibility. Hour on hour the fight is held along this front, no respite for the aching exhausted people choked with smoke, the hairs scorched from their arms, quietly swearing at the relentless play of wind. The ancient ironbark falls with a splitting crash, carrying its huge bouquet of flame across the creek. At one touch in that hot air, the surrounding bushes leap alight, trees squeal like animals in the embrace of fire; the population, arms raised to shield their eyes from the heat, edge towards the spot, then a dozen men charge among the flames risking their lives. The last reserves of water are desperately poured about. Some older folk give up with tears, they are collapsing to that blank of no longer knowing why they should keep on, and haven't they lived through enough?

Then. Suddenly. There's nothing else to do. The tree is a corpse. Burnt blots lie in the grass around it. The roaring and popping of the fire has fallen quiet. The black wasteland hangs in rags, empty of life, silent. The mountain stands up stilly in the evening. Smoke trickles free from the guttering wrecks of gums. The fallen ironbark leaking smoke. An hour's walk away, through a charcoal desert, the new front of the fire blazes with vast waves of flame sweeping away towards the foothills, the swamps and lakes of the plain. The people sit. Their eyeballs are scaled with flakes of soot, their hair stuck out stiff and clownlike with smoke, hearts beating painfully from the strain, a profound sense of well-being in the blood, and smiles breaking out on their white-caked lips. They go back home to a peaceful evening scene of sluicing down the horses, water plashing, quiet voices sounding hollowly, the stamp of a hoof, the pleasurable snorting of a beast that looks back at its long glossy body.

For the rest, autumn changes nothing at Main Ridge. The whistling eagles have flown elsewhere to escape the coming cold. The last hot day is filled with a milky haze and stifling dampness: the people hang about, thinking of each other as locals, lethargic, waiting ... till the rain begins, rain created slowly for the first time in creation, an ache in the air, the drops pattering independent, the land and its creatures gasping at a witnessed miracle, staring like lovers towards the banking clouds and the rainbow with its companion standing up straight on the earth, dissolved in the rush of a downpour. So the drought breaks and storms pass leaving a fresh chill in the air. Miners rug themselves as warmly as they can at night and wear blankets for ponchos in the early morning when they squat along the creek swilling pebbles in their sluicing pans, splitting quartz with little picks or winching mullock by the bucketload from their miserable hand-cut shafts. The travelling teacher begins calling once a month, teaching in the open and sleeping among the books in his canvas-hooded four-wheeler with red spokes and TRAVELLING SCHOOL DEPARTMENT OF PUBLIC INSTRUCTION on the side. Young Whitey discovers a way to the waterfall and proposes a plan for irrigation. Nothing comes of the plan, but by way of consoling him they begin to speak of the discovery as Whitey's Waterfall.

So winter invades with unmerciful thoroughness. The Dead Reef is nothing but heaps of rusted iron pipes now and half a dozen shacks lived in by those families determined to stay (Swans and Brinsmeads among them), diggers who are already mutating back into farmers, spending their days cutting fenceposts, wiring their properties ready for the spring, and initiating secret practices of incest to revenge themselves on the society they came from. Old Michael Brinsmead and his son set their horses to drag timbers by chain up to the crest of the hill and measure the ground for a homestead big as a palace, the wings of the house to stand round courtyards and overlook a squad of lesser buildings for use by some clan of serfs to come. The patterns of this doomed community are already set. While across the valley a girl-child, born crippled, is a sign of permanence for a cripple must have a home and can't be carted round the country willynilly, nor make her own way on crutches.

So winter brings houses, a crop of ugly wooden mushrooms at Main Ridge, tuberous and mullock heap houses, houses like forest accidents and upturned carts. Tent by tent the canvas dwindles and those who stay stake out gardens, put down stumps for a foundation, raise the floor, the walls, expend energy on the pitch of the roof and devise prop-out window-flaps. The traditional rivalries for gold are still evident but now there is also domestic rivalry, the pride of homebuilders. Granny Collins buys a dark brocade curtain splendid enough for Queen Victoria's own drawingroom and hangs it on a melaleuca rod hammered to the slab-timber wall of her shack. The hillsides of forest trees are ringbarked to clear the land for pasture, tree by tree the ringbarking work goes forward, the sap dies and leaves fall, bark flakes away and white twigs are blown off by the wind, the trees stand as simplified skeletons, now and then crashing down with a dry splintering thud, while grass invades their territory and sheep and cattle wander in, minds heavy with mythology, to eat the grass. Though it is only a few years since they murdered an indiscriminate sampling of Chinese diggers to teach them what's what, the locals now subscribe generously to an appeal for funds to finance a Christian mission to China. A rifle club is formed, with the intention of setting out each season in pursuit of quail. The digging of gardens is undertaken almost as furiously as the digging of claims, manure being collected by the cartload, and seeds ordered. Mr Ian McTaggart, discovering he hasn't the temperament for leadership, devotes his life in recluse to designing a garden of concentric circles so as to be in harmony with the celestial bodies and draw on their power, the last of all gardens, the very antipodes of Eden. And overlooking the lesser structures of the new town a commodious two-storey public house is raised amid general admiration, a hotel named The Mountain in competition with the mountain itself; the visit of a band of Baptist missionaries is denounced by the publican within a week of the opening, denounced from the upstairs porch of his palatial establishment with enough dignity for the Pope. The town's women grow strong and handsome with clear eyes and independent manners, the men grow cruel as nature. The women have sweet breath, the man have thick beards and low brows. The women laugh like the nobility and move in their easy manner. The primeval men seem overpowered and knotted up in their own muscle, sinews binding them with vines and creepers, their eyes are the eyes of innocent creatures turned savage by bewilderment. Life's refinements are being lost! becomes the catchcry of the vigilantes for British Values. In consequence a cricket team is convened, players assemble and swing the bat, make nice points and speak politely to the umpire (a McAloon with one eye and the only man sure of the rules); but having no rival team to play, the cricketers embark on a course of civilizing the natives from a Koorie encampment on the plateau beyond the mountain ... till eleven earnest fellows with mobile expressions magnifying every fluctuation of their fortunes, decked in linen pants and cotton shirts, flailing the imported willow bats with plenty of enthusiasm, come to the true faith of empire calling the holy name of *Howzat!* as to the manner born. A wives' floral society conducts meetings exactly as if this were Cheltenham or Durban. And a power struggle between the Lang ladies and the McTaggart ladies brings the downfall of the Country Women's Association branch which votes itself out of existence at a meeting stacked by visitors from the staging-town down in the valley. The Mountain Hotel flourishes as a great establishment, guests arriving, the rooms occupied, a continuous jostle, management decisions, cooks and maids in a flurry and money changing hands. An impressive majority of miners and their families vote for the belief that they are camped on a mountain of solid gold. The State Government discusses building a railway as far as Yalgoona; and the Whitey's Fall house of assembly has plenty to say on this score. But foreign capital is not impressed, it looks like an ordinary mountain to them, so the loans fall through and the project is

112

shelved. The search does not stop. Sulkies and dogcarts line the street, even the hermit prospectors are drawn by the excellent beer at the Mountain Hotel and the blazing fire on a cold night. A variety of shops now cluster along both sides of the street, including a tobacconist with his insignia of a black boy skirted and crowned with tobacco leaves. There is even a public streetlamp (fuelled by paraffin oil) set up to illuminate the hazardous homeward journey of late drinkers leaving the Mountain long after they were expected for supper. Houses now dot the surrounding hills. The bullock-dray arrives each fortnight so that this scarcely feels like the outback any more. Flares smoke and flicker in their brackets at night as the dray creaks to a standstill garlanded with the breath of the animals. People with hurricane lanterns mill round the sweating beasts whose great eyes gaze frightened and wide at the half-seen threatening activity. Walter Schramm the publican, filled with the pride of office, gives young Annie Lang a pat on the bottom as a compliment but she dongs him a beauty so you can hear it through all the noise, everybody cheers and goes on with the unloading in a better humour than ever. And shopkeepers stack their shelves with goods from the Sydney marketplace at goldfield prices. The bullock driver known as Uncle (though he can't be more than twenty) has fallen so far in love with Annie that he builds a house for her, she having nobody, being the black sheep of her family as she is, a prospector on her own account. And as it happens, this is the last house built there. The town itself is officially named Whitey's Fall in error, due to a drunken brawl involving the government survey man. Then a School of Arts is mooted by the leading families and someone is fool enough to call for a forum to discuss the idea, so they pass a motion and an architect is invited to submit plans, which he does, from Melbourne, but when the citizens are told how much the hall will cost two committee-men resign, another has a stroke, the plans are declared a scandal, the architect sues them for his fee, ten percent of the estimated cost, and wins his case, the crown officers who eventually wend their timorous way up to the town to enforce this decision are met with a hail of stones and abuse, so they rethink the bounds of duty and retreat

113

into a campaign of threatening letters which remain unopened and unread in a sack nailed to the side of Mr Michael Brinsmead's dignified desk (to be passed down, in due course, to succeeding oldest inhabitants as a public treasure). The locals set about designing their School of Arts themselves, seventy feet long by thirty feet wide; then work begins, all voluntary, and the haphazard drawings translate themselves surprisingly into a stumpy lightless block of a place without a back door, so to avoid too many steps at the back on account of the steep fall of the land a hole is sawn in the east wall, masked by a trellis, and a side door fitted, to everybody's satisfaction it seems by the lack of complaints. The opening of the School of Arts is a gala occasion, a Christmas fete. The crippled McAloon girl, Edith, is regularly paraded in fancydress, her wheelchair loaded with bows and flowers, decked out as a centrepiece to all festivities, so that she discovers her vocation, and in every family photograph album are to be found snapshots of the relations smiling down at Edith or Edith smiling up at them. Occasionally the Yalgoona railhead debate is revived and lapses. A petition earnestly prays for the Post Master-General to open a Postal Receiving Office at Whitey's Fall Provisional School; yet the bullocky rages drunkenly through town swearing that the post will be the end of independence, the incursion of an indolent British monarchy into their private affairs, and that the school itself cannot be justified either. But they have a vision, these are services the people want and they get them. So then the town appears on printed maps of New South Wales.

Families still at Dead Reef, feeling deprived that Main Ridge has developed into the community of Whitey's Fall, re-name their own place Wit's End, declare themselves the local aristocracy and make much of their larger ideals and more firmly established sophistication. Indeed, Mr and Mrs Michael Brinsmead go so far as to claim royal descent on both sides of the family when traced far enough back. Really, as the mother declares, she should be heir to millions if there were any justice and Mr Brinsmead ought to be Lord Somebody of Somewhere with a country seat and more servants than you could whip in a month. Instead of

114

which they have a kitchen table where the family affairs are conducted, an ancient desk for their papers, two children large and beautiful as gods who drift about in a perpetual dream they can't be woken from, a rack of cumbersome overcoats caked with clay, rubber boots, also those less material effects: Brinsmead's drunken rages, his rum fantasies, his artificial manners, and his wife's incurable delusion that fate has dealt her an undeserved blow. Then comes the shock of young Sebastian finding gold he won't say where, and whispering confidences to his sister, the two of them sneaking off in the dark to stake their claim together, not minding how their mother grovels on the floor, mouth working in a brilliantly simulated epilepsy; Felicia going to Sydney with her brother, the pair of them coming back eventually and moving into that shack among the enemy at the less salubrious end of Main Ridge or Whitey's Fall as the officials insist on calling it. The very place where the Chinese joss-house used to be, as if you wouldn't expect nightmares. No one knowing a single thing about their claim; them not seeming interested in the gold now by some strange quirk, not digging, nothing; growing more secretive more odd by the month. And a few years later, the accident of some government having a road bulldozed up the mountain to enter the town at their end and them finding themselves at the centre, opening the house as a general store and making it successful while others go out of business, so successful every five years they travel abroad, leaving for good some say, but always coming home after six months or nine, having appointed a deputy to keep the shop running and the funds (you may be sure) rolling in, travels to New Guinea and the Hebrides, weeks in Poona and nights at Raffles in Singapore, travels reportedly across the Arabian Desert to Aden and up the Congo to where Mr Stanley intruded on the retirement of Dr Livingstone, travels so exhausting that the time comes when poor Felicia at the age of sixty-one arriving home at night has to be carried into the singing grumbling shop covered in a pile of blankets, said to be sick and near her death with tropical fever. And each subsequent voyage ends the same till folks say: that's what travel does for you, that's the penalty for gadding about where civilized people have no business poking their noses.

Now the paint is peeling from weatherboard walls. Uncle finds bullock driving doesn't pay, feeling weary into the bargain, regrets he married the wrong woman and has no respect for his only son. Cars begin to make their appearance and call in for fuel and to restore the ravages of the climb before attempting the downward slope. Even the original mountain tracks change, the triple-ruts made by horsecarts (one rut for the horse, two for the cartwheels) imperceptibly becoming the double-ruts of motor vehicles. As for the main north-south highway snaking far below along the valley floor, it's given a bitumen surface which appears either black or white according to the time of day. And each curve of that newly bulldozed road coiling down the mountain to meet it is echoed by the old hand-hewn road, faint and following a parallel course lower on the slope. The heart goes out of Uncle when his darling Annie marries one of the McTaggarts and leaves town to nurse in some ratbag Churchill war, reconciled with her wowser brother to make matters worse. Edith McAloon the decorated cripple has died and celebrations are not the same without her, no one to be paraded that you don't see every day, the decorations appear trivial, and who can you smile at when you don't quite know what to do next; most disturbing, the whole idea of her beribboned wheelchair comes to seem macabre, even shameful. A barber's shop opens, Gents Haircuts, First Class, Tuesday and Friday. The diggers are despairing, packing away their pans and cradles, dismantling primitive machinery, putting off their charismatic characters as prospectors, accepting again the dun routine personalities of farmer, of labourer and trades-man. Their wives invest in bead-work table runners for when they might have a diningroom.

Churches stand empty. The Wesleyan chapel falls down, the Church of England is bypassed by the parson on his fortnightly rounds, the Catholic Church barely has its roof nailed on before being abandoned, never to be consecrated. The population gathers for occasions at the public bar where Felicia guides them in a resurrection of the past. Exotic luxuries and violences rage in the mute bowed heads, all human endeavour (even Whitey's Fall and Wit's End even) are understood to have meaning. The Rememberers contemplating their pots of beer hold absolute sway in town and the longest-standing family feuds may be set aside in the interests of the service. So the closing of Mrs Ping's schoolhouse and the enrolment of the few young children of the district at correspondence school is seen to be the work of destiny, a destiny remarkable for its rich heritage. Thus even the fading of those painted initials A.S. and A.L. framed by a heart high up on the School of Arts has meaning. The general decrepitude of the residents and their residences is respected. Thus the death of Mercy Ping becomes another occasion for exercising the power of Remembering so it can be accepted as fitting the jigsaw where nothing else would do; so that the disintegration of the British Empire itself is seen to depend for its meaning on Mercy's fatal determination to save her cow further pain. The inter-connections are essential. You cannot take away a single hair, a single leaf (that is to say, subtract it somehow utterly) without the entire fabric of the world collapsing. Into that hair-sized, leaf-sized void in the molecular fabric of the universe all else must disappear, including Mount Everest and the Pacific Ocean. Without Mrs Ping's failure to save her cow Alice, the history of our peoples would be meaningless. So Mrs Collins and Mrs Collins, Miss McAloon and Mrs McAloon, Mrs Buddall, Mrs Buddall, Mrs Swan and Mrs McTaggart make Annie Lang's grandniece welcome in their kitchen circle. So Felicia Brins-mead, hearing her shop groan *miserable miserable*, knows she has one terrible secret for which she must some day submit herself to society's judgment. So Fido also has a secret to guard with vigilance if he is ever to have the satisfaction of revenge. So Mr Ian McTaggart takes charge of unexplained letters still sealed in their government envelopes and keeps them safely in a drawer. So Billy Swan has found out something which puts a burden on his conscience and drives him to the general store like a stranger to ask for gelignite. So Uncle explores love again and settles down for a cup of tea when the Yalgoona police finally roar off with whatever information is required by law, and the motorist

117

who drove Mercy to her death has walked out of the place in peace. So Tony trudges wearily downhill to work, still aching with the failure to experience anything religious, still embarrassed to recall the night he learnt to sing. So Mr Ping works at his trade, creating molten suns, a shell of the man the young Felicia once worshipped. So Sebastian greets each day as God's revelation, every object as a thread in His design, a detail rich with the meaning of eternal purpose; even his paternity of Fido and his sister's wicked delusions being there in the Almighty's inscrutable project. So Jasper, heir of Walter Schramm, spares his customers the indignity of watching him drink his own assets to assuage the pain of being the victor in an argument of the blood. So the memory of Annie Lang's violin is woken afresh by that instrument once more sending bony-kneed jigs skipping across the rain-soaked paddocks. So the ghost of the famous German band at the gala opening of the Mountain may flit into mind at a phrase from some Ländler or Palatinate country dance in Vivien's book *Tyrolean Favourites*. So the populace takes mute notice of such bad omens as the all-night electrical storm crackling along the rooftops in miraculous silence and dryness. So Bill Swan won't rest at night and finds his days disturbed by suspicions and a debility he can't locate, so he puts aside his mission and all but forgets his conscience, so he is bewitched and knows himself a lesser man. So he sweats it out digging post holes and repairing gates, patching his moralistic father's property, believing it ought to be his own. So he wastes his Sundays burning through the tranquil countryside on his motorcycle, skimming round corners, causing the horizon to lift and sway at his touch like a gentle sea, revelling in the roar of throbbing metal, hot, thick rubbers in his hands, the dipping forward on the springs at a touch of brakes; the pathetic timidity of car drivers killing each other without the thrill of risk, wallowing along to death unruffled by wind, oblivious of rain, already in their coffins. So Billy one day turns off up the mountain track instead of heading home, bounces miserably along the rutted surface, stones popping from under his tyres, cuts the motor dead at Vivien's gate and sits there, watching; pride forbidding him, absolutely, to make the next move.

Two

In the quiet that followed when the engine cut, flies whizzed this way and that between dollops of dung, birds too shy to show themselves twittered in the four great lonely tired trees around Vivien's house. Far off a dog barked once, a hound, perhaps Uncle's Bertha, an unwelcome nudge to Billy's conscience. The cows were nosing grass, their calves inquisitively gathering along the fence, batting their ears, cretinous with goodwill and paying no heed to warning moos from the old dams. He propped the bike up and turned towards his task: only to find a block of space between himself and her house. A month had passed during which he had seen Vivien nine times. On several of these occasions they had even acknowledged one another. Senator Halloran made his appearance two successive weekends, he and Vivien walking easily together, laughing, his grey suit as creaseless as metal, and his broad pink face, his boyish sheaf of fair hair which slumped over his forehead and had to be continually pushed back out of his eyes, the eyes themselves dodging and darting looks, his big soft hands kept dangling at his sides with the fingers spread wide, while his spongey-soled shoes padded along, toes turned out at a laughable angle; and most of all, his habit of chuckling softly, a short signal of a chuckle indicating that he would be enjoying himself if he chose to.

Now nothing could be simple any longer for Billy, with Uncle raving on about her, praising her in the pub so that everybody smiled behind their hands, hanging round her like a peasant, giving her his prize cauliflower, introducing her to his dog, ogling her and being found sitting at the roadside afterwards declaring that his time had come and he'd be the last to complain if Death chose that precise moment.

The block of space compacted. The bike ticked as it cooled. Little flurries of wind set the grass tossing. A raging misery was in him. When he thought how much he had already been through it seemed impossible for her to exercise the least influence over him.

Vivien pushed wide the kitchen window and stuck her curly head out.

– Hullo, she called cheerfully. Come on in why don't you?

He grinned with disgust at his reaction. His fingers jostled the latch, the landscape swimming away to the lip of the waterfall. He fought the gate open and went kicking his ankles up the path, his mouth a zoo letting little creatures of sound escape. She watched him approach with his swift powerful steps, his open face casual with goodwill, and found she was resenting his intrusion.

– I'm in the kitchen, she called tartly.

Billy hated seeing women in shorts, however in her case she had firm downy legs that he viewed with interest. She knew he was watching her even behind her back. So cocksure, was he?

– At last you've come to visit. Everybody else is nice to me but you.

– Yeah? Billy contributed, unable to adjust to conversation that switched about like winds down in the valley.

She had nothing but contempt for such a bucolic idiot, so she banged the tea-caddy on the sideboard before slapping some tealeaves into the pot.

– I was wishin, he went on, his voice uncannily like Uncle's. Wishin I'd've seen what you saw. You know, under that wreck.

– What on earth for? she shrieked in her English accent. This

120

was odious. And the way he sprawled, tilting the chair back, with his knees against the table edge you'd swear it was his kitchen. There was a pause. He intended to laugh, even to offer some obscene words, but his voice came out as natural as you like.

– The way things are, I can't believe it, can't believe Mrs Ping's dead, except the smell ... she was the teacher here. For us younger ones, she was the only teacher ever. Just seeing her hand ... it's hard to believe in.

How direct he was. Her fingers fluttered round him, giant butterflies afraid to alight but fatally attracted by the honey hidden in him.

– Ah, she replied gently, I can understand that. I suppose it's our fate that we always have to know.

He looked at her, at the calm well, the intelligence. At the tightening of her breasts inside her blouse, at her slender hands, her oval fingernails. The kitchen was a white box floating on a gentle sea.

– I'm so glad you've come, Vivien added, amazed at herself for having found anything to criticize in him.

– I didn't think you wanted me to, he sang.

– Oh yes, I wanted you to.

– I thought you might be too caught up with Uncle. (That's right, she deserved a bit of telling off.)

– What can you be meaning? she flared.

The sun slid behind a cloud and the white kitchen walls were painted yellow.

– There's a dance, he said, on Saturday down at Yalgoona so I came to ask if you'd like to go. With me.

What a relief that he had come prepared with an excuse. She smiled and he recognized her as a different person in her pink kitchen.

– On the pillion of that deathtrap out there?

– Yes. And he remembered her pressing softly and warmly against him. But she kept putting him in a position where he had to make assessments. There's nothing about her I already know, as he did finally explain to himself four days later.

– I'd love to. Thank you Bill.

– Bill? he asked, toying with this unexpected evidence that he did have some objective existence. She blushed with confusion.

– Well you aren't going to insist on being called Mr Swan, I suppose! she replied with spirit. His heart clamoured for attention.

– I might do that, but.

– You might get a box on the ear too.

– I might give one, he crowed with excitement.

She withheld her smart retort. Check. And they sat panting from the exertion of communicating.

– I'd better pour that stuff out before it stews, she offered with false jollity. He was already wondering what the hell he'd do at the Yalgoona dance and how he'd go pushing a hefty lump of female like her around the floor when he was no good even with the expert Suzanne Jessop whom his father wanted him to marry for some unexplained reason. Especially as this one would shame him by being a couple of inches taller.

– I'm an accomplished dancer, she said. He flashed her a glance of hatred and fear. But she wasn't looking, her attention on the pouring of tea. And he saw instead the perfect arch of her neck, so smooth, so tenderly tucked in under the jaw.

– Bill, she spoke this time much more at ease with his name. I do know what you mean about Mrs Ping.

Now she watched him, he was fighting for breath as a wave of blood rose up carrying him with it, held him, and broke, washing through him. The room had blacked out. Red birds flickered past him, hunting for fish.

– Bill?

– I don't know what to say, he said eventually, his lips soured by the tea.

– Are you sure, she challenged him pointblank. Sure you want me to go to this dance with you? You mustn't be polite with me or I shan't forgive you. Her voice sounded so very English that she became aware of it herself and the dangers of primness, so when she continued she made certain to seem brutal if possible – I suppose you're about twenty-three or twenty-two aren't you? Well I'd better warn you that I'm thirty-four.

Her hair crackling with golden sparks.

This time she succeeded in shocking him. He twirled the cup on its saucer in a way that would have irritated her with anybody else. She had imposed yet another restriction: now he mustn't tell her he was nineteen last birthday. Not because it would be too discourteous but because deeper in himself his body had its own purposes and he was afraid this would destroy them; his arousal might survive such a blow, but he wasn't sure hers could. Whatever else, things had changed for the worse. He even accused the way he felt: there had to be something the matter with him to be attracted to a grandmother.

– I wished I'd seen Mrs Ping under that truck.

To know her age freed him, on second thoughts; any sexual connection impossible. The wind through the frail house braced him, so he grew light-hearted. Vivien watched the room caress him in gentle blue shadows and saw brilliant flecks in his eyes. She watched his strong throat as he threw back his head and barked with laughter, his clean pink mouth and young teeth excited her. She was breathing quickly. His own abrupt reactions surprised him. The moment the laugh was out it triggered a chill of shame; he had a responsibility toward her which could not be denied. She was a wrinkly, so she mustn't expect too much. He controlled the volatile mood seeing her colour so high, yes and she was undoubtedly attractive. She was beautiful. Was it wrong? He reached out to touch her hand. He had never found skin so fine, nor anything so elegant as that hand, the glossy nails, the long smooth joints.

– Thanks for tea, he said. And gulped it down dutifully. He stood knotting his fingers, interlocking the gristly knuckles. Don't forget next Saturday will you?

– I won't, she promised though she knew and he knew it was all over and this had been his apology, his chivalry.

He stumbled out of the green kitchen, his shoulders colliding with the doorjambs one then the other. The fool, the fool. Seeing imprinted at the back of his eyes a picture of her breasts swelling gently against her white cotton clothing. Sunshine emerging from cloud poured into the room with the prismatic dazzle of a fountain. Vivien sat in it, aware of crystal scabs flaking from the old cabinet, a diamond where his lips had touched the cup.

You imbecile, Vivien wailed to herself. He didn't understand a thing. Was it for this she'd waited and hoped without admitting she hoped? She heard the gate click shut. She heard the motorcycle cough eight times and then roar into vulgar life, skidding through the gravel and blaring away into town announcing where he had been, leaving it to anybody to deduce what he had been doing there.

That evening Bill Swan failed to join his usual school at the pub. He was far up the mountain track, lying on his side watching yellow squares of light pop on here and there across the countryside spread out below him, and in some cases the tiny blue glow of a television bringing the challenge of faith to a darkened farmhouse. One splinter lodged in his mind: she was thirty-four years old, like a lost sister in disguise, making turmoil of his emotions. If things had turned out otherwise he might have been glad of the notoriety of being seen with her. But as it was, he'd never forgive her for being so old.

Billy lay there and the hillsides faded, the country starred with domestic activity, all those crocks so busy in their tumbledown houses, he challenged the simplicity of these thoughts. She was beautiful, yes, tender and strong. He had noticed how shy she was as well as being self-assured. And you saw straight away, for certain, she was the kind you could rely on to face any responsibility.

He sat astride the bike, rubbing his fingers across the tank which was already cold and damp. He must go back and cancel the invitation to the dance. The motor jumped to life at the first kick for once, as if it had been waiting, the machine humming and pulsating against his thighs. He snapped the headlight on and allowed the bike to tick away down the slope, drifting not driving, easing her round the bends, stars scratching vivid quivers across his rearvision mirrors, the night breeze insisting on making his body feel good. He stretched his legs and rode with his boot-heels scuffing in the dust like one of those panama-hatted swells last century out for a spin on the pier, walking his cycle along. If it can be imagined it can somehow be done. The motorcycle rolled quietly down to the clearing, past the dump, to the first houses, the dead butcher's, past the Mountain where bald light-globes sparkled and a wedge of cheerful sound had been driven into the heavy silence of the street: he passed through it like one solid body through another, miraculously simple. Down among the abandoned homes and shops he coasted, then past those still occupied, swinging off to the right by Brinsmeads', engaging the motor and plupper-plup-plupping up towards the southerly spur at a comical jogtrot, to where four cypress pines spread open their embarrassment of hands for whatever the night had to offer. The motor cut. He was perfectly businesslike as he swung from the saddle and stood on his own two feet. He walked normally up the front steps on to the verandah. No need to knock: she had opened the door inviting him in.

– I came back to say . . . , he said.

– Am I disturbing you . . . , he said.

– Perhaps it's nothing that . . . , he said.

– I was up at the mountain, no not the pub, when . . . , he said.

– This idea . . . , he said.

– And it seemed such a . . . so . . . it struck me that . . . well, why . . . , he said.

Vivien offered nothing. She supported herself with one wall of the house and waited.

– I was remembering, you see . . . , he said.

– About this and that and Saturday and when I said . . . , he said touching her hair and lips, placing his hand on the nape of her neck and letting it slide down.

– I was up there, he explained gently against her, feeling her yield and rally. Lying on my side in dirt, feeling, I don't know . . . , he spoke through a curtain of curls what he had to say. His hands praised her. She held herself, determined to be in control.

– Are you shy! he whispered, breathing each other's breath.

Three

Again she confounded him. He couldn't believe she was at all surprised. She appeared neither excited nor ruffled that he intended making love to her. It was an act of resistance. Billy parried by avoiding her invitation to make plans that included her. Instead he risked the immediate truth.

– Yair. I'm going to buy some gelignite.

One o'clock in the morning; Vivien and Billy still sitting at the top of the steps, wrapped in the one blanket, the tartan holding them in its huge net, their voices sounding easy and mellow.

– Have you heard of the Golden Fleece? he asked, braving a final leap into reality.

– The argonauts? Ulysses and Jason?

– No, the big seam of gold supposed to have been staked by Seb and Felicia Brinso a couple of hundred years back. But they never let on where. And then they disappeared, so the story goes. You can imagine the talk. It still goes on.

– People never forget, she agreed.

– Some say they went to Sydney. The whole town knew. Famous in these parts. Another thing, their old dad was a drunk; and one night, knocking back the pots up the road at the Mountain with people there to witness, in walked his son Seb and said here's what I owe you, and he put down a lump of gold on the bar, the whole town saw it, a slab of a nugget, pure gold and weighing maybe two pounds. The old drunk left it where it was, he was famous for his dignity when he was sober, and even more when he wasn't. And for his big ideas. He went out back and hung himself with the belt of his greatcoat. Up in the john he did it. Next drunk needing a leak found him still warm and stinking. Mr Schramm had to cut him down, our Jasper's father it was then, though a good age himself, nobody else would touch the job. He wouldn't either if he hadn't needed the lavatory for his customers. The nugget went to the wife along with the corpse, never to be seen again, she disappeared the day they put him underground. No there wasn't any doubt about the Golden Fleece, that piece of gold was pure, the bar full of experts, Uncle among them, he was already a man in his thirties so he wouldn't have been imagining things, I've heard about it a dozen times.

Vivien's surprise gave way to an unaccountable disillusionment.

– And you want to find the Golden Fleece? she asked for the first time doubting him.

– Why else would I need gelignite, he jibed bitterly. No, I learnt a secret, that's all. And it won't let me alone.

She took his hand and resigned herself to waiting; soon enough she'd get it straight. His agitation over the gold wasn't a threat, being unconnected with her. They sat, shoulders and hips touching. She refrained from asking why he didn't approach the Brinsmeads if gold was needed so urgently. His talk was not allowed to interfere with the touching. Peace flowed to her powerfully from the land and the night. Who cared about any Golden Fleece? But she liked the steady baritone of his voice.

He was musing; remembering the same subject coming up in an argument with his father not long ago. At the time the very unexpectedness made him jump. I know what you think! His father raged as he rocked on the balls of his feet in that typical small man's habit when angry, trying for extra height to invest his words with authority, some element of threat. You think you've got more right to this farm than me. Bill admitted silently and precisely what he thought. Not just that he did half the work, the fencing and repairs, the dairy, that he and no one else drove the tractor. No, it was more that his father never seemed free of resentment against the place. It suits me better than it suits you, was what he thought. And his grandmother, Miss Bertha McAloon, once overheard complaining the property still belongs in title to me you know though I'm sick as Jesus of George and the way he runs it. Added to which Bill's grandfather, Uncle, had accused him of doing the mug's work: you can't call yourself a man till you front up to your father and demand your due. If you're so hungry for money, Mr Swan had snapped misconstruing the motive, get out and crawl to old lady Brinsmead, you might get her to leave you the bloody Golden Fleece, she can't last much longer, filthy state she lets herself get into, then you'll be able to talk son, then we'll all do some listening. He had jeered sarcastically in the way of fathers who suspect the truth. You'll be so rich they'll have you on television.

Bill had laughed at the jibe because he recognized it. What's more he knew how to handle himself so why shouldn't he laugh? He felt unique. Not clever, not talented, simply the possessor of a knot nobody could unravel, least of all his father. Laughed also because a madcap scheme had come to mind: what could be more infuriating to an already enraged parent than a public rort? Most of the boys were migrating to the city, this would be the last chance to do something together. The idea left him mute with delight and surprise. Yes, they'd go prospecting, a real trip, taking the Bedford truck. This was six weeks ago. He recollected the details.

– You going to use the Bedford this weekend Dad?

– It's broke down as you bloody well know.

– Okay, Billy offered sweetly. Suppose me and Tony go down the Yalgoona road and patch her up and get her going, can I keep her?

– Not on your life.

– For the weekend then?

So it was arranged. Mr Swan rankled with never going back on a decision. That's how the prospecting trip came about, a jaunt

128

for the Golden Fleece, as Billy explained the idea to the others: Tony plus the ones about to leave town for good, Lance and Maggot, the twins Pete and Dave. Naturally they'd all be in it. They'd hitch a ride down the Yalgoona road with the cheese delivery. Yes, they'd take picks and sleepingbags, Tony'd patch up the Bedford, they'd load her with food and grog and head back this way, then off along the overgrown gold trail, up the north face of the mountain, round behind the reservoir, across the saddle to the disused diggings and eventually home to Whitey's Fall on the eastern face. One last weekend together before making the break to escape stagnation. With most of the gang gone, the future could not be imagined.

So it had been decided, a fossicking trip. Billy remembered how he promised himself more than the mere scourings and scavengings the others talked about. Why not the Golden Fleece, or at least a clue to where it was. In retrospect he mocked the naive way he had hoped for what he now most feared.

– I can't lose, he boasted. Because once I get my hands on that truck nobody's going to get it back off me.

Six weeks ago he was a kid.

Going down ahead with Tony on the motorcycle had saved waiting about, he explained to Vivien. Once the Bedford was going again, despite a nasty rattle in the motor, they stowed the bike in the back along with watercans, rucksacks, lamps, boxes of tucker and prospecting tools that the boys brought with them when they arrived in the cheese truck according to plan. They were off, driving into the deepening darkness. Tony as mechanic occupied the seat of honour up front beside Bill, not that this was much of a luxury with the rear wall of the cab cut away to open directly on to the load. The advantages were psychological, plus a sprung seat.

– I'm just thinking back, Bill explained to Vivien and drifted among his memories of the other youths huddled, rugged up on the open tray, ready for anything, seeming to have a better time because of their closeness, their shared lack of privileges, which is how it always is. The humour of the private soldier. A great deal of adolescent laughter vanished out into the night as they lumbered along the bitumen, headed for the logging track at Dry River and the mountain of gold beyond.

– We've got to get this thing off the road by tonight, Bill yelled to Tony barely making himself heard above the engine. If the cops catch us they'll have us cold: no rego, one headlamp, baldy tyres, me without a truck licence. He laughed delightedly at the thought of his offences. Kick the mudguard she'd fall off, wipers won't work, you name it we've got it, blue smoke, offensive noise, steers like a crane.

Tony bounced beside him happily, gazing at his friend's profile, then out to the road where that one headlight poked its shuddering beam at an eccentric angle illuminating only the trees. He looked back over his shoulder to the others crowded in a steamy group.

– You guys okay? he asked kindly in his soft voice.

– Up your arse, they remarked.

– Give us the third class any day.

– Yeah, pity the bosses.

– Shift your hoofs Pete I can't stretch out me leg.

– Got a smoke Maggot?

– What anothery? You eating the bastards?

– Hang on a tick I've got something better anyhow.

Light mist washed past the vehicle, creaming like seawater. They blew a joint together, the dream and the companionship. They conversed in their peculiar mountain accent, an old language tired and cracked at the joints from too much exposure to rain and sun.

– Skiting is it? Maggot shouted suddenly. I'd fuck better than you big useless bastards I bet. Me and Stump there. That's skiting if you want to hear me skite. We'd beat the lot of yous, him and me. You know the saying: big man big cock, little man all cock. Wait till you're married, he threatened gleefully. Your wives'll come sneaking round to my place for a decent screw.

– Up yours you midget, Lance boomed, his huge arm strangling Maggot. I'll have a woman so big you won't come up to her knee let alone kiss her fanny.

The twins chuckled mirthlessly to fulfil their obligations.

130

– I'll tell you a tale, Lance declaimed in his grammar-school voice, reminding them that he was the only boy ever to go away as a boarder. Of the six heroes of the mountain. A tale of olden times, fabulous monsters ...

– Yuk, bullshit, Jesus, get stood on, siddown, pull yer head in yer mug.

– And beautiful maidens ...

– Yahoo!

– ... valorous deeds.

– Who's she?

Another joint passed around and they sucked at it greedily. Maggot amused himself surreptitiously unbuckling rucksack pockets and feeling for what was packed there. His kleptomaniac fingers assessing apples, boots, underpants, a sheath-knife.

– Good on you Lance mate, tell us, Billy called as the truck jolted and clanged over a pothole, jostling the passengers so they catcalled. Roaring its geriatric note the Bedford sounded like a mobile zoo, terrifying frogs, waking birds, bringing startled wallabies to a halt at the roadside. Billy drove sublimely, grinning with pleasure and bowling her along. Maggot eased the knife out of its sheath so he could test the blade. Whose was it? The sheath felt new.

To everyone's surprise one of the twins took up the story-telling; usually they were secretive, avoiding too much talk.

– Well there was these blokes in the backblocks. Now they was square-eyes like everybody else and green-eyes too. Like everybody. So one day Stumpy, son of Stumpy, out of Stumpy's Mum, tore himself away from episode ten of The Bushranger's Revenge and reckoned he could cheat his old man out of a truck and got his mates to help by promising them a heap of gold. Well these mugs let themselves be talked around. They packed up camping gear and that garbage and risked their necks being thrown about in the back of this bloody useless wreck of a truck.

– Right on! yelled the others enthusiastically.

– Remind me to break your jaw when we stop off, Billy laughed, his words partly lost in the racket and wind.

– You and who else?

– Come on Maggot, Lance said in a condescending voice covering his feeling of being slighted. Your turn mate.

– If you insist, Maggot consented graciously, his hand still in someone's rucksack. It began with this broke-down bomb ...

No sooner were the words out than the truck sighed with comic appropriateness and slowed to a halt. The motor died. A hemisphere of silence trapped them. The headlight went off and there was no moon yet. The knowledge of calamity sank in as they began to hear a hissing in the engine like a leaking balloon. Maggot edged the blade back in its sheath which he slipped out of the rucksack where it belonged and into his own pocket.

– What the hell was that then? came Bill Swan's voice.

– Let's have a look. Tony already had his door open.

– Torch!

A torch was passed down instantly, giving them a vaguely excited awareness that despite the horseplay and the mild muzziness from smoking grass they were well prepared and capable of anything.

They crowded round Tony offering advice and peering in under the bonnet with the wincing expressions of experts, while above them whirled a conference of bats disturbed from their feeding, tatters of black skin caught in a whirlpool. Tony pondered the problem, then without haste removed the distributor cap. A few minutes later he spoke in a flat hopeless voice: Okay Bill give her a kick. Billy climbed in and pulled the starter, the Bedford spluttered. Again Bill. This time the motor wheezed into life. They raised a cheer (which was heard a long way across the paddocks at a forgotten homestead by a forgotten farmer's wife in her eighty-seventh year, so that she was more pleased with the evidence of her good hearing than alarmed by what she heard). The young men boarded the truck as it lurched forward, its one crooked eye scanning the treetrunks again. In the back the passengers settled down to enjoy being jolted about in comfort. Spontaneously, as if taking up an unwillingly suspended dialogue, Peter and Dave the twins began singing.

When first I left old Ireland's shore, the yarns that we were told
Of how the folks in far Australia could pick up lumps of gold!
How gold-dust lay in all the streets and miner's right was free.
'Hurrah,' I told my family, 'that's the very place for me.'

The voices moved effortlessly into simple harmony for the chorus.

With my swag all on my shoulder, black billy in my hand,
I'll travel the bushes of Australia like a trueborn Irishman.

– Bushes? squawked someone in disbelief.

Other voices now joined in, humming, trembling and hiccupping as the Bedford trundled along.

For many years I wandered round to each new field about
And made and spent full many a pound till alluvial petered out.
And then for any job of work I was prepared to try,
But now I've found the tucker-track, I'll stop here till I die.

With my swag all on my shoulder, black billy in my hand,
I'll travel the bushes of Australia like a trueborn Irishman.

– Come on Tony mate, sing! Bill urged full of the joy of freedom and success, bouncing the truck purposely into a gutter to make the bastards jump. But Tony only smiled regretfully and mumbled something about not yet, or not drunk enough, or didn't know the words.

– You're a bloody piker sport, that's what you are, Billy responded with unction. She's a beauty this old truck, he added consolingly. I'll get her for myself. You'd better stick around so you can keep her going for me. Billy glanced across the silence to see in the dim light a private satisfaction print itself on his friend's face.

– Hope the police don't grab us, Tony offered at last.

– They wouldn't dare.

– What's that? demanded Maggot, poking his head between the seat backs, one hand on the stolen knife in his pocket. The cops won't stop us, no way. Not on your life. Plus they'd be too bloody amazed. They'd drive plumb off the road, hypnotized by that one headlight. God's truth that is. He reaped his harvest of laughs and ribbing.

– What about the rum? bawled Lance, still a schoolboy.

Maggot it was, as expected, who produced the bottle and leered puckishly at them with his freckled face and mischievous eyes. Unscrewed the cap, took a stiff gulp and then passed it round. This was a scene from some hearty German operetta, the up-ended bottle, the thigh slapping, the good humoured neighing, the chorus lurching from side to side in unison with never a thought for tomorrow.

– Eureka! yelled Billy, his voice from the cab hollow and metallic. Look up ahead.

It was the turning, the logging track. A hundred yards and they'd be safely out of reach of the law.

– Go Billy.

Had he said nothing and quietly turned off the road when the time came, this leg of the journey might have been entered without further mishap. But the spirit was in him. To give them a thrill in the back, Billy swung over suddenly. Too late. The bonnet slumped and pitched up, the rear wheels went down with a thud that threw the passengers sprawling along the open tray. The Bedford whined as it began to cant and came to a standstill, engine running, tail deep in a drainage ditch.

– Jesus Billo, someone swore, tears of frustration lurking in the voice.

– A man oughta bloody thump you, another offered. This turned out to be the Maggot. Tony grabbed his arm and volunteered to floor him. The victim wriggled away delighted, having coaxed this affectionate relationship into the open, as always just escaping a gentle swipe from one of those huge hands.

Billy insisted they take a cheerful view. Weren't they within an ace of escaping the main road and beginning the real trip? How were they to cope with the difficulties higher up if they didn't get some practice down here? The derision this provoked died in an instant: far down the black tunnel of night a flash lit the road then swivelled straight at them. Headlights approaching.

A car, rescue, hope. Yes and the car pulled over, good man. A voice from the dark asked if they needed a hand.

The stranger helped wedge rocks and branches under the wheels, showing them a technique for lifting the vehicle on the jack and building the rocks up stage by stage under the wheels. In fact he assumed command of the operation. Only once did he offer unwanted advice, suggesting they should have the headlight adjusted so they could see where they were going. No one rose to the bait. He'd been so obliging they decided to let him off this time.

The job was done. The Bedford heaved itself heroically free of the mud and sat purring on the track, nose towards the mountain. The stranger, dusting his hands, invited them to call on him if they had further trouble ... at the police station in Yalgoona. Constable Pope. Yes, and he hazarded a guess they'd be the Whitey's Fall crowd. Thought I recognized you. A last fling for some of you? Getting a taste of leaving home? Enjoy the sins of Sydney! When he drove off, perverse as it might seem, the boys felt downcast. What if there were no risks, nothing to be really up against, nothing to test a man, always somebody to rescue you? And was that a jibe about leaving home? Did he mean the final break would be no more than this? That cutting blood-ties could be so casual? The truck jolted up the first incline, slewed across ruts, jumped and clanged, the driver slamming it through the gears.

– Bloody hell, Maggot challenged them. Who says give in? Pass the rum. Go for your life Bill. What about the gold! We're madmen to trust ourselves to this old heap, they'll be looking for our skeletons twenty years from now.

Quite suddenly the episode with the policeman was funny, obviously funny. Laughter broke from the rosy well-being of rum. The night flowed together behind them. Trees edging past, some sly some guilty, made them laugh more. They laughed at nothing, laughing because laughter was in them and loneliness too. Stars dipped a lowering flag, an owl swooped blankly down. Snorts of laughter broke from them, the twins taunted each other with it, Maggot punched the Bedford with it, Billy and Tony spilled trickles of it, chuckles and mumblings of the laughter, the universe began to sway and rotate, trees tipped, jumped, a prismatic aureole hung round the headlamp beam. Dizzy moths whirled in. Every damned thing they thought of was funny. They could smell the warmth of company, even the bottle was warm with passing from hand to hand.

When they stopped to make camp they built a fire and planned to sit watching the embers till dawn. Still their strident voices trumpeted self-assertions into the night, the forest rang with whoops and screams, boasts went shouting down along the creek to the witness of an amazed tribe of frogs, hurricane lanterns were hung in the branches creating an ancient wall of forest, below which the invaders crouched discussing plans of campaign, courage, loot. Their fire crackled and danced spiritedly, illuminating the Bedford where it waited some distance away, an armoured weapon. The twins were wrestling playfully so that the others began laying bets on who would win; and what had started as a game became a serious matter of money. It was always worth a gamble, they were evenly matched and fought so skilfully that even Tony or Lance who were taller and heavier would hesitate to take them on. A space formed near the fire for them, their breath came in spurts, their faces excited and laughing, their eyes glittered with flame, sighs and grunts escaped them, red handmarks on their chests and shoulders, sweat coming, the veins standing out along arms and necks. Finally with a sharp gasp Pete lay helpless, surprised, body twisted so that you could hear the joints creak, the suck of damp skin. The onlookers cheered or booed according to their fortunes.

– Who's next? demanded the loser when he'd given in and dusted himself, grinning in an evasive way which could be put down to pride.

It was decided Billy and Maggot must have it out and they set to with a fine show of vigour, Billy quiet and quick, the Maggot cheeky, boastful and game. More bets were laid but the cash had scarcely been thrown into the circle when Maggot was pinned. Now the wagers began in earnest, there being no escape for the heavyweights. Reluctant as they were, Lance and Tony pulled off their jackets and shirts, locked arms and hands. There they swayed, ridiculously clumsy, straining and heaving, feet planted wide apart, hissing and snorting, a single eight-limbed thirty-three-stone creature. The effort of remaining immobile budding as sweat. Clumps of muscle rising and shifting across their backs as the strain altered. Then without warning Lance ducked to one side tricking his opponent with a judo hold he'd learnt at his gentlemen's school. Tony's legs buckled. He rolled in dirt, with a two-hundred-and-twenty-pound fanatic dropping on top of him: Lance, only seventeen, the youngest of them all, who now crowed in an ecstasy of narcissism. That long training for the school eights had had its reward. As he got up he placed his foot on the goodnatured Tony's neck, an elephant shooter with his bag. The only gambler to collect money on this victory was the Maggot.

– Just look at the bludger, Billy roared. Can't get his thieving hands on the cash fast enough. He couldn't help being a bit ashamed of Tony.

At this they all set on Maggot, dragged him about and pummelled him till he begged for mercy and reminded them he was technically their uncle, which was true, and that uncles deserve respect.

– The winners cook the tucker, declared Peter drunkenly sprawling in a prime spot near the fire. The rest of us've got to recover. Speaking for myself I've got three broken ribs and a dislocated shoulder.

– Great deeds, droned Lance in his grammar-school voice. Will be perfo ... performed on the morrow.

– The what-o?

– Morrow. And he flexed his muscles, touching them lightly here and there as if a stranger, unaware of the thornbush antagonism around him, that by some unspoken consent it was agreed he had over-exposed his education this time.

– Hey get moving you lazy pig you're one of the cooks.

– Rum, more rum, Maggot called from the luxury of indolence, hoping to change the subject because he was the most tolerant; watching as the night trees, the truck, the fire and friends

137

began to spin and roll in a carefree manner. I'm dying of thirst. Wylie, where's my faithful darkie guide, Wylie save my life mate, pass me the bottle of Bundaberg, this desert's killing me, time enough when we reach the coast to fight off the Temperance League; if there is a coast.

Steaks sizzled on the fire and fat hunks of bread passed from hand to hand following the bottle. A simple meal of strong flavours. As they ate they loved each other for this closeness. Their language became even more raucous and abusive. Later that night they spread sleepingbags in the truck, wriggled into them, hauled a tent over the top for a dew sheet and were immediately asleep. After an hour or so, Maggot called out quite loudly from his dream – Show 'em!

The first shock of the morning was how stiff and hung over they were, how the cold struck up from the metal chilling their backs. No one had a civil word to say. The second shock quite eclipsed the first: they were not alone. Just along the track stood a hut with a drift of smoke issuing from its chimney pipe. Inhabited. They decided a deputation should attend to the matter of contact with the natives. Billy and Dave struggled out of their bags and jumped about to get the circulation going.

– It's bloody warmer out here than in there, said Dave.

They set off for the hut.

Four

– There was this fellow, Billy told Vivien eventually. An old fellow.

– Yes? Having released her hand from his she played with his hair, parting it, combing it with her fingers.

– We were driving up the gold track behind the mountain when we came on a hut. Dave and me looked in at the window. There was an amazing guy sitting at the table, a real hermit. He looked up at me and then turned his head away. No wave, no surprise, even though people never use that track. Like he was expecting us. Nothing, except maybe his eyes showing he already knew us. And he didn't think much of what he knew either. Round we went to the door, you can imagine us, and we knocked. No answer. So we knocked again, of course, because we knew he was there. Then we opened it in case he was deaf and we called out goodday.

(This one night he'd lain in fear of hoodlums, hearing them cavorting round the place, lighting a fire without proper caution, he'd gone to give them a piece of his mind and send them packing, but saw the firelight flickering on half-naked bodies twined and straining together. It was a fucking orgy. And you could hear the drunks and their drunken betting, so he sat up to be ready for them, placed his rifle on the table, one hand on the butt, sat through the dark, eyes swollen, sleepless and heavy with the dark, hearing a sinister quiet, imagining what they could be doing. Surrounding the hut? Then praying they might have gone, only to hear one call some code: *show them.*

(Through all the years he'd complained who cares about me? knowing this was a blank he had never filled. In the same way he'd say one in, all in! Yes, not above a bit of a joke, living solitary as he did. The serious side being his principles he'd lived by in the days when he'd needed them. On principle this and on principle that. My duty as I see it, no one can say fairer, straight from the shoulder, not one to mince words ... these props shored up his sparse Irish inheritance and on occasion concealed his lapses into goodwill. Lately, deluding himself out of the stifling fear of death, he would add I'm half the man I was last year, as if six months might be a passing phase.

(He sat aching, chilled, moving only in order to toss a fresh log in the stove. Next thing it would be dawn. The sound of tramping footsteps. Close. Now. This was the time. They were coming to get him. He glanced at the window in time to see two delinquents staring in, one of them seeming to laugh. That'd be their style alright. Boots on the gravel ... towards the ... door as ...)

– He was dead, poor old coot, Billy explained. Already dead. Just in that moment. You couldn't believe. And his hand on his rifle. We opened the door, Dave and me, just in time to see his head flop back like the neck was broke. He began to slip off the chair. And his rifle went bam! Gave us one hell of a fright, I can tell you. The bullet buried itself in the wall, we found it afterwards. Vivien's fingers asked him what he did then. I rushed up to the table yelling you stupid fucking bastard of course. But he was dead. We only wanted to ask some advice. He was an old prospector you see. He could have helped us.

(He died knowing the sun that moment would be rising at

Whitey's Fall, light striking the highest houses filling their windows with gold, where they overlooked pits and hollows still flooded by an outbreak of despair issuing from abandoned diggings. His rusty corpse sprawled, jammed halfway under the table still waiting for what had already come. Not aware that at this moment three shrivelled gold diggers who'd known him better than themselves tidied their campsite on the opposite spur, sipped stewed tea in the early twilight, pissed scaldingly among the ferns and trudged downhill, pans in hand, to their separate destinies. Trudged, their backs to the disused mineshafts that they themselves, and he who had died, helped work when there was still anything in them. Tramped downhill towards the dark creek where they sifted and sluiced the dirt for whatever former hopes history might spare them.)

– Who was he? Vivien asked, feeling herself inadequate.
– Uncle used to know him. McAloon. A bad case, the gold got him thirty years ago. Before that there was a war he went to and turned nasty when he came back, dug up a corpse. Gold makes you suspicious. Nice little place though, he must have got a kick out of building that hut. Solid.

(As McAloon died, dairyfarmers at Whitey's Fall, their elbows on kitchen tables of their own, blearily admired wives who had already stoked the stoves and called in the cows in the old fashion and had ritually set aromatic teapots ready beside the altar of the alarm clock; farmers who drowsed where they sat, contented and yet with the anguish of prisoners, hearing the cows anxious for relief in the milking sheds come nuzzling and breathing at the gate. As Mr McAloon's dead hand fired the rifle, Mr Brinsmead and Mr Ping shuffled to doors of their respective establishments, grinding the stiff bolts and releasing cats to drift out in a balloon of warmth. Up the hill at the Mountain Hotel, Jasper the publican banged the first of his golden windows up exactly as that bullet hit the hut wall, and stood helpless, a man sculpted from dough, surrounded by a crowd of up-ended stools. Haunted by the years of ambition when he fought his brother in the courts, he coughed and spat into the street, into the dawn. Spat, oppressed by the pub's tradition of good times. Whitey's Fall, a town to be proud of, knew nothing about the death of James Richmond Ellis McAloon, for thirty-four years agent of Their Majesties the sovereigns of Great Britain and Northern Ireland, inspector of mines and tyrant of the licensing regulations, and twenty-nine years layabout drunk, who died frightened and sober, besieged by the hooligans he heard about on his Astor mantel-model till the valves gave out.)

– What the hell! yelped Dave.
– Fuckingbloodybastard! Billy jumped in to restrain the man at the table. But Mr James Richmond Ellis McAloon, known as Kel, was dead. His finger, still hard against the trigger, the rifle butt slipping down from where it had struck the chair-back. That look of terror and recognition totally wiped from his eyes, the face a sudden drained white. The stove with its firebox open, burning energetically, the clock going and in good order, and on the walls one smoke-cured calendar of a lady without clothes beside a hand-drawn map and a rack of pans and prospecting tools. The two youths, now certain the hermit was dead, tried unsuccessfully to sit him back on his chair, then opted for moving the table and stretching him flat on the floor, it seemed wrong to leave him in this doll-like indignity.
– I'll stay with him, Bill Swan offered. You go and get the others, Tony'd better use my bike and fetch that cop.
Dave answered like a dutiful recruit, thankful to take orders and not have to think, and went.
Billy knelt down to speak to the corpse: you poor old soldier, with your life. Didn't you have anything but this then? He experimented at touching the gluey eyelids. Then he did a really unaccountable thing, he stroked the man's face with the back of his hand, tenderly perhaps, feeling the stubble, the curious bony structure of it, the stiff sunken cheek. Oh man, he breathed. Oh man. This was something awful. The dead right hand in his, he was shaking it.
The corpse wore a jacket over pyjamas and a greatcoat on top

142

of that. Bill Swan did up the neck button on the pyjamas out of concern for the dignity of man. He reached across to the bunk pulling free a grey blanket to flag over the body. Oh man, Bill Swan said gently, almost admonishingly. You got yourself into a mess and never found a way out. This was a real corpse. In Whitey's Fall so few ever died, they all threatened to live as long as you could imagine. And he began to understand it wasn't death from age you puzzled about, but death before you were ready.

He left the rifle where it had fallen. Somewhere down the track he heard the crouping of his motorcycle followed by a dwindling drone. With only a minute left of undisturbed intimacy with the dead, I'm sorry, he said to the corpse, sorry for everything mate. Rats could be heard resuming their routine activities under the floor, a tiny blue wren fluttered into the cabin and hopped about pecking at this and that, perfectly at home. Billy watched the sunscoured head so grim and bitter. He couldn't help thinking of the contrast with Uncle, Uncle's merry brown face. When Uncle stopped smiling fans of pale sunless lines appeared round his eyes like a network of scar tissue, so even at his most severe he couldn't keep it up, his customary expression still printing its disruptive ghost on his features. Yet Billy had a wry suspicion the two of them might be related.

– What's going on here? Lance swaggered in newly aware of his own importance since last night's wrestling match.

Dave ushered the others into the presence of tragedy. Bill was on his feet and had his back turned, casually studying the calendar woman. A yawning power filled him, rising and subsiding: he had been with a dead man. Would his friends discover signs if he let them see his face?

– Who was he? Lance demanded.

The corpse exercised terrific presence, his tired face so tired, his clothes filthy and rumpled, dust ingrained in his hands.

– Where did the bullet hit, Dave?

– See? Buried right in the wood.

– Twenty-two.

Bill tinkered with things on the shelf: badly dinted pans, an auger of the old hand type, an iron mortar for dollying, two torches, some cold chisels and a battered notebook. He took possession of the book.

– That's official isn't it? Lance challenged him (so he'd been watching, suspecting).

– The johns'll get it if we leave it here.

They faced each other as enemies, then allowed the moment to deflate. Bill pocketed the book.

– What's the smell? asked Lance sulkily.

– Shit his pants I reckon. Looks like it's soaking out on to the floor.

The old cove, yes, who knew about secrecy. Whatever gold he found he must have kept the news to himself.

Lance wrinkled his nose at the blot of clay-coloured fluid. He stood so tall and secure and uncaring, aware that Bill Swan needed a punch in the head before he'd stop bossing other people's lives, same as Uncle the loudmouthed stickybeak.

Bill looked across the gulf.

– If you ask me, there never was a Golden Fleece, Lance sneered with the intention of wounding. Those Brinsos'd be certified anywhere but Whitey's, for sure.

(Food had been one of Kel McAloon's torments. He suffered a chronic gastric complaint which first robbed him of appetite and then rendered useless most of what he did manage to eat. He hated and feared his bowels. Some evenings he'd have fits of wind, knots in the gut becoming severe shooting pains, then the steady lead pipe stuck down through his chest to his groin, and he'd dry retch till he could induce the first wind to break. The following four hours he'd be absorbed in twisting his body, squeezing out balloons of gas, arching his belly, bending his back, reaching out his arms or curling up to hug his knees, tensed, stretched on his back, on his side, a man on the rack, while burps barked and farts fluttered. If the indigestion came on him severely, a violent diarrhoea would result, after which he'd collapse and lie exhausted well into the next morning, muttering obscenities at the injustice of his fate. Or else it would be followed by bloated visions of himself and the mountain swimming together

144

underwater, changing shape and mass, exchanging shape and mass, wallowing and merging, forest trees the bubbles of his own breath, his shoulder the numb mountain, a ridge his arm, his legs stuck deep underground.)

By eleven o'clock the formalities were completed. The police took charge of the situation. There was nothing more to be done. The boys were free to leave. The whole forest screamed with cicadas as the Bedford whined unsteadily up the hill past the dead man's hut into the dense enveloping bush, leaving the police car behind with its blue light flashing. The track grew steeper and hugged close in against the rockface. The vegetation took on the character of rainforest with long tendrils of vines draping the eucalypts their full length, clusters of treeferns, a canopy so thick the sun never penetrated it.

Billy drove, the steeringwheel jolting pleasantly in his hands. But the smell of that hut haunted him, the shock of having been shot at kept his heart pounding. The Bedford, the bush, the birds, the logging track itself, all were clean and restorative. The power of being touched ebbed. He was struck by the oddity that secrecy might grow with knowledge. Had this McAloon found gold?

– What next? Billy called so they could all hear him. A few grunts greeted the question. Wind flustered and went sighing among leaves, a pair of gang-gangs squawked cheerily, took to air scattering olive and scarlet among the branches. Dust feathered up behind the tailboard. Occasionally the forest parted to allow glimpses of cattle country below. The motor thumped like a paddlesteamer, goldgoldgold. The temperature indicator crept into the red, Bill tapped it to show Tony.

– Better take things easy ay?

– Yair.

Those in the back joggled about, mulling over the possibilities of their future, their careers in the city. A future meant you could succeed or fail. In Whitey's Fall nobody could fail. That was the difference. That was why they were going away.

Five

– Remember when we climbed down that cliff? Billy spoke very softly delivering the words right in Vivien's ear as she rested her head in his lap. I suppose . . . I was, well, jealous in a way. Because you could look at Mrs Ping while I was killing myself holding the truck. His breath came in hot puffs that left her cold afterwards. I wanted to face up to it.

– But you knew her, that's worse.

– When I saw Mr McAloon I was angry because he shot at us. But excited too. Billy sat up, separating himself from her.

– One thing . . . she began, discovering his hand.

– I know. His roughened fingers cradled her face but he didn't dare look at her. The moonlight was now brilliant and he couldn't be sure of himself. I know, you're going to ask why I said: what if I pushed you off the rock?

You were climbing down with me even though you didn't know me. As if everything had to be alright.

– As if you couldn't be dangerous?

He nodded, the hobbledehoy who trained his hair to stay flat and to work up a signature he could call his own.

They smiled together. Vivien felt his hand cup her ear, one fingertip probing, ruffling the tiny audible hairs.

146

– What next? he asked.

She was too astonished to attempt any reply. Billy thought of the contrast between them. He felt wise and mature. He knew from television what her world was, but she could have no knowledge of the mountain.

Vivien strove to relate the tenderness of his hands to the bullying voice.

– Are you married? she asked. It made him snort into the great night of cities and ships. Her despairing fingers cruised inside his shirt causing him to arch with pleasure. But fear warned him she was stealing his will. Some theft of this kind had happened before. A suffocating heap of flowers. An enchantress among her pigs. He'd suffered shipwreck for the sake of her song, a dozen years of enforced indolence robbing him of his prime.

– It's the place, he apologized.

– The place? she echoed bitterly, breaking contact, standing. She led the way indoors to the bedroom. Slowly she walked, not to strain the thread of her power.

Stubbornness kept him where he was, cold on the boards by himself, the storm of excitement subsiding, listening pitilessly to a giveaway shoe falling empty on the lino, a sigh of lost breath. He was mesmerized by half-forgotten lessons: the jangling touch of rapiers, an expectant crow, a bell clanging far off for early mass, the rapiers whipping together, nose running, the whirl and sting of the first engagement, blood. He could smell the dew, he wanted the business over. Voices told him, watch out Billy, man. He lay on the verandah and contemplated falling asleep.

Vivien had sacrificed the initiative. And this is the first night, she despaired. She caressed herself with disgust, her hands carried his smell when she clapped them over her trembling mouth. She should go out and kick him in the face as he deserved. She wallowed in bed, weeping, smothered by the pillow, her past cancelled, her future a hole of night. He was so deliberately in command.

Excitement settled among the company on the mountainside: the old man dead, the shot, the police, and now the engine temperature rising beyond the safe limit. A few grim smiles were exchanged in the bright morning sunshine. The forest closed behind them, trees bounding away like camouflaged guerrillas, the clayey slopes heaved ominously, outcrops of granite observed them from antiquity. The twins hummed a tune, gradually clarifying it into words and a definite rhythm.

For day and night the irons clang and like poor galley-slaves,
We toil and toil and when we die we shall fill dishonoured graves.
But by and by I'll break my chain and into the bush I'll go
To join the brave bushrangers there, Jack Donahue & Co.

– Another of their mad colonial raves, Lance complained.

Maggot, beating time with his free hand (clinging to the truck with the other to save his life), leaned across to yell in Billy's ear.

– Give her the gun, mate.

The cut-away hood shuddered, the motor whined, the gears grabbed. Soon they would have to stop to let the truck cool down. But every man was impatient to get ahead that morning, to crawl up as high as the Bedford could, short of actually exploding.

The difficulty of holding to a sense of scale stimulated them. The mountain, as they now saw it, so enormous and their collective insignificance an insect. Huge treeferns met overhead forming a bower for their rowdy smelly passage, a pale green tunnel with a larva nosing up towards the sun. In every direction spread generations of trees, ridge after ridge dense with them, trees utterly untouchable the panorama held so many of this dinosaur of plants, so that the truck's progress was not only as ridiculous as a ship at sea, but equally meaningless. Yet the will was strong.

– What we need is my grandfather, said Tony. The plants talk to him, so he says.

– Strange things happen, Bill conceded.

– He was in his garden talking to the cauliflowers. He woke up I was there but he didn't mind. I tell them they're beauties, he said, and they tell me things.

– What things?

– Their sort a things, was all he'd say. You can even catch him kissing flowers.

– Sooner them than me!

– He grabs hold of trees to save his life.

– I believe it.

– I once went to chop down a stump for firewood, nice wood, grey and dry, you know, just asking to be burnt. I swung me axe up in the air, ready, when the stump turned round. It was him, grandpa. How would you feel? He didn't say a thing, only smiled with what he knew.

Billy spared a glance for the rearvision mirror where the track slunk away behind them into a wilderness of vegetation. He could hear Lance's voice.

– Bet me this is the largest vehicle ever to get this far up? Who's game? She's a bloody beauty this Bedford, Lance added by way of making his peace with the driver, this time getting it right.

– She is too, Bill muttered happily.

Once they wheezed to a standstill. The party in the back leapt over the side and, in the competitive way of young men, jogged up ahead, eyes everywhere, but soon returned with nothing to report. The motor cooled off in the shade. The forest moved, dense with life, cicadas throwing up arches of song, sudden peaks and towers, a whole cathedral of sound bewildering in its detail.

Bill took himself off to a secluded spot, squatted on his hams and quietly emptied his bowels among pebbles that possibly bore gold. He took note of his surroundings, grunted, sighed with the pleasure of it, remaining there a while to make the most of his comfort. Then he recalled Kel McAloon's diary in his pocket. Stolen goods. Here was the seclusion he'd been waiting for. He opened it:

kept clear of the filthy basterds from the day they come. Now there gone the place still stinks fair horrible. Nothing here anyhow, nothing left but rubbish. They go through every last shovel full twice over AS WE KNOW. Rubbish is all they'd leave us of Australia if we let them. Dirty little pooftas youd want to ring there necks like a roosters.

Billy shut the book. He put it away, his mind uneasy, shown

149

some ugly angers in himself. The scrub had grown denser since last he looked. He heard a shout. He scrambled up, kicked some dirt into the hole he'd made, zipped his jeans and yelled a reply. Others could be heard crashing through the bush converging on a creek where the Maggot stood cupping his hands for a megaphone. He and Peter had filled the watercans ready to carry back, then they'd had a dip in the icy water. But why call out? Bill, Tony, Dave and Lance watched their clean damp faces, questioned the sunshine glistening in their lashes. Was it gold? Was this what they'd come for already?

– Look, Maggot ordered as he led the way to a shallow cave in the cliff. An iron camp-oven stood at the back. He removed the lid with a flourish. Dinner's up! he announced, reached in and drew out a woman's dress.

The dress had been folded for so long a grid of creases squared the cloth as he held it up: a pink cotton frock of a long forgotten fashion. Lance whistled. Maggot bunched his fists and inserted them in the bosom of the dress while the others tittered. He held it against himself and modelled it, pirouetting in the narrow space, pursed his lips, crossed his legs and vamped over his left shoulder. Doing well.

– Next! he called as he tossed the dress to Peter and produced a petticoat. Next! he called again throwing the petticoat at Lance's head and taking out a pair of white bloomers. These he unfolded gingerly and displayed. They were disfigured by a florid brown stain.

– What's happened? asked Tony in fear.

Lance turned away, disgusted.

– Looks like someone got raped, Dave suggested.

– No, Maggot pointed out. No, she folded the clothes herself.

– That's her period, Lance taunted them, his mouth full of wolverine teeth.

The young men gaped at the bloodstain, that huge dark blot. So this was the period, this was what they'd heard about in Yalgoona.

– Such a lot of blood, Maggot marvelled.

Not to be hurried, Billy examined the bloomers till sure he

had missed nothing. It didn't appear puzzling to him that the clothes were left and never claimed. Satisfied, he passed the evidence to Dave who hastily dropped it back where it belonged.

– That's been a long time, Tony observed of religion as a whole.

Peter folded the dress and Maggot folded the petticoat. The iron lid clanged a loud bell when they replaced it.

Unexpectedly he was there, he had come into the room, yes, to be part of its dark angles. She could hear him breathing, then slipping off his clothes and leaving them where they dropped. She heard him go back and pick them up, surely not folding them? His belt-buckle clinked against a chair. He opened her bed, peeling it back gently. His warm rough body beside her, her own treacherous warmth flowed out to him. But she volunteered no response to his invasion. Bill propped himself on his side to see her, chromium-plated in the moonlight from the window. Eyes bright and dark, nose defined with exquisite sharpness, she did not move. Fully clothed, she lay silent. So he was horrified at what he had done, and done without motive. Once at that first meeting climbing down the cliff he asked what she'd think if he pushed her off. Now he had. No reason then, none now. Couldn't she guess he was ready to offer any apology if only she'd turn and forgive him? Even a sigh would grant him leave to comfort her. He saw she was beautiful. Recumbency hollowed her cheeks, suffering gave depth to her eyes, the oblique light picking out explicit details. Previously he had seen her body as a body of actions rather than shapes. The hair massed round her brow with such life its very stillness appeared astonishing. He was not skilled in these matters and, since he was also inexperienced, continued supine and helpless, embarrassed by nakedness. Ready to do the right thing, also a little petulant at her refusal to resolve the deadlock. With a start of surprise it occurred to him he might appear to her much as his father appeared to him: a stocky, mulish, dissatisfied and baffling being.

Vivien was back in the Berkshire countryside, a village child scooping handfuls of snow and pelting them at a rumpled assembly of other village children; then came a sharp pain in the side of her head and at the touch of that one gross superthumb of a mitten, the knitted wool blotting up blood, her cry of anguish that it was at *her* somebody chose to throw a snowball loaded with a stone, that she should be the one to excite malice, that it should be her pain affording them triumphant amusement; that the butcher now saw fit to come waddling out of his shop, stomach tightly strapped in a hideously bloodied apron, and shake his sharpening-steel at his nephews and nieces, chasing them off and referring to her as a sweet charming little thing. He had led her into his shop for protection, so she stood, an utter stranger and outcast, shoes scuffing in the sawdust, rolling the occasional bloodball, her head filled with the obnoxious odour of fresh carcasses, eyes fascinated by forms of death and dissection. In addition to which there was no way out. How was she to get home? The time must come for her to confront those children the kindly beastly butcher had declared to be her enemies and inferiors. Proper gentleman your father, he'd said by way of consolation; so that now she knew what she must do.

Lying in her own bed stiff as a wax figure in the Chamber of Horrors, again being an outsider foisting herself on a community too small and insular to cope with her foreignness, Vivien relived her reply to the butcher, the words having seemed through all the years important. Thank you for helping me Mr Chap but I think I must go back to my friends now, she'd said and squared her eight-year-old shoulders, set her face against crying, refused her mittened hand permission to check the wound again, walked as steadily as she was able to the door, pulled it, dragged at its handle, struggled against stiff hinges and the spring holding it shut against flies, staggered outside and called in that high precious voice she now heard for the first time as hateful as it must sound to others – Where are you? Please come and play. It doesn't hurt. I don't mind. And when the first snowball whizzed out of nowhere to splatter on the shoulder of her red coat with the black velvet collar, she found the knowledge to laugh. Ya boo! she laughed with hysterical derision as two more surprise snowballs narrowly missed their mark. Then came a silence. A robin danced prettily out of the hedge between the butcher's and the grocer's. Nothing but her laugh, now a laugh of scorn, and the unconcerned robin busy about the necessities of worm spotting. Then they emerged from hiding, surrendered all together, sidling from behind gates, facing her from doorways. Are you the new kid then? they asked. And she said she was, gladly yes, she was an identity, the new kid in person. So one girl came and put her arm round her neck. You're on my side, she announced.

– My father, Vivien had informed them, beats me. Though not true, this was inspired.

Billy didn't arrive at a decision, he simply acted when he felt released to act. His hand hovered. His face close to Vivien's, but with a natural delicacy not actually touching.

– This is the first time for me, he said healing the rift instantly, when it has meant anything. His hand curving to her shape, adventuring.

Mrs Ping once read from a book that if matter could be stilled, the molecules arrested in their perpetual movement, two solid bodies would pass through one another, whole and unharmed. His hand swept through her, oaring down, as, in the same manner, her head rose, teeth and nose spearing up through his jaw, already past his ears and eventually breaking free of the skull so she could take a deep breath at last and feel it serving both pairs of lungs. Her thighs rising from the back of his legs lazarus-like, pallid and cold. So now she levitated above the bed and surely her clothes had been lost somewhere along the way. For his part, he experienced a crimping of the scalp, a slight draught as she floated out from his back, and a tingling when she re-entered in the same way. Their eyes saw the act of seeing. Their double tongue unravelled coupling snakes, licking through and back through each other. They were instantly inheritors of two worlds of knowledge; he thought and she thought together:
the speckled feather, a treasure of generations unchanged
axes   different trees different tunes   rhythms
the great ship lurching into a beggar-filled port
laughing rabbit   nice in the gunsight
the first day lived in the swank of stolen lipstick

steam from a frog's back   December
the emergence from fire of a porcelain figure of repose
transparent roof of a fish's mouth
the hunt for pussywillows on a hill that smells of fox
blaze of blood   the motorcycle   perfect cornering
the fear of not knowing what a cow's eyes see
knowing what a cow's eyes see   afraid
the strowing of leaves on Palm Sunday, the plaited grass cross
last bird of a migration   hasn't led at any stage
the mystery of greed and the odour of loneliness
simple   sparkplug
the candle going out and the canary keeling over
toenails of an old lady   her fingernail picking them
the loss of one leg by a three-legged stool
a horse's shit   cloud shape
the sadness of an addled egg
water frozen in a boot left out all night
the one tuft of boy's hair that won't lie flat
someone falling down   joke
the blindman beating his seeing-eye dog
waterdiviner's fingertips   trembling
the nose and teeth spearing effortlessly through another skull
still body   swimming down

Not yet daylight. Trees dipped into mist and branched up from
it. Despite the damp air you couldn't say it was cold. Boots glossy
wet, Bill Swan and Vivien sauntered uphill with all the time
before them. Already well above the house and at the verge of
the forest they wandered, thoughtful. Outcrops of granite
hunched, speckled with lilies. The mountain could be seen best
reflected in their eyes. They were listening to the rustle of their
own progress, inattentive to the birds who now sang, casting each
note singly like a fishing line. The sky clean glass filled up with
water. Neither spoke. There was no plan. The flies had not yet
woken. All night the wind stayed gentle. Branches veiled in mist
signalled to them. Soaked to the knees, the lovers climbed the
mountain slope, in among treetrunks too ancient to bear scars.

154

Glass chips fell starlike from the leaves far up out of reach. Wisps of steam began to form on their clothing, the incline rose steeply ahead. They stopped and listened. Nearby they could hear the chirruping of a kangaroo grinding its teeth. Bill Swan's world was filled with Vivien and Vivien's eyes. They let each other's hand go, then joined them together tighter.

– Are you cold love? he asked hoarsely, feeling her coldness as deliciously fresh and unfamiliar.

– No, she lied so he'd be told she loved him.

They climbed till they were met by two massive rocks, tall presences carved to the sweeping shapes of wind, gouged and smoothed, loud with birdsong, standing with the absolute stillness of time itself. Mist played tricks of substance and illusion. But Vivien pushed through the bracken to the foot of one rock and placed her hand there, palm chilled by the shock of stone. William Swan of Dead Reef placed his hand on the companion rock and they were joined then by the mountain itself, the mist vanishing from around them. All colour being leached from the sky, the foliage jutted black and sharp silhouettes with white outlines. Somewhere water gurgled. The cold cut at them. Together they willed the sun to rise. The horizon gathered its remembered resources of blue into wings and swooped towards them. Then the first shaft of light blinded them. Insects swarmed through the air, a plague of mosquitoes drifting down, flies whirling up, grasshoppers launching themselves with the trajectory of bullets, flocks of white moths escaped from dark hollows and disappeared into the sun. The ground underfoot showed as four crescents of rainbow moisture while beneath the grass shadows ants patrolled the hard soil. Leaves flickered and sparkled in the wind. The distant petrol motor at the cheese factory stammered to life and settled to its heartbeat.

The full company once more aboard, the Bedford rasped into action, crawling up the steep slope. Bill drove, attentive to the revs, considering the question of coincidences. Each detail of his life revealed as strange if you got close enough to it. His own name Swan, for example. Who could have thought of the letter

W, let alone an *S?* The rattletrap corkscrewed into a grassy clearing where two treeferns had placed their strange symmetrical forms as if in a plot of parkland. Behind them the sky blossomed with thundercloud. The last short climb lay ahead, then from a saddle in the horizon you had to explore on foot; leaving the return journey winding eastward round the mountain, downhill to Whitey's Fall.

– Come on Bill, shouted the Maggot. Before the rain hits, mate.

They accelerated, bounced crazily across the turf and rumbled up the steep incline. The first drops starred the windscreen. The men in the back huddled into waterproof jackets, one-handedly stowing their dry gear under a tarpaulin, clutching the vehicle's lurching sidewalls with their other hands. Rain fell in brief cold gusts. Then they were there. The Bedford had made it to the top of the track, and only just in time. A wet surface might have meant disaster. The east wind struck in from the sea with a message.

The party sprang out and began walking, heading for the southern peak. The silent slopes of forested gullies immediately filled with a theatrical crash of thunder, massive as the mountain itself, re-echoing round ridges and valleys, a gorgeous sound rolling solidly this way and that, a colossal glossy boom heard in glass caverns. The view below took their breath, superb assemblages of rockfaces and ravines plunging to a fan of valleys filled with treeferns and threaded on sparkling wires of creeks.

While the young men stood listening to the thunderclap ricochet among the complex of soundingboards, repeatedly leaping alive, a patch of mist floated across and blotted out the whole panorama. All sense of prominence lost, the explorers were stranded on the bluff, and for the first time took note of the soil itself. There was no sign of any track. The space about them splintered into raucous squeals: a flock of black cockatoos swept past, alighting in a patch of trees, ripping at the branches with strong beaks, dropping chunks of bark as they tore them off. Back they rushed in a flurry of argumentative discontent, storm birds with long bodies, yellow patched wings and faces and fan tails, sounding like so many creaking doors among the trees, a township of dead prospectors opening their decrepit dwellings to show what they had in common.

The rain peppered down, sharp drops knocking a passage between the leaves. Behind them the forest reared smooth trunks washed dark green by rain streaming down them to form puffs of white foam at the bottom. The six young men were too self-absorbed to feel uncomfortable, though their shoulders and the backs of their legs got soaked. Boots silenced by rubbery lichen. The route they chose towards the south peak led through low scrub and airstreams of scent, now acrid, now floury, now cloying, now clean eucalyptus, now nostalgic mimosa, and finally the neutral perfume of seeding grasses. So they climbed, lungs heaving, blood thudding at the base of the skull, feet slipping. Below them the well of space lay filled with cloud, so that a cold insecurity tugged at the ground underfoot and set damp wings trembling in their hair. They plugged on, socks squeaking in their boots, dribblets inside their clothing meandering down over the swell of chest and belly, the raindrops ticking resonantly against their sodden gear, woollens giving off a whiff of sheep oil as a reminder of the spirit. The rain pelted so solid it appeared not to be falling at all, but to be myriad wires by which the mountain was lifted up, cloud-shaped and giving voice to thunder of its own.

They had impertinently treated the mountain of gold as an obstacle, so the rain beat the cheerful talk out of them; then even their complaints fell mute. They plodded ahead, not looking around nor thinking of why they had come.

Six

The rain stopped. Pure citron sunlight filled the space around them as the mist finally rose and dispersed, trailing ragged ends and leaving threads snagged on the trees. The eastern and southern slopes spread faint and watery beneath them. Collectively they were God dividing the waters from the dry land and the waters above the earth from the firmament. Shutters slid apart, Australia blazed with light. They stood stiffly, gazing at the new land; deep steaming gullies choked with burrawang palms, pink-tipped crowns of great eucalypts crowded with shifting shadows, hints of watching faces, the spirits of those who'd gone before. Across there at the second level of ridges they spotted two clearings, then a third: mines. This was what they'd come for. And lower down something else, more formal but less distinct, disturbing and exciting, almost the ground-plan of a settlement, a village. They smiled at each other from under plastered hair, swung their packs lightly on their shoulders and stepped out with fresh enthusiasm to find a way down.

Once there, you saw the rotting grey windlasses sprawled on the ground, bolts rusted in their joints, limbs splayed out of kilter. The naked pits humbler and more squalid than expected, rough holes of greed.

– They must have been bloody desperate, Lance protested with a hint of fear. It was so. The forest rustled indifferently.

The lip of the first shaft lay sticky and bright ochre in that end-of-storm light. Easy to imagine men, carefree with familiarity, losing their balance and slipping, falling into such a shaft. Accidents all over the goldfields. Bill already lay on his belly working his way backward, legs first, his face imprinting a quarter of its shape in the soft clay, feet waving like a beetle's feelers till they knocked against the top rung of a ladder let into the shaft. Unsafe, no doubt, rotten. Cautiously he eased his weight on it while Dave went to get a rope for him and the others watched, glad to be spectators, occasionally offering the reassurance of humorous suggestions. He was testing the next rung, and the one below. Four or five more. His head lower than ground level, so when he thought of something to say to Tony he had to crane his neck.

– Tony, he ordered. Don't for christsake stand on this till I'm all the way down, it's shaky as buggery.

– Give us a hoy, Tony replied placidly.

– Something running across the wall here. Rat maybe, Billy's voice came up damp and hollow. They could hear him breathing, also his shoes and the curious stone-on-stone noise they made. He spoke muffled words, but they did not answer, understanding that he was simply giving himself courage.

– Okay Tony it's only about thirty feet deep, came his blurred report. I'm here.

And down in the dark Bill Swan stood back waiting for Tony to join him. The walls were very roughly gouged and none too safe. Pebbles rattled against them, a moment later pattering round him. Most of the light blocked out. The space where he waited seemed confined but evidently led off in several directions. The uneven rock floor was slippery with mud. He listened, anxious that the ladder should not give way, annoyed that his friend should be so large.

It was better when they both stood at the bottom together, shuffling about to explore how wide the pit might be. Hands stretched in front, they groped their way into separate chambers.

In two lobes of a lung they stopped, blind, making no noise. Each turned his invisible head, nose detecting the unseeable, the untouchable approaching.

Utter dark clasped Billy in a suffocating mass. Something small moved through his hair. Sweating, he breathed the air of loss, the blackness with its forgotten odour. Gaps in the ladder to safety preyed on his imagination: even the rust of the rungs smelled forlorn. He had to break out, move, back into the dim spotlight of the shaft. Once there, raindrops baptised him. He opened his mouth to let out his fear, closed his eyes and welcomed the good moisture trickling on his tongue. He would confess none of what he had felt.

Tony remained among the warm black feather-shapes. He wished for nothing more. The place surprised him as a homecoming, earth gathered him into itself, the mountain had something to share with him, he picked it as a beating sensation in the air, the slow regular vibration he dreamily accepted. Yes he opened his mouth. Tipping back his head so the shaft of darkness plunged right inside him, he was a shell of skin suspended in darkness. The dark lay soft and glossy inside him. I have not been like this for a long time, his body said to him.

Next moment. Torches clattering down, tied to a cord, clapping against the shaft walls. Bill was there to unite them and call thanks. He was there to switch them on, dissolve the black chambers with watery light. Tony accepted a torch resentfully, watched his mate so glibly showing this to be a couple of squalid holes dug in shale.

– See the seams of quartz, said Billy.

– I felt them, Tony co-operated curtly.

– Not much left.

– Pretty worked out, Tony agreed feeling a little ashamed of his surliness.

– I've got a few samples to take up. Let's get out of here.

– In a minute mate.

They heard a sound they had never heard before, a large body of air hooting down the shaft into their cave. Afterwards a soft heavy flop and their eardrums cricking. By torchlight they discovered the exit to the shaft blocked with a heap of slushy clay. They were shut off. Tony nodded his acceptance, curiously unable to feel any panic. Here he was with Bill on equal terms. He stuck his foot in the soggy clay as it advanced into the chamber oozing over the rock floor.

Billy's body was a flock of birds in a net. He edged back, knocking his skull on the ceiling. He breathed the knowledge that air was limited. For a second he swore he could hear voices. His knees trembled. People don't die like this on our mountain, he protested. His father coughed irritably in the dark. Billy considered the advancing clay. His courage being marshalled, he knew how to behave.

– We're the ones who decided to stay on the mountain, he joked.

This maddened Tony, who couldn't stick the conventional bravado. The darkness was his death and he wasn't going to have it stolen by Bill Swan who had stolen so much else from him. All the years of loss, the little concessions of pride, of giving in so perpetually he couldn't put a shape to his own character. This at last was an insult, this he cared about. Tossing aside his torch, Tony lunged at the clay, lying on it, swimming on it, surprised to find it quite warm.

– Shift the fucking stuff, he ordered. His powerful arms scooped it into the chamber round his feet. Gradually he sank into the muck by his own weight. Billy's torch wavered on the scene. Wrong, crazy, a waste of precious strength; but it was something to be done. You couldn't stand by. He tucked the torch in his pocket, then also threw himself bodily on the enemy and felt the earth clutch him. Panic took over. He exhausted himself in wild threshing that resembled an effort to escape, breathing as shallowly as he could. Anyhow the air was nothing but a clot of hisses, sucks and slaps; sounds of drowning men.

Tony's voice occasionally grunted get in get in ... to the mud itself.

That was the logic of it. Bill clung to the idea, the direction. Thicker than the forest, deafening as an explosion.

They felt the body of soil living and sliding under them. Hard as they fought forward they floated gradually, relentlessly, back. Billy sobbed with rage, he battled against the unknown quantity of clay. Maybe the whole shaft had filled in. He saw visions of second tunnels, backways out by other means. Fantasies, he knew it, having already touched the dead end stone wall of the cave sculpted a century ago by miners who thought themselves lucky. He could hear Tony working methodically, rhythmically, victim of prehistoric instincts. His own broken nails scooped at the rubbish he knew so well, his elbows banged on a memory of drunken years ago when his father and Uncle punched each other in the hope of murder. The slocking scoop of mud brought him face to face with Mrs Ping fingering her globe of the world when she sucked at her teeth with disappointment. He tasted the earth, he felt it, he breathed it. He was being shot at by a dead man and shovelled under.

At the end of his life his eyes opened, cracking the clay lids itself apart and he saw a blob of light, white, blank, completely alien to the dark, a mysterious ovoid shape of light, stretching, widening with power. Billy wriggled, flailing like a yabbie, something catching at his hair and jerking his face up. Then his eyes seeing the miraculous crystal plumage of a rainshower, hands tugging him and busy under his arms, a shocking tightness around his chest and his whole body lifted agonisingly free of the sucking mud.

Lance and the twins yanked him up on the rope and heaved his boneless, sleepy body over the rim to safety. They untied him and lowered the rope again for the Maggot down there to rescue Tony.

– Christ O Christ, were Bill's first words as his oyster mouth gaped. He wept and trembled. And even when he lay beside the creek half an hour later, washed and changed into the dry clothes they found for him, he couldn't suppress the trembling. His old man's hands fumbled with the mud-sealed pockets of his discarded trousers, extracting lumps of quartz he had collected before the cave-in, samples strangely more interesting than they'd looked in the torchlit mine. One knob bore definite flecks of gold. Then he retrieved the torch itself still palely glimmering, and his watch.

– It can't be only nine o'clock! he shook the watch in disbelief, in anger. Up above, a King Parrot made progress among the branches, stepping with rigid dignity, moving his scarlet thighs as if earth could not resist him.

– Three hours till food! Somebody wailed to cheer them up.

Bill Swan, the runt, turned to look at Tony who sat nearby, and found himself wondering, is that my cousin? Of course their mothers were sisters so in the usual sense the question was rhetorical, but it disturbed him because he was aware that, unless more closely related, everybody was everybody else's cousin. This kinship with his friend seldom came to mind. In the general course of events his main discomfort was that he kept meaning to acknowledge Tony's loyalty but somehow it came out as sarcasm or indifference. Now he watched the big man haul himself upright, stretching, and he knew something had happened for Tony that hadn't happened for himself. A new knowledge sharpened his critical observation. Tony had not been afraid as he had. A break had taken place. Like a perfectly strange friend Tony asked – Are you going down the next one mate? His high voice coming strongly and (Billy couldn't tell how) independently. That's it, the runt noted, he has got something going for himself.

– A man would have to be a mug. Like those guys up in satellites.

– You reckon? Tony pursued his disbelief. This had nothing in common with his own feeling. Billy felt the burden of awkwardness, the constriction he had carried with him for two years or more, begin to lift. When he had least expected it and had done nothing for it, the burden of Tony forever wanting something from him began to evaporate, painlessly, like mist dispersing though you cannot feel the slightest breeze. While their companions discussed the advisability of trying out other mines, Bill reached across and put his hand on Tony's boot as if about to ask a favour. Tony, who had longed for such a gesture an hour ago, scarcely noticed. Instead he smiled the way experience smiles at ignorance. I'm free, I'm free, the runt sang inwardly.

– Are you laughing? Tony inquired, his privacy enhanced.

– Did you hear me? he threw back his head shakily and guffawed in the open.

– You want to take it easy mate, this could be serious! Tony tapped his forehead in the traditional joke which at the same time was a dismissal, watching a moment, distastefully, the roof of his cousin's mouth, almost transparent, the cleanest thing in the world. Bill laughed his laugh of the motorcyclist swaying free and feckless round the mountain, lay back in the wet grass and laughed all the blackness out, laughed out suffocation, the cloying earth, the taste of clay, the stench. Tony wandered away, nursing the power he had earned, refusing to be diminished by irritation.

The party visited six other mines, approaching them with caution and not staying down long, more to fulfil an obligation than enthusiasm. They took turns, being lowered on ropes, landing thigh-deep in water, ankle-deep in mud, with bruised shoulders, grazed knees, they chipped at the rock and filled bags with worthless samples. All in all they found the day challenging beyond anticipation and enjoyable. Towards evening they set out to find a campsite. A curious mood seized them so that they made their way independently, straggling, no two together. If you were close enough to observe fine points, you'd find all their eyes had some expression in common, guarded, closed, warding off interruption. Reliving the day in their diverse ways they found communication impossible. Tony McTaggart, leading for the first time, made his statement walking into the evening, leaving behind him the diagonal sunlight as it broke through the day's cloud to stand in silence between the treetrunks, so intensely had the experience of being buried in the mine worked on him. You began to suspect there were things to achieve. Nobody could have explained to Tony what he experienced at this time. The dependencies of the past were finished yet he was without fear. He put it this way: I feel good. So he walked ahead into the bush, the others watching him stride among the trees, for a moment blotted up by the shadow of a giant woollybutt. He did not look back. Had he done so, he'd have wondered at what he saw: Maggot the mocker,

Maggot who so often told him what to do next, Maggot his own age and yet his uncle, his mother's youngest brother following his lead, not even peering into the remaining mineshafts to assess the chances of easy wealth, bypassing opportunities to scavenge what their forbears had left behind in disgust or panic. Each in turn the friends followed; Lance the rower, the new heavyweight champion of Whitey's Fall; Peter who had chosen to become an aircraft pilot; Dave lost in a fight with loneliness; and Bill Swan who refused to go down another gold mine after the first. So they shambled past the windlass stumps, the inviting holes in the mountain, each gold mine a monument to suffering, appropriately a monument of nothing, a column of lightless air stuck in the dirt. Tony was leading.

They tramped into the forest, away from the evening sun, dark green shadows again wrapping round them. They were dotted among the trees like a drama of statues; to be glimpsed and gone, to reappear elsewhere for another momentary tableau. The sun went down, drawing warmth out of them, leaving them shivering till they grew used to it. Unseen water gurgled. Cold air cut at them. Separate, each with the space of his own body insulated from contact, not speaking. Soon enough it would be too dark to press ahead any further. The thirst for privacy possessed them, thirst for the power to understand. The abstract forest swept around them, moving up the mountain, hustling and chuckling as it went.

The town no longer existed. Daytime noises fell into extinction. Flies stopped worrying at the window. Light itself had no source. Back at the house Bill Swan lay in a globe of luminescence, not even aware of the edges of the bed, the air still and heavy as tepid water, his leg cocked across Vivien's body, his arm on the pillows of her breast, his mouth smiling on her smiling mouth, his head filled with her sweet intimate breath, ears hearing his own blood as rain on a tin roof.

Then she slipped out from under him to go to the bathroom. Instantly he drowned in sheets. Swam to the brink. He hung over the side of the mattress watching her white feet delicate and fresh

165

without the protective shells of shoes, edible feet on the bare lino, watched their swift silent placement, feet so eloquent he wanted to cry out with joy.

– Ah feet! he groaned, surprised at himself.

– What, love?

– I want to eat your feet.

She ran off laughing, kicking up her heels in a lovable parody of alarm.

As he hung out of the bed savouring memories of the past few hours, putting the clamour of his pleasure into some order of priority, Bill Swan noticed the lino scattered with garments of various kinds and colours, Vivien's skirts, underwear, shorts, jeans, blouses, more underwear. To his distaste they were all dirty.

She came back pearly and soap-fresh from the bathroom.

– You can't live like this, he told her. It's not hygienic. Those things are so bloody dirty. You never catch me treating a place this way.

– Maybe you don't see what matters and what doesn't, she retorted tartly.

– What! he shouted. Cleanliness not matter!

– Right, she turned it to a moral issue. Could be a sign of hating your own body.

– How can I hate my own body?

She only laughed gaily and kicked her sweaty clothes in a heap and bowled them to one corner out of the way. Then she kissed his knotted forehead.

– Tell me, he invited because he wanted to understand. About your childhood.

She answered – I loved the days of the week.

Yes, she had loved the washing rituals of Monday, steamy soapy sheets grown cold and still flapping in the damp English air by the time she came out of school. Tuesday the first day of the desert that stretched monotonous dunes of arithmetic, botany, geography as far as the future. And yet the very next day known to be Wednesday, the halfway mark achieved, with the downhill run ahead and still time for playground plots to hatch. Thursday black with boredom and made blacker by an afternoon of com-

166

pulsory sports for character-building, hockeysticks snickering, ankles viciously bruised, short skirts flying up round thick girlish thighs and girls' faces thuggish with teeth. Friday and the class was a dream in the tired teacher's mind, nagging but tolerated, the smell of sour milk, the clash of empty lockers. Then the catherinewheel of Saturday jerked into action and flowered dizzily, the gang on the loose, the hectic squandering of breath, climbing, chasing; her household duties at home, even, a reprieve at the end of afternoon joys. But Sunday she specially loved because she must submit. The town walked round in a hush: shutters and blinds drawn across shop windows; the pavements wider than on weekdays; chimneys smoking already by ten in the morning and at midday the aromas of cooking lunches mingled, lamb and dumplings hung about the sacrificial streets; loafers on crossroads hurried for cover; and sure enough crowds of ritually hatted and overcoated citizens swarmed out of the churches to the strains of Handel and Parry (the bells above still rocking), their voices squabbling peaceably as sparrows, lured by the smells of their own ovens, emptied of the vice of patience by the sermon, promenading down the middle of streets to assert the timidity of cars; the well-fed afternoon ahead, lounging in fleshy grass and watching the canal turn in its hundred-year sleep, tipping blue and green dragonflies into the fringes of wild parsley; a bar of elderberry wine under the bridge; the fear of giant pike in the mud and a single sparrowhawk stamped on the sky, a coupon in the blank rationbook of excesses of the flesh. Ah to roll lazily in the dirt and know it was Sunday, to hear and smell Sunday and have Sunday feeling up your skirt and puffing your blouse out like a woman.

– Touch me like that again, she invited Billy, who did his best though his confidence failed him.

At the rim of a rocky slope each man found himself looking down on a grassed clearing, human evidence, the place he had wanted to reach all along, that ghost of a settlement, the worn remains of foundations, groundplan of a village, the blurred grid

167

of civilization already observed earlier in the day from higher up the mountain.

Faint as an overgrown Roman road, the grassed carriageway cut an improbably straight line along the flank of the ridge; hummocks of greenery stood at intervals on either side, igloos with clusters of daffodils around them, the alien presence of a figtree; a dead sulky reared its shafts in a burlesque threat against intrusion, causing the visitors to hesitate, alert for evidence of more recent habitation, seeing only the ghost of a town as it lay printed in the green dusk washed across the clearing; and the question unspoken, what town? and why like some prehistoric relic, a mere ten or fifteen miles by the crow from their own safe, dull, unsuspecting homes?

They would camp here, why not, filled as the place was with departed times. The ruin had knowledge of its own; the deepest secrets of civilization set out in the symmetry of streets, the parallels, right angles, the centrality of large sites, the defensive eminence of location. You could fill your lungs with the perfume of a place once loved, while the eye lingered on its regrets. In a letter Lance wrote his girlfriend in Sydney he put: you could feel the people really lived there.

The men did not build a fire, nor did they talk. The party had fragmented, only the twins went together. Bill Swan who had a sense of living presences, a nose for ghosts as his grandfather put it, was first to carry his pack and sleepingbag in search of a place to lie down and think and sleep ... wandering, a solitary black shape in the cloud-diffused moonlight, a figure in quest of Beauty or Truth or Honour or some such medieval Dignity; and attaining the stature of a courageous man, the character of the pitiful.

For Tony McTaggart the night journey into this vanished community was a time of apprehension, not because of the lovable commonplace of night, nor the unfamiliar surroundings, nor being alone; no, he sensed an aura of snake around, and he had never been wrong about a snake, perhaps a premonition that he and the dead town were destined to be linked; so he walked the perimeter of this lost refuge with a knife in the small of his back, scrotum painfully tight . . . the body ready for an emergency, he held on to the coins in his pocket.

Dave the wrestler lay in his sleepingbag fingering his body, exploring the smooth muscles of his arms and hairless thighs, rubbing, kneading at his groin, gazing half-blind, his own warm skin setting up shivers of pleasure and delicate strokes, his back beginning to arch, the ridges of his abdomen like flat river stones under his hand, loneliness glaring down on him from empty space, hand flicking at his penis, the bow of his spine taut, the arrow poised; then the need for love being stifled by that warm private liquid across his belly, while he sensed the mooning whites of his brother's eyes.

Billy was shocked to recognize old McAloon's dead face high up there sliding backwards after that nerve-hammering bang; the sky a blackened timber ceiling with knotholes, the moon's mouth gaping in toothless funk at seeing Dave and himself, the veiny eyes, the shocking angle of the face tilted up, with the rifle jammed between chairback and tabletop before it sprang free of his grasp and bounced clattering on the rammed earth slab . . . not to forget the soles of his bare feet, themselves dead moons in their own right, the pale dead balls of his feet with their tidemarks and craters, never seen before, things mystical.

Lance had a girlfriend in Sydney and he kept her a secret, she hated touching him, frightened by his size and immaturity and wasn't keen on having him maul her either, but for the sake of knowledge allowed him now and then the ration of a hurried fuck, during which she would whisper: hurry up, hurry, somebody might come, somebody's there, oh Lance have you done it yet? and she was a little ashamed to be three years older than him, as if this meant something she'd have to live with; Lance smelt the memories in this abandoned town, smelt the record of despair and resilience.

Tony McTaggart willed himself in his waking dream to face the sun suddenly there, let it blaze in, the lining of his skull a limitless shining blot of gold, but then he screwed his eyes shut in pain, conceding to his shame as acolyte that the sun had failed him, that it too was a face, resting there above the horizon, what's more it was a particular face, Mr Ping, and Tony McTaggart was not responding as himself, for Mr Ping appeared to be more than just an employer, a figure of godlike power and presence risen from the east: Tony was the first asleep.

Once upon a time nine inches of rain fell in one hour. The ferocity of water raged down from the higher slopes of the mountain and carried away live goats, overturned sulkies, silted up machinery, broke one paddlewheel of the crusher, poured and trickled into the ill-sealed homes people had made, set up such a roar on bark roofs that the town dogs began howling in unison, and ducks cowered in fear looking up sideways as they do when eagles are about; so the entire population went with picks and spades to dig the stormdrain trench where the Maggot now lay dry and sleepless.

The long voyage to New South Wales transformed the known world: after three months at sea the shape of a hill was reduced to a quibble of oil-paint on canvas, the taste of fresh water a craving vicious in its liberty from moral control, conversation with a stranger a forgotten art, the elementary act of walking had become perverted to a grotesque dance compensating for the dipping, swaying deck; even the basic appetite for food simplified its reactions to distinguishing between salted meat and salted fish (apart from that brief shock of Cape oranges).

Pete lay floating in moonshine, illusions playing unwanted games with his imagination: he had seen the film *2001*, so right now his capsule spun headlong among the stars, vast reaches of space hurtling past, cleft by his face, new forces threw things out of known relationships, they were beyond him to think out ... he worked his capsule sideways and lay gazing at himself as someone else, unable to believe the convention that this was his brother Dave engaged glassily in some ecstasy, independent unlike a miror reflection, but as intimate as a shadow.

Without warning the twins faced each other, abandoned their dreams, confronting a face feline and androgynous, brutal and delicate, clean eyes, crisply outlined and bearing a brilliant moon floating on the dark surface, lips parted giving a hint of tooth, lean hollow cheeks ... as they lay, the eyes beautiful as objects, but set like boxers' eyes, wary, aggressive: so the twins lay alert, few cruelties could be put past the man with such a face, hideously thrilling animal despite its feminine fineness, what could be more male than the set jaw, the wolf eyes among the lashes?

Bill Swan sat up to assure himself of where he was, he stared gratefully at the soft igloos of soil and timber, at the vines and grasses growing over them, at the sulky down the way raising its frail antennae at the soft wash of moonlight edging the flat granite slab under him, while he reached one arm out into the cold and allowed his fingers to trace the neat incisions, so that above his head they read the letters I N L O V I N G M E M O R Y O F A L B E R T S W A N D I E D 1 8 t h N O V E M B E R 1 8 9 4 and at the right side of his chest O U R B E L O and at the left side N D F A T H E R.

Seven

It was a Sunday morning and nothing had happened; the known world restored. Already the mist was busy creating a forest and trying out its ideas of a mountain. The six young men were up early, raucous, cheerful as they packed their sleepingbags and boiled a couple of billies for tea, the steam mingling with camouflaged air. Talk ranged over yesterday's experience and they agreed not to waste today scavenging leftovers from worked-out mines, the purpose was to find clues to the Golden Fleece, the black motherlode of gold. Sixty years of bushfires might well have laid bare what was previously hidden. Or perhaps converging wallaby tracks would lead them there. Or the big rains of 1952 could have washed the soil from a seam of quartz once covered up, or a landslide revealed it.

This, at least, was the way they talked. Yet being on the spot you found such hopes hard to credit now the mist had finished its work and dispersed, the mountain towering massively impersonal, the bush so dense, the unexplored areas dominant. Where could you begin? How could you survive?

Except for Tony. Since yesterday Tony was floating, the mountain a giant wave buoying him up. And he knew that Billy sank, shrivelled to a solid weight, cousin to the rock he sat on.

– Worthwhile for what we've seen already, Lance the tourist suggested, ready to leave and trying not to think of the corpse among things seen.

– Come on you piker, Maggot challenged him. There's hundreds more places to look.

And Tony loved him for it. Naturally he had a softness for Maggot, Maggot being the one who had ideas and made things add up. But this support he had not anticipated. The mines called him.

– I reckon we're going to have our work cut out getting the truck home by nightfall, Lance grumbled.

– Can't be more than twelve miles at most. Downhill! Dave sneered because nobody was going to talk him out of becoming a millionaire.

They set off to the creek with plates and mugs to be washed, their boots kicking at stones, their strong bodies breasting the undergrowth, whistling shrilly and discordantly among the trees.

– Well mates, Maggot declared as he sluiced his plate in cold swirling water. This'll be our last expedition together in any case.

– The last, Lance confirmed, awkward in his haircut, his cheerful shirt, with his knowledge of judo, already out of place as a plainclothes policeman.

The others busied themselves with cleaning. Even those who enjoyed planning the future didn't talk about it now. Words were not their way in a case like this. There were pitfalls in words; they might find themselves having to talk about friendship, they might even thank one another for something, or enter the treacherous waters of putting a name to affection. No. Instead, they stood, flicked the drops from glistening fingers, and sauntered back, outlaw fashion, the way they'd come, whistling among those ghosts of a forgotten security, the grassy hummocks and ditches, foundations and streets put there by ancestors. And packed up.

So they pressed on, touched by yesterday's mood, a whole generation, the youth of Whitey's Fall, and all males. This was the death of Whitey's without a doubt. These young men going away for careers. There'd be no youth coming in to take their place. Outsiders never understood the district, they wouldn't fit in even if they wanted to; Yalgoona people spoke of it as the ends of the earth. Nothing could be done about this. Not since they were small lads screaming after the mystery of what girls *were* did it have to be thought about. You couldn't explain it. The flower of Whitey's Fall. The last flowering, the curse of the male child. And so many boys already gone away before them: the three weedy McTaggarts, John, Ross and Brendan, the blond Buddalls and their cousins the dark Buddalls (dark because their mother was a McAloon), Stan, Ray, Kevvie, as well as their poor in-laws who lived in the timberyard shack, Greg, Ricky, Jack, Cec and Les (Maggot's bullying half-brothers), all had gone now. That plague of males migrated, carting off their parents too. Opportunity lured them to Goulburn and Bathurst, to Tamworth and Wollongong and even to Eden. But they left their grandparents and great-grandparents behind. They said they'd come back someday to visit. But sorry as you were to see them go, they weren't wanted in their Holdens, flaunting their new aimlessness, their cash, their tales of wall-to-wall, hot-and-cold, steel radials, their soggy hands, their hardness softening down so in a horrible way they'd become great hairy kids, and their skins pale as if they'd been sick a long time and indoors under the mosquito nets breathing balsams that steamed your pores open. Once they went away they weren't wanted back. You saw enough of casual visitors from the towns as it was, no week went by without at least one intruding car, and the only local who knew how to handle them was Felicia Brinsmead, old crow, madbag Brinso, hairbag the witch, who gave them the evil once-over, showed them the dead mice among her lollies, kissed the cat, told them their business, switched on a fake expression and packed them on their way glad to get out of the place uncontaminated.

– Yes this is the last time together Lance, Tony drawled with equanimity, recalling his pang of surprise when he felt the vigour of that young man's body, upsetting everything you could depend on, for a Lang who'd always been one of the younger kids to toss him on the ground. Within a couple of weeks Lance'd be gone, so would Maggot, and the twins with their little ones. Let them go. Bill would stay, so what the hell.

– When we were at school, Tony continued eventually. There were twenty-two of us. Remember that? And all blokes. He folded his big arms and inspected the arms, their matting of blond hairs.

– There'll be you and me left mate, Billy contributed without expression, looking over to where the forest marched steeply downhill into a lake of blue air.

As they collected their gear from round the fire and headed back to the Bedford, Bill Swan wasn't thinking of those twenty-one other schoolboys, no. Cut into the foot of that grave, he'd found a riddle *Fear not, tis only I*. We're all just relations, he realized bitterly. He watched Maggot's back; the jaunty angle of his disreputable hat, the scruff of bright ginger hair sticking out from under it. Yes, he wished Maggot would stay. He wanted to tell Maggot how much he would miss him.

– Get a move on, short-arse, he shouted.

– Up you, you conshie, Maggot replied happily.

The others grinned with relief from their haunted thoughts of the hermit's death, and what he might have feared, the scorn of that policeman leaning out under his flashing blue light to say, oh Kel is it, Kel McAloon the dirty scab? The corpse would not forgive, lying on the floor with his mouth sour and pulled to one side, his eyes staring at nothing so you had to check for yourself. The resistance of the mountain itself making you unwelcome, the weather brooding in sympathy, cloud banking up again and compacting, light rain beginning to set in.

– Shit. This could ruin everything, Billy foresaw.

Near where they left the Bedford, they discovered a pair of gateposts and the relics of a fence leading north and south.

– There's writing on the post, Dave said. T W something something T E Y.

– T. Whitey.

– Might be nothing there.

The house was so hidden behind a rocky bluff they didn't spot it till they turned to go back. It was a slab hut with some of the roof still on and most of the walls. Wild clematis wandered among the rafters and the chimney spouted a dense cloud of leaves where a young tree had grown slender and straight in the fireplace, the window trembled alive with light, the garden was scattered with animal droppings.

They clustered in the house, trod rustling across the floor now deep in grass and weeds. The walls, spongy with plants and fungus, in any other country would call to mind enchantments, kidnapped children, ancient practices subversive as they were innocent, unspeakable appetites and a dislocation of the natural order.

– Mr Whitey's house.

They all knew Tom Whitey. He had died only two years previously. Persecuted by trivial signs of indifference, dictatorial towards the young, discoverer of the waterfall, visionary who planned a whole city and an aqueduct to supply it with fresh water, he was the man a town had been named after: how often do you meet such a person.

Some furniture survived, gaping at the joints. An iron mangle rusted over a washtub; underneath, the owner had propped one panel of a red lacquered screen pilfered from the Cinese josshouse. A clock eaten by verdigris declared a permanent amnesty at two forty-four from the mantelpiece. While in the fireplace itself the young treetrunk grew up into the black hole of the chimney. A dismantled bed, stacked against one wall, began its seventy-eighth year of awaited removal to the new house. Maggot Buddall picked up one of its rails, a hefty lump of metal, and swung it for the sake of swinging it, hard against the wall, thud into the thick off-cut timbers, knocking a grey slab loose. That made him feel good, he'd done something to satisfy the anger under his cheerfulness. Why not? Even the brim of his hat trembled with discovery, his red hair thrilled electric. No one spoke a word. The place had come alive at the touch of violence. Lance took up the other rail and with his superior strength smashed the next timber clean off at a single blow. Billy brought in a lump of granite to hurl at the clock which flattened with a pop like a burst paperbag. The twins pulled off their shirts and swung agilely up to the ceiling and out on to the remaining roof where they began ripping the iron loose. Tony had hold of the mangle which he wrenched from its mounting and used to batter down the doorposts, each tremendous blow booming from all parts of the buildings. The place creaked and yawed to the accompaniment of protesting howls from those inside and on top who suddenly found themselves in danger. Billy hauled the last remaining window off its hinges and threw it down with a fine clash of glass. This was a game, a heady game. Lance and Maggot worked as partners, belting out the wallslabs one after another, taking turns and developing a rhythm wak wok-wak wok-wak wok. The twins strained at dislodging a rafter, their young bodies glittering with rain. Competition ran fierce, at every success they'd utter a jubilant wahoo. Sheets of roofing sailed down among splintered timbers. Billy levered up the tallow-wood threshold and used it to sledgehammer the lower part of the chimney. As their excitement verged on frenzy they threw away their tools and worked with hands and feet, rending and kicking, revelling in the physical effort, the pain, drunk on the narcissism of destroyers, flaying the building with bruised flesh, Viking flames among the monasteries, wooden saints and the virgin falling like King Charles's head, Ned Kelly's hideout, down it must come. The chimney collapsed round the trunk of the smoke-tree leaving it naked and pale. The entire frame now leaned so dangerously the catlike men on top leapt to safety. The final assault was launched, hands bleeding. They wrenched and shook the ruin. So intense was their excitement when the house sank camel-fashion one end first then the other, they cheered and danced together, stamping on the fallen victim, liberated from restraint, pounded Mr Whitey's handiwork flat among the weeds of its own simple floor. This was good, purging the darkness of the mines for some, purging the light for others. Leaping and prancing, veins swollen, nostrils flared, their bodies sang. By christ they were going to miss one another. Then they realized Lance was sprawled to one side, rolling on the dirt screaming out, not in hysteria but in agony, a heavy cornerpost pinning his leg. He struggled to shift it. Billy also heaved at it but one end was jammed under the weight of

177

the fallen roof. Lance shouted incoherently, frantic with pain, pleading, sobbing. It was Tony, wrenching at the post with all his strength, who finally released the injured leg.

– Don't touch it, said Dave. I know what to do. We've got to get the boot off without shifting his foot. It wants a razorblade to cut through the laces.

– My new knife, Lance gasped. It's very sharp. In the front pocket of my pack.

They tipped the pack upside down, sniggering at a dog-eared *Playboy* in the bottom. But there was no knife. Maggot was particularly definite about this. The victim lay contorted and afraid of the consequences of moving. Tony found some aspirins and gave him a handful with the dregs of the rum to help his pain. Lance became almost as distressed about his missing knife as about his damaged leg. Bill took charge and ordered all packs and pockets to be emptied to find the most suitable tool for the job. The twins set about this with the enthusiasm of customs officials. Too late for Maggot to dive in and save the privacy of his guilt. They rummaged in his belongings and came up with a flashy sheath-knife.

A currawong sang through the silence. Dust still hung in the air round the fallen house. Lance's voice sounded harsh and more mature than ever before.

– I'm glad it's not lost. Who's going to do the dirty work?

– Jesus Maggot, Bill complained. Are you still at it? Why the fuck don't you wake up to yourself?

Dave sliced the laces expertly, opened out the boot and slipped it off. The foot seemed undamaged after all. He slit the seam of the injured man's jeans and laid bare the brown leg already bruised and swollen where the bone was broken.

– That's it then, said Dave. But how do we get him on to the truck?

– Lift him up on to his good leg, Tony suggested. And I'll carry him from there on my back.

Maggot the thief was entrusted with re-packing all the bags and took charge of the laceless boot. The twins went ahead to clear a space on the Bedford and make a bed of sleepingbags.

Tony took the weight, a curious joy filling him. His superior strength was in kindness not combat. Lance's arms around his neck, that large handsome body lolled hot and helpless on his own. Bowed down but triumphant, he edged up the embankment to the vehicle. Lance hissed with pain at each step, the puffs of breath hot in Tony's ear. Even as he strained to be gentle, Tony was conquering his rival with flashes of anguish.

By the time Lance had been installed as comfortably as possible, half the morning was gone. The Golden Fleece forgotten, the journey home would be difficult. They stretched a tarpaulin for a tent over the injured man as the mountain drew heavy rain from the white air. Already the track had turned into twin runnels of clay-water trapping the wheels to lurch first into one rut, then along the other. The earth gave out its glorious wet smell for purposes not guessed at. Frequently they had to stop to unload the chainsaw and cut through trees fallen across the way and rotting there, moss-covered. All about them water poured down gullies and into holes, dripping, gurgling. Abandoned automobiles stood rusted into the landscape, empty windows and stripped axles an omen. One ridiculous wreck sat dignified and upright, a chassis with steering column, still sporting a white wheel-cover. Lance lay groaning freely in the back, so private he could weep for his beautiful, broken body, because the others had taken to walking ahead of the Bedford, clearing the way. Rain soaked in round their collars, dripping off eyebrows, squelching in boots. They bowed and crawled for the truck, scrambling among stones and dirt, slaves smoothing a path for a cripplingly lavish chariot. Rain under their arms and down their tender sides. So as descendants of slaves they knew how to be slaves, without rehearsal they had every cringing gesture exact, every envious look and rebellious surge of anger and helplessness. Yes, they were ready for the cities and careers. The Golden Fleece forgotten, already a myth. Bill Swan sat erect and vigilant high above them behind a shimmering glass screen, taking to himself the manner of rulers as his hands controlled those tons of steel, at his will the motor roared like a crowd sending echoes out across the immense valley, given the sovereign privileges of dryness and power he was carried along the path their bruised hands cleared for him; and at his shoulder, the sobs of the giant in his custody.

– Why the fuck don't you give someone else a go at driving, a voice complained anonymously from among the sodden bent figures.

– Keep working, Billy shouted joyously. Or I'll run you bastards down!

– You would too, the dissident Maggot commented, half-serious, and Peter slapped him on the back to signal that he was forgiven all else.

Lance lay joggling in the back on his bed of sleepingbags, absorbed, become a bloodfilled balloon of pain, preoccupied with remaining passive, words too much trouble to form when anybody spoke to him. Even so, once the time came to call a break for lunch, the boys were cheerful, sheltered under an overhanging slab of rock. They passed round hot tea, fruit and hunks of bread. Not so bad then, the morning could be looked at as an achievement. The truck this far down the track, there was a limit to the suffering. Used to hard labour, they soon recovered their strength and were eager to be off. Bill, alone, being reluctant. Apparently safe in his high cab, he knew the lonely burden of authority, anxiously watching the fuel gauge. The journey wasn't all down-hill, the motor had to be driven hard to pull clear of boggy patches and sudden rises, the heavy going used more petrol than anybody foresaw. Periodically they had to stop to let the engine cool and refill the radiator from the many cascades frothing down the cliff faces. Wollongong's going to be bloody lovely after this, Maggot the optimist promised himself.

So the young men from Whitey's Fall, heroes of the Golden Fleece prospecting expedition, looked only a yard ahead, lashed at the scrub, reconstructed the track where they had to, hands crusted with blood from demolishing the empty house. Nothing mattered but this stone or that log as they stooped and slaved for the Bedford; for the sake of getting back to the place they longed to leave, they submitted to the injustice of Billy's privileges.

– Are you alright up there? somebody called affectionately.

This was how they felt after their second scratch meal and as evening approached, each yard the truck advanced a triumph for them all. They knew why the motor had been switched off, why it was coasting with quiet squeals down the slope, no need to ask or have it spoken. Occasionally they'd look up to catch the driver's expression so their own fate might be guessed. They accepted that nobody knew where they were. By now they dared not leave the Bedford. Progress slower and more painful. Periodically the motor coughed into life so the vehicle could crash up a part-cleared rise, then able to creep, free-wheeling down the other side.

Just after dark, they rolled on to a gravel clearing so flat you'd swear it had been graded. They climbed aboard and found this was a properly kept road, smooth as metal, wide and engineered, yes, with a line of white surveyors' pegs visible in the twilight down one side. The party raised a cheer, a yell of victory and relief. Yet at the same time they felt uneasy. They were safe, true, but why was this end of the track graded, foreign and unknown to anybody? The Bedford roared round the first polished curve and fell silent except for the howling tyres, the motor dissolved into air. The fuel had run out.

Sunday night. Rain stopped. Thick cloud still covered the moon. The six friends sat becalmed, their decision made for them by Lance's broken leg. It wasn't possible to move him before daylight. They still had no idea where they were. Not a single house light could be seen to guide them. Their last shared experience, now at an end, suddenly precious, the wild sea tossing behind, schooldays remembered.

– Looks like we're pretty well stuck, said Bill.
– Yeah. Your dad's a moral to read you the riot act.
Lance groaned.
– You going to be okay Lance mate?
– It's only a broken leg, Lance replied, rising to the occasion.
Billy and Tony joined the rest huddled in the back for warmth; also to comfort the injured man. This was a gift, a chance to talk through the night. To watch the dawn without cows to bother about. The curse of boy-children would soon be a fact of history;

it was a chance for skiting and confessions bringing them closer than they'd been since they were young kids. Being the death of something was perhaps what charmed them most. They lasted till three in the morning when the talk lapsed into a dreamy state of surprise at how the prospecting trip had turned out. Lance stifled his grunts to join in the banter. Had they found what they'd wanted?

– When we make it as pilots, said one of the twins. I reckon we're going to look back on this.

– There's school for the young ones, the other apologized to those who wouldn't be going to civilization.

Life was unimaginable without the twins, those secretive daredevils no one could outrun or outjump. Though you never claimed you actually liked them.

– Well I always did say, Billy announced in Uncle's voice. Sydney would be the only place to rival Whitey's. Winnin form!

Tony, who could never take emotional difficulties in his stride, admired this. Lost and screwed up, clay stuck in his throat, while the night wore on, he drifted far outside his hulk remaining jammed between Bill and the forgiven Maggot, only just in earshot of their murmured exchanges, surrounded by emptiness, alienated by it, lonely when the flock of moons came up behind the trees into the void of a televised Buddhist monk in Vietnam who burnt to death sitting crosslegged in the street. The monk poured kerosene over himself from a gurgling can, it coursed agonizingly into his eyes and the secret sores of his body. Tony saw the man soaked, robe sticking to his glossy skin, bald head running with the stuff, the shimmer of evaporating fumes a halo ... saw the foolish moment when he groped for the box of matches where he thought he had placed it, living the likelihood of pathetic failure, found them with gratitude and horror, still blinded, struck a match and then had not known what to do. But the flame knew; leapt straight from his hand all over him before he could make the gesture of applying it. His eyes, momentarily black, opened at the piercing clasp of fire. Mouth a twisted hole. This burning man should be enough to shame any God worth believing in. And as cameras photographed him, his act took fire

182

in Turkey and China, in Warsaw and Valparaiso, in Newfoundland and at the Cape of Good Hope, even here in the Australia of his own brain. What word in the language was there for it? Tony opened his mouth to the dark, and sounds came. His throat and chest throbbing. Night air poured into his lungs and poured back out as a black sound, his voice rose and sank, swayed and leapt from him into the void he ... was raising his voice ... was singing. His song streamed blood, to carry through the hell of nothing. This alone declaring truth because there were no words. He sat straight, the long notes reached and dipped their red-brown tones, reached higher, each for the first time exploring some sensation of action. The kerosene flames danced and flickered. Tony was answering that dying monk. The voice swelled with astounding strength, without end to what he had begun. The skeleton became a tree in flames and the voice from the burning bush cried out. The singing unravelled its long thread. The flame of one man spoke from the war of many: I AM THAT I AM, the labyrinth in which is all that ever was, and the world's knowledge of it.

Out there the dark moved around Tony, who had never achieved a Remembering. His voice must carry through the uncomprehending years to where Chinese gold diggers had been lynched (as had Jesus) for not being like everybody else. The night seethed with faces, composed of faces as matter is of atoms, and among them hideous cancers. A tremor of eyes, the flutter of countless mouths gaping. He, Tony McTaggart, had no defence but his voice, this new-found weapon. He sang without form, simply sang as an assertion of singing, of life, loyalty, love, until he was exhausted. He grew hoarse. His entire body shook with the effort. When at last his voice gave out and he slumped back, the others again felt their own presence but chose not to move, not to speak. Lance had no sensation in his broken leg at all. The cool night manoeuvred itself around them. They had secretly and humbly, at their different times, acknowledged the desire to weep and to rejoice, their bruised hands stiffened to the permanent shapes of longing. When Maggot felt Tony's sleeping head loll against his shoulder, he did not move it. He did not even dare touch it.

In the cold of the morning Billy rode his motorbike into town to get petrol and bring help for Lance.

Eight

– Are you always going to live in Whitey's Fall? Vivien asked him. They strolled in the overgrown backyard.

– How do I know?

– But Bill, a few hours ago you began to tell me.

They lay in hot grass breathing dust, stubble pricking their naked skin. In their minds, those two great rocks, dry and domineering, hummed with magnetic forces.

– You know something about you people? Billy said but not unkindly. You're always wanting to be told things last for ever.

She laughed and he watched her belly tremble deliciously as she did so.

– *You* people? she burbled to cover the possible injury.

– Yes, you people who don't belong in Whitey's.

– I hope I do though.

– Would you stay Viv?

Yet the question caught them in an undertow, too late to escape having gone too far. She allowed herself to be lulled along by it, she didn't care, had never been so happy, so secure.

– With you I would, she murmured letting the sun's heat fondle her. She could see the pulse ticking in his neck as he bent to kiss her. He'd begun to rise again. His virility excited her and

185

excitement made her beautiful. She teased him, talking her interfering words, her questions.

– Well those friends you've been telling me about, they
thought of the future and they were Whitey's Fallers.

– Not any more. They've gone. We shan't see them again.
Tony and me are the only young ones left. Once they started
thinking about nothing . . . plans and that . . . well then they were
gone. They'll be pilots soon and engineers or bums or clerks,
something useless. And they'll be stuck with talking about the
future all their lives till they haven't got one left. You can never
get there can you? Each day tomorrow is a day further off and
then you don't have time to live today or yesterday.

She noticed his legs, brown as the soil, furry as an animal, she
watched them as he drew his knees up, tufts of grass around them;
they belonged like the grass belonged. And to prove it a little
blue wren came picking among his toes. Flat on his back he
stretched out his brown arms, his brown chest a simple hill. Vivien
was astounded by the sheer breadth of him, the sense of lung-
power as his chest lifted and subsided and lifted. Exotic as a Chinese opera-mask, she imagined her face must appear when she
placed it there, first one cool cheek then the other.

– Well, she persisted, laughing once more and now avoiding
his lips so that he laughed too. Well, in that case why did you
want the gelignite? You never told me.

– For the Golden Fleece of course, he replied surprised. I did
tell you, that's what I've been telling you about all this time. I
found it in Mr McAloon's diary. I know where the Golden Fleece
is. Right in the middle of Whitey's Fall. Right under our noses.

– How are you going to get hold of it? Her mind filled with
fantasies of wealth.

– I'm going to blow it up.

– . . .?

– Close it for good. This is our mountain Viv. Us Whitey's
Fallers have done everything here. There's no one needs anything
they haven't got, except Tony and me: the rest are too old. What
would happen? Golden Fleece'd finish the place off. Once word
got round they'd be here in their thousands.

186

Naked, he needed nothing. She knew then that she wanted to be part of his world, that the finest thing imaginable would be to blow up a gold mine and bury it. She thought back to her German lover, how greedily he would have shown off in a Lamborghini and hung a hand-wrought chain round his pale muscular neck. Bill Swan had thought of this one thing worthwhile doing, that she wanted to do. Vivien closed her eyes as they joined, nothing in her mind, no memories, no fantasies, no fears; herself and Billy. That was all. She looked again and the sun filled her head.

They lay listening to the mountain. And somewhere, faint, true, the planet delicately throbbing unravelled its harmony. Bill Swan recognized it. He dared not speak or the spell would be broken. Gold, ringing with the spirit of the people who first thought of it. Far down below the disguise of everyday soil, caverns of the precious metal gave tongue to the least shift of earth's crust. They listened to the priceless bells.

In the heat of the morning they walked into town, together.

BOOK THREE

Seven Figures Without Landscape

One – The Maker of Circles

Suppose there'd been a chance to bring you to Mr Ian McTaggart's garden before everything changed, what then? Here you had to stand absolutely still to learn what you could. So much the place offered, and so unlike any other garden. But it would depend on how sharply you see and hear, as well as how sharply you almost-hear, how much you'd pick up by doing nothing but remaining alert.

Mr McTaggart's garden formed a circle, huge cool and rich in perfumes; perpetually muttering water could be heard and the music from a profusion of birds among the leaves. When he was at the centre, the plants in order of kind made concentric circles around him. And because the plants in each circle were a stage larger than those they encircled, the waves of what he grew widened around him, swelled and loomed, blossomed and fruited in a crescendo of height and splendour till they extended to include the surrounding bush, the continent, the whole earth. While at their tender heart squatted the most aged man of Whitey's Fall working among the mushrooms in his shirt sleeves with dark patches of sweat under the arms, or weeding beds where frail spikes of dill were encouraged into the sun, soon to move on to the circle of lettuces, to water the capsicums or listen to

191

the potatoes, fondle the nipples of young Brussels sprouts, sing to his tomatoes and in turn be fingered by bean plants, breathless among passionfruit, fumbling along his emotions out where the fruit trees grew or the nut trees beyond. Circle on circle the garden burgeoned, the accumulated bounty of five continents.

Mr McTaggart's notion of family followed a similar pattern. He could see how the generations welled in overlapping circles, even from himself. But of course he was not the source: no, you must look a long way back toward the centre of the circle. For a start there was his mother and her clan. As a boy he'd worn the MacDonald tartan, his grandfather on his mother's side having been a MacDonald of the Isles as was his grandmother; the Murrays of Tullibardine could say what they liked, no clan was older or nobler than the MacDonalds. And then of course on his father's side the Ross clan and the McTaggarts had married with the O'Neills who could trace their family back to Hugh O'Donnell, Earl of Tyrone, who came as near as damn-it to freeing Ireland totally from the English invaders (after the battle of Yellow Ford and the arrival of the Spanish fleet at Kinsale anything could have happened, liberty was in reach). The age-old struggle against authority, the refusal to knuckle under.

He liked to hoard things too. His house was stuffed full of bric-a-brac, even to a drawerful of mysterious letters stamped with official seals and never opened, which had come to him as the oldest man, some recently, many passed on by Paddy McAloon's widow when Paddy died and which he'd had from Tom Whitey before him. Certain of these letters were addressed to the Progress Association, an ugliness unheard of in these parts; others to the Postmaster though their post office was no longer in operation; and one was addressed with a despairing wide-shot to The Citizens. They were reliquaries for the mystery.

Mr Ian McTaggart need only close his eyes to be back in the days of horsedrawn ploughs, hearing the clonking churchbell like a giant lost cow, the sweet festive family gatherings with drunken men weeping affectionately and hanging on to each other, the ladies laughing fit to burst, the bleating of sheep, and a brass band practising with the hall doors open so the uncles inside could be watched puffing proudly and tapping their feet, frowning at the task of squeezing out a work of art, undoing their collar studs, whispering hang it! and sorry! if they missed the beat. Such days, and so fresh in the memory being carried about the garden: a cosmos of sounds and emotions whirling harmlessly between the Brussels sprouts and the Jerusalem artichokes.

You wouldn't get much idea of Mr McTaggart, seeing him in his garden stooped over the herbs, drugged with their whispers of dreary Aeolian music, nor even in the process of making his marvellous way among the rows and paths with the ease of a builder of labyrinths not willing to believe he does something other people don't do. But you might at least guess that for most of the day, crouched among plants, Mr McTaggart could scent well-being in the air, his fingers working the soil, his pet budgerigar perched on his head like a single brilliant blue thought emerging.

From time to time his crippled wife called to him from the house to summon him back from eternity. She called, her thin voice habitually carrying over the complexities of his maze of living things, with some single piece of homely information or other: it's eleven o'clock, it's eight o'clock, perhaps we'll have a drop of rain, my but it's a sticky hot day, I shall be ready with tea soon love, Olive just dropped in to say goodday, those damn parrots are back again this year I see, have you got your hat on the sun's a killer, five-and-twenty to two, you haven't seen my spectacles I suppose, a body gets tired easy these days, I'd be wearing a scarf in this cold wind if I was you love, bread's come, I shall cook up that roast tonight I think, are you alright?

Because of her deafness, Mrs McTaggart could never hear whether or not he answered, but she kept calling when the spirit took her, knowing he needed her, calling into the sunny rainy windy silence.

For his part he did need her, it was true, and whatever she called out became part of his dream. While his fingers intuitively ministered to the needs of his circles of plants, he dreamed. There was a funeral and himself saying the words that needed to be said, while somebody's child in the coffin waited to be put away, but

193

as he stood in the dream saying the burial words, he was dreaming within the dream, dreaming he'd got his knee in the small of a man's back, yes, he had him down on the ground, himself a strong young fellow kneeling his full weight there and sawing away at some minor thing with a knife, an ear could it be? while the victim bled and howled and had to be hit; yet even as he sawed at the human ear to get it off the head, he was dreaming within this dream too; of standing on the mountain, watching a building which had been built to withstand that one constant wind, when it dropped for the first time ever, like a prop knocked away, so the building sagged to one side and collapsed; and yet, even while he watched this building fall in the dream inside the dream of cutting off the ear inside the dream of speaking burial words for the unknown child, he was dreaming of the mountain itself no longer there, gouged out by giant machines, and to be seen only in certain lights as a mountain of stilled air.

– Those lads came back, called Mrs McTaggart. Came back in George Swan's truck this morning with young Lance's leg broke and bringing a tale about a road. You wouldn't believe it, a new road love. What does it mean?

For the joy of where he was, the budgerigar began twittering. The oldest man, as if he had listened to her and was letting the bird answer for him, stood up, shaded his eyes against the light, looked towards the house (or beyond, to the mountain?) and ambled along a hidden path to another circle of his heaven.

Two – The Violinist

My great-aunt Annie always was a plain woman and a sensible one. She said she had no patience with the past, no not in any shape or form, no patience whatsoever with it. You take my word, young Vivi, she used to tell me, if you waste time trying to relive times you never lived properly in the first place, you'll never have time to live today either. I always thought this the best advice I was ever given. Live for the wonder of living, she'd say on other occasions. Or else she'd say live for the wonder of the world about you. Or don't let a moment escape if you can help it, you won't get it back, not that one, phut gone, and once gone gone forever. And stand on your own two feet my girl, she'd instruct me wagging a finger. Don't you let anybody go living your life for you, you fool yourself if you think you can live through others. I've only got one regret, she'd say, and that doesn't matter now either.

Outside her livingroom window I could watch the English rain pelting against the street, people running for cover, and a portly gentleman sauntering along beneath his varnished umbrella with a beadcurtain of raindrops swaying down about him, a maharajah on an elephant. Peonies grew in my great-aunt's tiny garden, big voluptuous bushes that sprouted blots of vulgar taste against the housefront. Aunt Annie cradled the flowers as they died. I would come in one afternoon to find her on her usual chair with the machine-lace drapes a veil behind her head, and in her cupped hands one huge pad of crimson light. The peonie rested there as if it knew about her. See how the tips go brown poor darling, she'd croon. Like a heart of feathers and old stale sunshine. Then I'd look out past her in embarrassment and notice the rows of squat terracehouses and I knew her house was no different and I'd feel sorry for the world, being afraid of going home into the wrong front door. When the Lord created the peonie, she'd say, he had a message for mankind. She'd press the bright withered lips against her own.

Do you want anything at the shop Auntie? I'd ask. Lord love us the darling never forgets me, she'd answer. And that was the way we were, Aunt Annie and me. Of course she'd swindle me, she'd sidetrack me with tall stories, she'd trick me into feeling sorry for something I hadn't done, she'd bribe me with affection into taking her side in any dispute, she'd bulldoze me into thinking what she was thinking, but next minute out would come some favourite saying: stand on your own two feet my girl, you can't live your life through anybody else. That's for sure, she'd add just for the comfort of being right as usual.

There she'd be in the front room with the clock ticking tunefully, surrounded by the frail possessions proper to a lady of refinement. Her huge fingers closing with exquisite care on some glass object, she'd appraise it and replace it. She'd sigh with pleasure, her arm a megalithic carving among the demure Dresden faces and filigree knick-knacks. Bundled massively into the flimsiest silks or nylons, guipure lace sleeves, tulle skirts, muslin bodices, she carried loads of flowers on her bosom, in her hair, clutched in her handbag, for tuppence she'd tuck a lily in her belt for a trip to the baker, or a crocus behind her ear to cheer up the Court of Petty Sessions when she went to hear the dramas, just for a fig she'd wear an arum lily in her hat too if it suited her. Whatever she could conveniently steal she would wear. The neighbours planted wallflowers and Auntie took up the wallflower in her own way, her hand cruising through the privet hedge, fingers nipping off a choice bloom. The stationmaster tried out pansies in his windowbox and lo and behold Aunt Annie had a pansy on her collar the very first morning those all-purple ones were out, the ones she liked best. The geraniums at the dentist's suffered annual losses in spite of being tucked away behind two fences and a brick wall. The parish church itself had to countenance Auntie turning up devoutly sporting a daffodil or two exactly matching those outside the vestry. Even the policeman's alsatians could not deter Auntie from sampling his irises.

When Mrs Pye down the street accosted Auntie, I was seven or eight and clinging on, dying with shame as Auntie answered, What rose? yesterday morning you say? yesterday? no no, I can't be bothered remembering, the past is the past Mrs Pye, all gone and buried, I've no time at all for the past, but are you fond of roses then my dear? just hold on here, don't move, I'll slip back home, I've just the thing for you, a little beauty, wait here Vivi, talk to Mrs Pye and don't pick your nose or suck your thumb darling. Sure enough she came back, glowing with excitement, with the pleasure of gift-bearing. Here you are then, she declared and handed Mrs Pye the prize *Prince de Bulgarie* she'd taken from her garden twenty-four hours earlier, I'll bet you couldn't match a blossom like that! Not since yesterday I couldn't, Mrs Pye whined spitefully. Never mind, said Auntie, but don't ask me how it's done, that's somebody else's secret, I'm sure I couldn't say, they just seem to come up like that of their own accord. Then she recollected something and I felt her hand harden horribly about my own. Now Vivien my duck you expect me to buy you a nice cream bun at the shops I dare say well we must be getting along then have you anything to say to Mrs Pye before we go? Surely you're going to say good morning Mrs Pye I hope you like Auntie's rose? Yes? There's a good girl. We have to teach them, Mrs Pye, they don't learn by themselves do they? Bye-bye and do have a sniff of the scent, lovely, I hope you're pleased with it . . . any time!

I have only one memory of my mother and this was the sight of half her back, it's to do with the way she sat at the table I suppose, as if she had her plate in her lap and ate with her back half-turned to me and my father. Perhaps she had something wrong with her face. Perhaps she hated us, shutting us out of her life. I don't know. This was one reason I wanted to talk to Aunt Annie about our family, because she'd known them all so well. There were no shadowy figures in Auntie's life. What was great-uncle Joe like, Auntie? I asked her sometimes when I looked at his photo on the mantelpiece surrounded by a minuet of porcelain pompadours and backed up by the gilt clock with its square bevel glass door. Old Joe, she'd answer, also gazing at her husband in half-hearted black and white, just like his photo he was. But what was he like to know? I asked. Now that I don't remember rightly, was her stock reply. But I knew she did remember. She was only pretending, because she could be so definite about it.

The only other photograph on display was a brownish one of herself standing beside an ant-hill taller than she was, holding an earthworm six foot long and draped across both outstretched arms. That's in Australia, she said. That's in Whitey's Fall where I come from. That's a worm and that there's an ant-hill behind me. This was the vision of Australia I grew up with. If anyone asked me what it would be like, I could describe it perfectly.

I didn't spend all my time with my great-aunt. Indeed, not enough of it to my way of thinking. I lived with my father in a procession of flats. We never occupied anywhere long enough for me to get a grip on it as home. Perhaps this is why Aunt Annie's house (always the same, with the same smells and the same things in it, the same routines) is what I associate with the settled aspect of the word home. I helped my father set up house from the earliest times I can recall: looking over the cold new place with its worn furniture and dingy walls, wrinkling my nose at its dead air, and hearing my father speak of his resignation to an unjust destiny by asking me where we should put this and what could be done with that? I arranged everything, divided the knives forks and spoons, hung cups on hooks, brightened the bedrooms with our own coverlets, stripped curtains from windows and put up Your Mother's curtains, trying them for length, placed the gay vermilion tablets of Lifebuoy soap on basin and bath, plugged in our wireless and made it sing; the wardrobes stood open and naked to the world so I filled them with our clothes (while my father sat shaking his head at the magnitude of the task of unpacking) and closed their doors. My parents' wedding photograph was placed on a prominent sill. Grief had never been part of this photo for me. I didn't know my mother. I had a rich history of childhood griefs but none to be called up by this picture. I thought it was funny. My mother looked stupid in the unbelievable fashions of 1930. Also the men in penguin suits. Even the ground covered with dead leaves outside the church. Through all our moves, this comic familiar wedding group had always perched some place prominent and mildly ludicrous.

Thinking back a long way I have a clear memory of waking once during the night and actually saying to myself – The war is on, I will remember this. I was no more than four perhaps. Later I woke again seeing my room floodlit, a golden glow blazed and fluttered against the walls.

– It's Peace! I whispered, recognizing. So I was not surprised when neighbours began banging at the door and shouting. I lay there hearing Daddy in the front room stirring. He coughed a horrible thick cough so that he might be choking on phlegm; and then thud, bumping into the walls, staggering out to answer the callers. What had gone wrong? While I held my breath to hear better, he barged into my room, snatched me up in his arms, blankets trailing and tripping him; ran, joggling and hurting. Outside, the cold air grabbing at my feet, I could afford to wake so I opened my eyes and found them filled with a sky of flames. Then a large black hand swooped across my sight and blinded me so that only the familiar smell of my father's skin saved me crying out in alarm. Out across the yard we went, with neighbours plucking at my train of bedclothes, out over the threshold a giant bridegroom and with his fire-blinded bride in his arms; fragments of blazing wood pattered on the ground as we ran. Once he removed his hand so he could brush a red-hot ember from my pyjama-sleeve and, unafraid, I had seen everything including two lumps of timber rushing like comets overhead plus the bakery roaring with flames. Flames circled the silhouette of my father's head; and when he turned to look back they filled his open mouth, then as he glanced my way I even saw a tiny flame in each of his terrified eyes.

That period of my life came to an unpredicted halt. My father began to behave in an odd way, seeming to be occupied with some problem he couldn't grasp. His hair was grey and he complained of feeling sick. We were never free of father's sicknesses; if it wasn't migraine (which he sometimes called *mygrain* and sometimes *meegrain* according to whether he had one or not), it was the gastro, or his nerves. His friends who used to arrive periodically in the evening to play cribbage ceased to call. The day came when I knew they'd never play cards at our place again. I hated his sicknesses, I had no sympathy for him. All the energies inside me longed to be free of them, with their disgusting symptoms and the burden of his helplessness. So I began playing truant instead of going to school. I went down to the railway line to look at the trains. When this became boring and I was getting too dirty in the sooty grass, I walked a mile along the canal bank to steer clear of the houses and sat in the sunshine, wondering about things, the way you do with still water and insects skittering on its surface. I told myself not to feel hungry at lunch time, because I'd eaten my sandwich hours before when I couldn't resist though I knew it was too early. But by early afternoon I decided I could risk buying a bun somewhere on the outskirts. And besides, I had become obsessed with the clock. I had absolutely no idea what time it was. The morning stretched enormous behind me, the afternoon too. It could be four and school out, it could be two, or twelve or five, or the police could be on my tracks.

At last something new was happening to me, success as a habitual truant. One evening my father came in as always, shabby but neat, bringing with him an event. I detected the signs of despair deepening in his face. He was tired out and feeling ill (when wasn't he tired and ill?). I answered his questions about school. Yes it had been alright lately, no there wasn't any more difficulty with geometry now. Suddenly my father was weeping at me, sitting across the table, wetness dripping into the dinner I had cooked. Tears seemed to come from somewhere far inside him which he himself didn't know about and couldn't control. His face looked puzzled as much as anything. But a terrible pain lodged in his eyes and this I shall not forget.

– You've been playing truant, he sobbed. I saw your teacher. And now you'll never do well. You'll never be able to fend for yourself and have a decent life. You just don't see how important school is.

How could I explain I did it because of him, because I couldn't stand his horrible helplessness? How could I explain I did it because I found I was beginning to sneer at him in secret, my father who used to know everything, the one who stood between me and the dangers of the world?

– I want you to be able to do well, he said. You've got to be able to. You have to think of *me*. Otherwise, otherwise ...

I ran, I just ran, out along the passage and up to my bed where I hid, never to come out or be seen again or take up my life as it had been before. How could he let me see him crying! I was so wounded and disgusted. My father's tears were nothing to mine, the sheet and the pillow sopped them up, silently I howled into the warm womb of darkness, I ached as I lay in my tears, till I could die. Curiously, what I remembered before falling asleep was the end of a seaside holiday, it was a holiday from the year before, a farewell to the lovely sand and rocks and the seawater with its awful taste, the mysterious world of caves and rockpools, and goodbye to the excitement of that one day helping fishermen drag in a net full of kicking fish, and most of all good-bye to my friend Mandy I'd been with for the fortnight, whom I'd met there and probably wouldn't see again, that sweet charm of a chance friendship. Daddy was so irritable after packing the car (we had one that year, a battered Singer) he didn't allow me time to say goodbye to Mandy, if Mandy wasn't home I'd have to content myself with telling her parents and asking them to pass it on. So we drove off. The gap between me and Mandy suddenly, casually, total. I begged him to stop. He didn't understand till he saw me blubbering. And when we looked back, there was Mandy pumping along behind us, red in the face, making a heroic run. She came up to the car, still frantic and tear-stained, waving a scrap of paper on which she'd written her address. We swore always to be friends and it was the most wonderful moment of the holidays. But I had to wake to the horror of life with my weeping pain-racked father. The next I knew, morning had already taken possession of my room and things were not the way I might have wished them. Great-aunt Anne was at the chest of drawers packing my things into a suitcase, tiptoeing about, her huge careful form butting soundlessly against my furniture, treading like a great weightless shadow on my fallen books and clothes. Because I wanted to die I pretended to be asleep. Eventually she had to wake me.

My aunt Annie is a remarkable woman, sensible and strong. Wake up Vivi, she said, you're coming to live with me and I shall love to have you. Let me tell you everything now so you'll bear it all at once and never again, your father's dead, he simply couldn't bear the pain, so he did what any sensible person would do, he put a stop to it. He just said, I won't stand for any more. She packed another pile of my things in the bag. The clothes looked so small. That is to say, Aunt Annie said, he swallowed a handful of the sleeping tablets he had for his pain. He left one tablet over. Now that's a marvel. As though he might need it later if things didn't work out.

I was too stunned to cry. My feeling, at the age of twelve, was recognition: I'd always known he could be dead like this. But it would be unpardonable if I did not cry, for Auntie's sake as my relative. So I burst into a loud hacking and moaning. She folded me against her, another thin rag of clothing to be packed, and she said, you're such a good girl Vivi, you don't have to cry in front of me. Then I really did cry because I didn't have to.

In his coffin my father looked exactly like himself but with one eye a bit crooked, and his cheeks a shade too pink. The thing that made me believe he was finally dead was the cottonwool he wore stuffed in his ears and nostrils. He was dressed in his suit, his splendid formality. As a child what preoccupied me was how had he done it: did he dress before he took the pills? Perhaps I might have been more shocked hadn't there been so many flowers in the room: Auntie's signature. I hardly dared imagine where they had come from. So I watched him sealed away and buried, exotic as a tropical bird.

My aunt, determined to console me at whatever price, promised me the most precious thing in her house to help me forget. I imagined the clock, the ornaments, some lump of furniture, her black cashbox. When she brought me the gift from upstairs, explaining that she kept it under her bed, I was surprised to see it was a simple wooden case which for one painful moment resembled a miniature coffin. Open it my dear, her voice trembled with excitement, I can't wait! Inside lay a violin. Now, said Auntie almost crossly, do what I say or you won't be any good at all.

She took up the instrument herself and tuned it. Imagine my astonishment. She was the last person on earth to have a violin. Then to watch her wooden fingers lifting and falling like mechanical hammers and her whole body trembling as she swept the bow its full length this way and that. I could have laughed because she handled everything as if she knew what she was doing. The violin gave out a simple spritely dance tune, stiff and rough but somehow filled with feelings that made a lump rise in my throat. Auntie, I gasped in admiration, you never told! When she finished the tune she put the instrument into my hands. Tuck it under your chin, she said grimly. Like this, now take the bow like this, no like this, no, thumb there duffer, no, knuckles in a straight line, no the two small fingers don't touch it, no, fingers together, no the horsehair at a slant, no the other way, no square to the strings, no wrist higher than that, wrist not elbow, elbow down wrist up knuckles up fingers relaxed, horsehairs on a tilt … now draw the bow gently down, down further, keep going. To my utter astonishment the bow produced a long clean note from the violin with only two hitches as I lost confidence. Suddenly Auntie smiled. It's yours now Vivi. She turned the smile away to a dim corner of the room. And if you don't use it right and practise I'll put you out on the street to beg.

Come on Aunt Annie, I cried proud and delighted with the note I had made, Daddy already buried and forgotten, teach me, teach me to play. No, she replied and took the violin away, you're going to learn from someone who can really show you, you're going to be a famous violin player, before I die I want to buy a ticket and hear you play in a concert, you can sit me in the front row so I can catch your eye when you get it right. I wished then that the future would allow me to do something for Aunt Annie, something really spectacular to make her gasp.

What do you remember about the old days? I cajoled her because she was now an enigma. The old days? she answered vigorously. What old days? I don't remember a thing, what do the old days matter when there's today to live and tomorrow to think about? A little while later she added, relenting, I made one mistake in the old days and I'll never forget that, I married a man who didn't love me and I refused a man who did. Can you think of anything – now my great-aunt was shouting at me – anything more criminal than that, to wreck two lives, to make a good man miserable all his days and make my husband miserable too, as well as myself into the bargain? I've got two pieces of advice for you my girl and you'd better take note: don't let other people try to live your life for you, and don't get married. So I asked her who was she going to get to teach me the violin then? I know who, she said, I've had my eyes peeled for some time and that's a fact.

Auntie found me a violin teacher. She dug up someone who had played with the BBC Symphony Orchestra, she prised him out of retirement, she carted me off to his cottage and sat me in the porch, she set him up in front of his music stand and called me into the room when she was ready. Now, she announced to Mr Rosenbloom, this is my grandniece who will become a violinist and this is her violin. He peered at me over the top of ridiculous half-moon spectacles like the most perfect absent-minded professor. Really, he said and held out his hand for the violin. I passed it to him. Good morning, he said to the violin. Good morning, I answered for it. Extraordinary, he commented having twanged a couple of strings and hastily corrected the tuning. And where might I ask, Mrs McTaggart, did this instrument come from? From me, she replied promptly. Yes but before that? he asked, fingering it. So far as I know, she replied, it came from French Equatorial Africa in the 1890s. Indeed? he looked at me.

French Equatorial Africa? he said cautiously and twanged it again. Yes Mr Rosenbloom, my father brought it from there to Uruguay where he was living for a while with some Scottish folk. Uruguay, eh? said the violin teacher. That's right and from Uruguay to New South Wales. New South Wales in Australia? asked Mr Rosenbloom. And then here to England with me, my great-aunt confirmed. To England, he spoke to the violin, now that is extraordinary. He gave it an apprehensive twang. I risked a glance at Auntie, mortified on her behalf at what she must be suffering. But there she sat on a cedar chair, flounces of crimson organdie piled up from the seat to the deep ruff round her neck and the drooping crimson coyly fluttering at her shins. Her face red with pride and happiness, her great brilliant eyes met mine but she could spare only a moment, the occasion being too momentous for anything to be missed. I knew then that she was glad to be old, proud to have got there.

At last Mr Rosenbloom managed to tear his eyes away from the instrument and looked straight at me. He was piercing me with that look. Miss Lang, he said, would you kindly stand up. He spoke English with the exactness of a foreigner and his pronunciation distracted me so much I had to think before I could understand him. I leapt to my feet dropping the handbag Aunt Annie had given me the week before, so that it fell open on the carpet spilling its contents: three coins, a pencil, a left-over wartime lipstick I'd purloined, a powderpuff deeply impregnated with Lucy Urquart's powder, a lucky charm elephant, a piece of chewing gum and a grubby handkerchief I had been meaning to wash for this occasion but had forgotten. Instantly I was on hands and knees scooping everything back into hiding. Unfortunately my energy somewhat outdid my aim and the lipstick was sent flying across the room to where it rapped Mr Rosenbloom sharply on the ankle. His hand approached it gingerly. He passed it back to me and then permitted himself to sniff ever so briefly at his fingertips, propping at the perfume. I had stood to retrieve the lipstick so I remained standing, which was what I had been asked to do. Turn to your right please, said Mr Rosenbloom, no don't hold the handbag leave it on the chair, yes, now tilt your chin up, now put your chin down but keep your eyes up like a Duchess ordering the dinner, good gracious, now show me your back, now still with your back to me sing this note (he played a note on the violin), I sang it. I see, he said, now sing me these two notes. I sang them. Now sing me these four notes. I sang again. Come here child, he said, and show me your hands. He took hold of them and it troubled me that his fingers were hot. Mrs McTaggart, he said mournfully in his perfectly foreign English, this is not what I had looked forward to. How awful: I glanced at my great-aunt, seeing how much it meant to her, that she was nervous, for there was not a flower anywhere on her person. No indeed, Mrs McTaggart, as I explained to you I came to the country to retire not to teach. This was too dreadful, so ashamed I felt and so sorry for Aunt Annie as he handed her the poor shabby violin she thought such a lot of. Miss Lang, he continued as if introducing me to my aunt, is beginning too late perhaps for us to hope for really great things of her, which is regrettable as it is past remedy, but she has everything a violinist should need so far as one can tell, an excellent ear, a sensitive disposition, supple hands, a sturdy constitution, and modesty. The petals of Auntie's dress shuffled slightly as she breathed out ... and you could tell then she'd been holding her breath. Of course, said the teacher, I shall sacrifice my retirement in part and accept her. On condition, he added quickly, that you mention it to nobody else, I would urge this promise on you. When can you bring her to me, he concluded, and can she come twice a week? Great-aunt Anne became as dignified as Queen Mary, if a little fuller in the figure. We shall come Tuesday and Friday afternoons at half-past four, she said for all the world as if she knew what she was talking about. Provided that is convenient. Perfectly convenient, Mr Rosenbloom snatched his half-moon glasses off his nose, snapped them shut and clipped them in a metal case. Excellent, he declared. Oh and the violin, he added, was made by a respectable Italian house but is a rather eccentric instrument, still it will serve well enough for the present.

As Aunt Annie turned to check that I had closed Mr

Rosenbloom's garden gate after us, I saw a splendid white carnation blazing on her crimson bosom.

– I knew he'd be alright, she said. I picked him for his name.

For seven years Martin Rosenbloom taught me, coaxed, bullied and encouraged me. I passed my examinations with credit; but when it came to the final test, I would never be a professional.

Aunt Annie was impatient with all forms of compromise. Forget what's reasonable or respectable, she said, if you're going to change, change completely. Either you're right or you're wrong. If you're right stick to your guns and if you're wrong stand up and say so. I knew she spoke from experience, that she had once risked her life, changing her mind out loud; it was through Mr Rosenbloom that the story came to be known. Aunt Annie recognized the Great War, the Depression and the Second World War as a single event, a symphony of human suffering and endurance, cruelty and resistance. The movements were different, yes, but they belonged together.

When she was twenty-nine she changed her mind about love and walked out on Uncle to marry Joseph McTaggart, well known for his liberal distribution of white duck feathers around the Whitey's Fall district. Luckily for their marriage these unsuited people went immediately to Sydney to enlist in the army. The year was 1915.

So I come to a letter found among my father's papers when they were surrendered to me on my twenty-first birthday. In a shoe box containing his treasured oddities, a glider altimeter, an ivory slide-rule, golf tees, collar studs and a pair of shoetrees, was a package of correspondence addressed to Mr Archibald Lang: in the main, letters from Great-aunt Anne to my grandfather. This one was dated 1917:

In the afternoon I arrived at the Casualty Station; three tents, a marquee and two Swiss Cottage tents. Everything was deathly in the countryside, snowflakes drifting down through the air. There were some rocks in front of the tents black rugged silhouettes standing against the snowy fields. The patients were huddled outside sitting on ammunition boxes by the clerking tent, while the staff scuttled about, you could hear voices echoing across the snow from an old bunker on the hill where I was told a couple of our boys covered the retreat of the injured with a Vickers gun, and the wounded were arriving in a hobbling column all the while.

The men leaving the dressing station, one by one, dipped biscuits into their pannikins of hot cocoa. Then I noticed them halt, biscuits poised in the steam, and a roaring filled the air, this great plane came swooping down no more than twenty feet above the tents, its guns firing at us! Shooting at our wounded! I couldn't believe such wickedness.

It turned out that the men they fired at were our machine-gunners on the hill. We had no defence and the airplane was turning in a wide circle to attack us again, I grabbed hold of the nearest soldier with two legs and we ran to see if the gunners needed medical aid. They were beyond mortal assistance, Archie, God rest them. We crawled in beside them to take cover as the Jerry swooped in again with his guns rattling away and I prayed our helpless lads would be spared, and I can tell you I demanded the soldier with me should fire the Vickers and bring down the airplane, it was flying low enough Lord knows, only then I realized he had both arms in plaster! But he knew how to work it, so I told him to teach me, I got down in the mud and did exactly what he said. Next time the hun flew in low over the Casualty Station, I opened her up and blasted him with as many bullets as the gun had in it, it was enough to shake the flesh off my arms and I only realized afterwards that I'd seen chips fly off the wing. Sure enough when we looked as he passed, there were splinters and tatters. My soldier went wild with excitement. You got him, sister, you got him, he shouted and I truly believe he waved his plastered arms. The airplane swooped up in the sky steeply, then it seemed to falter and a puff of black smoke floated out, by this time a whole crowd of crippled men had struggled up the hill to help me, but now we realized the Jerry was going to fall right in among us, you could even make out the pilot wrestling with the controls trying to pull it out of the dive. Would you believe those fools went on cheering? In the sunset light the flaps on the wings and tail switched this way and that, like flashing signals, I shall always remember this, next the pilot's body came tumbling out, falling ahead of the machine. I shut my eyes, but that was worse than having them open and as I looked up the wind was blowing the airplane aside like a kite, mercifully away from us. Just before it hit the ground the engine dropped out and my tummy dropped with it.

As I was escorted to the hospital in triumph, the acetylene lamps were being lit, so that put a stop to the highjinks, it meant there was a batch of operations ready. I had to get busy, though I felt sick as a dog.

Great-aunt Annie didn't see active service in the next world war, being fifty-three when it began, but she still had her part to play. In 1937 her husband's small-time import-export agency was based in Bristol and he went to Germany to negotiate a sub-agency with a Bremen firm. Annie was with him.

Mr Rosenbloom took me to a restaurant for dinner one night and during coffee adopted a pensive expression. I have something to tell you, he said, which no one else knows. It is written here. He passed me an envelope. Here you will find pages from my diary I kept years ago, I have translated it into English for you. There is no need to say anything more to me about it; also I give it to you trusting you will never mention this to your aunt, it is simply *entre nous*. He toyed with his empty wineglass, twirling it to catch the light. When he was ready he looked me in the eye and smiled, so that I was nonplussed: he was pleading with me. Coming from this worldly person it appeared so very unlikely. I was young. That night, sitting up in bed making a ceremony of having waited till then, I opened the envelope and read what he had given me:

Travel all day by train, expecting to arrive Bremen late pm. Hannah and self. *(my sister Dr Hannah Reuben, married to Dr Benjamin Reuben a famous surgeon.) Opposite sit two foreigners, married? large woman, small husband. Hannah and woman in animated conversation in English. Too fast and fluent for me. Occasional words suggest wide range of topics. Becoming friendly, what a bore. Perhaps becoming personal. H. condescended an aside to me that they had much in common, wartime service, medical ideas. All put me out of humour. Short-tempered: a fault. Uncomfortable, being excluded. Left compartment. Now in the dining car. Coffee and bread. Tasteless. Spent the past hour studying score for SSS (Saint-Saëns Septet). Not really to my taste. Looks best for the piano. Rather regret accepting engagement. Clever though. And Dieter asked for me ... so.

Approaching Bremen. Raining as always. Streaky brick. Passing mile on mile of grey slate roofs all wet, metallic, depressing. Back in compartment. When I commented to Hannah about dismal Bremen: How can people live in such places? H. shrugged. But large woman answered (grotesque accent): 'Yet we all must live there.' End of conversation. Her tone of voice as disagreeable as her interference. Ignored her.

Not yet 4.30 pm, but the street lights going on. Lime trees dripping in the rain. What a place. The buses, black cars. Lights, lights. The road a mirror of lights. Far up ahead our locomotive lets out a melancholy howl. Even the carriage lamps in little yellow shades come on above our heads, swaying. Cold out there. Warm in here, stuffy. We're comfortable it seems. Is that what we wish above all?

Something dreadful. The conversation. H. very angry. Expressing disgust, outrage. Snapping words in English at the foreigners. They are suspicious of me writing. H. now staring with absolute hatred. Tells me the woman said she found fascists really quite nice people! decent, clean and full of good sense, she says. Says people spread wild fears about them. Says she has been obliged to modify her views of Hitler and Germany at large.

Look at H. to signal: trust you haven't told her who we are. H. signals back: do you take me for a fool! Bremen station now. What lies before us?

We live in fear. Bremen a trap. Look at yesterday. Yesterday when we got off the train, we joined the queue moving with luggage through the turnstiles. General bustle, very busy. Somewhere ahead raucous young voices were singing *O du schöner Westerwald*. A brooding atmosphere in the place, not just due to rain. Suddenly there were shouting men and people pushing towards us against the mainstream. I suppose my violin case gave us away. A gang of youths clustered round, isolating Hannah and myself from the rest. They began to denounce us, challenging us to deny we had been members of the Communist Party. When we admitted that once we had been members, as reasonably as we could, they hurled insults at us and demanded to know why we were in Bremen. They stopped the queue and called on the whole crowd to witness what monsters we were. They shouted at us that things were too dangerous for them to keep quiet and leave us to our 'work'. One leapt on a wooden crate and waved his arms telling everyone the city was in an explosive state. Perhaps he just wanted attention. He certainly got it. I was shaking. He shouted: 'People like these traitors put us all in peril.' There were officials in uniform around us now too: police among them and a few military. The platform was crammed with people, all listening, many stopping to stare, others hurrying past with their eyes cast down, some joining in abusing us. Perfect strangers! They seemed to be respectable people turned savage animals in pinstripe and velvet. Their leader on the crate went through the standard routine of denunciations: 'You are the well-known Jewish agitator Martin Fischer and she is your sister the notorious communist scientist Dr Hannah Reuben, where have you been Dr Reuben, selling military secrets to the enemy?' The situation had become extremely threatening. I wondered if they'd trample us underfoot there and then. A lout tugged the violin out from under my arm. Ridiculously he and I stood struggling for possession of it. Then he had it off me, my precious instrument. At this moment something swept through the air narrowly missing me. I realized my assailant had been struck across the face by an umbrella, a sharp painful blow too. It was that foreign woman from the train. Without any show of embarrassment at her unladylike behaviour, she dropped her umbrella, grasped my violin case with both hands and wrenched it away from him. I noticed how enormous her hands were, like a farmer's. We were all astonished, a complete hush fell, so that my saviour had time to harangue us in a mixture of nearly incomprehensible German and strange English. Nevertheless she made herself clear. No doubt about that. She had been deceived, the scales fallen from her eyes, she towered with her anger. She confronted the man she struck as if he had wronged her personally. She pinched a sample of his brown shirt between thumb and finger, held it displayed like some soiled article. In the midst of my fear I loved her for that. She spoke out: 'I have changed my mind!' she said so that everybody was even more surprised. 'Up till today I thought you Fascists had a lot of sensible arguments on your side. But I was wrong!' Then she turned on the people watching. 'All you people over there,' she called in her terrible and understandable German, 'are being led to the butcher like a lot of silly sheep. These people in their beautiful brown shirts are amateur thugs. I never believed it possible. But anybody can see the truth of it right here.' She handed me my violin as if awarding me a prize at a ceremony. 'I am a player myself,' she said. 'Now,' she called out, 'you policemen come and earn your keep. These people and ourselves require safe conduct to a taxi.' She bent over, unself-conscious in a way I've never seen before, retrieved her umbrella and led the way to the gate, even instructing one of the officers to carry her suitcase. Showing him her ticket like orders from his superiors. So we passed, a charmed procession, away from that angry gang of nazis, straight out through the gate and into our respective taxis – under official protection. A policeman closed her taxi door like a footman. I wasn't even able to thank her or say goodbye. In our own taxi Hannah dumbfounded me by bursting into tears, a thing I had not known her do since she was a child. 'This is the beginning, Martin,' she whispered, 'What will the end be?'

Postscript:

So my dear Vivien, and that is all I knew of our saviour. I shall not say what happened to us afterwards, the experiences in the ghetto, the local postman who saved my instrument and my papers, the terror, our arrest, life in the camps and cattle trains, torture and so forth. But I survived. I'm afraid my sister died; nothing has been heard of her all these years. I came to England when the war was over. I worked with the BBC Symphony, then I retired, leaving London and moving down here. One day a neighbour called to say a lady was enquiring for a violin teacher. No, I said, absolutely no. I was in the grip of death, you see. A week later the same neighbour pointed out this lady in the baker's shop. I was frightened. Fear, yes, that was my first reaction to anything unexpected. The past flooded back in all its horror. I knew her. At once I decided to allow her to recognize me. Whatever came about, this was England, at least I would pay my debt of thanks. You see, during the terrible decade of Hitler's rule many people, maybe dozens, had similarly marked my life ... but she was the first I had stumbled across in the years since. I was watching her as she turned away from the counter with her bread in her hands, those farmer's hands. For a moment I had a panic, thinking I must be wrong. She looked full in my face without a sign of recognition. But it was too late to go back, already my attention must have seemed rude, so I stopped her and asked her if it was she who had been enquiring about violin lessons. The moment she spoke, I knew without any remaining doubt that this was the same woman, a voice in millions. Fourteen years had passed, I'd become a shaky old man in that time. Yet it is hard to believe I'd changed so much. But of course it might not have seemed such an important event to her, anyhow. Often I catch a glance in her eye, an expression, a tiny hint of this or that, and wonder whether she hasn't known me all along. Who can tell? She was lucky to escape from Bremen, we all were, all of us who did survive.

When it became obvious that I'd never make a professional violinist, Aunt Annie presented me with the keys to her house in Australia, also a packet containing the title-deeds and papers. You may as well make do with what you've got, she told me ruthlessly. All you need do is get yourself to Whitey's Fall, New South Wales, and tell Brinsmeads at the general store to show you Annie McTaggart's house because it's yours. Had she never thought of returning herself? No, she replied, I'm someone who can't go home; I've made my bed.

Australia seemed an outlandish suggestion, but I persuaded myself to take it seriously because I loved her and I could see how she valued her gift. Meanwhile I told the old lady I'd be moving to London to look for a flat and a job. To my surprise she was delighted and advised me for the umpteenth time to get busy and stand on my own two feet and not let anyone make up my mind for me. As I was leaving she took my arm. We kissed: not like affectionate relatives of different generations but like conspirators, her strength flowing out to me. Whatever you do, Vivi, she told me, if you decide it's not right for you, have the guts to give it up. Say: That's enough, I'm not going to waste my life. Do something else. It's only too late to change when you're dead!

So you're a schoolteacher at last, I knew you'd make the grade! she exclaimed delightedly when I visited her a year later, as if I hadn't failed in all I wanted to do. She picked a fresh peonie for me. From her own bush. She gave me a wonderful welcome disguised as a stern lecture on my previously aimless ways. I remembered her keys, her house on the mountain. That was the moment I knew I would come to Whitey's Fall some day.

Last time I saw her, Great-aunt Anne had shrunk into an old old woman half her proper weight. It was pathetic to see her so gaunt, how long and fine her nose, how high her cheekbones. In a macabre way, under the thick overlay of wrinkles and dying skin, she was being reborn as a beautiful girl. In vigour she hadn't aged a scrap. She sat in her same chair, the street going about its business beyond her window, the people, the flowers, maharajas under umbrellas beaded with rain; and still she refused to reminisce. What's the use of the past, she declared, it never did me any good.

213

Live for the present, my girl! A lovely young woman like you has no business with the past. The only thing I remember is a river called Dry River. Now that tells you what you need to know.

I promised I would think about it. And then announced my surprise: I showed her my airline ticket to Sydney with the keys she had given me. There and then she wrote a letter of introduction for me to take. Her slanted writing dashed waveringly across the page.

Dear Seb,

If you have not forgotten an old acquaintance, you will surely do me a favour. I dare say you are well in command of Whitey's Fall by now, you have had sixty years to make it since I saw you last, all said and done!

This letter is being brought by a dear young woman who is buying the old house off me. It's no use to me now. Please be sure she manages all right. I am certain that I may depend upon you, of all people.

Give my love to all my friends, and most of my blood relations.

Ever yours. May the Good Lord bless and keep you.

Anne McTaggart

When she finished, she slapped the envelope against her tongue and wet it thoroughly, her fingers stroked the flap closed, then she banged it shut on the table. She watched the letter pass into my hands and her eyes were blurred with tears, I saw the slack rims fill helplessly and tears gathering in her poor stunted lashes.

Can I take any messages, Auntie? I asked.

Yes, yes, she replied eventually, to my darling Arthur.

Arthur who?

Just call him Uncle, everybody does, it grew on him. Say to my darling Arthur ... her voice failed her, but she swallowed hard. Say, she began again ... Give him a warning from me, if him and his rowdy mates get up to any old buck, I'll be after him with a big stick to sort him out! Say that, she said downright, her lip trembling in its delicate feminine curve.

Three – The Narcissist

Why are you standing at the mirror with that look on your face? said the man inside him.

I've just seen what I've seen, replied Mr Rupert Ping.

What is there to be seen?

The years.

You look like something not properly made.

That's because I won't agree to grow old.

How many years are there then? asked the man inside him.

Seventy-four, there are seventy-four, that's why I'm standing at the mirror.

That's why you're looking like you are.

Mr Ping stared at the wall the mirror was screwed on to. He had screwed the mirror there himself a very long time ago so that he'd be able to see himself full-length when he wanted to.

I know what to do though, Mr Ping said. At last I do know what to do.

You won't forget to have it really sharp, I hope?

I won't forget.

If it's blunt you'll never be able to see this through.

I know.

Then take off the rest of your clothes or you'll get weak and regret it.

Mr Ping slipped his singlet and shorts off. He stood in his underpants while the mirror spared him nothing.

Did you want a drink first? asked the man inside him.

I look like something not properly made, don't I?

Do you want a drink?

Yes perhaps I need one.

It's the years, all those years have done it.

Perhaps I won't have a drink after all, said Mr Ping stropping his cut-throat.

If you'll take my advice you won't begin with your arms because that'll make the rest too messy.

I see what you mean. Legs first then?

Legs, the dear legs, first.

Let them go first. No I don't want a drink. I'm ready now and after a drink I might not be ready any longer.

Take it steady then, perhaps you should stand on a towel.

Obediently Mr Ping reached for a towel, folded it and stood on it. Then he bent over and began drawing the razor lightly across one leg, lightly across the calf, up around the thigh, cutting a little deeper.

It doesn't really hurt after the first shock, said Mr Ping.

You seem to have it sharp enough then?

I won't look in the mirror yet.

Do the other leg first, that's my suggestion, then it won't be any different from this one.

Mr Ping stooped over, attending to his other leg, drawing the razor this way and that, crisscrossing from the foot up so that blood started out suddenly like the thonged stockings of a medieval peasant.

My trouble is, said Mr Ping sadly, I can still recognize them for what they were.

Keep going then, the man inside advised him.

How many years did we say there were?

Seventy-four.

Should I start on my chest before I look?

Seventy-four is a long time when you come to consider it.

Yes, I think it would be best to work on the chest now.

You're making a nice clean line there; things wouldn't be so simple if you had body hairs.

I never did have, he said proudly. (The blade gave out a sound which filled him with horror, a faint sibilant whistling, as it sliced through skin and flesh.)

Can you feel the blood running down your legs?

It tickles a bit and my feet feel sticky, but I haven't looked yet.

Mr Ping stopped what he was doing. He stood alone in the bathroom of his house, wearing nothing but his underpants, arraigned before the large mirror he had once installed for his vanity. Finally he looked up to see what had been accomplished so far.

It's an awful shock I know, the man inside him apologized hastily.

O God. What am I doing?

You're doing what you have to do, and not too badly, except the cuts could be a shade deeper if that can be managed.

It's so shiny.

Better start with your stomach before it gets too messy and dripped on.

I don't think I can go through with this, I'm feeling sick.

Answer your own question, Ping. When I asked you before what there was to see, you replied, the years nothing but the years.

I understand, already that's forgotten.

The blood, the blood.

I understand.

Just cut a little deeper, not so much as to really hurt though.

I don't care if it does hurt. I only care about whether it will work.

Keep cutting, it's a question of faith.

The razor trailed with a gentle almost lazy motion over his wrinkled abdomen, the old sagging skin producing berries of blood startlingly young and fresh.

You see, said the man inside Mr Ping. The blood doesn't age, watch the blood come young as it ever was.

217

I was betrayed you know, he said as he punched at himself with his knuckles, before slicing the skin delicately.

You really have a case.

Nothing else has gone. I'm fit as I ever was. Look at that for shape, proportion. You can feel me anywhere and not an ounce of fat or softness. Just this hanging skin.

You look like something not properly made with that skin.

The razor decorated it with a swirling red line. Mr Ping set to work on his arms.

Got to be a bit careful of the big veins though, he said.

You could make it a work of art. You could exhibit what you've done. In the city they'd pay to see you.

What if I leave my face alone?

There's no point in doing anything if you leave your face alone. That's the worst part as it is.

Mr Ping's bare feet puddled in the rucking bloody folds of the towel. He looked up at the mirror.

I'm pale, he said.

Then he stroked the blade across his cheeks. Harder, so it bit into the flesh. He dragged it up round the side of one eye socket and across his forehead, back and across the lips so that the warm flesh opened out and something mysterious was happening inside him.

I think you've done a good job.

Yes I think I have, said Mr Ping.

He stood in front of himself, engulfed in a howl of fear and horror. At that instant he recalled how his wife had come to the open door a few months previously: Mrs Ping had risen from her afternoon rest, woken by a premonition, she had stood there and watched through the bathroom door, watched him inspecting his body and face, watched him inwardly weeping for what he had been. Their eyes had met in the mirror. In her look he could see at last what the mirror was trying to show him; he could also read the compassion she felt for him; angrily he saw that she did not hate him; worse, that she understood, that watching him touch himself and pinch at the slack skin she'd recognized what he felt for his own body: disgust. She who had lived all these years with the insult of his self-love, the pampering of his own physique and skin, had now witnessed his disgust, his admission that age had defeated him, that he'd become grotesque. On that day Mrs Ping said nothing as she returned where she had come from, carrying with her the dreadful load of what she knew, the burden of her freedom, her victory, her sympathy for him, and the knowledge that he did not deserve it.

She was exultant, said the man inside him.

She got what she wanted, he agreed bitterly.

Giving her such a victory as you did.

Who's to care, said Mr Ping. She's dead now.

She would never have been able to watch this.

I never wanted it to be like this. That's the trouble, he said.

It's been a crime against you all these years, keeping you in hopes.

Now Mr Ping suffered afresh at the hands of his own narcissism for he could not resist the fascination of staring at himself, the hideous tatters of skin, the streaked gluey blood. Just as self-love had once stripped him ridiculously naked and wrinkled in front of the wife who was martyred to what he'd been. Standing in the bathroom, Mr Ping thought he heard noises in the house, as if somebody moved stealthily. He listened with concentration, unable to tell whether the breathing was his own or not. Who could it be anyway! The idea absurd. No one knew he was up here. No one had been in the house since Mercy's death. Only himself, endlessly with himself, with his decaying flesh and his rancid thoughts. The sound of movement came again; plainly the house creaking in the midday sun. He turned his attention to the mirror. The voice inside him seemed to have died. He felt ridiculous, a mutilated scrawny old man imagining he'd been talking to himself (which he probably had). It was not Mercy but Felicia Brinsmead who could claim his greatest moments anyhow. Felicia who was once beautiful as the morning, a year younger than himself and half a head taller, she, the loveliest woman he'd ever seen, had kissed his feet and praised him, hadn't she?

His body was shivering. As the shivering began he felt himself wrapped in a lightning flash, the agony zigzagged around, every nerve burnt by a freezing charge. A man on fire. He ought to have been afraid. But instead he accepted this as proof: he knew it had been done now. Very slowly his slashed face crept into an excruciating lopsided smile.

At last, at last, he breathed.

You're free then? the man inside him asked anxiously.

It's been prison.

You've set yourself free alright?

Free. I've thrown it off.

Aren't you sorry for what you've done?

No. I'm glad thank you. I'm relieved.

How will you face the people in the street? They'll ask.

The cattle? Mr Ping replied with a sneer. Those cow people? A sharp thud came from the bedroom. No doubt about it this time. It had to be some large animal or an intruder. Mr Ping hobbled into the passage, dried blood cracking along his legs. He threw open the bedroom door. There stood Bill Swan, arrested halfway from the wardrobe to the window, clutching a black tin cashbox. Billy gaped at the sight of that bloody naked figure.

– Can I help? he asked.

– What are you doing?

– Stealing this box, Mr Ping.

– Why don't you look at me?

– Stealing a document, that is.

– Why don't you look at me?

– I just came for one thing. I'd have returned the rest safely.

– Haven't you seen an old man naked before?

– I wasn't stealing it for myself.

Mr Ping hobbled in, steadying himself against the bed, his feet making curious suckings on the floor. He reached for the cashbox, took it and placed it on the oilcloth-covered table. Still working with one hand he juggled the tiny key into its lock and threw open the lid.

– Take what you came for, he said in his nasal Australian voice. Bill Swan stepped forward, sorted through the papers in the box, extracted a manilla envelope and held it up as if for approval. Bright red fingers grabbed at his wrist and held him.

220

By an immense effort he did not resist, nor attempt to free himself.

– This, said Bill Swan.

– Tell me, Swan, have you ever seen a freed man before?

– ...?

– A man who was not free before. A prisoner?

– No.

– What did you want with that envelope?

– It's the history Mrs Ping wrote out.

– I know what it is. You haven't answered me. He let go of the boy's arm.

– We were afraid for what Mrs Ping wrote here, in case it would be lost.

Mr Ping sank to his knees, teeth chattering violently. He knelt, trying to think what he must do. Shook his head. Hopeless. And rolled unconscious on the worn lino. Bill Swan considered the alternatives. But there was no easy way, he knew. He lifted the old man up, small and light as a child and, after a momentary hesitation for the fate of the bedclothes (which were immaculate), stripped off one blanket, laid him there and covered him up. He was breathing alright. With an unthief-like confusion, the young man looked for the kitchen and barged right into the bathroom instead. Blood was everywhere, blots dribbling down the wall and the long mirror, a trampled mess of it partly sopped up by a towel, footprints of blood leading out through the door. Bile gushed into Billy's mouth. He spat into the washbasin. He stooped there, rinsing his mouth, hands trembling, bewildered by such depravity, something so impossible to imagine. But there were things to do; he found the kitchen and carried a tumbler of water into the bedroom. The free man, who had now regained consciousness, lifted one hand to help guide the glass. Bill propped his head up and helped him drink. Disgust must have been written on his face as he did so because that is what Mr Rupert Ping saw and that is why he smiled a piercing, grateful smile.

– It's not bad son, he said. I'll be alright after a bit of a sleep.

You can tell anyone you like. They'll see for themselves soon enough.

Billy backed out of the room.

– Bill, Mr Ping whispered and his eyes indicated the manilla envelope which lay forgotten on the bed. It's for Miss Brinsmead, he whispered. He rested there as if asleep, feeling the dry blood sewing his body back together again, that clumsy patchwork of skin, he felt the threads being drawn. He was so tired. He knew everything was alright now. Young Swan could be heard walking out into the yard, coughing. For a while there was nothing else. Gradually the cold ebbed from him, as a terrible ache took its place. He felt aged beyond anything imaginable. There was nothing to be heard now: no human, not even a dog, not even a cow. Then one blowfly seesawed into the room through the open window. Mr Ping lay listening to it smacking into the walls.

Lovely blood, he said.

The blood came young as it ever was, the man inside him confirmed the fact.

Four – The Doubter

She was packing, yes packing, and that's all there was to it. No matter what anybody said, let them put it in their pipe. The decision had been made, thank heaven. Come here Susie and help me a moment darling it's just a bit too much for me to manage alone while Daddy's out with the stock. Especially with Fred forever asking are we going to need this in Goulburn and are we going to need that in Goulburn, so I hardly know what to answer. Thanks darling yes I'm alright now. Are you? Well don't worry about me for another half hour at least, I shall be getting into the lowboy and clearing that lot out. Take Freddie with you will you?

She was packing. She had been a force in the town, no doubt she would be missed. But she didn't congratulate herself. Though she knew her worth, she wasn't vain. She was the kind of woman you could find packing in almost any part of the country, in tin shanties out in the semi-desert with her face set on the comforts of a border town, or in the wealthy suburbs of Adelaide you could find her ready to shift her possessions into the luxury suite of an ocean liner bound for Acapulco and a life of glamour. You could find her in Brisbane mopping the sweat from her forehead and reading newspaper reports of a cool change in Sydney, in

Bathurst you could find her kissing her mother goodbye with anguished tears because the old lady might never live to see them all again once they got to the supermarkets of Campbelltown, you could find her on Norfolk Island going to Tasmania, in Tasmania bound for Melbourne or Perth, in Perth stepping on a plane for Canberra, in Canberra hustling her husband to get a diplomatic posting to Japan.

Elaine was packing. A force within her compelled her to pack. The twins had been sent ahead for the sake of their careers. But what had gone wrong she didn't know though she knew she must set off in person and see to it. They needed her after all. Anyhow this had always been the plan: she and Eric and the younger children would follow. Pete and Dave were to rent a house big enough for them all. The great thing was to get away. Away, out from under, free of what was expected of you all the time. There had to be more to life than this. Had to be. Whitey's bloody Fall. It was the stagnation that depressed you and gave you headaches. Never mind about risk, no, never mind how the furniture stood round open-mouthed like a lot of friends seeing the real you for the first time. It'd make you laugh if you weren't so nervous. With the children upset and all. Not that they have any friends their age, but Merv is attached to Grandpa Ian's budgerigar, Fred's got this thing he loves and Susie's got that. And so it goes on. Mum's in tears of course, so's Auntie Doreen. Even the mad Brinsos at the shop looked as if they'd have something to say when they heard.

Elaine McTaggart was packing for the sake of the future. One day she'd had a revelation: there's nothing to stop me leaving. She flung open the cowshed door on brilliant careers for her children. The twins could be pilots, and spacemen had to be born somewhere so why not at Whitey's? Susie could be a filmstar. Merv might make a doctor, with the free schools and universities. And Fred, you never knew, why not a knight? An education gives everybody an equal chance.

She was packing their old clothes. But as soon as they had new ones, out these'd go and no mistake, taking their memories with them, on to the rubbish heap. She was excited. Once her mind had been made up she could be cheerful about the insecurity, she'd have risked moving that very day and without any place to go. Just the whole of Australia! she told herself with a laugh. It's all for the future. She was a ball of courage and the envy of her cousins. What was good for her and her children was good for the nation; money and progress. You can't stop progress, Mother, the world has to go round. Which it does, thanks to America. Of course we'll write. Will we need this in Goulburn? Not again! There was Fred in the doorway with, my God, what's that thing? No, love, I don't expect you'll find much use for a dingo trap in the city, whatever this Goulburn is like.

She was packing and her thoughts came back to the subject of Susie, always to Susie because the moment Susie was born Elaine predicted they'd have to move: one girl, the first girl in twenty-seven years, the only girl in that plague of boy children. Yes, how she'd lived in terror of her little darling being molested. The great hulks of teenage boys around the place with their tongues out and their eyes bulging lifting up Susie when she was no more than five or six and throwing her to each other, a game a game a dreadful game, black and brooding, throwing her and catching her, wolves with a morsel of deer, and her squealing at the delicious daring, the fun the panic, from these huge clutching hands to those, those to those. At one time there were three dozen prospective husbands. Oh yes you couldn't miss the way they watched her wondering what made her a girl. But where was the use in saying it was only natural? Cold comfort that would be when the time came for them to pack-rape her. You could say this was only natural too. What wasn't natural if it came to the point? Well what wasn't natural was something else, something she wanted no further proof of, thank you all the same. It was this. She'd passed the twins' room one night when she couldn't sleep and swore blind she'd caught sight of activity. Activity she didn't ever want to know more about. So urgently did she *not* want to know, she hadn't gone back to investigate, instead she'd kept on her way till outside, till she stood in the cold kitchen, already a collaborator, her mind electrified with messages, directives to get them out of here before it was too late, before anyone in the town could guess. Because after all, were they to blame, with no girls their age closer than the Yalgoona gossips, no women younger than herself? And never would she dare hint a thing to Eric or he'd kill them for sure. You only had to hear him on the subject of the television to know. It must not happen to Fred or Merv. Never. Yet she was so proud of the twins, such handsome young men and such champions at sport. They weren't cannibals were they?

Elaine was packing and thinking about that strange woman coming here to live. Why would a person? Unless she was hiding out, on the run. The rest of the town could believe her cock-and-bull story, but anybody could be called Lang. And not a week after the Vivien creature had arrived young Bill Swan was in at Brinsos asking for gelignite so the whispers had it. Now what would he want gelignite for? And Elaine saw them together with her own eyes, the jezebel hanging on to his body like a leech and speeding away down hill on his motorbike. The very day Mrs Ping died, Mrs Ping who was so kind to Elaine and never went anywhere else for her eggs. And Mrs Ping's house no further than a couple of hundred yards up the hill from where that woman lived. Also when Elaine had taken Uncle Swan aside to have a quiet word with him, he'd gone mad at her so she thought he was going to hit her, and said some dreadful things. In any case he was such a trouble to talk to at the best of times with his deafness. Not to mention his nasty habits. Whitey's Fall was the place to get out of.

So yes, she was packing, shutting from her mind the relatives she loved. No good stopping in this hole, this dead end, nothing would ever happen here as long as that bloody dirt track remained the only way to get into the place. Nobody in their right mind would drive up for pleasure. She'd grow as old as her mother, grandmother, great-grandmother without anything waking the town up, and then perhaps she'd die in this very same house so she'd feel like suffocating. Oh no, not her, not this cookie. To be cramped in here with the hopeless furniture, flies buzzing in and out and cattle mooing on the hillside and that blasted wind blowing the grit in your tea, paralysed on that bed (she thumped

226

it). You've got to have a sense of humour her brother said the other day and she freely admitted hers wasn't the sharpest, well there's more to life than a sense of humour. Oh yes she enjoyed a good joke when there weren't so many worries. But she would never make another Bessie Collins: but then Mum hadn't roused the energy to get out for the sake of her kids.

Now she had begun packing she saw herself for the first time. Is this the woman I am? Have I been waiting for the chance all these years? Tip the lot out, burn that, give those away, how beautiful, how bare, how exciting, I'm so nervous. Mind you she knew that when the time came she wouldn't be able to look back at Whitey's as Eric started the van or she'd burst out sobbing, but she also knew she wouldn't weaken. She and her family must see it through to the end. This was a decision. She must hurry. Maybe they were moving too late as it was. Would there be room on the ladder?

Whatever is the matter Susie, don't cry sweetheart. I'm busy with packing. I know, I know you're worried, but there isn't any need. We won't be going for good, you'll be seeing Nanna again and Grandpa yes and Myrtle and the chooks. We'll come back to visit. Wherever we go we'll always know there's home here and we only have to drive up the road to be back, everyone'll still be here to give us a welcome. It isn't halfway round the world. And just you think of it: where we're going you won't only have animals and old people to play with, you'll have friends your own age, other girls like you, it's true. How does that make it worse? Won't it be wonderful? What's that about Merv? But why darling? Well of course there'll be kids in Goulburn with their eyes a different colour. Goulburn's got everything.

Elaine McTaggart was fitting her household in boxes, folding her present reality away. You couldn't miss the tone of her ceremony, the ritual ownership. This was her denial of belief in the airyfairy theories of the locals. She never understood what others saw in their Remembering. Had no patience with all that stuff about the past. Was there a crumb of evidence you could pick up in your hand? There was not. Where was the past anyhow, when Grandpa Ian could remember a time before the first buildings were put up at Whitey's, when it was all trees and the wreckage of gold fossicking. Ask him for yourself, he could give you the drum, screwy as he is. One day I'll fly in a jumbo jet, she promised herself. She was definitely ready for the fortune-telling computer, and nuclear power was the power she wanted. Wait till she could get some nuclear in her kitchen, then watch out. As for the silly chickens whingeing about radiation, what did they know? She'd never seen radiation. People were too timid. The minerals were saving the country. That was the future. The past was definitely a lot of hooey. The past was her old clothes, as far as that went. What's more they were only good as long as you could still use them and couldn't afford better. She was folding them away in boxes while she planned the future. I don't know why I left it so long, she reassured herself, ruthlessly squashing a tear against her cheek.

Elaine McTaggart was packing.

Five – The Victim of Ambition

The faint bagpiping of Tom Whitey's hollow skeleton was so subtle it did not disturb even the corpse of Kel McAloon newly installed in the next door grave. But Tom Whitey's spirit heard. And heard the skirling as a question.

Well we're all different in that respect, replied the spirit. It's true most of us have white swan-type wings, but some have big swallow's wings, parrot wings, even eagle wings.

The bones droned hopefully.

No, the spirit apologized, I didn't score eagle wings. Well, since you ask, it's like being able to breathe underwater and . . .

At this point a merciful flight of red-backed parrots swept through the cemetery carrying Tom Whitey's angel away with them. The bones were left moaning, content with the memory of roasted swan's meat and having a plan for a viaduct to Dead Reef, a television tower on the mountain, and a major road down to the coast.

Six – The Shape-Thinker

Fido occupied himself thinking he was where he always was. And thinking what he had thought all along. The mountain picture developing to a flurry of pale green, a smudge, an exquisite veil, a memory of Corot's France transmuting to ochre, a haze, a grain of light, with a sky bleached negative and grey and not mattering beyond the unfocused lace edges.

He was changing it so that wet clouds came up and stood over the mountain with plum and brown underbellies, the mountain leaping to the challenge with its dark earth red and aggressive, also giving away touches of mauve and purple.

Fido wasn't going to put up with this at all. Not any longer. He wiped everything he had thought so far. A fresh beginning. He discovered there was room for possessiveness, sentiment. That's right. A cheerful mountain touched by a plume of blue smoke doubtless rising from some man's camp where work was going ahead, trees felled, fences going up, and a future implied in every choice of line, with birds diving through the intervening space to show all was perfectly perfect.

Actually this didn't satisfy him for long, being a boy and expecting so much. The trick was to treat the mountain as an interior, a screen, the idea for a decoration, sweet in its outline, attenuated

230

ridges falling as blue hair to the scooped-out gullies, whimsical ghosts of a Europe long dead frolicking among the trees to the ice-green of flutes, the irresistible art-nouveau spotted gums, world-weary beginnings and a childlike nervousness.

He had another idea, an old one, much handled, a stone buffed smooth as a pebble in a creek, it was possible. And the thought so slippery. Strange because it oughtn't to be like that: an uncle ought not to be a father. The idea worn glassy by constant thinking, washed over by his fast-moving imagination, still-life, solid with planes, actually shaping the mind round it. If the stone were taken away, he would be lost. Fido had observed them at lunch, woodcuts of people; Adam and Eve repining, gazing back through a trellis at the forbidden garden. He thought, supposing I were the angel with a sword I would forgive them, I'd say I know the famous secret you are ashamed of, so you needn't be ashamed about it with me. They never do understand I could kill them like this so they'd crash together, china plates, smashing to bits as they kiss. And he realized this exact design had been in his mind when he set them up with corned beef on their forks and talk of cooks burnt to death, for him to wind up the clockwork of love and release them so their fatal kiss might happen.

I wonder, he wrote in his diary, what this benighted shop looks like from outside.

Once the family came home from India, that dreadful trip, he'd been so ill, Uncle Sebastian got the moon times wrong and they were caught in a full moon like daylight, the van had to be backed right up to the door while Fido's mother huddled him into cover loaded down and disguised as a mobile heap of blankets in case some stickybeak might be awake and prying, which was likely to be the case. He had glimpsed the shop; and it wasn't so different from the two distant houses to be seen out of the kitchen window.

Hanging above me as though it would topple, he wrote.

On another occasion he wrote, I read everything that happens but nothing happens to me. This is what I think, that people don't think there are other people thinking.

The mountain in this dilemma rushed upward, a surface of chewed tatters, then revealing itself as a writhing mass of beastly

231

heads, a clash of energy, a tangle of horns and wings in the desperate throes of murder or escape. Fido faced it clear-eyed, curious and without fear.

Try as he might, although there were a million words in his brain, he needed a couple more he couldn't find. Take the case of his father whom he had to call Uncle Sebastian. He wrote in the eternal diary, I have to call my father uncle. What he needed was a word he didn't have; because, of the two words he did have, who could say one was true and the other wasn't? He pictured it this way: an uncle-uncle, great ragged shapes of wormy wood with a rock falling out of his eye for a tear, facing a father-uncle living grub-like and pallid in the seclusion of a chrysalis not noticing it had split and his damp fatness might be tempting a ravenous Fido on black feather wings.

Refinement, Fido read in the *Town and Country Journal* of October 28th, 1876, is not fastidious. It is not luxury. It is nothing of this kind. It is far removed from excess and waste. A person truly refined will not squander or needlessly consume anything. Refinement, on the contrary, is always allied to simplicity and judicious and tasteful employment of the means of good and happiness which it has at its command.

He imagined a burglar coming to steal his gelignite. In the dim room, lit only by the luminous mountain remote as the moon, intruding eyes big and white with intentions, his shadow paler than himself, a ghostly bride on his muscular arm. He wished the burglar would come so somebody could see him and be given a shock. So somebody would notice him and speak. Fido vowed to scream if the burglar wouldn't sit down and tell all about himself. And listen also. I would write him in my diary, Fido promised, and never tell on him if he promised to come again. On a new page the boy set out these words:

> How are you going? Are you going with me?
> I love you. If you love me, write back.
> love
> Fido

Fido was thinking he was where he always was, but with a difference. Uncle Sebastian planned to change the world by drilling a hole in the den wall for reconnaissance, a truly refined alteration, tasteful in its promise of good and happiness.

– Yes, Felicia explained. The shed fell down years ago, you wouldn't remember, but somebody might come sneaking round to find out what's buried there underneath and you're to watch through the peephole as often as you like and give warning.

This promised to end the tyranny of the mountain picture. There would be other things to see once the hole had been drilled. Fido threw his paint at the window and smeared it across the remote glass with the straight-edge of cardboard. A judicious simplicity. In this way he dragged the paint into a semblance of the spirit of the mountain. It was the best day he had had for ages.

Seven – The Webster

Miss Bertha McAloon was swimming. Yes, she enjoyed a swim in the dam as long as she didn't have to walk home afterwards, and young Peter Buddall would be coming for her before sundown in his Land Rover. You could depend on it. The water in the little dam warmed by muggy air. She didn't care a fig for the world while she floated there, not on your life. She had her own way of swimming too, the Bertha McAloon style, a backstroke tending toward sidestroke, allowing you to ferry yourself around like a distressed raft. When she was swimming she was anywhere you like, so there. It was no good thinking: Miss McAloon is in the dam at Buddall's where the cattle drink, not minding the rain, working her way across and back. No good at all, because the Empress Marie Louise was in fact placing one foot on Napoleon's stocky neck and daring him to lay Russia in her lap as a Christmas present, a White Christmas my love. It would be a dreadful mistake to say there's a crazy old lady floating naked in the dam, because that'd be Mattiwilda Shenandoah the forty-stone black freak with three breasts each big enough to feed four healthy babies, also with the stump of a tail too, that she'd only show as a special favour and then no one but men of good family, right now queening it in a stately home overlooking the wide Missouri, at a birthday party for herself, dressed in luminous green oh glory and how her eyes sparkle and how she laughs and wait till they want to see my tits. Anyway, as it was, nobody need look at the dam if they didn't wish to, the peeping toms, nobody need see her ferrying her starved grey body round and around, let them mind their own business into the bargain, so what if her scrub of grey pubic hairs surfaced now and again, so what, she wasn't even looking herself. She's the Pope and they all come humbly to kiss her toe, no mistake about it, the bosses of the Mafia come like three wise kings with their gifts, followed by Isadora Duncan who is Bertha McAloon's double would you believe, and then comes that bitch Annie Lang now rightly being given the raspberry by his Holiness herself, what else? Who does she think she is? Next please, put your hot lips there Rudolph Valentino my dear, I think I'll have another off you while you're here. How did that Annie Lang get into my cathedral in the first place, clap the guards in jail, if they can't spot a heathen by now they don't deserve their jobs, just wait to one side Rudy and we'll have a private chat when all this bowing and scraping's finished with for the day, I don't mind admitting I'm longing for a cold bath in my crystal tub, I'll show you how I float, oh yes suck me there, why can't I forget, oh yes you've got it, oh that's lovely, I needed you. What's the matter, I can't forget, I can't grow old, cold.

So she lay in luxury, Miss McAloon, swimming while the warm rain pattered on her and hissed into the yellow water of the dam. She could not see the mountain, she made sure she couldn't even see the banks of the little dam itself: there was simply water and water falling gently into water to keep it there and keep it fresh. Hisses.

She lies on a heap of cushions dressed only in beads, fantastic skirts and bodices of beads, jewels in fact, her head caged in jewels, her arms weighed down by the bloody things, and a hundred boys of fifteen years kissing and petting her with their half-grown hands and their tentative roughness, ah, and rolling her about like a game and yes they're so strong and so fresh you could slap their thighs hard, such fat hard thighs you'd never believe, and them being only boys with their chests not yet filled out, oh

235

Lord so beautiful, let me have you all, but the things they want, you can't teach them a trick these days, I'll have you all, enough semen to fill a cup perhaps, a jug, yes all of you, a quart of semen, a gallon, I'll have it, I'll have it flowing out of me and keep some for breakfast, each one bigger than the last, good as a bull, hurt me if you can, I'm eighty-one you rotten little sneak I should tan your bottom, oh help, how strong, mercy, ooh, delicious, all spurting it out for me me me me and I can't have enough, I'm slopping around in it, lovely, see the hairs coming like goats their legs already thick with hairs, they've got no shame, look at this one's balls hanging like a black fig and his thing as thick as my wrist, whose son are you then? You're better than your father was and your grandfather for that matter, I've had them all. Why don't you bite me? why don't you come back when you're seventeen and kill me with it? Now don't you try putting it in my mouth you pig, I'm going to drink you up for breakfast in my own time, you make me cry, those long eyelashes you evil thing and your spotty face. You want to come again, you'll have to wait your turn. But no man's big enough to give me satisfaction. As for boys, don't make me laugh. Here take a jewel for doing what you could. How much have I had so far: a hundred boys of fifteen years, a gallon is it? Twice each and no one failed, raped by children, raped by grandnephews and grandchildren, a jug filled up with their two hundred children, children's children, and I'm to drink the lot instead of eggs and bacon in the morning, you think I won't but I will I'll taste them all, they've broken my back for me and still I haven't had enough. What a bitch that woman is, the cow of a thing. I'll make her hop before I've finished with her.

Miss Bertha McAloon inspected her soggy fingers with their mauve nails and swollen joints. She floated on her back, one hand held up close to her face. The water framed her in a dozen concentric circles of yellow and silver, a dear old picture of time past. There was nothing above her and nothing below, the rain raining upwards and downwards. Untouched, she dipped her hand back like an article she had decided not to purchase and resumed the Bertha McAloon stroke.

She is revered for her wisdom, disciples come from the Himalayas that's correct to visit her cave at Whitey's Fall, she can't even ask the time without it sounding profound. And yet she's so beautiful she has to caress her arms all day and her legs too. All over herself she strokes freely feeling the firm soft beauty of what she is, while she says these things that bring the disciples and keep them listening. And this puts rubberlips Madam Brinsmead's nose out of joint and no mistake. Not before time, the whore. Professors come to learn what she knows, and she doesn't even have to try, doesn't need to think even, but out come the sayings they'll be turning into hymns a thousand years from now. She dresses herself in light, wears it like a fashion, swathed around her in lengths. No one would touch. Too holy. They get the idea. Naturally I'm pure as far as that goes; moral, must be, especially with Indians who set such store on being gentlemen and do it so well. Sir I cannot let you touch me, not so much as the hem of my garment, but do please show me how you lie down on a bed of nails, I admire you for looking so relaxed and breathing easy the way you do. Up your bum Felicia Brinsmead if you think you can read my thoughts! She's got her own secrets, never you mind. You hear her calling that dog of hers, you hear the silly devil calling Fido Fido, but who has ever seen the dog? I wouldn't go so far as to say she's drunk oh dear no, just raving bonkers more likely. If you ask me she's dosing herself up with whatdoyoucallit, that drug stuff. She's not all there at times, young Felicia isn't, I'd testify to that, screw loose, nutty as a fruitcake, your Worship.

Into the clayey pool the new rain rained gently, blurring boundaries, also the world: an open egg where Miss McAloon lay contemplating the life to come. It would be a crass mistake to say that more than half a century ago she'd married Arthur Swan and borne his child. Even worse to say she'd been cast off by him because he never loved her. Lies, hideous slanders. Who ever said such things? Also that she'd wept and crawled, begged and screamed. Snap out of it. She was Miss Miss Miss McAloon proud daughter of Paddy and Nell. Paddy whose head was filled with the Mabinogion and all those dreadful stories of people being right and wrong, perhaps because his own father had been a strict bigamist; and Nell Swan the aunt of Arthur and mistress of two languages, who could recite the 'Idylls of the King' and could give 'The Ode to a Nightingale' backwards from finish to start. And of course of course Bertha had a talent of her own a dreaded malforming possessive lumpish talent which filled her with shame so she'd sooner disown it when she could, when it let her, but she never could forget. Not to mention her own child too, the steamy embraces of her son George who hadn't the gumption and wouldn't revenge her when she wanted, ached for, revenge. The avenger slopping in a tin bath of suds, the games and the catapults. Possible. So that she'd whisper why do you think I named you George? And now I'll tell you the story, Saint George is your very own saint and his job was to save this lady in distress and kill this dragon, see. Oh yes, Bertha fed her son and nourished him so he'd grow strong, she made him sleep outdoors to toughen him up, she supervised his exercises with a copy of *The Sandow Technique* and had imported a Sandow chest-expander for his sixteenth birthday while she dreamt of his father floating in a pool of blood, an axe in his skull, or writhing on his promiscuous bed with the cord being tightened relentlessly round his sweaty neck, or howling into space as he fell from the top of Whitey's Waterfall where the boy had picked him up bodily, lifted him above his head and flung him to justice, or broken his spine across his knee like that, snap. But what had she got? Bloody George the dumb ox who wouldn't know a good revenge if it stabbed him to death. Sneak thief of her love and trust, letting her build such hopes of peace all for nothing, who went round at the age of fifty would you believe boasting that he'd learnt to ignore his father. That's the *last* thing. I want you to hate him, to murder him, to see the lifelong injustice of these years I've suffered and watched. Does it mean nothing to you that he sleeps with every woman but his lawful wife your mother? Does it mean nothing that he abandoned us to our own devices when you were a little boy, to survive as best we could while he went trumpeting round the countryside on his bullock dray, on his truck, on his bus, skiting about his fame so you'd think they'd

238

put him in the *Guinness Book of Records* for sheer bloody stamina and for a champion liar too, I hope? Does it mean nothing that all the years since your marriage to that idiot Rose I've lived in a cowshed nobody wanted, when I should have been in a palace by rights? I've given you everything, but what do you give in return? You owe me this. There's only one thing I want and I want it. I'm living for it, that's why I won't die, and I won't die till I get it. Yet you don't give it to me. You dare to mention my talent as if it's public, like a toilet anyone can visit and piss in. I'll shoot you God support me, see if I don't. Anybody comes snooping round'll know what to expect from me. Talent. Dirty word, another failure too. You don't get out of it that way, because I remember. And I even told you straight – George I wish you'd kill your father. Him, you had the gall to answer, sometimes I feel like doing it too! Well why not, why not for heaven's sake get on with it? Has he got to lie down before you'll step on him! It's forty years since I gave you your axe and sent you across to Ping's to learn how to keep it sharp. Have your brains addled or something? Then your Uncle Kel taught you to shoot straight, I sold my milker to buy you your rifle but what did I get for it apart from ten years' free supply of rabbits? The Lord is my witness George you turned out to be a worm. And don't dare talk to me about your own layabout son, that's a sore subject, he's the worst poison of all, hanging round his grand-father like a lovesick cow, with a tell me this and a tell me that and a how does the other and why and when and what does it mean granddaddy. Disgusting. Whose fault is it? Whose fault could it be but yours and your silly mouse Rose's. Don't ask me what put it in your head to marry her when I wanted an ally who'd urge you on, to shame you for wearing a heart so white, a fierce big giant of a woman not afraid to mess her own hands with the blood, I wanted an Amazon and you brought me Rose! I wanted her to be strong enough to educate her son in case you failed me. But she tricked you, she's smarter than you, she made young Billy love him, she did it because she's a mouse and afraid of me. I should poison your dog and I just might come and shoot the horse to teach you. I'd sooner have anything happen to them than have this happen to me, that's for sure. Where is there justice to be had? What does it all mean? Don't talk to me of my bloody talent, I've given it up. Fat compensation!

Peacefully she paddled herself about in the gentle rain, somebody's mother, somebody's granny, enjoying the warm clayey water of a dam, humming and mumbling, propelling herself forward.

BOOK FOUR

Tree-felling

One

The trees of Whitey's Fall have gold in their sap that rises from the deepest taproot to fountain in leaf-veins sparkling at the wind, tantalizingly out of reach like the laughter of people. But not beyond Mr George Swan who traps as much laughter as he can, burns it in a crucible and collects the precious metal from a long retort. Laughter is not frequent in his house, especially the day he plans to fell the tallow tree until (because felling is the most risky and thrilling vandalism) his own golden laughs escape him and flock freely home to the mountain.

This venerable eucalypt, standing further south than is generally allowed these days, acts as cornerpost for hilltop paddocks not far from a farmhouse at Wit's End. Blossoming in season, the tiny flowers cast out gold dust with their pollen. On hot days cattle gather under this tree and wait for the intelligence to be bored. Even on a spring afternoon like today, the sunshine throws down an immense shadow on dust milled by patient hooves, with the aplomb of a Brinsmead casting a lace cloth across a round table.

One knee in the dust, the other on the body of a chainsaw, Mr George Swan sweats. For the twentieth time he pulls the starter-cord and the motor stutters dully. A leaf twirling down touches him on the shoulder. Mr Swan squints up at the tree.

Looking towards the south, the township of Whitey's Fall, tucked in against the mountain, appears two-dimensional. The houses have no depth, their faded grey timbers are silvery layers of gloss applied to a painted mountain; and the mountain road wriggles away in a flicker of the artist's wrist.

The chainsaw bursts into life, its hideous rasp reeling out across the valley into the verge of forest. As the blade touches the trunk, pale woodchips gush from its edge and two eagles launch themselves from their platform of broken branches in the crown of the tree with an alarm impossible to detect beneath the cry of their menacing dignity. The eagles wheeling in a wide arc watch and they are not alone in this, the sound of the motor has brought to the open doorway of the house someone who stops there, hands in hip pockets, restraining his disgust. He looks up and, following an eagle eye, knows he must face this out.

Mr George Swan completes the sleeve-cut. This is the end of the tallow tree. Little nodules of that oily wood so often worn from steps and thresholds form a heap round the destroyer's boot. He too knows he is being watched. He wants to smile, surprised at his simple pleasures. He swings the spinning saw away and shouts at the house.

– You better clean yourself up hadn't you?

The person in the doorway seems not to have heard.

The blade makes a diagonal cut and a wedge of wood falls out. The eagles circle. The motor, a magnified version of the ever-present flies. Then the blade bites into the other side of the trunk, a little higher up. The watcher has to admire the judgment of this cut: already they know where and how the tree will fall. The blade slices deeper into the noise. Mr Swan withdraws it hastily and steps back with an agility which calls attention to itself in a man his age.

The tonnage of this tree is now weighed in air. The familiar shape tips slightly so that you see what it is for the first time: a miraculous solution of balances. The eagles levitate as the nest of their generations sways, wind combing out a few loose twigs and the most intimate places being shown in a strange light. The mandala of shadow slides rippling across the ground to mutate into the outline of a family tree.

The man in the doorway scans the stiff brittle tallow and then tries to read the message the eagles spell out on the sky. His father stands back, happy from his handiwork, hearing the leaves rush, the branches tear helplessly at nothing, crashing bone-like and skeletal, no longer sensitive. The tree lolls on the ground, its severed trunk kicking up once. Under that impressive ruin the eagles' nest becomes a paltry heap of rubbish fit for burning. The eagles themselves already see things differently, searching the catastrophe for prey. As they float round, each checks that its mate is unharmed, the hooked beaks again tender. The saw is switched off. Silence paints the foreground into the same picture as the mountain. Mr George Swan drags his forearm across his brow, collecting the sweat.

– You better clean yerself up hadn't you? he repeats.

No reply from the man in the doorway who takes his hands out of his pockets. The tree lies exactly as hoped, but posing an inconvenience all the same. Mr Swan blames himself for a fool. He glares at the man watching him, his bugger of a son, Billy, who won't be told. The father pulls a tobacco pouch from his shirt pocket, extracts a flimsy cigarette paper from a packet, holds it between pursed lips. For a moment it flutters there, a frail apology. Then he rubs the tobacco, lifts the paper off his lip, rolls them together, licks the gummed edge and seals it. The noise of his match striking can be heard from the house. The first luminous trickle of blue smoke shapes in the air a miniature ghost of the tree.

This is the complete picture as it was.

– What you do, said Mr Swan, is your business I suppose.

He touched his saw blade between finger and thumb, quickly, assessing the metal's heat.

– It was getting to be a danger, that bastard, he added.

They knew this to be a lie. The tallow had attained only its first maturity. The gap between them seemed too far, but the quiet desultory comments carried clearly. Meanwhile, beyond, the mountain fleshed itself solid, lifted its peaks more remote, the rock an aged blue with blue wrinkles: shedding enough air to drown the two human figures.

– What's the strength of me getting married? Billy demanded remembering Uncle explaining, You grab a hold of him and say what's in this marryin shit for you.

The flies drew puzzles of straight lines between them. Mr George Swan, who had not expected a direct challenge, pulled at his cigarette, deeply. When he spoke again, each syllable came as a puff of smoke.

– Looks like her car, coming up the track.

They watched the car shimmering with sunlight followed by a drift of dust almost catching up with it.

– What's in it for you is what I want to find out, Billy insisted so that his father should know the expression of his eyes, even without bothering to look.

– Always wide of the mark, you are. Like that weird stuff in the pub, it's not normal; drunk out of your minds, standing round having DTs, and Baggy Brindle leading it. Fair makes my stomach turn. No wonder your mates cleared out.

The cigarette smoke drifted up in a succession of four more tree-ghosts before the visiting car turned at the gate and rattled in across the cattle grid. George Swan mopped his brow again, preparing to receive a young lady on behalf of his son. The car stopped in a haphazard manner, the driver puzzled by a great tree across her track. She switched off the motor and bounced out decisively enough, her hair also bouncing and her nice plump breasts bouncing too, her hazel eyes smiling, her free hand waving, her engaged hand tugging at an unwilling handbag.

– Have you cut the tree down Mr Swan? she asked.

– Yes. Yes I have.

– Hullo Billy.

Billy returned the greeting defensively, having nothing against her except she was stupid and his father wanted him to marry her, no doubt because she'd inherit a farm soon. She wanted the marriage too. Bad luck.

– What a mess, she exclaimed. Sooner you than me clearing

it up. She swung her bag over her shoulder in a slangy television version of what it's all about.

Bill despised her vulnerability. She was one of those people who just miss. Somebody had told her once she was a bright little thing and a ball of fun and Lord help the boys when she grew up; and He had. She was twenty-two and not a serious prospect. All the fault of Yalgoona, dead hole with its four thousand dreary inhabitants at an altitude of two hundred and twenty feet above sea level. Mr Swan picked up the chainsaw, resting its weight against his thigh so it stuck out in front of him, an absurd penis wavering as he advanced towards the visitor. Bill stood back against the open door to invite her in, but his gesture was spoilt by his mother making her appearance and coming out. Mrs Swan scurried down so as not to be caught up on the stairs. With seven skips she reached her proper level, where she paused meekly.

– Oh I do like your hair! she said and started forward to reach up to touch it.

– I just had it done, the girl bowed with pleasure.

– She never lets us down does she? Mrs Swan turned meaningfully to her son but he had his back to her and was slouching in along the corridor.

– She never does, the father filled in for him, hoisting the heavy chainsaw and pushing it on to the verandah floor.

Suddenly Mrs Swan clapped her tiny hand over her mouth. She closed her eyes to shut out the sight of the fallen tallow.

– So you did it after all? she whispered.

– You didn't hear!

– I heard alright. But I never imagined.

– Progress is progress, Suzanne Jessop was inspired to say.

– I never liked that tree, Mrs Swan commented, making her own doubts smaller than anybody else's.

They all three looked at it as people will stare at something new.

Once indoors, the parents indulged themselves by referring to Billy and Suzanne as that collective phenomenon You

Youngsters: you youngsters don't appreciate how easy life is these days – so you youngsters go and amuse yourselves while me and your father get a bit of work done – why should the youngsters have to put up with our oldfashioned opinions Mother – you youngsters can please yourselves but the scones won't be ready for another quarter of an hour – you youngsters take too much sugar in your tea for your own good it's bad for your teeth but what's the use of telling you – youngsters your age believe everything the television tells you – you young ones ought to take more interest in politics for the sake of the Country Party – you youngsters had schooling laid on like water out of a tap, if it had been like that in our day we'd have shown you a thing or two ...

Billy was ashamed for the girl's sake that his parents allowed their designs on her to be so transparent, and by doing it in this manner seemed to implicate her as a conspirator.

– I nearly forgot, Suzanne exclaimed, digging in her handbag and pulling out a long white envelope. The Post Lady asked me to bring this up to save her the drive, it was the only one for Whitey's Fall. As she handed it to his father, Billy noticed a government crest stamped in glossy blue print. Even Mrs Swan couldn't help being surprised when he stuffed it unceremoniously in his pocket with only the briefest mumbled thanks, instead of ripping it open in an economy of self-importance. Not long afterwards, Mr Swan offered excuses and went to clean himself up, as he put it, showering away the last clues of sawdust from his hair. He returned smelling ostentatiously clean, in a fresh shirt with his going-out trousers and a pair of felt slippers. So he was ready for tea and scones, ready to set an example.

– Shall we have a hand of euchre then? asked the mother as a plea when the afternoon tea things had been cleared away and the thick brown cloth smoothed over the table once more. She protected her husband from ever suspecting she was a far better player than he was.

– You youngsters can play us oldies then, George Swan conceded as he assumed his privilege of shuffling and dealing first. I'll carry you, Rose.

– Hold your cards up Bill dear or I'll see.

– Pass.

– Pass.

– I'll order it up, said Bill promptly, looking his father in the eye, seeing his father as his father was: a short healthy man with brilliant blue eyes, boyishly curly hair, definite features, a man of sixty, his face too angrily frustrated to look disappointed, one of those people who live to work tomorrow. He sat there, George Wilkinson Swan, shackled by duty, glancing at the clock on the wall to check that time still cheated him. He was a man of principle, a Presbyterian without religion, who boasted that alcohol had no more passed his lips than day-dreaming crossed his mind. He found his son looking at him from above a fan of cards. The look he received was boldly questioning, the look he gave back was defiant and inquisitorial. He tucked his chin down against his neck.

– You would! he growled, annoyed at anyone stealing the initiative from him. Diamonds it is then, he instructed them in case they hadn't followed. Cards were played: Mrs Swan's artful indecision, Suzanne Jessop's bemusement, Billy's gambling for higher stakes, and his father's torment as if each card played were his own hand lopped off. Poor Mrs Swan did what she could to rescue his luck with a succession of fumbling masterstrokes.

– Will we win a march? asked Suzanne excitedly.

– You won't win anything unless you put down a card, Mr Swan complained. She giggled at the possibility of a joke. She looked over her endless succession of numbers, knowing that it was normal to enjoy cards, yet the hateful jack of diamonds challenged her with those bulging thyroid eyes. She stared at the numbers searching for some obvious move to stand out, and herself as the queen of spades flipping through movie journals for young filmstars she could bite.

– The ace of spades! Billy groaned tolerantly so that she pretended not to hear. Mrs Swan trumped it.

– That's a trump you know, her husband told her.

– It's our trick is it? the little lady darted her bright mouse look, sure her astuteness had not been detected. You only made a point then, she remarked quietly as she gathered the pack.

249

– Next time they order us up we'll euchre them Rose. You just keep on fluking this winning form. That'll teach them. Good as ever, he declared tapping his head.

While his wife bungled the business of shuffling and dealing, George Swan glanced out of the window and saw pure sky. He sat looking in the direction of Venus, his blood turning to glass. This window he had known all his life, framing the obscure sky, shattered through him and the tallow tree had gone. He had created this blank. Energy surged back, causing his chair to creak. And as he met his son's eyes he knew the connection.

Billy grew uncomfortable, a meaning in the exchange of looks which he didn't like and last saw when Elizabeth Macarthur pushed him off his farm and he had to take to the bush as a shepherd.

– Pass.

– I'll order it up, Bill said because to be passive was to die.

– You sure you know what you're doing? his father demanded, spurring his horse and marshalling the mistress's rouseabouts around the only water on the property. One more move and we'll nail yer.

Suzanne took her teeth out of Warren Beatty tasting her new knowledge of his ankle to glance from Billy to his father and float back on the undercurrents she could smell in their strong male odour. She set Robert Redford beside her fiance-to-be. They were punching each other with vicious whacks. Her admiration of Billy was reduced to momentary distaste by a little roll of snot in his nostril, hanging there among the black hairs. This is silly, she told herself, refusing to let Redford deliver the final knockout, it could happen to anyone. But it showed her things in Billy's face she wasn't prepared for. She had the rigours of marriage.

– We'll euchre them this time for sure Rose.

– I don't say I can George, she looked very timid and willing.

So the game progressed. Mrs Swan put her side well in front. Her husband's cleverness became author of the entire game – Your play Bill – Now you Mother – Mother– Hope you've got the ace for your sake – Cop a load of this – You're holding us up Rose – Look lively with a club Suzanne – Isn't anybody going

to take up the trick? – Me is it? – *Now* you play it! – Your deal
Mother – Your lead Bill – How am I supposed to make head
or tail of that for a lead? – Stone the crows! – Play up young
lady – You youngsters want to be glad we're not playing for thousands – One more round and then we'll finish ...

So the game was over, the youngsters routed, the blank sky
in the window touched with a hint of pink when an eagle floated
into that empty frame. More tea was brewed, Suzanne sighed an
admission that she'd better go home, Billy at last blew his nose,
Mrs Swan sat down every time the others stood up and Mr Swan
carried his cold chainsaw to the shed, Bill and the guest went out
to look at the ruined tree, some beast bellowed remotely from
the direction of Whitey's Fall.

– See that little house just this side of the pub, said Billy
becoming companionable now the visit was at an end. Well that's
where my grandfather lives.

Smiling happily into a haze of shortsightedness, she couldn't
even make out Whitey's Fall itself. All she could see was the
mountain hunching into a pointless blue sky. But she nodded,
proud of Billy's keen sight. Though she wanted to stay she knew
what was expected and bounced out to her car, her pretty face,
her pretty plump breasts, her eyes smiling through the windshield,
her firm little hands on the wheel, she was a creature being
hounded to Antarctica, and away she drove, drawn to the glacial
loneliness of her own bed, her teeth aching with recriminations,
her heart fair set for failure.

They waved till her car ratcheted out across the cattle grid.
Mrs Swan said what a sweet girl. Bill said nothing.

– You seem to get on well with her dear, Mrs Swan made
another try, her eyes on the fallen tree and her voice suggesting
the world was getting out of hand. I always think it's so unfair
that the ones with most to give get treated unkindly, she observed
seeming to speak of others.

– Pleasant afternoon that, Mr Swan remarked.

– Is it her father's farm? said Bill.

Mrs Swan disappeared into the kitchen.

– You listen to me for once, his father counter-attacked.

Sooner or later you've got to grow up. And that means having principles. You can't just please yourself and to hell with everybody else in this world and if you try you'll be sure to regret it in the next so you've got to know right from wrong and I've been meaning to have a man-to-man yarn with you for some time now about the way you're going and the life you're leading hanging around the pub with fellows like those McTaggart twins when everybody knows what's said about them not to mention young Paul Buddall ...

– Maggot!

– Who's a proper crook caught thieving I don't know how many times. You see his kind on the news. He'll end up in court and so will you if you don't wake up to yourself. You're nineteen now for God sake. Bloody good thing when that crew packed their bags. As for you you ought to be thinking of the future or you'll turn out a no-hoper too, you've only got to look at your grandfather.

– Uncle!

– Don't tell me I don't know about my own father, shouted Mr George Swan. It's because of him my mother went mad. Cadging drinks at the Mountain, that's my father and I'm ashamed to say it. Not to mention the punishment in the hereafter. You'll never have to be ashamed of me.

– If I thought I could be like Uncle I'd be laughing.

– I wouldn't be in his shoes when it comes to facing our Maker. And I'm not being damned for bringing up my son like that. Me and your mother discussed it.

Billy stared at the wreck of the tallow tree, smelling the fragrant sap. The mountain shaped itself expectantly. He could hear Uncle talking about him a couple of miles away. He could imagine how he'd describe all this to Vivien over a meal of home-shot rabbit.

– I don't believe you, he said quietly.

– So we've come to this! his father raged.

Bill faced adulthood in the clear nothing of a parent's eyes.

– So we've come to this, his father repeated. You'll spend your life in the gutter, you bloody little drunk.

252

Mr Swan had gone too far. Billy, fury coursing the hot young blood, the war of Jenkins's ear, punched him a single jolting smack on the cheek. Mr Swan struck back with the joy of a man liberated from doubt. Poised on the brink of their first communication, at last they were to find pleasure in one another. Billy feared this was an intimacy he might never escape. His bunched fist white with readiness, he saw how easily he could be trapped into love and strove to check himself, stop. Clenching his jaw he mastered his temper, head shrieking with memory, breath hissing in his flared nose. Mr Swan as a matter of principle waited to be hit again so he could have his turn giving him another. But Bill had the curb on and did not crack. One look in his father's eye and he would lose his advantage, they'd fight to a standstill because neither would give in.

So Bill flung off into the house with a few mumbled words to his mother to say he was going. Then who could imagine he meant leaving, that night, going to live with a foreign whore? Shortly before dawn he went out to his motorbike, filled the saddlebags and strapped a bundle on the pillion. His parents lay in their bed, painfully awake with starlight, the three lumps of furniture leaning against the wall, uncomfortable at a family squabble. Mr George Swan and Mrs Rose Swan his wife, a home-made quilt pulled up to their chins, eyes alert in immobile faces, holding their breath, concentrated on what their singing ears told them; guessing, tensed ready to leap out of bed and stop the boy with promises of chocolates and lullabies. The dark blood of the dead weighed them down. The motorcycle tyres crunched the gravel by degrees, powered by slow footsteps, until they rolled on to the soft dust of the track. Two thousand heartbeats later, quarter of a mile away, the machine kicked into life, revved and sang, a single knife of sound drawn continuously through the flesh, a sibilant screeching that faded into the warm bath of oblivion. The echoes in a stone ear rasped on and on. They lay, rigidly alert, ceremonial figures of the futile King Henry VI and his lady wife on a tomb in a forgotten decaying church. Clothed in respectability, naked in grief, embalmed in the perfume of defeat and deserved neglect. Had the cry finally gone? Was the pain past repair? The dying whine of the motorcycle tightened round their necks.

Then a voice broke the spell, shockingly near and human. Mr George Swan's wife speaking on her own account.

– You were wrong George.

He lay deciding, his stone eyes closed against the starlight. Five minutes later the dawn crept into his hand, her five fingers meshing with his. He would certainly kill her, he said. The years grew green stems and their flowers exploded into nothing. His hand curled round hers gently. And outside, another branch of the felled tree gave under the strain as the trunk settled closer to earth.

Two

The only tallow-wood left in the district was a stunted specimen in Brinsmeads' back garden. In the late evening its shadow stood fully printed on a blank wall of overlapping timbers. Inside, the imprisoned Fido stage-whispered *miserable miserable* so he'd be heard in the shop and rescued. He discovered the tallow only when testing the peephole Uncle Sebastian drilled for him. Eye to the hole, squinting and wanting it to be good, his mind filled up with dusk, the purple-stained grass, a feathering of shadows complicated and delicate, a collapsed shed, and one tree burning in dead sunlight.

– That shed, his mother explained intruding as far as the den door, is the whole idea. You're to watch for something to happen.

He expected a helicopter landing, a squad of terrorists crawling out on their bellies dragging a millionaire tied up and held hostage for ransom.

– You're to call and warn us, said his Uncle from the kitchen.

Fido stayed silent in his private submarine. The memory of the garden fluttering through him. Then he saw, miraculously printed on his wall opposite the peephole, a play of shadows, tones he recognized, the violet, the musk, and down near the floor the complex tree: the garden world seen upside down. The delicate mirage laid its gauze over every grain of the wood. Fido sat mesmerized inside his camera. His heart stopped so he wouldn't spoil the photograph. When he applied his eye to the hole again to check, he unscrewed his fountain pen, he wrote in his diary:

Gold is mauve

Green is red.

He winked the peephole-eye to try it out and see if it had turned a different colour. Still the same. Once, lying on his tummy in the shop on a Sunday, he'd seen through the letterflap a boy with one eye blue and one eye brown, which made him afraid. He put the other eye to his new peephole to even things up, so if one changed they'd both change. He was a spy. People with guns tiptoeing round corners. Ha ha. Fido accused the room, even so I could blow you all up the way I hate you. And when he opened the wardrobe too, the crazy mirror cast thirty silver scales around his face. He slammed the door so the little dangling brass handle jittered. He exercised as usual, heaving the heavy cases around, touching his toes and doing some rapid push-ups, the heroic survival of his healthy body in these cramped conditions. He smoothed his pale perfect skin admiringly.

Smell those newspapers. Papers in the passage, papers in here. What you don't know Mummy is that I've been reading them. Love the murders, love the weddings, how people stick the knife in when they can't bear it any longer, and how they dress up and throw stars on one another and have their photograph taken and their mothers cry.

What if some spy the other side tried looking in through this hole? Would he see the bed? No, I'm glad. Only my train set plus the museum. Got a V.C. for sleeping on a box of dynamite. Bullets in the pillow. Ssh. Must shift that chest of drawers, if the spy fired one shot the whole place might go up when I'm not ready; can't get a grip on it; that's better, over here. Three doses of thirty push-ups tomorrow. My muscles are twelve inches but I don't know if that's good. I feel strong enough to smash through the wall with my fist. You wouldn't be able to see the bed no matter how you worked your eye around. No, except the mountain sees. Once I asked my mother for a room that didn't look out this way, but she was cross and said she had no patience with nonsense and the mountain was the one thing I must learn to see. As if I couldn't see it all the time. It moves. When I looked before lunch it was like being in bed with my mother, the mountain settling herself to sleep. Sometimes I've seen it pink and I remembered Amsterdam and that art gallery, I said to the man in uniform Rubens is the only artist who truly makes me sick. The other day I decided to put people on the mountain but I can't be sure if this worked. Whenever it moves too close I get scared and ask it to be the usual old thing. That mountain is out to get me.

Pictures of my father's saints, all face to the wall, spiders sew them there and I haven't looked for ages. The Tropics painted on their backs by me myself, where I'll live when I escape so I can feel big butterflies on me and the sun for my museum. Who cares. Two hundred different coloured cockroaches and not enough pins for them. Impossible. Do they want to be caught? Perhaps they fall in love with the ones stuck on my board. Suitcases, awful empty drums, some of these I've carried on a Sunday when the foreign people are shut away in churches, cases full of things for the opera and swimming.

One day I'll tie up my parents and run away while they're calling for help and they'll have the bruises I've given them. Then I'll put all my dynamite together and blow up the mountain. We'll see if it's made of gold or not. I'm a prodigy. The policeman will come and be my friend, he'll say they deserve it and let that be a lesson.

I've got to find a way under the icecap and this sub can sail for months. It has been done before, it can be done again. Brains. We'll go down now: submerge the ship, pass me the periscope, sea's all dark and especially that big shadow under water, that is the flagship I'll have you know. Ay ay, sir, all ready, don't move a finger you men till I give the order, action stations, but quiet as a mouse, no one knows we are here, they're in for a shock, O boy are they in for a shock, we've got them in our sights we can't miss, helmsman hold it like this, on course, there's a lot of stuff to go up in this bang, I can tell you. Keep your eyes skinned.

Three

One day no one in Whitey's Fall had heard of the new highway. The next day the whole population crowded up the hill to stop it coming any closer. Jasper Schramm locked the hundred doors of his Mountain Hotel with a hundred keys and set out to join his neighbours. Afloat on a Sargasso known only to the brotherhood of drinkers, rocked by profound depths of bitterness, the green regions writhing where octopuses made tangled love, negotiating obstacles here and there in the empty street, he pursued them carrying his own time scale with him, plus an emergency flask of scotch.

The names of the people there included the Collinses complete, some of the Langs and McTaggarts, all the Buddalls, the McAloons, a few Swans and of course the surviving Brinsmeads with the exception of Fido who did not yet officially exist, to the number of forty-one of the forty-nine residents. The matriarch of the McAloon family, Nell, at one hundred and fourteen, wife of the legendary Paddy and mother of the legendary Bertha, moved to the divan on her porch to declare herself with them in spirit, daft as she was; there she reclined wearing her quilted skin for the great occasion.

News of the highway had caused a calf at McTaggarts' to be

born with five legs during the night and now waiting to be shot. A party crammed on a dray had trembled up across the paddocks: Felicia recognizing the sight as Medusa's head neck-deep in a green wave, bristling serpents. Men presumed dead emerged from a mineshaft high along the ridge to join the protest. These mountain folk stood in the gap newly gouged out of their mountain, their faraway eyes searching for the familiar horizon. Trees swayed either side of them and crashed into a fresh grief before huge, grinding machinery clanking massive steel plates.

Mum Collins remarked that this was the first time the whole town had turned out since that amnesty for draft evaders and deserters when the population of the district met the crown officers halfway, the men eager to be on the list of pardons and their women eager to see them there. Only to discover it was for the wrong war. So impressed were the officials that the amnesty was extended to cover them all. This is how it became generally acknowledged in Country Women's Association branches throughout New South Wales that Whitey's Fallers could handle the Queen Elizabeth's men. These same defiant people exercised their cracked voices despite the angry warnings of bulldozer drivers, like black cockatoos in a storm with the air already thundering around them. Ponderous machinery lumbered in tight circles pushing heaps of dirt, puffing out balls of black smoke, lifting scoops of rock, and stinking of burnt oil. Then, weaving its dextrous passage among them, a blue car came gliding along the smooth foundations of the highway. The driver parked it to one side and got out.

– That's the Honourable *I AM*, Uncle sneered as Senator Halloran approached. With a head too big for his Yankee hat.

– Good morning, called Felicia Brinsmead through the din, officially recognizing the visitor. Good morning Senator Neville Chamberlain. Have you brought your scrap of white paper?

The senator stopped, disconcerted.

– We have met you before, continued that lady at the top of her voice, her scabby bundle of hair nodding independently, patting her like a friend. You came here a few months ago trying to sell us paint to prettify our houses and cover the nasty symptoms of death. And now you've come to smash them down altogether so we hear.

– Ladies and gentlemen, yelled the senator deciding to ignore Miss Brinsmead rather than argue the point. I am pleased to have arrived in time.

– Last visit you arrived in time, Felicia screamed through the bombardment of noise, motors and crashing trees. To drive poor Mercy Ping off. The road to her death!

So then the locals paid him more markedly unfriendly attention than he might have hoped.

–... in time to reassure you, the senator persisted. Benefits will accrue. As a result of this highway. Whitey's Fall to live again. Does that mean nothing?

– Nothing, Sebastian Brinsmead confirmed.

Caterpillar treads squealed, engines throttled and lumps of the mountain lurched before blades as big as faith.

– People will come, the politician roared. New families. Will settle. Children. The school. Trade and money. The life will. Town. Saved, they heard him say.

The old people formed up into a choir of heavy breathers, confronting him in a manner calculated to arouse his anger.

– Our government, he made a fresh start, but the renewed din overpowered his attempts at persuasion. He gave up. If he had used this time to observe his antagonists he might have learnt a remarkable fact. The younger people still watched him. But the great majority of the old were dreaming, their eyes fixed blankly on something beyond. He could hardly suspect they were hypnotized by the cutting itself. At the bottom of the sheered rock a stratum lay bare as a straight black line. Gold. The roadbuilders, heads down, conscientiously doing a job, saw only the road they were employed to lay. And even when they switched off the giant motors and blinked at the sun, they were no nearer to knowledge. As the sounds of the mountain rushed in to cover the wounded silence, the politician seized his chance of finishing what he had to say.

– I know this leaves it rather late to explain the details of our regional development scheme in person, but I have been arguing your rights in the Senate for months. I want you to believe that. And finally the Commission authorized me, as one of your elected representatives for the State of New South Wales, to come in person and lay it out before you. You have nothing to fear. You wouldn't be protesting if you understood. It is a forward-looking scheme to help everybody and build for the future, for your kids and their kids.

Workmen, no more than lads too young for such responsibility, jumped down from the cabs of their crushers and levellers.

– This will put you on the map again, Halloran promised, a buttery tone intruding now he had freedom to play his instrument. The Buddalls, the McAloons, the Brinsmeads, the Collinses, the Schramms, the Langs, the Swans and the McTaggarts confronted him with their stubbornness. On the map, he repeated to emphasize their present obscurity. He was kindly disposed toward them and wanted them to be pleased. He was, after all, working in their interest, he represented an enlightened view. Mrs Collins stepped forward and fixed him.

– Tell me this then son. What *are* our interests?

– I'm sure they're of the same standard as everybody else's, he responded. Reforms to provide all the amenities necessary for the quality of life.

– Qualities, Mum Collins agreed promptly thinking of fullness of heart, loving children and good health God willing.

The workmen avoided looking any more, so as not to intrude on a funeral.

– Yes indeed, public services, Senator Halloran said into the very air they charged with awareness of the gold. His sermon was a flapping of seaweed tongues, a lunar riddle.

Mum Collins came back at him with her final dismissal.

– If you was two-faced, she said. You'd show the other one.

Vivien hung back, cautious about butting in. The senator's soft male hands which had enveloped her own on the afternoon the police came to take details of Mrs Ping's death strangled each other briefly. Fury and impatience were stamped on his every feature. He despised Mum Collins, whatever she was saying. Vivien felt a surge of anger against him, a protective energy on behalf of that darling old lady who'd been the first to make her feel welcome, then she noticed Billy struggling with electricity, she recognized jealously when she saw it and smiled faintly. Were her reactions to be interpreted by him? Because she had criticized Billy in public, she had no intention of consoling him now with an attack on his enemy, so she resisted the desire to rush over and take Mum Collins's part.

Birds flocked in to fill the empty air with wings.

– Miss Lang, the senator called, relieved for here was an educated person who could be his intermediary. Miss Lang would you please explain to these good folk how the new road will be a boon to them.

– The poor coot, Mum Collins whispered. He does try, you got to hand it to him.

– Will it be a boon Senator? Vivien asked.

The assembled Whitey's Fallers knew how she'd first met the government man to address him with such assurance. Next thing the workmen were gathering in conference just out of earshot, baffled by the idea that anybody might want to obstruct their job.

– The first prosperity for Whitey's Fall since the goldrush days. The business prospect will be very promising, petrol stations, more shops, a boost for the pub. You know what I think would go really well? An antique Devonshire tea shop.

– With us in it, Miss Brinsmead cried out.

– So that's an idea for you. And once things get going there'll be money for other projects. It can't fail.

– You don't need me to explain that, Vivien said lightly to disavow any right to an opinion.

– It seems this lady here thinks I do.

– I think nothing to do with you! Mum Collins fired back.

Mr Ian McTaggart slapped his stone thigh with a stone hand, dislodging a little fall of dust. The cobwebs across his lips stretched and tore as he opened his mouth.

– There's plants that eats vermin.

– Winnin form, Uncle cheered.

– We've never found a better life anywhere the world over,

Felicia Brinsmead declared, than we have here. And that's the bitter truth.

– I understand, ladies and gentlemen, the senator addressed them collectively more easily than he could speak to individuals. I understand that you're concerned for the future of your historic township. You are absolutely right. Please believe me when I tell you you have friends throughout the nation. Your government is concerned too, and that's what really counts. You may be sure we're doing what is best for you. I'd like you to think of this. We are bringing you a priceless gift: communication. Ecology is a web. This road will make you part of it. That is what these men here are doing, building for your benefit. You'll be put in touch with the rest of the country because the secret of communication is mobility. Let me cite the tragic accident on this ... murderous ... road so recently. Mrs Ping. You know what I mean. Tell them, Miss Lang.

– We know exactly, she answered in a tight voice.

What was that supposed to mean on a rainy Christmas, Uncle would like to be told. He shot a look at her, seeing her for the first time as someone unknown, possibly an enemy. Grief sucked the strength from him. He had to lean his whole weight on his walkingsticks. He'd trusted her as if she was Annie. But she was not Annie. A distant boom of dynamite sounded the approaching war.

Felicia concentrated on the meeting of roadmen, in case they might be discussing life in Acapulco or the Amsterdam diamond market. But no, they turned their backs on the motherlode of gold they had uncovered. Even so, she braced herself because they were now advancing in deputation order.

– Down with the amenities, said Sebastian Brinsmead and with the hauteur of a ruined Nordic hero set his face toward the mountain, snubbing the senator.

– Down with the government, the two Mrs Collinses agreed joyously.

– Walk gently on the land, Ian McTaggart warned the labourers.

Jasper Schramm shook his head to clear the confusions of half a century's peace of mind.

The people, the fat and the crooked, malformed hands dangling, ancient simple clothes, men's hats and women's hats, those doughy with age and those carved of worn wood, shuffled past the senator to meet the destroyer, raising puffs of dust and escorted by their squadron of miscellaneous pets, dogs, cats, a budgerigar (travelling on Mr McTaggart's head) plus a cow who ambled along on swollen ankles knowing perfectly well what to say when face to face with mountain wreckers.

Nobody knew what to say. Trembling and wheezing, they simply confronted the men. Still in a state of shock, they had reached the bend in the road bed, staring with disbelief at the mutilated land, the horrifying scope of destruction sweeping a hundred miles west over the range to the cities of the plateau. Vivien supported Mum Collins whose flesh caved and shrank from the impact. Even Senator Halloran's services were accepted by two ladies, burdening either arm. The cow, weighed down by the assayable gold dust in her milk, sat in the dirt with an unashamed sigh of relief. The foreman of works hitched up his shorts, pulled in his beer gut and stepped forward.

– Sorry folks you can't come any further on the site, he said mastering his astonishment, his laughter. It gets a bit dangerous up the way, what with the felling and the blasting and that.

– *We* can't? one of the locals roared in a cavernous bass, his tone not exactly conciliatory. On our mountain? What's your name?

– Milliner. Hughie Milliner. And all I ask . . .

– Milliner? Uncle took up the name, passing the criminal's identikit round for possible recognition. Anyone heard of it? I never have. No Milliners in this district. I used to do the mail run, what's more.

– Well I never lived here, Mr Milliner replied reasonably. My people's from Queensland. Up Biloela way.

– Queensland! Uncle was not convinced the panjandrumate existed.

– Never heard a Bill O'Wheeler neither, the publican spoke up, positive on this point.

– O'Wheelers is from another neck of the woods too then? Uncle suggested kindly.

The workmen closed ranks, large healthy specimens with friendly eyes, massed footballers confronting a team they don't have to play.

– Come on grandma, what's your problem? one of them laughed.

– How much for a drink of milk off of the cow? asked another.

Plainly it was time for Senator Frank Halloran to introduce himself, which he did, to whistles of approval from the less respectful elements among the road men.

– These are the people of Whitey's Fall, he explained. Luckily I arrived in time to join them and hear their point of view.

On being invited, Foreman Milliner squatted to make a drawing in the dust of where the highway would pass in relation to Whitey's Fall: right through it. He answered the senator's questions and expressed himself perfectly satisfied it could bring only good and become the greatest boon since gold. Uncle looked up sharply. Frank Halloran spread his large white hands, it was true, open and above board. The workmen prepared to amble back to their earth-moving equipment.

– You've had your say mister, Uncle stepped up in front of his party. Now I've got somethin of me own to put. We know one another, all us locals here. His gesture included his second cousins, his nieces, his grandson, his brother-in-law, his grand-nephew and his half-sisters. No amount of talkin is goin to fool us, he said.

– Good on you Uncle, shouted Billy.

– Good on you Uncle, other voices encouraged him. The cow added a weary moo.

– What's happenin here, said Uncle a fine anger burning him (you know what these old bush people are like). What's happenin here is a whole mob of outsiders and Hallorans, O'Wheelers, Milliners and Christ knows who, has come along with bulldozers to make a muck of good hillside that we don't want touched. No fancy words'll change the truth a that. My father, he shouted now to prevent the senator from interrupting, lies buried not far from here. And the grandfather too. I don't suppose many of yous young fellows would know who yer fathers was even, let alone where they was buried! These fighting words sent a tremor of delight through the defenders.

– Now you look here sport, a grader-driver advanced his menacing expression so that Tony pushed his way to the front to block the man's way. Uncle went on regardless.

– And if I was them I wouldn't want to own up to siring the likes of yous neether. That's a fact. Come bulldozin through other people's country. Haven't you learnt no manners? This is our bush up here. We always had it. We know every yard a this scrub we do. (You could see him trembling with rage; and inwardly he was also trembling with the premonition of defeat.) Now I've come with me mates to tell you somethin. We haven't come to be told. No, we're doin the tellin. We haven't come to be reassured about our fears like Senator Whatsit says. No. Speak for yourself Senator, or keep you mouth shut sonny. We know what's ours, we understand alright. If we don't talk it's because we got good manners and don't like tellin you what's in our minds.

The workmen, creatures of their machines, used to the isolation of high cabs, deliberate thinkers on the whole and unaccustomed to insults from helpless geriatrics, gaped angrily while Uncle concluded what he had to say.

– We come to tell you somethin in person. And this is it. Get off of our mountain. You done enough damage and more.

Mr Ian McTaggart sniffed disgustedly. In his opinion Uncle talked too much. As for himself, it was a point of honour not to blab. He turned his back on them and shuffled down in the direction of his garden, the bright blue bird sitting pertly on his head, all expectation.

– Let's be calm and discuss this thing, Senator Halloran suggested, looking them over, these tough flap-eared hairy-nosed coarse-skinned grannies, struck by the fact that most of them bore

266

marks of family resemblance, even the two ancient mongoloids (perhaps the oldest in existence) holding hands at the back. The exceptions were the publican with his face of a drunken cake from a cold oven, and the Brinsmeads set apart by their large aristocratic features, fine-boned cheeks and noses. He realized at this moment that the Chinese welder was not among the protestors, a fact which he filed for future use. He continued to lecture them.

– We're talking about growth and productivity. We're talking about tourism and maybe some non-polluting cottage industry.

– A boomerang factory? Miss Brinsmead suggested acidly.

– Now there's an idea. That's the spirit. The old days of isolation are finished. It's no good trying to crawl back into the burrow. Today's lifestyle depends on mobility.

– You've got to have mobility, the foreman of works agreed.

– Everybody owns a car these days and the country's opening up. The wonderful thing for you people in the bush is that you can continue to live in this beautiful pollution-free environment while also enjoying the benefits of city life, the extra sophistication, the money, the public services.

– It's the dust *I* reckon, Hughie Milliner contributed.

– Quite right, said the senator.

– When the road goes through you won't have all this dust in your tea.

– We've got to live with progress. Turning a blind eye is kidding yourself. The better the roads, the cheaper the transport costs on commodities like your everyday food.

– Don't say *Miss Brinsmead should know*, said Miss Brinsmead.

– Miss Brinsmead should know, Senator Halloran argued. The problem is that ...

He did not finish his sentence, for Miss Brinsmead, coughing her surprisingly girlish cough, fixed him with one of her fifteen expressions and dumbfounded him by announcing the angry thought coursing through his brain.

– You're still deluding yourself that we haven't understood. From his face you could tell this hit home. The trouble is, she went on, that though you've been elected to office, you haven't grown into it, you haven't related power to responsibility, nor perceived the opposition between the morality of dialectics and unprincipled passion. I dare say Mr Swan or Mrs Collins could teach you a few things if you knew how to listen. Instead of which you condescend to us, you persist in reassuring yourself that since we do not agree with you we cannot have understood.

Remember your history of campaigns, Julius Caesar advised her.

– That's right, she said. We understand with excruciating clarity Senator Greek. We know precisely what your wooden horse is worth. We will not be talked out of Troy. As Mr Swan so rightly explained . . . and do you understand him? . . . even if there were something to be discussed it would not be with you, nor with your bulldozers and your dynamite. We are the ones to say whether or not any discussion is appropriate and you already have our answer. Mr Swan (if he will forgive me for repeating him, and I only take this liberty because it seems we are dealing with a singularly obtuse class of person Mr Swan) has said we're here to tell you, not to be told.

The invader's principal weakness is that the soil will never be his, Julius Caesar confided.

– We're not here to have our fears allayed, Miss Brinsmead went on and her creaking hair agreed. We're asserting our rights. It's perfectly accidental that you are here today, you've done nothing for it except drive your vehicles. But we belong. We've made this place and been made by it, that includes those who hate it as much as those who love it. We won't accept that we've been sacrificed for nothing, you know.

Put a road through, Caesar explained. And you've changed the terrain.

– One can't damage this mountain without damaging us. We know you're sent by people who don't even want the bother of cutting their own bread. People who'll do anything for convenience; they don't want to drive up and down mountains, so you gouge a great slice out of the top thank you. Tomorrow they won't be willing to drive round corners, you wait and see.

A valuable weapon, Caesar explained. Is the envoy whose job

is to put the people's fears into words. Their ignorance is worth two cohorts and forty horses.

– We know who you represent, dispatched here to reduce us. Yes, creaked the good woman's burden of hair.

– This is what we have come to say. If you have sufficient intelligence to understand, all well and good. Otherwise, as I fear, there will be more to be said and in different ways . . . she allowed her voice to trail off, murmuring private fears. As for gold, she added an afterthought. You're crass enough to speak of gold as a boon. Watch out we don't put the curse on you. All you'll be left is stories to tell in the ruins.

– Yes madam and you seem to live by yours, he retorted, a touch of temper showing.

– Do you think you don't? It's just that our stories are more interesting. Even a mathematical equation is a story: $2x$ plus $3y$ over 5 equals the imprint of an elephant's foot in a controlled tray of sand. Ha ha, I'm with you you see.

During this speech she digressed to pick up objections as people thought them, slipped in a sketch history of Greek imperialism, plus a philosophy of gardening as model-perception of the land (Mr Ian McTaggart, she said, could verify her point), criticized obedience to orders and the performance of duties by those ignorant of their consequences. She opened her propositions to any objection, but it was she herself who listed alternatives and then refuted them. By the time Miss Brinsmead finished, as I've mentioned, with private mutterings that there would be more said *and in different ways*, the main party of Whitey's Fallers had already begun staggering homeward, finding the going even more exhausting than the climb, leaning back against the slope and tottering along in tiny steps. They had no call to stay, their point had been put.

– That Felicia, Mum Collins suggested to her neighbour, gets a bit carried away. Considering, I mean, he's a good-hearted swindler.

For Uncle, his eye on that vast mass of gold, more was needed. Into the bargain, speech-making came easier now without Ian McTaggart pursing his lips at so many words.

– Listen Senator I've got somethin else on me mind, son. A moment ago you was throwin round a few fine-soundin sentiments: prosperity wasn't it? and security? and progress? So what are they when you come down to it? Prosperity is nothin more nor less than greed. That's a fact. I know that one for sure. It's havin more than you need, so's you're not obliged to go on doin honest work. Correct me if I'm wrong won't you? What you call prosperity I call sin. We see your prosperous people up here time to time. Look at yourself; you're what you'd call prosperous. You took more thought this mornin to what you'd wear and how you'd make the right impression than how this would upset us. And what did you mean by progress? Don't be surprised if we're wonderin. It's progress I'm really wantin to tell you about. It's on account of progress I'm havin my say and I want this lad here to listen. I've had somethin to do with progress in my time. There's been a few outbreaks of it even up this way. My own son's one of them progress people. Silly as a rabbit. And young Tony's father, he's another. But I've never stood for a bar of it myself. Didn't I fight against the hospital? They wanted to put up a hospital here. I said home's good enough for the healthy it's good enough for the sick. We hadn't even got a blacksmith at the time and they wanted a hospital. Progress is a way of gettin you out of your homes when you're too sick to put up a fight, I said ... and chargin you money for it too. I fought the hospital when I was a young man and there was a lot more livin here than what we've got now. There used to be close on a thousand in Whitey's in them days. And another thing they wanted was an old people's home. I fought against that too. We won that one as well, and thank God we did. Imagine me or Miss Brinsmead here in an old people's home. We'd have been dead long ago, dead of a nasty bout of progress. Every time there's been plans and schemes to let us out of our family responsibilities, I fought em. I fought against the police station being set up. I did, I fought against school too, even though Mercy Ping was a little darling thing with the youngsters and gave them curry when they played up. By God she laid about them! I fought against the draft and I fought against any number a government johnnies like yourself. The school's the only time I ever lost out too. Mind you, it was never just me fightin: people here has always been against progress. Strong against progress. They're a good little community, no doubt about that. We wouldn't let them put away our old people, nor our sick people neether. And what did we need a policeman for? If anyone got out a line we'd soon put them straight to our satisfaction. There's always trouble when folks live together; no reason to shut bad ones away. We've got to live with them. They've got to live with us. That's it, isn't it? They're no more happy than we are about it. But prison's the worst thing you could think of, I shouldn't wonder. Now what you're callin progress is a new road. Right? A lot of fools killin themselves in fast cars, lot of fat people with full bellies complainin about being hungry; lot of empty heads gawkin at ordinary folk as if they was in the zoo; lot of empty hearts hoping to fill their lives with trinkets and souvenirs of where their cars have been driven through. Your progress means money. Noise. Stink. Death. Correct me if I'm wrong. We've lived here the way we've lived. Nobody's bothered us up until now. And this is the way we're ready to die too. I hope you've understood me. We deserve that: to die our own way. We're old. He slapped the blade of a bulldozer. Greed machine, he said.

Tony shuffled uncomfortably. This was all beside the point. He sensed the argument was not having any effect. He alone of the Whitey's Fallers could tell this was a mistaken approach. But he had no words of his own. And Bill stood nodding as if giving a public lesson in appreciation.

– We never asked anythin of yous, Uncle concluded. Don't want anythin. No good moanin it's too late, road's begun. It isn't finished is it? If you'd had the common decency to come and ask, we'd a told you we don't want the road in the first place. So you'd best arrange to take it another way. Just skirt round the bottom of our mountain. There's the T-ridge forks off north a couple of hundred yards from where we are right this moment. You could take your graders down that way.

– But this is wholly unreasonable! the senator burst out. For the past fourteen years we have been writing to you and never had a reply. Then two years ago we published the regional development scheme. It was discussed on television. It was in the newspapers. He allowed himself the luxury of a lapse into sarcasm – I suppose the papers do reach this far? You had ample time to lodge an appeal. No government could have been fairer. The Aesthetic and Historical Resources Commission wrote offering to restore your buildings.

–And my brother replied on our behalf to say no, said Felicia.

– Exactly, the only response we had. Which is why the Commission asked me to come and see you while I was in this area on that first occasion. Surely there you had proof if it was ever needed of the government's concern for you.

Billy joined the dispute.

– Did you do anything? he asked.

– About what?

– Well, you wanted to paint the place up. Mr Brinsmead wrote you a letter to say no. So what's happening?

– I can tell you, Senator Halloran answered this enemy with a lizardlike flicker of the eye which made Vivien loathe him as the sort of official Aunt Annie would attack with an umbrella. We noted that decision of yours. We regretted it, we thought you were wrong because it's not just up to you, this highway will serve the people of the whole nation, but we noted it. It's not simply a question of the selfish interests of one tiny town on the way; still, we accepted your decision for what it was worth. Then, of course, the other letter arrived and changed the complexion of everything.

– There was no second letter, Felicia said.

– Well this represented the views of other citizens of Whitey's Fall, the dissenting view you might say, or more properly the assenting view, he joked mirthlessly. To suggest we set up an impartial inquiry, a very sensible idea which we are in the process of implementing. If Senator Halloran felt uncomfortable while delivering this considered opinion, it was because that mad woman with the filthy hair was giving him such a peculiar look, eyes boring at his, examining the fine print.

– The letter, she said squinting to read the signature at a dis-

272

tance, is from George ... Uncle! she turned accusingly. It's from your George.

Temporarily the protestors were in disarray, baffled by George Swan's treachery, ashamed: Uncle of his son, Billy of his father, Tony of his uncle by marriage, Felicia of the boy who had once threatened her he'd bust in one night and find out all her secrets.

The mountain muttered and the gold pushed up to draw attention to itself.

– Leave him to us, Billy said grimly. His father had strained filial loyalty beyond endurance. He had actually written a letter to the government. A family would break over this, break permanently. The form of the tragedy was known and established long ago.

– I must say, Senator Halloran was speaking again. I'm more than a little surprised you'd have any reservations about the upgrading of a road that's a danger to you. Heaven knows we're all aware of the fatal accident on it recently. He looked from one wizened face to another, each void of expression, the eyes chinks of glass. What's more, he oiled their resistance. This village is a national treasure. You don't seem to realize what you have here. The asset, I mean. It's like the last surviving relic of the Empire, it really is a link with those days.

The irony of these words sang to Felicia, so she clapped her hands. Uncle snorted dismissively, fifty years ago a man in a morning coat had called him and his bullock cart a national treasure and had the opportunity to reconsider from the new perspective of being flat on his back in the muck. But the words didn't register with Billy, preoccupied, caught in the crosscurrents of how to disown his father, yes and he remembered Suzanne Jessop bringing an official envelope for him that day he felled the tallow-tree, remembered the crisp paper rammed into a pocket out of sight; then he thought of something equally uncomfortable, himself and his friends joyfully smashing Mr Whitey's empty place at London. If Milliner's men were vandals why not him and Tony?

The two old people accepted the matter as settled and in Billy's hands. They set off together, returning down the long track home, comrades-in-arms, not needing to talk, heads cocked for sounds a stranger couldn't hope to interpret. The deep strength they shared could only be guessed by those who knew how they hated each other, their relentless antagonism through the years to this moment.

– You told them Felissy, Uncle said eventually. You told them good and proper my dear.

– I saw it was gold, Felicia whispered with uncharacteristic caution. I can tell what you're thinking Uncle.

– And it was. They just got down deep enough with them machines of theirs. But considerin they don't know what to look for, and never guessed there'd be anythin worth lookin for, they just levelled her out and made her ready for the bitumen.

– Until somebody comes along who does know.

– I think, said Uncle fossicking in his pocket for his pipe. I think it's worth a punt. Keep their minds off what's under their feet, and they'll go ahead and cover it up for us.

– My lips are sealed.

– Somethin I been meanin to ask you about Felissy. That tobacco of mine. Did you ever track down the old brand? I'm gettin jack of this new scented muck.

– I hope to have good news for you, I can't say more than that.

– Well it was four years ago come Christmas I put me order in.

– I have always paid due respect to your virtues, Mr Swan, she countered chivalrously.

A storm of dust smothered them as the senator drove past tooting his horn and nodding nervously, mesmerized by the horrors of the surface he had to negotiate, but proceeding on their assurance that the track was clear right down to the town, his nice shiny car kangarooing across the bumps, slurrying in gulches, leaving a skirl of dust droning in their ears.

They stopped for a blow while the consequences of civilization abated. Uncle treated himself to a couple of well-rehearsed hawkings and spittings. Felicia watched him with ladylike composure.

He began to distrust his own optimism.

274

Thus Fido:

SECRET. Diary, this is what happened. You know I was going outside to find somebody, well I went today and it was horrible. Uncle S locked the shop and told me they'd be away for the day and to keep out of sight but I could play the radio quietly. I let them go because they may as well go for ever for all I care. So I got the idea the time had come and this might be my chance. I wasn't afraid, I felt really excited. I went out into the garden. The sun was dreadful, it hurt my eyes so I couldn't stop sneezing. I used to love the sun I think. But I said there was no going back so I went on though my hair kept blowing in my eyes. There wasn't anybody about. I looked at our shop which is going to fall down any minute, then I ran back because I thought I heard a sound. You see what I'm like? I had dust all over me. Anyway I went again to find somebody up the hill to talk to. The biggest place has The Mountain written on the wall, but it's nothing compared to India. And outside I met Boy, he was watching me from inside a car, barking at me and I jumped. Then I could see there wasn't any danger so I tried my whistle on him. He liked it better than they do here because he stuck his ears up. I talked with Boy through the glass. Then I went on further but still there wasn't anybody about so I began to get scared of course and ran back. But Boy barked for me so I had to stop. I've seen Boy with that man who used the telephone, and I know he lives in the city. I planned to get in the car with him and lie down on the floor in the back and that's how I'd escape. So I opened the door but Boy snarled at me and I slammed it shut again. He wasn't a friend after all. And I was having trouble with the wind too. But the worst thing was when I wanted to run home. I told myself I'd get caught, some person would ask me my name and where I live. The only thing was to stop the man getting away in his car without taking me. That's why I'm panting now and dizzy so my writing's wonky. The thing is I did it, I did go out by myself. I definitely don't believe this is Australia. I haven't found a single men-tion of Whitey's Fall in all those newspapers or a picture of boredom like this. Australia in the papers looks like everywhere else, but this doesn't look like anywhere I've ever seen. I'll soon know because I'm determined Boy's owner will not go without me. I let down the tyres to hold him up. It worked just the way those boys showed me in Naples. He can't go until I've smuggled a message to him. This is an adventure.

Fido wrote this when safely back home, not having noticed the matriarch McAloon asleep on her divan out on the porch where she'd had herself put to see the townsfolk off to stop the crown flunkeys extending the empire into their front yards, asleep like a heap of waterdamaged paper, a dinosaur of the insect world, a scatter of ironing, appearing no more alive than the remains of the bog princess, and snoring in tune with the wind among leaves.

Four

By the time Uncle and Felicia arrived back home it was found to be already evening. The town lay hushed with fear, the curse of gold on everyone's mind. Cells of conspirators and covert alliances discussed how to claim against the Department of Main Roads, how to keep it a secret for long enough to get it out of the ground. Meanwhile somebody, impossible to imagine who, had let down the tyres of the senator's car. Such a thing had never been thought of. It was a foreign idea and an uncomfortable one. In the dim rooms lamps were being groped for while fortunes were planned. One houselight, apart from all this, shone at Wit's End, which filled Billy with shame for his parents. Also a feeble twinkle winked deep inside the welder's workshop as Rupert Ping performed the ritual of joining an element to itself. When Felicia Brinsmead poked her nose in where it wasn't wanted, a goggled Mr Ping applied the oxy flame to steel: miraculously a sun began to appear through the metal, a gold-white molten blob of sun, the unthinkable brilliance of it. And Mr Ping, creator, priest and communicant.

– You weren't with us Rupert, Miss Brinsmead's voice floated on oil.

– No. He didn't look up, holding in his eye what he must not lose.

Four or five wars ago, Felicia promised she would do herself an injury which she could take to Rupert Ping and show him, even some cut-off part of her hateful body, perhaps have it delivered into his hand, something awful needing no explanation. Yet it was he who eventually did that, slashing himself for the world to see. Remotely, she heard her brother's voice speaking to her from the roadway.

– They've come before their time.

The lights of the pub flooded on simultaneously, so the empty shell blazed against the night's shadow.

Senator Halloran was explaining that after he had driven ahead of them he parked his car outside the Mountain Hotel and took a walk to explore the beautiful countryside and find the waterfall etcetera but when he got back, right on dark, this is what greeted him. He poked the toe of one Italian shoe against a sagging French tyre. Otherwise he restrained his anger at their childishness. Vivien felt mortified, not yet being close enough to the community to trust them completely. She dared assume her neighbours might be glad about this spiteful gesture. Was it their bucolic humour? Yes, she was ashamed. Coming after the pride of hearing Uncle's speech and Miss Brinsmead's great harangue and at the very moment she felt she might permit herself a parting shot at officialdom on their behalf. She regretted this let-down keenly.

– I shall need to stay overnight, Frank Halloran said accepting the situation with a certain largeness and leading the way to the pub, where he ordered drinks for everybody and, wowser though he was, had one with them. It seems you're so upset with me you don't want me to leave! thus he made a joke of it to save face for the elders who grimaced and jangled their heads.

– You should have a word with Mr Schramm, Uncle growled gloomy as a McAloon.

But Mr Schramm latched the door marked GUESTS ONLY, the empty rooms upstairs echoing.

– You don't stay in my hotel. I'm full up. Regret. Can't be helped.

The senator ordered another round to play for time. Outside the cold wind called him. The last of the evening light faded. An unseen hand switched on the single streetlamp. He turned again to his drinking companions and raised his second glass. Smacked his lips with distaste, the beer nauseatingly bitter and wallowing in his gut. He gulped the remainder to be rid of it in one dose. If he knew where to go he would have made his getaway, duty done. Perhaps return to the workers' camp? But it was a long way in the dark on the mountainside. He stayed.

Bill Swan wouldn't touch the drinks set up for him and paid for by the enemy. They bubbled quietly side by side.

– Here, Uncle took one of the glasses and thrust it into the senator's hand. Get this into you. It's a short cut to bein human.

All eyes watched as the statesman assessed the situation, studied the poisonous brew, thirty years since he had last tasted alcohol. He sipped. At this rate the torture would last all night.

– I must go, he announced.

– Not before you've had a drink with us.

This was Ian McTaggart's round, being the senior citizen, and then Basher Collins's round and after that Jessie McAloon stood one for the ladies, which you couldn't refuse without extreme discourtesy, and young Tony McTaggart on behalf of the generation of the future.

– I saw your grannie Bill, said Basher. Floating in the old dam bare as a plucked chook.

– She's a talented woman alright, Billy said.

The visiting politician eventually struggled off his bar stool and assembled himself in a departing position. Silly Robbie McTaggart, forgetting who was on whose side, got carried away with sentiment and tucked a little flask of whisky in the man's coat pocket for the sake of goodwill. Uncle, Basher, Vivien and Billy took him by the four corners and helped him out, the men accidentally giving him a kick in the shins and a clout across the head on the way. They stood in the dark street once more, balancing, and at a loss. What could be done with the mongrel? There was no one barring George who'd have him; and they weren't allowing George that pleasure either, or they'd never hold up their heads.

– Senator, said Vivien Lang. If you're willing to make do with a blanket and an uncomfortable sofa you're welcome to stay at my house.

An absolute hush followed this offer, during which you could not hear his acceptance nor his thanks, as if an explosion had deafened people. Uncle's head chimed with Elaine McTaggart's words, words she spat out with such venom he couldn't comprehend at the time – I saw them don't you realize, Billy and her together, and say what you like Uncle Swan that woman'll be the ruin of somebody I shan't say who, she won't be satisfied till she has the whole lot of you at one another's necks, I know women and I know her type.

The telephone inside the pub began ringing, the sky shivered to black shards that pricked at their skin. Basher escaped back to the bar. Vivien stood her ground against the pressure of Whitey's. Bill struggled with a storm of outrage, and yet he was also tantalized by this way she had of reacting impulsively and getting things wrong. She didn't appear to care what anybody thought of her, which attracted him and held him in check.

Vivien blamed herself for a clumsy fool. But how could you go back on it without sinking even lower? Nothing more than politeness prevented her modifying the invitation with some impossible condition. But she had an intuition about Great-aunt Annie and her self-imposed exile instead: might she be ashamed ... and at the same time proud?

– I'll bring the gear up from my car, the visitor declared sedately. He opened the door of the deflated vehicle and out bounded sixty-seven pounds of woolly black dog, sole witness to the crime of harassment, and trotted off to lay its tribute outside the pub. The senator recovered his centre of balance and liberated a suitcase from the clutches of the back seat.

Vivien was very much at home in the tension she had created; forever the new girl, teased and tormented, an outsider, her father's face streaked with shameful tears that dissolved her confidence in the world, and something about her mother they kept her from knowing, oh yes, and when she wanted very much to suffer it, to survive it.

Jasper Schramm again appeared on his porch silhouetted against the bright smoky air of the bar.

– Billy, your dad wants you on the phone mate.

– Tell him, Uncle growled as Billy bounded across the road. If he comes in range a my place I'll shoot the arse off him.

What was this hope that lifted him to such lightness? And coming now, when he was most sure he had successfully broken free of his parents? Billy skipped indoors.

– A bad business, said Tony joining them outside and shaking his head at the mystery of the deflated tyres or Vivien's stratagems; so agitated that even by the streetlamp's glow you could see he blushed at what remained unspoken.

Vivien made her getaway. She thought of promising Uncle she'd work on the senator while he was at her place, but wisely changed her mind. It could never sound right. Instead she said Goodnight goodnight, and was gone. So that Frank Halloran, slamming and checking the doors of his car, had to trot drunkenly after her, his cumbersome suitcase banging against one leg and his dog slinking along sensing trouble.

– Well Felissy, Uncle spoke at last in the tenderest voice he'd used to her for forty years. This could be the end I'd say. We might be seein the end a Whitey's.

She conceded that we might.

– Who'd have thought it, he said.

– About Miss Lang?

Uncle looked at her slowly, distrust collecting between them once more.

– Miss Lang, she repeated. Is deeper than I thought. How she hates that senator!

– Does she but? he didn't bother to conceal his hope.

– Mr Swan you are blind as well as deaf, the old lady exclaimed spiritedly.

Billy emerged from the Mountain emanating grim colours, the railing ducked as he sprang over it. He ran to the car, checking that its owner had gone, and Vivien too. Vivien, his thirty-four-year-old mistress making the biggest idiot of him. What if, he thought, her hair had been dyed and she was really fifty?

– Here's another fool, Miss Brinsmead commented as she left them.

– I'm coming home with you Uncle if that's okay, said Billy no longer free to consider Vivien's house his own. My father wants me back!

– Christ, Uncle grumbled happily. That'll be the end of my peace and quiet for the night. Noisy bastard like you in the house.

– Are you coming Tony?

Though he would have liked to do so, Tony obeyed some obscure sense of honour in refusing. So much was happening. As usual he had been one step behind. And now it looked possible that he and his best friend might find themselves rivals in love, of all things. Only the highway, the future of the town, holding them together. Vivien's snub to Billy had given him hope. A false gesture of sympathy would be something he might live to regret.

– I need another drink, Tony replied and left them to their lousy exclusive friendship. He'd have liked to make a defiant gesture, but knew nothing in this line beyond childhood, the urge to thumb his nose or stick out his tongue disgraceful for a man of nineteen. Stiffly he left them, dissatisfied with himself.

Frank Halloran, snoring pure alcohol, fitfully tossed around on the tired sofa in the Langs' back room. He was watching Senator Frank Halloran cutting a white tape tied to the doorhandle of Brinsmeads' store in Whitey's Fall, that godforsaken windy hole, and tied at the other end to the trellis at the side of the School of Arts in the same town. The tape stretched right across the road and he was there in the middle cutting it, yes an old Chinaman had given him a large pair of scissors but they were proving difficult to manage. Meanwhile, each side of the tape, uphill and downhill, stretched cars and cars, a traffic jam decked out with bunting, meeting here at this point and waiting only for him to snip the tape and release them, each line of cars to where the other had come from. However, as he watched his hand striving to open the scissors, sunlight flashed on the blades and he looked up because his eyes were dazzled. He could also smell something blossoming apparently, but didn't recognize it to put a name to. He looked up and what he saw filled him with fear. The mountain itself was changing. The Whitey's Fall general store remained the same as ever though perhaps cleaner, even the scrolls painted on the doors were identical with the way he remembered them: HASHERDAGGERY BOOTS & ALL TRESPASSERS & PROSECUTED, the Mountain Hotel was exactly the same. But the roadway appeared to be a vast barren surface. There was a chicken apparently enjoying it, a white chicken stepping across with its neck jerking in time with its tread as if the cars would never move. Then the mountain turned a curious shape and much larger, dark too and covered with people. And the roadway which the cars had come down was swallowed in a mess of trees, a jungle nobody had cleared, thick vines strangling the houses, monstrous growths. The whole mountain a community of groping shadowy shapes which filled up the sky. And afterward all that was left was this mountain which wasn't even the colour mountains can be and a pair of dazzling scissors. Then car tyres screeching and a woman ... That's how he woke into the night-time, the dark room spinning and himself flying on the bed, the lovely alcohol still at work. Yes, with sensuous deliberation Frank Halloran careened and banked, whirling away, glimpsing the gold roofs of a castle keep where Vivien Lang would be woken from death by a kiss. He lay in the dark, wondering why he didn't do this more often.

In his mind a question stood solid as a witness in court: why had she invited him to her house to sleep? He addressed himself to this question, respectfully.

You are waiting for an answer to me, the question said.

Tricky, Senator Frank agreed. The point is, she's single, he added, impressed with his grasp of fact. But not even the infant Samuel was more mystified by the voice he heard in the night.

The point is, said the question at last, finding his slowness tiresome and passing him a tangible glass proposition. There's only one bloody motive she could have.

The darkness hummed a swarm of bees.

Senator Frank took the hard fact and turned its crystal, peering for enlightenment.

Could St Peter himself deny it? asked the question. When you can see right through it?

He uncorked the fact and took a swig of whisky. In any other way but that, he admitted. She has to be worse off for having me here.

Jesus! the thing that amazes me, the question accused him, is you in this house, *waking up* in the middle of the night.

You mean I've already been asleep?

You've got to be joking.

F.H. consulted the bottle, realizing with some outrage that it was half empty already. I see what you mean, he admitted. Frank, Frank, he berated himself despairingly, tenderly, his chalky feet rubbing together and powdering the floor. He was permitted another swig. But is it too late? Is it ever too late while it's still dark?

An insensitive cockerel crowed in the distance.

It's a myth that they wake at dawn, the question soothed him.

Being the cautious, responsible individual he had made himself, Senator Halloran lay a while longer on the spinning, gliding sofa to debate the nuances of the situation, the personal, social (and yes, political, even national) consequences of action or inaction. His drunkenness holding him back with its usual moralistic scruples. He listened and the silence sang a gloria. Even so, microsonic sighs and creaks also reached him from elsewhere in the house. He slid off the sofa nearly cracking his head open as a result of the blanket diving for his legs in a rugby tackle. Extricated, he sat for a dignified half hour composing his nerves while the couch whisked him through a quick tour of New South Wales. He listened again for the giveaway murmurs of a woman frustrated in her desires, his prehensile ear clutching each sound in its little fist.

What the hell, as the question pointed out. Action is preferable to the deadly sin of sloth. If you do nothing, it reasoned, you'll always blame yourself afterwards.

He moved, a herd of nubiles galloping off in the hysterical distance, their sweet bare legs and gentle buttocks a vision. The floor swung up to meet his feet each time he took a step, feet so impressionable they could feel the pattern on the lino. Give him his due; once decided, he proceeded with the same firmness he would adopt to enter the senate chamber when he knew everybody was watching. This was a theatrical occasion. In the dignity of his singlet and underpants, Senator Frank seven-leagued it out of the back room into the ruined passageway where a huge shaggy bear leapt up at his throat. He struggled with the black brute. The heat of it hugged to his chest, teeth glimmered in the dark. Then the vicious animal began whining Brahms's lullaby in his ear. He knew it. Ocker! His old mate Ocker. He converted his desperate wrestling into caresses. For a moment there he sank in the morass of affection. But the call was on him. He accepted another slug from the bottle which had thoughtfully stuck in his hand. What if, the objective in view and the lady ticking off her ecstasy with his every footfall, this bloody mongrel were to jump in after him and bark the frigging house down? Not cool. Not cosmopolitan. Might easily ruin his pitch. Best take preventative action. His free hand groped for the dog's collar while the impertinent creature sniffed enquiringly at his breath. A policeman in every dog.

– Shush, he instructed it.

Sure enough, someone had thought of the problem already. The dog was tied up on a long rope! Had he accomplished this when he got home from the pub? His head wagged with respect. Marvellous what you can do without even trying. Unless she did it, thinking ahead. Well, it was better to get rid of the animal altogether. Both hands were needed for the knot. He put the bottle on the floor and concentrated. Ocker recognized freedom when it came his way and shot out into the night and the pleasures of perfect camouflage. The senator expressed gratitude to the chamber as he collected his brief and stood erect in his pants. He took exact bearings to navigate the rocking corridor. He wavered at the bedroom door. Actually there was no door, just a conventional opening. Frankie boy occupied this opening with his large blurry form, intent, feeling for sounds.

She lay breathing on the bed. If you didn't know better you'd nave sworn she was asleep. She even gave a realistic groan and that dry-mouth inducement of saliva common enough among sleeping persons.

– Are you asleep? Senator Laurence Olivier murmured.

She turned on the bed discontentedly. He peered at what little could be made out, listening with his whole body.

– Are you asleep? he asked more firmly.

She turned again, again discontentedly. He began to feel cold, the merry-go-round slowing down.

– Vivien are you sleeping? he asked with more urgency. Nothing. He balanced on one foot and then, the virtuoso, on the other, his dry soles brushing the floor audibly, his pulse deafening, his nerves emitting a shrill scream.

– Vivien, are you . . .?

– Mnnh, she moaned.

– Are you asleep?

– Mnnh. Mnnh. She tossed the other way, facing the wall. She had stopped breathing altogether. So he stopped too. Then she started again. He breathed.

Amazingly enough the bottle had arrived back in his hand. This would not make a respectable impression so he stood it on the floor and left it there, giving it a pat to indicate that this time it really must not follow him. And then he ventured his first step into the room. No effect. Another. Missing the support of the wall, he wavered, too soon beside her bed, his bare thighs rustling. Safety firmly put behind him, bridges burnt, the floor crossed, his lot cast, alive with the theatricality of the absurd, he reached for the bedcovers. This time she made no response: a definite encouragement. Gingerly he had opened the way; the principal remaining problem was her position, lying as she was, right on the edge of the bed leaving no room for him to slip in . . . unless he climbed over her and lay between her and the wall. Frank Halloran held the petrified sheet and blanket while he rummaged for a decision. Surely she would move over? Very gently, very cautiously he placed his hand on her hip and tried pushing her over. Breathing fire, he pressed so carefully that he might have been some natural phenomenon such as gravity. At first she gave a bit, but then resisted. Just as gently she matched his push, she was pushing against him. She was teasing him, her face still to the wall. O ho! a delightful game. He pushed harder, her resistance firmed. Alcohol tapped him on the shoulder and alerted him to a problem: if she was awake, this had to be a challenge he must meet or lose face; but if she was actually asleep, any more definite attempt would surely wake her. Right. And after all, Honourable Senators, had he not already attained advantages too precious to let slip? Wasn't he ready to get into her bed, satisfied with having taken the initiative, in as strong a position to gain his pleasures as any young hoodlum with a shag-wagon and the charisma of a rock star? He lowered the bedding and considered other means. Thankfully, the merry-go-round jerked into action again, rumbling and a comfort. He delivered his verdict. How could any woman sleep through this? Okay so that meant he had the go-ahead.

Being a tall man though inclined to fat he opted for the second approach, lifted his large soft leg and stepped right over her recumbent form, placing his foot in the middle of the bed. Then grasping the bedhead firmly, eased his weight on to that foot. The bed sagged in alarm, springs squealing. He was determined, admirable, he didn't flinch. She rolled into the pit, against his calf. He froze. At that instant a clicking of claws on lino announced the return of the faithful Ocker voluntarily putting aside freedom. The mongrel clattered cheerfully in to fetch him. Still balanced on the leg being burnt to the bone by contact with the lady, Frank Halloran waved his best friend to hell with what could have been mistaken as ferocity. The invisible beast waited politely for this wild activity to cease and then licked his master's hand with a hot loving tongue.

–Go *away*!

He heard the idiotic thing wagging its tail, thumping the floor like a bass drummer, the night's nerves soon to be tortured with the skirling of a hundred bagpipes.

– Go home, he ordered the puzzled darkness. He hissed, he growled, he went cold at the thought of what Vivien must be expecting as she lay there waiting for him. Was he to be the snarling biting mutilating kind of lover? You stupid dog, he whispered for her benefit.

Ocker whimpered.

There's nothing to equal intelligence, thought the senator proudly, though his muscles were beginning to seize up in a chain of cramps from his shoulder to his heel. The dog was heard to slink away and settle outside the door. Once again Frank Halloran could feel the warmth of Miss Lang's body lolling softly (you might say nestling) against his leg, smelling deliciously of drowsiness. The calm of Johnnie Walker suffused him once more. He took the final plunge and lifted his hind foot off the floor. His underpanted form straddled across her head, a pale colossus, a lover, a falcon hovering, an angel. Without warning, her body contracted in a spasm, next she flung herself out straight again, on to her back, then catapulted violently against his trembling leg. The knee gave way. He clutched desperately at the bedhead. But his fingers slipped on the varnished wood. He was gone. His intruding leg kicked up as he toppled, and with a terrific thud he crashed to the floor on his back. He lay there stunned by the noise and the cold, the hugeness of the catastrophe in that room of whispers and sighs. Secondarily he lay stunned by pains in his lumbar region, his shoulder and, come to think of it, his arm too. Expecting her to laugh or preferably to comfort him: or else wake and scream murder if she really had been asleep. One thing for certain, it was not humanly possible to sleep through such a din. The Honourable Senator, so proud of his priorities, sprawled on the floor of a scarcely known lady's bedroom while the bruises gathered their sap and blossomed. The house regained its composure. Night poured thick and blue into the room. He congratulated himself on wearing neither glasses nor false teeth.

– Mnnh, the temptress moaned. Mnnh. Mnnh. She stopped breathing (and so did he). She started breathing again, deeper, more regularly.

The criminal sat up slow-motion, knelt, bowed his head, eased his crucified body upright and tiptoed, hobbled to the door with infinitely delicate tread, a nation of righteous matrons howling for his blood if he should make a single slip and be caught. This cushioned step, then that. He was master of the thunderous Niagara. He was Blondin stepping off a wire attached to colonial Canada and placing his crippled feet on Goat Island, USA. He was there. The portal to freedom, the gates of heaven, the exit from Eden. He collided with the whisky bottle which maliciously torpedoed the faithful Ocker who had been lying patiently awaiting the next insult and now leapt into action yelping with pain and rushing away out of the house forever.

– Who's there? Vivien shouted from the bed, in one movement throwing off the covers and sitting up rigidly. What is it!

The bottle lay flat, dribbling and disowned in the passageway.

– Only me.

– What? Who? she shrieked.

– Frank Halloran, Frank Halloran gasped in terror, spinning round so he'd be facing the right way. I tripped over the dog I'm sorry. I'm looking for the bathroom.

– Oh. She sank back, one hand to her forehead. Oh, I remember. Well it's not in here. The next door along.

He stepped back, too hasty with relief, and trod on the bottle which skidding wetly under him whisked him away straight out on to the verandah and down the five front steps to crash in a gravel-rash on the path.

Her mind picked up threads as he ghosted away at high speed.

– But if it's the lavatory you need, she explained in an afternoon voice, you'll have to go out in the yard.

– I'm there already, he called feebly, unable to move.

She sighed – That's alright then, that's alright. And she sank back to sleep gratefully.

Five

Next morning all the old people of town were still bemused by knowing they'd been right through the years and the mountain under their feet was pure gold. Yet by some perversity of the human spirit this robbed them of purpose. Not one among them could rouse the energy to stake the claim. Meanwhile Billy Swan, who did not recognize what had been laid bare before him up at the cutting any more than the roadworkers did, felt filled with urgency to put his secret plan into effect. He would save Whitey's Fall single-handed from progress. He presented himself at the general store after watching Mr Ping jack up the foreigner's car and begin loosening the wheels. He ignored the protesting floorboards, and slouched in among heaps of decaying merchandise, boxes of hats, colonies of biscuits, a parade of inscrutable gumboots, till he stood by the towers of unopened newspapers (somewhere among which lay yellowing pages of public announcements concerning the Regional Planning Scheme and calling for submissions from interested parties). Miss Brinsmead waited in her usual place, one hand flat on the mint papers, ashamed of the date, her moony face already prepared to arrange itself in a suitable expression. And behind her Rastus the cat half-sleeping among the aromatic lollies.

– Miserable, miserable, whispered the convolvulus.

Come along, thought the lady impatiently, speak up Mr Swan, I know it all, the wound in his red face gaping, come along, ask about the gelignite; speak up, wound.

– Half a dozen sticks of gelignite please Miss Brinsmead if they've come in yet. The short ones will do. And about twenty feet of fuse. A dozen detonators too. Or, he added helpfully, dynamite would be okay instead.

What do you want it for? she seemed to ask. He glanced round, reassured that they could be overheard only by Saint Sebastian up against his wall awaiting fate's arrows.

– To blow up a dead bullock, he lied weakly. At this the saint shook with cultured laughter.

A bullock indeed! To blow up your father you mean, Felicia knew: she had the pleasure of guessing, she didn't even need to concentrate on finding out properly. It was inevitable Billy would come to this, she had predicted it all along.

The saint lapsed into chuckles, paying attention but not understanding. Half a century ago people said the town would fester to a sticky end, the wickedness of the world being unparalleled, he could believe it. Before the year was out he expected divine vengeance in the form of human folly, or foreign invasion. Something to cut the thread and finish God's tapestry. Failing these, why not the Black Death of Whitey's Fall carried in the fur of fleeing bandicoots, converging on the mountain, displaced from their habitat by a proliferation of cities along the coastal plain to the east and on the plateau to the west.

Lord Kitchener's Favourite brand Gentleman's Relish maintained a stiff upper lip.

– I'll have the gelignite for you this afternoon Billy, Miss Brinsmead promised decisively (recalling the day this boy at seven had shyly asked if he could give them a present, handing Mr Brinsmead a photograph of President John F. Kennedy cut from a magazine; it was a large glossy picture which might have been designed for sub-branches of Rotary and though Felicia saw in the face all manner of frightful deceits plus the cruelty that accepts something less than complete knowledge, she recollected her manners and thanked him, polite as Ivan Turgenev receiving from Pauline Viardot a ticket to one of her peerless performances of bad taste) ... she perceived, from the orange lights he now threw on the cellophane-wrapped packets around him, that some monumental despair was brewing, such that a person of his stamp would express in anger and go off to the war if there was one luckily, or the South Pole if not. Billy said nothing, merely slapped the counter with his labourer's hand, a gesture of satisfaction, and walked out leaving the shop trembling.

There was work to be done on Uncle's place where Bill had taken up residence, as the late Mrs Ping might have phrased it for the benefit of culture. Yet something more urgent nagged at his attention, something he didn't want to know about. He concentrated on the comfortable guilt of work not done; he'd promised to repair the fences in the little paddock today so animals could be put there and not get out, the tools were ready in his saddlebag, the motorbike stood as usual against the monument to the unforgotten dead, he anticipated the jaunt across the hillside to where he'd be working, a blood-rousing bone-jolting shortcut. Yet a gnawing undermined his life, eating away, flowing, unsettling, something desperately important. Business at the shop complete, he slung one leg over the greasy machine and kicked the starter. Bloody Pommy heap of scrap, still had a kick-start, never heard of the starter-button. Motorbikes'll go into museums before those dickheads catch up with the Japanese. He kicked again, savagely. The dumb brute hung between his legs without a shudder of life. Kick. You bastard. Kick. Cunt. The mountain wind blew unceasingly, set his hair dancing. Kick. This time he dismounted and kicked *at* the machine. Impotent. Found himself already walking. Walking fast and knowing exactly where he was going. Going with the undercurrent, the urgency. Walking up the stony track, almost trotting now, a race to keep his anger hot, yes running, stumbling, swearing, fuming, just in the mood, watch out you smooth Irish prick, this is the end, talking won't get you anywhere. He was turning his ankles on the ruts, breathing great lumps of black steam, blood zoomed through his system, he threw open the gate with a clatter and left it swinging behind him (ultimate insult of the countryman). They were sitting preening themselves of course on the verandah, the two of them, sipping their little poofter cups of tea, munching the toast and marmalade, digesting the grapefruit and the mishmash of cereals, eggs and bacon, discussing the art market or the winelist or hospitals and their operations (comparing scars), or perhaps haggling politely over the price for selling out Whitey's Fall. Yes, that, even that. He stamped up the steps. The senator, to give him credit, sat cool and casual with his floral teacup and a last corner of crust. But Vivien was on her feet, crows going mad in her head, a relentless drum booming its torture, *accelerando*, her fingers working, a dark blot, swift negative, cancelling the sky, her voice already raised, the words out before you could think them, a damwall of loose dirt flung across the path of a flood in vain hopes.

– You dare come marching in here Bill Swan after the way you treated me last night and if you can't be civil in front of strangers, for God's sake grow up, and shut my gate, come stamping around like lord and master, where's your whip, do you think I'm going to be dismissed by you as if I don't know how to behave, should I ask permission to think, is this the ...?

He pushed past her, solid with purpose, she was his after all and such were his rights as he understood them. With the flat of his hand he knocked the cup away from Senator Halloran's face, vaguely hearing the tinkle of its twenty falling daggers, but an hour away from seeing the heart-shaped puddle of tea soaking into the bare weathered flooring, oh boy you've done it now, and a flash of grief for Mrs Ping and her hopeless patience at trying to teach him, her hand in the grass, reaching open, like his own, also the old cow dying of life, that new calf killing its mother to get out in time, and not making it. Billy emitted a bellow you could have heard in the main street (and which Fido, for one, did hear).

– Your car's fixed, you mongrel, we did it while you were snoring in ... there. Billy couldn't bring himself to mention bed, considering the circumstances. He went on. A man ought to smack you in the mouth. But he knew already that Frank Halloran had had a frustrating night, this was clear from his tension, his odour, and the way they'd been sitting when he arrived. Billy took a moment to catch up with knowing, but the effect was sweeping. In a volatile shuttle of moods he accepted victory though he had done nothing for it.

– Your car's fixed, he repeated and you could have detected a touch of chivalry in his tone as he seethed with energy. His perception sharpened, he saw that the senator's hair, the colour of rank hay, had been dyed. As a question of pride, no one would hear it from him; he wouldn't diminish the enemy he'd defeated.

– A man ought to smack you in the mouth, Bill said again to restore Halloran's self-respect.

A vulgar laugh fought up Vivien's throat. She struggled to suppress it. The ripples of this unpardonable cruelty tested her reserves of self-control. Like a child she concentrated on holding down that awful self who knew already. Now she must meet Bill Swan's eyes, for he had turned his back contemptuously on the other man and presumed to look straight into her. He was challenging her unpredictability, detecting the laughter battling against her courtesy. The wild girl within could at last be glimpsed. What more had he been hoping for? This was the inner Vivien, once before encountered, letting herself over the cliff edge heedless of danger. On impulse Bill faced Frank Halloran again.

– Sorry if I spoiled your tea!

Now the laughter did blurt free from Vivien's efforts. Just a momentary burst which might pass for a shock-reaction perhaps. But she knew no excuse would convince. She suspected with horror that her motive was a secret lust for blood. Could her devious mind have set this up?

– Who do I thank for being cleared of suspicion, you or your grandfather? she asked her lover harshly, invitingly, her voice rich with passion.

– Miss Brinsmead I'd say, he replied as he clattered back down the stairs. I'll tell them you're leaving in five minutes, he called, Frank!

The grin on his face caused her a painful leap of the heart.

– Please understand I am an outsider myself, she said gently to her visitor. I keep kidding myself I understand, but I never do. Would you like another cup?

One more cruelty.

– Don't bother, he answered miserably, the gravel-rash smarting and an ache felt through all his bones. I must find Ocker. He got loose in the night and seems to have run off. I really have tried my best, he added. I wish you could believe that.

– I wish I could, she agreed.

Six

– Gold! Miss Felicia Brinsmead exclaimed. Why should I speak to anyone about gold? Least of all you Miss Lang. I've more than that to kill myself talking about, I do declare. One need only think of the history of the world. It's in the furthest degree irrelevent how or when the stuff is unearthed. I might say, she added with a switch of expression to something little short of lascivious. I might say the more difficult lesson is the acceptance of home. When I think of the futility of the twenty-three times my brother and I have set off abroad never to return, twenty-four if you count the time our parents took us! You must have felt the same, surely? People of our kind cannot afford to waste energy. To make the most of what we have one really needs to stay as still as possible.

They were seated on ricketty chairs outside the store, struggling to extract oxygen from its aroma of mice and termites, sweet things and rubber things; so that the wind sweeping tons of dust over them was actually a relief. Vivien had folded her arms, appearing as a woman inclined to be prim. Miss Brinsmead by contrast sat with her knees comfortably apart and her hands planted on them sturdily, her elbows locked straight and hung with dimpled bags, her head thrown back, her fine eye rolling, and her bare toes casually rubbing ants into the concrete. With her skirt up, she'd have made a sight indeed for Mr Ping across the road if he'd bothered to look, not that she cared or gave a thought to him any more than to herself. People of our kind, she wooed her guest, linking them in deep anguished ways.

– Our young people, she went on, have gone, all but the two who can't. Billy thinks there's gold here, whereas what is here is destiny. His cousin the McTaggart boy has an inkling and mustn't be underrated. She shot her interrogatory look and was satisfied with the impression she had made, so when she spoke further it was to cajole. You know this, don't you my dear, you've been here before, there's no getting away from that.

– Are we related, Miss Brinsmead?

– Of course we are. My mother was, let me see, your Great-aunt Anne's aunt.

– That's pretty remote.

– All relationships are remote to that way of thinking, or equally close. I am a sister to Ho Chi Minh, for example, and to Adolf Hitler the clever little brat, as well as Stravinsky. You came here to give me Mercy Ping's papers.

– So you knew already?

– No I only knew just now. And young Billy got them for me, did he? Good boy. He turned out well enough despite his grandfather's ruthless interference. Poor Mercy Ping, she went on. Respectable woman, but needed to live with a failure and would have it that way. She took root, oh in the twenties some time, fresh from the city where her father grew a market garden, mind you her grandfather had been here before, oh yes indeed, one of our brave lads had stuck a knee in his back and cut off his ear to nail on the barn door, no mistake about that; so she had a vocation in a manner of speaking, to civilize us, and when she came she tripped in like a Chinese doll so dainty you could kiss, but you wouldn't dare touch, too fragile, too wounded, turned out tough enough however, managed Rupert and he was a god bright as the sun, he made me weep, I crawled I can tell you for his tight little body, and everybody's eyes a mirror for himself, of course he had no business settling, none of his grandparents had their ears cut off, not in this district anyhow, a tragedy for him that he met her and her longing to live with a failure. He was paralysed by thinking there was somewhere he ought to go, something to be done, but unable to discover what was worthy of his great opinion of himself. Tragic for him. Because he was stupid, it must be admitted, that was his besetting fault and still is.

– It seems to have been tragic for her too, Vivien objected with a shiver of disgust.

– She managed very well, dear, she was killing him nicely. A case of touch-and-go right to the end. Little intervention of fate, if one cares to believe in fate, which I don't unless you define the word as too big for definition. Now we're getting theoretical which I detest as much as anyone.

A counterfeit cloud intruded above the skyline at Wit's End with a billowy simplistic shape that invited suspicion from the outset.

– I wonder if you would explain to me about Remembering Miss Brinsmead?

– That's what we're here for. But when you come to the point there's little to tell, no theory, no theology. Have you read Mercy's testament? she asked as the younger woman took it from her bag and passed it over.

– Of course not, it isn't my business.

– What a miserable outlook! I'm sorry to hear such sentiments from you of all people. Of course it's your business. Everything's your business I hope, if you're truly alive to the world. Everything's a threat. Everything's your enemy. This pad of paper could be the death of you for all you know and you won't dare open it, simply for the sake of your genteel upbringing. I hope I shan't hear the like of that again in a month of weekdays.

– Well after all, Vivien protested, I am an outsider. And this I accept. I'm well aware it means exercising a bit of tact.

– Heavens, what will the woman say next? Miss Brinsmead asked the iron awning above them. Whatever will she say? Very soon we shall have to begin at the beginning if you go on giving me shocks. If you're an outsider then so are we all, Miss Lang, you have quite the wrong way of looking at it. The point is that

298

we are historic. Let me tell you I was the first in this town to come out in a picture-hat when they were all the rage in Paris. Such a fine hat too, a fluffy concoction of silks and feathers with a brim as wide as the average verandah. I manoeuvred myself out into the street on a Saturday afternoon when everybody promenaded, taking turns, arm in arm with somebody, hundreds were out, families you've never heard of since, and myself proud as you like in my picture-hat which had set the Bond Street galleries aflutter. And the whole town laughed. They fell about laughing so that I saw into their black bloody mouths and the hell inside them choking out ha ha ha ha, aimed at me, everywhere bloodthirsty ha ha ha's. I could see immediately there was no point in standing on ceremony, so I threw the hat on the ground where it belonged now I hated myself in it. They were correct, it was a ridiculous hat. Had I been living historically at the time I'd have realized that for myself. The boys used it for a football. What a game they had till it fell to pieces and one of the Buddall babies got tangled in the silk band and strangled to death. The trouble was, I thought at the time, that everybody had cousins except me. I felt deprived, I freely admit it. I was ignorant then and disgracefully vain. Had I had the least inkling that history is not a chain of things done, but a continuance of things been, a morass of heart-searching and despair might never have come my way. You should have seen us in those days, she sighed dreamily. Dancing for charity, dancing for fun and for our sporting teams, trying everything out. Nothing daunted us. The girls played cricket against the clergy, the men played the Yalgoona Aborigines who are coming back to invade this place; if it was just forest without our mountain they'd be back here today. We had Massey-Harris bicycle rallies, an orchestra of ukuleles, our teams competed at working the irrigation mill, the fastest treadmill in the civilized world, we had working-bees for sharpening gramophone needles, the birdwatchers' club was in correspondence with Saskatchewan. And everything we did, we photographed ourselves doing. Axemen would take a break risking death as the tree toppled so a friendly fanatic could record some action for posterity, girls smiled while they milked cows in case any moment a lens appeared beneath the beast and that's how Olive McAloon got her facial paralysis. Ladies would sit posing in a group while the men stood up and folded their arms in the annual society portrait. 320-bellows cameras were all the rage. We were quite the most *au courant* backwater in New South Wales, I shouldn't be surprised.

They sat, side by side, utterly at cross-purposes, confronting the stage-set of the School of Arts with its faint heart A.S./A.L. and the welder's workshop, the background of green pegged up on the studs of cows. Across everything a dusty wind constantly blew the lines of an engraving.

– You're disappointed, said Miss Brinsmead enjoying herself all the more, smoothing her thighs, thinking of her once-beautiful flesh now rotten with its secrets. But there was no response.

– Remembering really began with my grandfather, Miss Brinsmead explained feeling little flurries of love re-kindling. It's an idea so simple you don't have to think of it. You let go and permit yourself to live again, or *still live*, what happened at some other time and place.

– How far back can you go?

– As far back as you do go.

– Did your grandfather practise the idea, or did he just have it?

– What intelligent questions you ask. My family and yours are unusual, Vivien. But most unusual was Tom Whitey himself. Every other family intermarried as fast as they could strangle each other. But he never married, he was the sole and only Mr Whitey. One has to respect that. Next came my grandfather who had three sons, Albert, Michael and Edgar. Two of them died in infancy as was the habit in those days. He was stuck with Michael, who was my father and a miserable disoriented man. He and my mother set themselves the task of being the aristocrats of the district! Felicia Brinsmead shrieked with laughter, the shocking noise of a magpie in an eagle's claws, sending clusters of goosepimples crawling across Vivien's skin. The decayed buildings gave back wooden and iron shrieks. The old lady ducked her head with effort, her bundle of dead hair bouncing in distress.

300

– They were the vulgarest people, she commented eventually while arranging the dress across her lap. As was proved by my father's suicide and my mother's rushing off into oblivion with her single contemptible morsel of gold. My brother and I have never married.

They sat on their ricketty chairs, Vivien with her arms folded, Miss Brinsmead still hands on knees and watching her bare toes at their independent work among the ants. Above them the mountain put on an ostentatious display of large comforting shapes.

– I am told, Vivien said into the silence. There was a plague of boy children. She noted her companion flinch, yes perhaps it was a malicious thing to say to a spinster, also recollecting that boy's face peering out from the shop window.

– In those days, Felicia responded with composure (though given the lie by her thick voice). We used to pray for boys, needing to breed men for the work. Well it came home to roost. She stiffened her arms and her toes worked more ants into the concrete.

– Sebastian and I had no cousins, she announced after a pause.

The town had died. Only the washing hung out along a verandah up the road flapped restlessly, shirts and singlets strung across the front doorway tugging their rope line, wind puffing them full as ghostly fluttering petitioners.

– Miss Brinsmead, why do you keep coming back here?

– Because this is the only place where I can be in touch. I go away and feel free, but I lose control, I may as well be anyone from anywhere. Out there you have to adjust to what other people expect . . . She let her answer lapse, musing on the incompleteness of what she'd said. In any case the question wasn't of a kind to inspire respect for this person's subtlety. But to educate is an obligation, ho hum.

– The world's great cities are mostly shells, Miss Brinsmead added. Filled with people who scarcely exist. I've listened to what they're thinking. It's a terrible shock in a Geneva bus to suffer the magnetism of a real person getting in, or a San Francisco tramcar for that matter. Like having Savonarola for your corner chemist. But now you see you're thinking of yourself again. Too bad.

– I was thinking of my family, of family characteristics.

– Your family the Langs. Well the Langs could never abide other Whitey's Fallers. Norm Lang was of an age with my father and a drinking companion of his, he brought nurse Margaret Opie from the city to marry him. That's your great-aunt Annie's parents and your grandfather's too. As for Annie's nephew Geoff, now he was a typical Lang, took himself off down the valley to Yalgoona and didn't come back till Sadie Saunders agreed to hold his hand. He was always full of ideas, poor man, oh yes, you couldn't say a thing without his flying off at a tangent. Him and Sadie, a bright pair of miseries, and no mistake. Theirs is that green place up the back of you on the south track. And as soon as their son Lance could read and write they were planning to bundle him out of Whitey's and put him to boarding school. Long history of malcontents in the Langs.

– Me too.

– Yes, you too. But always had cousins because at one stage the family had girls who married all over the place with the Collinses and McTaggarts and who else. The girls were local alright. It's the men imported their wives: and a suffering mob of sheep they turned out to be, Miss Brinsmead sniffed at the thought of the wives.

– Annie went away.

– But she sent you back to fill her place.

The idea was so astonishing that all feeling drained from Vivien leaving her brittle and ricketty as the chair she sat on. Could she have been *used*? Could she have been sent back by Great-aunt Annie as a substitute, a proxy, a surrogate, a sacrifice? Without warning the world came rushing up to meet her, she sat tight, as if drunk. Was she such a dupe? Miss Brinsmead began talking again while her listener, her disciple apparently, hung on for dear life against a prolonged falling sensation, the old lady was talking savagely, sagely about how worthless it was to struggle with the deadening stupidity and goodwill of this bumpkin community, how she wished it were possible to leave though she knew leaving meant nothing, in common with so many beautiful human truths, how she doubted a sane person could stay sane long in such a backwater, how Miss Lang herself was joining the mad stampede to insignificance.

– Miss Lang! she cried joyously, her mood swinging round a hundred and eighty degrees. Are you falling, my dear? Is it true then?

Bending to peer right into Vivien's face, she examined the fear-locked eyes and saw the truth through deep water, moving steadily gracefully uncontrollably killingly down.

– Are you in love with young Bill Swan? the sibyl clucked so her voice alone might supply some security some sense of direction. Hold on to him, he's all you have. I know the feeling. After fifty-eight years, I should think I do. My poor mother never succeeded, her anger at her own life was such that she found it hard to bring herself even to say *thank you* for a courtesy. Now hold on Miss Lang dear.

Vivien's world filled with that hideous bland face, its lips two flaps sucking and blowing. Evil, evil.

– One must get used to it gradually. How right I was after all Vivien. I remember the day you arrived. I remember what I felt. Ah yes indeed. Would you like to stay a little longer before we try walking? You might be unsteady. Perhaps I could tell you a story? Miss Brinsmead smiled as she patted Mercy Ping's notebook.

Vivien tried not to hear, not to be corrupted, tried instead to think her way out, to save herself from this sensation. Yet she was powerless.

– Mrs Ping tells how she was captured and hung, back there at the old town. Poor Mercy, how hateful people are, Miss Brinsmead commented complacently, aware of the ambiguity.

They sat, it might be thought intimately, the listener with her arms prim, the speaker with head well back, shoulders propped on the buttress of straight elbows, knees comfortably wide and her toes grasping at the concrete. A warm wind swirled round them and off among the dying relics. The washing gesticulated and ballooned against the house up the street, a hectic repetition of empty gestures and rebuffs. Miss Brinsmead turned to the dead woman's notebook with its spot of Mr Ping's blood dried into the cover. She recited in a dreamy singsong.

– Hung without warning, pain jolting and stinging her through the length of her body. Even to the ten fingertips, she says. Did she have the presence of mind to count, one wonders? As if pain could be a light around her ... how she must have suppressed her taste for melodrama all those years. Admittedly she did always indulge her desire to see herself as innocent. That's true. As the injured party, few could touch her. Yet you know she never took trouble with herself in the way of vanity; and she'd go to no end of bother for other people. Not just because she was Chinese.

Vivien hugged herself protectively. She saw something awful: her darling great-aunt plotting. With herself as pawn. Aunt Annie giving her the violin for a reason, buying her an icecream and holding her hand for a reason, telling stories about a fairytale Australia for a reason, charming her, possessing her. And all this to use her life as a means of vicarious repayment. In Miss Brinsmead's words, she sent you back to fill her place: to face exile for the satisfaction of some fantasy, the women's role in keeping Whitey's Fall alive?

– Do you think we know what we are doing? Felicia enquired gently as she watched these ideas formulate.

– Auntie was too strong for me.

– In my opinion she would never guess her destiny, Miss Brinsmead replied, jumping up so suddenly she seemed a younger woman altogether. We are going, she announced. We are already late. This is an occasion; you and I will settle ourselves at the Mountain for our first Remembering together. Try standing, dear, that's the spirit. It's a question of balance and I shall be here to help, I do know what this feels like. Young Bill Swan will do well enough. When I was born this time my mother shouted *go away*, not a nice thought to live with. But she was afraid, she guessed I knew more than she did even then. Correct though she was, it ought to be nothing to fear. I've been in hell fifty-two years this time, becoming quite comfortable with it. You have to drift along, fighting won't help. You're starting a bit late at, what is it, thirty-four? but a lot better off than I was. Being without a brother.

– I feel quite well thank you, said Vivien disengaging her arm with some distaste.

– Good heavens now you don't even like me! she screamed a little laugh. Oh I'm used to that, you needn't trouble to hide it, thank you very much indeed. You can't be expected to look on things as I do.

– Do I seem ungrateful?

– Gratitude gratitude, chanted Miss Brinsmead. The sly Roman flatitude *maxima debetur puella reverentia.* All the same, she added, giving her colleague a tiny slap to show she was still hurt and offended, all the same the Mountain is the place for you at this stage. No need to tidy up, that's one thing the beautiful and the ugly have in common: nothing wasted on appearances.

The two women walked independently and without further conversation until they reached the hotel, the dust swirling under their feet.

– Now I should mention this, Miss Brinsmead broached the silence expunging all trace of wistful cajoling from her voice. At the Mountain one doesn't speak unless one's sure the person wishes to be spoken to. There's the television if you need an escape. A drink is helpful. Then you're on your own.

– You don't have to mollycoddle, Vivien retorted irritably because she was nervous. I wouldn't volunteer to come if I felt afraid.

– Hey ho, how tiresome, independence, the new woman, lady Godiva in modern dress, in we go.

Inside, some of the ladies from the morning tea club were there, the two Collins matriarchs and the spinster Dolly Swan. There were men as well, some a generation older than Felicia Brinsmead, while behind the bar Jasper sidled without raising his eyes from what his hands were doing so the top of his head confronted the newcomers.

– One shandy, Miss Brinsmead ordered.

The top of the head considered the order.

– A beer for me please, Vivien said distinctly, nettled and

ostentatiously more polite than her mentor. She was feeling conspicuous. They must all guess what she was here for, her initiation, her debut, her corruption. She took refuge in an interested examination of the room, the long bar, dark wood scratched stained and dull, the wall lined with shelves where a few sparse exhibits stood; bottles of extinct liqueurs crusted inside to a scum of crystals; a family of black tankards growing mould as if once edible; hideous mementos of forgotten occasions adorned the place, such as a boot now dry as a leaf which had once made violent contact with the buttocks of the last policeman of Whitey's Fall, some mirrors lied about the world of appearances, and a poster over the till, pasted to the bare timbers of the wall, proclaimed the benefit to the complexion of Pear's Soap, the ever-smiling model unaware the grain of the wood had grown out through her cheeks. A television, as promised, babbled cosily about the chocolate space-age and a shipping strike. Mum Collins's arm reached out of its own accord from the inert form of Mum, drawing Vivien to her side, taking her round the waist in that motherly way. You could not resist, nor wish to. Her jutting jaw thrust forward, her mouth also smiled at the bar, it was a gesture and all Mum could manage, the force pulling at her and no going back, she closed her eyes to save her young friend seeing what might be there.

– Starve the lizards, Mum Collins gasped after a highly charged muteness. That's shocking.

Fear laid siege to Vivien, the mountain folk around her in uncanny attitudes, their pursed faces and faraway eyes; one wizened figure carved in patchy granite already host to lichens and animal parasites, a yellow discharge seeping out from under his knuckled eyelids. Was he perhaps asleep? Her fear told her he was not. Nor was Mary Buddall, the cheery aunt, hunched over a tiny glass of sherry, blowing into her cupped hands, concentrating on something not there. You couldn't breathe for other people's breath.

The publican turned his back to pour himself a tot, which he tossed down at a gulp. Vivien realized only now that he had been muttering all the time and seemed to do so even while he drank.

The syllables slurred together sounding familiar but incomprehensible. Now and again he flung out an arm with the emotion of the scene. In contrast with the deadly quiet of hallucination, his condition was pitiable and not at all threatening. If her father had lived he might have become an alcoholic.

As she looked from one face to the next she learnt something. They have all watched the mystery of each other's flowering, they've been here on this little mountain every day and watched the signs of childish meanness develop into the dangerous urges of the spy, the thief, the gossip; they've watched shyness develop into modesty; they've watched cleverness become opportunism and possessiveness become nymphomania. And then they've watched the flowering shrivel, the spy withering to spitefulness, the voyeur reverting to a moralist, the opportunist becoming wise and the nymphomaniac tolerant. Till seedtime slurs these distinctions. The husk wrinkles hard. Family resemblances obliterate personal identity so that eventually there remain principal types: the McAloon, the Collins, the McTaggart, the Lang, developing towards one another with each generation. One day they would be indistinguishable, perhaps. A sad occasion. She shuddered, thinking of her own name.

Vivien, turning to Miss Brinsmead for reassurance, saw herself in that lady's eyes, her screaming plummeting fall through a void. It was absurd that she'd thought of Felicia as dirty. What could be more irrelevant to anything that mattered? Heroic to care for herself so little. Mum Collins still clung to her waist but more like a child overawed by the fairground than a rescuer; the support came from Felicia. Vivien herself whirling round screeching, yes she danced, mad with hatred, and no she wasn't alone nor was she vulnerable, she was winning, it was the other woman, the one they were holding down who uttered orange sounds, moonlit trees reflected in her eyes, her mouth a ragged injury.

– No, Vivien convulsed, shaking herself free. No, she gulped, trembling horribly.

– Miss Lang, whispered the leader and caught her again, meshed her in those strange soft fingers, stroked her, quelling her resistance, and drew her again to the place where she had been, to the untouched glass of beer, to the encircling arm of Mum Collins's ghost.

Vivien took up her beer and held it steady. She mastered the spiralling sensation. She was a tourist again among the faces; the lichened man a work of art.

– That's Mr Ian McTaggart, Felicia whispered. Tony's grandfather, one hundred and two last December. Capricorn: ask the girls. Over there, she indicated a beldam in the corner, is Miss Bertha McAloon, was Mrs Bertha Swan but went back to being what she started as, once she and Uncle had their falling out. You'll meet her. Ssh. The hand was warm on her arm, stroking intense waves. Vivien didn't care, after all, what was happening or how she might be thought of. (The French windows swung open and there she went, so all and sundry might observe her, out on to the balcony of ... is it the Kursaal? yes and she's recognized. Naturally she's recognized, and lets her ostrich-feather fan click open so she can hold it up becomingly against her chest, the tortoise-shell handle smooth in her creamy gloved fingers. She's smiling. They all look up from the foyer ... and begin to applaud her. She is, she is smiling. The dyed feathers quiver alive, she feels their tips fluttering at her throat. She has been recognized of course, she expected it. My husband says, she says, there will be no trouble if we all remain calm. They listen. The archduke, she continues in her clear high voice, is regrettably dead. He was held in high honour and we are all deeply shocked but we owe it to the rest of the world to be calm and brave and cool. She remains calm and brave and cool at the stone balustrade with that tremor of crimson at her throat, her aura of discreet Parisian perfume. My husband, she says to them, believes in your courage. As long as there is no panic. We have the diplomatic means to achieve anything. And we want peace, is that not so? The Kursaal foyer once again rings with the clapping of those people she does not know, agents? spies? assassins?, but who know her. She touches her taffeta skirt, the lovely blue fabric shimmers, her fan slaps shut, she bows her pretty head, they love her, they have heard what they longed to hear, now they can go in to the ball with easy minds. The orchestra strikes up a new waltz by Lehár, the rotating doors whirl and flash, the chandelier blossoms bubbles of light against the amber decor, she gazes . . .) She gazed at it and held its miraculous drifting forms close to her eyes. And took her first sip of beer. Miss Brinsmead had let go of her hand. She was afloat.

The pub door stood open. Something intentional about it. Bill.

– Can't you even love? he snarled in front of everyone. I mean, you make me so bloody angry.

She met his eyes but hardly heard him, not enough to be wounded. He waited in the doorway: a reversal of how they first saw each other the day she came to find help for Mrs Ping. He willed her to come outside and talk. But her supporters were her jailers and held her firm. He willed her because he could see she needed him to be strong. But still she did not move. And did not move even when Felicia Brinsmead relaxed her grip, Mum Collins held on all the tighter. So that while Felicia let go altogether, Mum's arm locked round Vivien's waist. Bill found himself collected by Miss Brinsmead and guided outside.

Mr Ian McTaggart watched, a half-smile cracked the patina of his face, lichens flaked off, his eyes crawled from side to side slow as clusters of parasites. He watched because he ought to recognize this young woman, and perhaps had a duty. Outside, the shopkeeper spoke confidentially to Billy.

– I'm glad to see you because your gelignite has arrived and I've put it away. Come down to the store right now if you please. These are difficult times and I prefer not to hold it.

His gelignite. Enough to make you laugh. It would be hers again when it blew a hole in her yard filling in the mineshaft. The first priority was to have it in his possession, claim it before anything went wrong. He'd come back for Viv. He concentrated on behaving warily; Brinso had her ways of finding things out by just watching you. He walked with impressive nonchalance and stationed himself outside the closed shop while she let herself in at the back. The building, decayed to this dangerous state, gave the survival of its owners a touch of the heroic. He stood near the monument to the unforgotten fallen of Whitey's Fall and

Wit's End: the names chiselled on the Roll of Honour were mainly common, McTaggart, McAloon, Buddall, Lang, Collins, Swan. Had ordinary people died then? The improbability of the idea surprised him. How did they come to know about the *glorious cause* in the first place? And why *For God, Queen, and Empire* (with King scratched in the stone above Queen by some punctilious historian with a rusty nail)?

Summer began that moment, the persistent wind warm as a river between dilapidated banks. No new buildings had been put up since 1903, but plenty had fallen down. Young Swan rocked on his heels, waiting for his explosives, trying not to appear suspect. Across at the welder's shed Tony was still working though it was lunchtime, working overtime out of pity for Mr Ping who hadn't recovered the full use of his arms, cut into lozenges and strips by the razor ... as he, William James Swan knew them to be, the first-hand witness. But these days he no longer waited for Tony as he used to, that lunchtime ritual a token of the past. They went their separate ways and you couldn't put your finger on the moment of change. Something broken beyond explanation. The last two of their generation to remain in town (already a month had passed since Maggot left and no letter yet), but the link you took for granted had snapped.

He didn't want to be seen looking too hard at Ping's or this might be interpreted. Instead he searched the hall for the faded heart with A.S./A.L., musing whimsically of Uncle as a young daredevil. The School of Arts groaned. And Mr Ping came to his door to watch.

Billy had been Miss Brinsmead's agent, her thief, when he went for Mercy's papers and found himself in the nightmare of that blood-spattered bathroom, and the naked man he lifted on to the bed exhibiting the art of mutilation. Your mouth felt like a hole in your head to think of it. The usual wind bombarded his legs with dust. He could face anything, he hoped. What came to mind was his father's lecture on Manliness and Uprightness; also his mother's stupid habit of nodding in agreement. He was freer away from them.

Miss Brinsmead clacked the side door behind her as she

struggled out through the thicket of wistaria that held up that wall. She brought him a parcel hurriedly packed, the cellotape already lifting free of the brownpaper and refusing to be stuck back. So the fateful gelignite changed hands. He felt its power race through him, endangering his plan because she did seem to be looking with her look and guessing something. His treacherous eyes evaded her and focused on the collapsed shed in her back yard where the Golden Fleece was known to be. The gelignite heavy in his hands, he escaped in disarray.

Miss Brinsmead didn't even hear the motorcycle fire into life, so preoccupied was she. How neatly she had kept him off the subject of Vivien, Vivien's new loyalty to herself, how adroitly he'd been diverted and sent about his business leaving her free to finish what she'd begun. She ambled with a lazy swing of her large hairless legs, back up the hill to complete the initiation of her acolyte.

Rupert Ping made what he could of what he saw: a transaction between hazy figures on the run, a revolution being triggered. The mountain, dull, furry and beastlike, brooded under a stormcloud almost as dark as itself. The summer air was bringing on the wet season. Bill Swan, nursing a packet of inflammatory leaflets, bent over his motorbike. Mr Ping flexed his fingers, the skin crackling along his forearms. Oh he was tired, at last he was tired. If nothing else, he had achieved tiredness. The barbarians were never tired though. And here was Bill Swan to prove it, blue eyes buttoning him into his red skin, virtually picking up the heavy BSA in his two hands, driving it by force of his own energy. And Felicia, bright star of so long ago, bouncing ridiculously off towards the pub, her whole figure an indistinct rhythm of careless obesity.

– Why am I here? Mr Ping murmured.

The motorcycle machine-gunned away. And out came Tony the ministering giant, smitten with loyalty, with an invitation to sit down and share food. Tony, wiping his black hands on a black rag, finding an excuse to be at the doorway, checking where Bill was going on his bike.

Seven

Bill Swan knew where he was going without working out why, he eased the bike along the rutted stony track and let himself in at the Lang gateway. He drove, bouncing gingerly over the grass, right up to Vivien's house stinking as it was with fresh paint. He needed her help. He might have asked Maggot instead if Maggot had still been around. Or Tony, yes a month ago he would certainly have asked Tony and not even thought of anybody else. But Tony was out of the question and somewhere among his insecurities he knew why. Uncle would be perfect if quicker on his pins and if he didn't fumble so much ... and didn't always want to be leader himself. The point was that Billy had no choice. This job had to be done. It was Billy's show. And there wasn't anybody else to help him do it. Also he needed moral support, which Vivien would give. He'd wait indoors. She would be home from the pub soon, for sure. He took the brownpaper parcel from his saddlebag and sat it on the outdoor table. At that moment he heard somebody inside the house (and thought for a flash of himself intruding at Ping's). Definitely someone was moving in there. He snatched up his gelignite and went in. But though he stamped across the floor so possessively, master of the establishment, fully within his rights and righteous, the interloper didn't seem to hear. There was no guilty hush. Billy hurried towards the sounds, right to the door of Viv's bedroom, his bedroom. And who should be inside but a stooping dotard with his back turned, poking around in the lady's open wardrobe. It was Billy's own back in a way, it was himself he saw doing something unspeakable. Intent as only the back of a deaf person can be.

– Uncle! he shouted, rage and betrayal giving an edge to his voice, the last curtains of respectful pretence ripped aside. He knew instantaneously what his grandfather was about, the old perv. The horrible thought of that decaying flesh still roused, against all probability and decency, to the calls of lust. Those hairfilled nostrils sucking at her perfume, the nicotine-mapped fingers fumbling tenderly among her intimate garments. All seen through the sickening realization that because it was his bad luck to catch the old man out, he would be forced to go through the full confrontation of accusations and, worse, the humbling of his so deeply loved grandfather. Finally the most painful thing to Billy was that he felt really angry, outraged and in the right.

– Hullo there Billo, said Uncle cheerful as you like and amazingly off-hand.

– What are you doing here Uncle?

– Just havin a little feel through her clothes and a little sniff at them.

Billy gaped: the coolness, the casual, factual complicity.

– What the bloody hell are you doing? he shouted again making his anger clearer than clear.

– I've been havin bit of a feel and bit of a sniff, his grandfather answered patiently.

But this was preposterous: the confession being made without trace of guilt, not even a snigger. Suddenly Uncle's face crinkled into a brownpaper smile, his eyes full of calm and compassion.

– Settle down mate, he recommended and advanced one walking stick at a time. I found out what I came to find out.

– What the bloody hell, Bill exploded again pompously. What were you up to?

– Findin out.

– You got found out yourself, but! You've been acting queer

some weeks now. Don't think I haven't noticed. And I don't like it.

The clothes hung straight and dead in the open wardrobe, all movement in them stilled. The room itself stood round the two men, naively inanimate as if its objects and corners and surfaces had been painted by a folk artist with a superb eye for detail but no sense of implied meanings, no perception of order in the accidental. The room was arbitrary as this misunderstanding.

– What have you got hidden in there? Uncle demanded reversing their roles and poking his stick at the parcel of gelignite so that Billy withdrew, nervous of the danger, protecting secrets, afraid that his plan might seem too extreme, fearful of being reduced to a comic inept character, a disjointed puppet of Bill Swan's supposed angry intentions. His tone of voice was exactly that of his grandfather a few moments before.

– I've been buyin a bit of gelignite on the side, he dared say.

– Gelignite is it? the old man asked rhetorically. Who's goin to use it?

But Bill recollected his own function as policeman.

– Sniffing what? he demanded finding he must consciously whip up moral indignation. If he felt resentful and at a disadvantage it was because of this effort.

– If I was to use gelignite, Uncle now seemed more than his ninety-one years. I'd want to know what I was doin first. Yes I'll grant he's a great puddin of pigshit, your father, but you got Rose your mother to think of too. No good endangerin her for nothin. Pretty as paint she is and better than he deserves.

Uncle remembered something. His face stricken.

– I heard, he croaked. I heard about the tree. Haven't trusted meself to go up there to the End and look. Couldn't believe what I was hearin. Couldn't credit the idea at all. As I heard it it didn't make no sense. Who'd imagine such a thing. Young tree in its prime and valuable. Even him I couldn't imagine doin it. Couldn't catch on. There always was that tree there ever since Bertha put it in as a mark of her happiness. I carried her over the threshold of that place and all. Eagles was in that tree when your father was a kid. Always eagles. There was lots of trees about

314

in them days, but they favoured the tallow. And even when more
and more trees went, that one stood big as you like and eagles
stopped there though everybody said they'd move. All the experts
round the place said so, Frank McAloon and old Archie and
Miles McTaggart, they all said eagles'd never stop with the forest
going. But stop they did. I remember them. Just the two. Always
in that tallow. And why did he cut it down? That's what beats
me.

Billy was caught between two currents. He could find no words
for either of his betrayals. This man, this blood relation, spoke
like an innocent even while the scent of forbidden clothing must
still be on his hands. Yet who knew the homestead and its tree
like Uncle and who else could understand what that butchery
meant? Then there was this house too, which Uncle knew better
than any man living because of Annie Lang, because he'd built
it. The four guardian pinetrees outside rustled as witnesses.

– I was sniffin her clothes, said the elder leaning forward on
his sticks so the rubber ferrules squeaked tiny sounds. Because
I can't never come up here again.

(Mr Swan, Felissy Brindle had said screwing up her mouth
like a baby's fist. You must be blind as well as deaf if you can't
see how Miss Lang hates that senator.)

– . . .?

– I'm handin her over to you, boy. Just for the favour. To keep
things in the family you might say. Though what she'll see in
a stump-footed stubborn little runt like you I'm hanged if I
know.

– You've got to be bloody joking! Billy checked to his relief
that at least she had cleared away the heaps of dirty clothing usually found on the floor.

– Memories. Memories, the old man mumbled, suddenly
vague and introspective. He kicked at his grandson's shins with
one of his walkingsticks. Memories, he shouted in his shaky bass
to prevent having to say anything more. Hadn't he once been the
daredevil who shinned up on to the School of Arts roof, stood
there, and hadn't he thrown back his head and bellowed with
triumph, hung out over the peak of the building and painted a

red heart to frame the initials A.S. and A.L.? By christ I was a troublemaker when I was your age, he confessed.

– I'm not planning to use this gelignite at home, said Bill eventually.

– Are you goin for Mr Whatdyacallit Milliner and his road machines?

– I hadn't thought of that.

Uncle pushed past and lumbered out along the passage.

– Got to get out of here, he said in a choked voice. You'll be right, he called back remembering there was a responsibility on him as head of the family and advisor to this young hopeful. You'll be right, he repeated. Only keep in mind that if you blow up their machines we'll have to take on the law.

Something now became urgent for Billy, he needed approval. Only one person could give it, or had the right to give it. In a moment the opportunity might be lost. Yet the words wouldn't come. He remained tonguetied about the very thing he must ask, and took refuge instead in more conventional matters.

– What were you sniffing, grandpa?

– Grandpa! Uncle wheeled round so fast and with such anger his sticks flew out and struck both walls of the passage simultaneously.

Billy himself felt outraged and excited by his insult too; but at a deeper level was that flush of satisfaction which comes of scoring a tactical advantage. Almost a slip of the tongue had turned out to be an inspired manoeuvre.

– I was sniffin her clothes, the old man said with sonorous dignity. Because I haven't sniffed a young woman's clothes for many a long year. Will that satisfy yer worship? He became thoughtful and at the same time tamer. Annie, he said, smelt different to that if I remember right.

The moment trembled between them as if one or other might disgrace himself with some show of weakness. They had little experience of this kind of thing.

– I came, Uncle spoke again, because I see you're back with her and that cuts me out.

– Cuts you out!

The idea was grotesque, his own grandfather victim to foolish hopes of a woman sixty years younger than himself. You ought to be laughing and not angry. Bad as the five-legged calf McTaggarts put a bullet in that morning.

– I'm going to blow up the Golden Fleece, Bill said on impulse.

– So's you can open up a lead to the seam, is it? Or are yer hopin to pick up lumps a the stuff? Better let yer father know then yous can go down on your knees together and make proper fools a the family. In this way he threw up a defensive barrage behind which his Intelligence Section got busy with the facts: it could only mean that Billy didn't know gold in the mass when it hit him in the eye, probably neither of the young ones knew what was laid out in front of them up at the highway site. Bill, being a steady fellow, should perhaps be told. But then he was young too, and the young have got their own way of looking at things. Could you expect him to turn his back on all the worthless rubbish a fortune can buy? Would it be fair? Would it be safe? And if that bugger George ever got to hear, there'd be no holding *him*.

– I mean to close the shaft, Billy said. Block it for good.

Rain cast a silvery net over the roof. They felt themselves trapped by what they knew.

– That's different then, Uncle apologized.

A gust of wet grass-odour swept through Vivien's house with memories of Annie. The pinetrees could be heard shivering. The passageway darkened. The mountain heavy and blind, a green impenetrable mass.

– What're yer thinkin about Billo?

– Whitey's.

– Who's goin to help you with the job? Uncle's clear diction gave him away: of course he'd guessed, Bill had her in mind.

The cloud from the mountain threw down its hot rain methodically now. They stood in the narrow passage, one listening, the other watching. Only now did it occur to Bill that his grandfather might be drunk; he recognized a whole farce of corroborative evidence, not least of which was the old cove's judicial slowness in all but that single whirling gesture of pain at his insult. He observed the shrivelled ankle bared between trouser-cuff and boot, a forgotten leg stuck out one side as Uncle rested on the tripod of the other and the two sticks.

– Soyouve foundiday? the drunken tribune munched his words. The Golden Fleece?

– I've found out where it is, he replied pedantically, slurred speech being contagious.

– Have you spoke to Missy Brindle or the saint?

– What do you take me for? Billy felt unreasonably irritated. And after them selling me the gelignite too.

At this moral problem Uncle coughed a few bleeding hunks of laughter. He spat into a crusted handkerchief and stuffed it incompletely in his pocket. The rain intensified, its drumming on the roof now the solid roar of wind through a tunnel.

– Their store shed that collapsed a few years back ...

– Is that where it is?

– Under that shed.

So Brinsmeads had known right through the years what the rest found out yesterday.

– Winnin form! They're an amazement when you think about it. All this time. You'll need a decoy then, to get them safely out a the way. Unless you do it by night with a smaller charge to be sure you don't blow up the house and that.

Watching his grandfather's face sent a chill of sympathy through the young man, reminded of something he'd seen not long ago. The old coot's skin lumpy and discoloured like a relief-map of mountain terrain, there were moles, and a glossy knob on his forehead held together with tiny purple veins, his ears stood straight out from a tufting of hacked-at hair, like a ruminant elephant he was, unpredictable, careless of what he might collide with. The lower lids of his eyes sagged, drained pink and rheumy. He held his head slightly sideways to make better use of the least deaf ear.

– God you're an ugly bastard, said Billy lovingly because he was afraid of what he now knew (that this was the face of the mad digger, the rotten corpse who'd fired his rifle after he'd died,

318

and you'd never have thought Uncle could appear like that, yet of course the chances were they shared a bloodline, like most other people, but oh my god fuckingbastard a lifetime of sickness for gold, not Uncle, the same gluey eyelids though ... there had been that dreadful rasping as he drew the back of his hand down Kel McAloon's cheek with its hollows set hard: this is what he knew).

– Oh man, he breathed his sorrow.

– What're you keepin me standin here for as if me legs was as young as yours? Uncle shouted against the din of rain pummelling Vivien's house.

– Are we related to the McAloons, apart from grandma?

– A course we are. Mrs Nell McAloon is my aunt. Though I don't know but she might only be an aunt by marriage. Why ask? The puzzle was too deep for him sorting back that far, and the storm too loud. What's more he hated the possibility of the talk turning to his wife, the troublesome Miss Bertha McAloon as she'd re-christened herself fifty years ago. He edged forward, nudging his grandson toward somewhere they could sit down. The changing light transformed his head to that of a Greek philosopher with eyes too deep to look into, a noble front of forehead, two vertical slashes of quick irritation between the eyebrows offset by fans of wrinkles pinching his cheeks into a perpetual smile, the wide sensuous mouth, broad cheek, the large simple question mark of his ear.

– Yes I've got gelignite and I'm going to blow it up, Bill Swan yelled with joy as he turned to lead the way out to the verandah. And was brought up to a sudden halt, face to face with a dripping wet Senator Halloran. Senator Halloran with the rain running off him in sparkling cords like those from the rotten gutter beyond, Halloran apologetic with wetness, his shoes exuding a secretion of water, his trouserlegs clinging and slocking.

– May I speak to Miss Lang please? the enemy pushed his request forward like a hostage between them.

But the showdown was past. Billy could only speak with fear for what this man might have overheard.

– Why don't you fuck off?

319

– I lost my dog, replied the statesman helplessly. He was a black dog, curly-haired labrador, had him with me a long time now.

What had he overheard? How could he have failed to hear? Gelignite: the plan? *I'm going to blow it up?*

– If we find yer dog, Uncle promised, you needn't worry because we'll definitely put a bullet through his head for you.

– Is Miss Lang here? the intruder demanded coldly in a voice used to commanding respect. Yet he was afraid. Law of the jungle. Movies about redneck violence. Easy-rider. Deliverance. You never knew. Lot of truth in the media.

They didn't answer. So Frank Halloran, friend of the friends of the needy and ally of Worthy Causes, turned his back. It was hopeless. He himself had chased the dog away. Who knows, Ocker might even now have set out on one of those heart-rending journeys across the continent, the symbol of loyalty on bleeding paws. And some wit had left a scrap of paper in the car with a mocking message, signed by a dog:

I love you. Do you love me. Then come and
let me out. I'll come home with you. Please
wait for my sign and be ready to leave
straight away.
    Love,
        Fido

He turned his back and retraced the puddles of his footprints out to the edge of the verandah. His shattered teacup of that morning still lay there in a heap, the faint tea stain around it. He didn't care to notice, couldn't understand callousness. He was keeping his eye on the enemy now as he delivered the parting shot of a state dignitary.

– The dog's name is Ocker, he said. They have my phone number down at the shop.

Rain rattled against his coat and he was having trouble keeping his balance on the steep sticky path outside, hobbling with the bruises of last night's shameful adventure.

– What sort a name is that? Uncle wanted to know. What's
Ocker mean?

The senator slushed away out of earshot, isolated in the world
of his intentions.

– Let him think what he likes, Uncle answered his grandson's
unspoken fears. Let him worry if he overheard anything. Do him
good.

They sat so they could watch the small birds dancing and
singing for the wet while above them one hawk spread the sodden
umbrella of its wings. The downpour wiped out the coastal plain
and made the mountain an island. Uncle spoke again.

– I had a dream last night mate and it's been nagging at me
ever since. Not that I'd do meself a favour wastin a good dream
on a rough little rogue like you, but I always was a generous cove,
and these sort a things has somethin invitin about them. I
dreamed I was standin on top of a hill, very smooth and grassy
with not a tree in sight, gazing out across a lovely stretch of
country, fields ploughed up and looked after so beautiful you'd
want to eat them. When I noticed somethin comin towards me,
still a long way off mind, straight as a ruler it come up hills and
down gullies, over creeks, never mind the creeks, it kept straight
like a religious sort of thing it was, just holdin to that straight
line was what counted and give the arse to everythin else. It was
a road, white road, I could tell that. Dream brought on by that
highway up there I dare say. But this road in me mind had a kind
of head like one of them furry caterpillars, sort of tufts of red
and white, and kind a rippling so that I didn't like her at all. More
of a nightmare than dream, a quiet one but.

Already the yard outside was awash, dead leaves and sticks
swirling downhill past the house. Bill squatted silently, waiting,
to see if Uncle had finished. He hadn't.

– It came a bit closer to me but never enough to get a clear
sight on them tufty things. That's what I don't like about a dream.
Not the same as Rememberin, with Rememberin you're always
right in it and you can tell what's happenin to you. Anyhow, whatever I was watchin made me wake in a sweat, I can tell you. And
I got up to ease me bladder. Just on dawn it was. And I went

to go outside for a piss when I caught sight a this man asleep on the kitchen floor. Well you see I'd forgot you was stayin with me. Felt me heart thuddin, I can tell you. Damn near waded into you with my sticks. You might a had a proper beatin whiles you was still rolled up in your blanket. My stars, I said, that's our Billy. And I felt better after.

– You got the highway on the brain Uncle.

– I dare say I have too, Uncle growled with dissatisfaction (the dream hadn't sounded right in the telling, when you put words to it you lost a hold of it).

But young Bill had the spirit in him, he knew what to say and how to go about it. He sat there jabbing the palm of one hand with a shard of china cup, denting the tough skin, ruminatively working at the sensation. The rain poured down evenly, so intense and purposeful you couldn't imagine it was possible to get above it.

– Who was Albert Swan, died on the eighteenth of November 1894?

– My old pa who married Louise McTaggart. Where did you see that?

– On a gravestone when me and the boys took dad's Bedford up round the mountain a few months ago.

– I know that gravestone. Not much left I suppose? I haven't been there in twenty years. Waste of effort, graveyards, if you ask me. Once dead you're dead. My old ma had that stone slab put there and a damn lot a good it did her. She made me promise to put one up for herself when she died but I never did; it was me livin mother I promised, and I'd have done anythin for her. Dead, I owed her nothin. Yes, I know the place you mean Billo.

– Foundations. That's the only thing left. And graves.

– Last to live there was Tommy Whitey. They named this place after him but he put off comin here and joinin other folk livin by the fall.

– What was the place called?

– London.

– London! Billy laughed with astonishment.

Something nagged the old man's memory, as an amputated

limb is said to weigh on the nerves, still passing faint messages. He was being observed by his grandson who pushed one big toe into a puddle left by the senator.

– I near smashed that johnny's face for him this morning, Bill said to help out. But it didn't help. His grandfather was already lost in a thicket of allusions and broken connections. So they lolled at ease, only the walkingsticks as reminders that anything had to be done. Having left home was such a luxury, able to forget the cattle, the fences, jobs crying out to be done, motors to be fixed and somehow kept going in the face of ruin, the filter to be cleaned, the bull bar for the Ford, Mum's new cooker rusting in the yard for want of a weekend's effort installing it. Things pleasant to think of, longstanding pressures cancelled out.

– Of course, Uncle began speaking. Whitey's used to have a mayor. Used to have a good couple a thousand living on the mountain one place and another when I was a boy. What's it now? Forty-nine? Forty-eight since little Mercy's gone. Plus this new girl, Annie's girl. Sorry to see Elaine and Eric pack up, those kids of theirs was a bit of life around the place. Specially young Fred. Had a soft spot for him, young fellow after me own heart. Yes, forty-nine and that's Wit's End included. We used to have a mayor all right. Wasn't Lord Mayor I don't think, just the plain sort. School of Arts was his office. Last mayor but two was the blacksmith. Died young. Big fat bloke and only fifty-seven. Used to watch the sweat come off of him, when he shook his head you'd see drops fly out good as rain. We never knew what took him. When he died the idea of havin a mayor went with him, you could say. Last of the line he was, for a while. Before him Shorty Collins was mayor but he never had the figure. No dignity. Specially comin only two after old man Brinsmead. Brinsmead was that dignified when he was alive you could have screwed a tap into him and drained the dignity off by the bucketful. Oh, years later, someone did get the idea of starting up the mayor thing again, there was a committee if I remember asked young Seb to accept the chain. But you couldn't expect it, so high and mighty Seb held himself though he wasn't more than thirty I'd guess. Now look at him (Uncle coughed as if laughing into a mug of pea soup):

323

storekeeper's brother and useless prop for the wall. Shorty Collins's son Ginger wanted it. Don't know why. So we gave it him on trial. He carried on for a year or so till he broke down cryin over the figure work. He never could sort figures out in his head. Nanny McTaggart reckoned her Artie was the man, a giant he was, like half the McTaggarts are. He looked his best when he was standing still. He looked good when he was praying or on the platform. As long as he didn't have to move quick and as long as he didn't have to speak, he was okay. It was him who had the great idea of a drinkin fountain for the poor. Put all his effort into that. And he had it built. Not that it ever worked. It never did, not even for the opening ceremony. When Artie died we put on a bumper funeral for him because there wouldn't be another mayor of Whitey's Fall. Nanny would've had the chain buried with him like them Egyptians did. She'd have seen to it too if it hadn't of been for a possum that crept in in the night before they nailed the lid and grabbed it out of our dead man's hands and made off with it into the trees. Next morning there was fourteen big ironbarks felled to try to find that chain. We never found the bugger. But I'll tell you what, there was enough wood in them logs for the whole town to stay warm through five winters. Those warm winter fires were Artie's one success as a public figure, his memorial in a manner of speakin. Who knows?

Billy started messing the chips of china. He loved to hear the old man talk, as a rule, but not today. Something of this unexpected irritation must have communicated itself because Uncle switched mood, hoisting himself free of the bog of sentimental times gone by.

– Help me up mate, he grunted. I'm going. He prepared to brave the rain. I'll tell you about London one day.

– Yeah.

– I knew you was in love with her right from the first, Uncle remarked, in the passion of the moment his words coming out with pedantic clarity. The day Mercy died young Elaine McTaggart came and fetched me from the pub you see and told me the two of yous was elopin on the motorbike. I told her to mind her damn business and leave me to mine. Ah well, this house'll be your place now I suppose. I only come up to find out. Only come up for a last look around. I don't doubt it'll be my last sniff of what a young woman's clothes smell like for a power of years. He turned gay, adding, What if I was to go up to one a them fashion judies, them tourists, and said mind if I have a sniff a your skirt! that'd give em somethin to think about.

Then he turned his hateful old back, bent legs capering, the headful of dirty thoughts nodding, one walkingstick dangling as he clawed at the rail, easing his weight from crooked foot to crooked foot, and tested the security of the wet ground when he reached it.

Bill could crow into the tomb. He was cock-a-hoop of a grotty little cottage. His ninety-one-year-old rival had gone down admitting final defeat. Down in the mud and out. You could signal for trumpets and put out the flags. The clouds had shifted and the dark mountain hung in fragments from the sky, an underwater explosion about to cascade pearl chandeliers into the paddocks, flat as the curved earth would allow. Only then did Bill remember what was worrying him all along: Vivien left back there in the clutches of Madbag Brinso and Mum Collins, her pleading eyes full of fear and surprise, her neck so twisted you could see the gristle of her adam's apple plain as a man's. He went back indoors, king, to decide what to do next. He threw himself on the bed because wasn't it his? Wasn't it?

Eight

As he edged on to the track, Uncle was shaking, not just from cold and rain, nor the scene with Billy and the appearance of the enemy government man, but from a memory of London. When still a young man he had gone back there with an uncle of his to get the wheels off an abandoned dray while they were still good. When they'd finished the job he wandered alone among the creaking rotting buildings while his uncle sat back for a smoke. Despair drove people from the town, you knew it and you could still feel it: not fire, not lack of water; they were not forced out, not evicted. Despair written on the place as it might be one day on Whitey's. Slow rot. He recollected the curiosity of finding a kind of fungus, small flaps growing all over the door of an unroofed barn. He'd looked closely. Couldn't remember what. Couldn't imagine what. Dry leathery flaps. Till he saw the nail through each one, old nails rusting into the wood. They're ears! he croaked and hurried for somewhere he could wash the hand that had touched. Ears. Nothing to worry about, as his uncle had smiled, only off of the Chows and the Blacks in the early days. But you knew the old fellow was already queer in the head and once had a tattoo cut from his arm by a Melbourne surgeon at a cost of nine pounds, and then paid a taxidermist at the museum to have it preserved and mounted on a plaque. Remember the plaque. And the tattoo which was a blue falcon. It must have meant something or he wouldn't have gone to so much trouble and expense to have it taken off ...

Uncle skidded. His mind had wandered. He wasn't watching where he was going. Like a beginner on skis his helpless sticks projected at odd angles as his feet went from under him and he fell. The land caught him in the back with a tremendous thump. He lay there winded and shocked. Of course he had fallen once like this when he was a boy, that fabulous year it snowed at London and the mountain vanished altogether into the white sky and ice lay thick on the ground. Himself and his mates skidding again and again along one slippery strip, creating a slide, running at it like bowlers to a cricket pitch. Then thump and he was down and couldn't get up for a minute, so the others laughed and then got scared. And here was this same little boy flat in the mud with warm rain soaking the front of his shirt. Next thing Annie Lang and young Bill were one each side of him like a pair of wonky crutches making headway towards the house. One of those pine-trees shaking down huge drops in the wind, I planted them pines, Uncle tried to say to establish some respect for himself. Mouth working at it. Sound not wanting to come. Now it was Uncle's turn to be installed in Vivien's bed, propped there like a huge rag doll no one would ever want. But first up ten steps and then along the passage. Heave ho. Careful.

They gasped and puffed in your ear, you could swear the two of them was bellows and a weak fire trying to blaze: o your fat arse they don't know what good times you had rorting and fishing and travelling through the weather here help that leg a bit up the stair no o lord love us there were you laughed till the tears ran and when the trucks came in you got yourself that Dodge and ran it and ran it what about picking up the ladies at Yalgoona and halfway up the mountain the damn thing boiled squirting steam leaving rusty powder all over the motor clicking hot enough to fry eggs keep it turning over love while I add a drop at a time and seeing the fanbelt caused it broken now then ladies you said like announcing an interval for icecream which of you darlings is going to be the lucky one to save us with her stockings a pair of silk stockings and you could fix this good enough to get us home at least and young Bunty Buddall giggling fit to give herself hiccups saying you did it on purpose to see my legs Uncle coming good with the stockings modest she went down behind a bit of scrub to pull them off but you catching a glimpse of suspenders dangling though you tried not to being a gent at heart darling legs as they were and her lifting her foot turning it inwards pretty as you like to roll one stocking over her ankle ah Bunty you're the heroine and you'll be awarded Queen Mary's Medal for female bravery if we have any say with Queen Mary take my word there goes the last stair on the flat at last wait wait for breath bloody fall like you fell as a kid on ice but never saw ice like that again thank you Annie kindly but a man's lost without his pipe you like a big rush of smoke the sweet flavoured stuff flake of course only ponces smoke mixtures where you can't taste what's in it and anyway half of it scent by the way it sticks round your dentures afterwards bad as cold fat no you give her a little pat on the shoulder helpless fingers she's helping you stand all said and done thank you lovey ah those Virginia swindlers run-down colonies new blood dangerous mix as we know here your worship mate money the root of it no doubt about that yes ta it does ease the back the spine to lie down again you know what you mean to say if you could find the words ta for the kindness gentle hands young Billy a decent feller though what his father means by murdering good timber you don't and couldn't make sense not to mention if eagles have feelings eagles without a home after all these years sticking it out once their forest was gone loyalty that couldn't be anything else o yes animals do have and birds as well well-known o lordy a beautiful rest darling but somebody ought to pick that leg of yours up off of the floor yes the foot down there somewhere you can't see lying back comfortable where you are yes that's the one too right you're alright now pig in shit they're leaving you so she can make a cup of tea and he can talk to her in private well fair enough you say no snooping old man with jealousies glad of the time because something deep is a problem you have to fish for and bring up room looks bigger from

328

a lying down position the tongue and groove ceiling got a bit of
a sag to it must be the weather seeping through though no sign
even with this rain and rain pounding so you're back son what're
you doing Billy why should they come off no man's going to take
your clothes off wet or not nor no woman neither come to that
so don't anyone get ideas you'll be right it'll soon work off as
steam and you can brush the dried mud sorry about the blankets
though looking forward to a minute's peace to get things straight
but your mother was just like that about wet clothes in the house
dry between the toes chills and so forth superstition water never
hurt anybody goodbye and thank you must clear the old brain
get all this muck out no good something deep there must think
good times with picnic races and the Massey Cycle Club when
cycles the rage though you didn't have so far to go at Whitey's
or else too far of course on a bike city man's invention really the
bicycle but the sport another matter and decorated cycles for the
girls in hats and flounces wearing white and their sweet soft pink
cheeks and white fingers you'd want to slip your own among ah
the treacherous past is treachery whatever felt better than this bed
you may well ask can't hear a thing problem with deafness big
enough earholes god knows who made them but gone brum crook
state of affairs when you can't move get up and see when you
hope like hell those kids have made things up but of course they
have no need to worry and is that you Bertha old girl nice wet
nose have you been asleep you lazy hound no that's enough licking what's got into you have you forgotten how to behave but
got something else to fish for down there somewhere hidden need
a piss rather urgent but can't move much wait nursey nursey take
my hand but look the other way you were steward at the picnic
races back in the conscription days a battle that was with the auth-
orities coming up the mountain road and nobody else to lead
public opinion ladies dear ladies announcement the government
agents are coming to take your men or put us in jail so look after
the race meeting my dears while the boys and me get hold of
shotguns and meet outside the pub in a trice the races turned
into the first all female handicap events in the history of New
South Wales with Grandma Collins at eighty as official starter

the skirts were off and the jodhpurs on before the government came creeping round the last bend choking in a cloud of mountain dust those were sporting days no question and then they set about taking out their nasty feelings by parading through the town all military show with brass and straight lines and stiff arms and up ridiculous towards the mountain paraded piff puffing but grim when the whole forest opened fire above their heads amazement the officers with their braid and ribbons running like a lot of madhouse christmas trees clink clank and their lovely boots looking like yellow velvet and shouting orders come out of there you cowards but they never saw a one of you and nobody got hurt so they retired to the racecourse in time to watch Bertha your wife-to-be come romping home on the skewbald gelding in the eight furlongs and stayed for the sight of Olive McTaggart bareback so mustn't have been so bad as expected human at least and even cast a bet here and there according to legend but next time they sent their requests by post demanding obedience and stupid Kel McAloon gave in and volunteered but not the rest they never heard you still existed even ten years after armistice there wasn't a man jack had filled in a government form for fear of letting down the side and afterwards you and your rorting mates diggers indeed coming yahooing whoopeeing down off the slopes as the dust settled behind the official cavalcade and the ladies refusing to give up their prize money for the races they rode and you had to grant them they carried the day with style ah the lovely creatures flushed and panting from the vigorous events plus the triumph of doing it and the whiff of sweat nothing more delicious to the nose and eyes old eyeballs all looking perving and brain click clack imagining while papa Walter Schramm came dancing down the street purple with rage shouting that some maniac had shot his chimneypots to pieces with about forty cartridges o boy you've got to ease this bladder somehow why not sit and swing your legs over first or call out understandable after all natural there you are Billy Billy you see it's like this I wonder Billy yes thanks didn't like to trouble or anything sorry it's natural and old timers have the frequent need as a rule you never knew Olive McTaggart son did you married Frank McAloon back in the twenties nor Gil her brother the most giant man could bend solid iron with his hands never seen a sight like it but jumped over Whitey's Waterfall because he couldn't understand anything especially not Jessie McAloon on her second time round with marriage who had her third time with his brother Paddy afterwards and Jessie said Gil had the biggest cock in the Empire and offered to have him show it at the harvest festival for a donation to the Indian Missionary Society though others said it was just for the chance for her to skite he didn't understand and a waste when you think of it a giant like that and such a famous two-pound cock thrown away on the world for want of an ounce of brain while the other ladies of town had a celebration of tea and easter cake thanksgiving for being let out of their sins of coveting and temptations of the flesh beyond what's respectable and him having given her three children by the time he was sixteen and you wouldn't have known D'Arcy Collins another suicide a bit too handy with his rifle was determined to prove he could hit the mark even if it was pointblank bit of a juggler too used to go in for fire-eating also a sword-swallowing act on the side done for the school concert every year ended up swallowing the muzzle of his rifle and practising clever things with his toes doesn't do to be too clever he was the one left a note on the kitchen table just before dawn milking if you want me I'll be down with the cows and so he was a half his head in the gutter of piss ah that feels so good yes finished now you can help us back if you will room turning touch giddy why the blasted hell this rain and going out like that more haste less speed Grannie said right she was too oh ahh better no need to stay fine just fine be up soon and right as rain don't suppose you ever heard tell of the Wit's End murder did you no well that was before your time too and never solved though everybody knew who did it baby dead of suffocation and nobody able to suspect the only suspect cute little girl of four she was and did it females not the same as us more jealous possessive feel more there's a fire in them we haven't got ah but the murderer grew up to be somebody's mum and somebody else's grandma and ate apples and drank milk like anyone else so aside from a touch of extra respect she survived got along like any other girl we all knew and knew she'd never forgive herself and not forget so why remind her can you still hear or can't a deaf man catch your answers no just as well blabber-mouth full of the useless past give us your paw Bertha old girl old faithful o lord love us yes ahh that's

The rain had stopped. Silence. Arthur George Ortrid (Uncle) Swan lay sunken in the bed where he'd once made love to Annie Lang. It was the same bed standing in the same position. He and only he had changed. He was smaller than he'd ever been, lighter and less noticeable, you could see through his skin. Annie had gone, he had changed. The rain stopped. He lay silently help-lessly sunk in comfort, thinking of the shortness of life, the trick-ery of ninety-one years. The wardrobe, painted green and heaped with cardboard boxes, filled one corner; there was a rose on its righthand door which Annie had painted there and promised to paint a matching one in white on the left door, but only ever man-aged the red one. The faint powerhouse of deafness hummed in his head which lay placed like a precious object of art on a white cushion in the brilliant air. Space had come to rest around him. Annie had not changed, she'd somehow found the key to living on. She turned her back on the past of Remembering but instead she'd achieved another more puzzling way of lasting, a jump across space: here was her rose still glossy red, her bed full of memories, even her same home-made sheets by some miracle res-urrected, her old lampshade none the worse, her choice of lino for those willing to stretch out and look, her very self renewed replaced duplicated, Vivien perfect as a double and even having her gestures, her look.

At that moment Uncle experienced what he later described as bein hit with the inspiration.

– We've got to fight them, he called.

The room was full of Vivien and Bill and of Bertha barking into the morning sunshine. Yes, the rose glittered and the world was sponged with new air.

– We've got to fight, he repeated. Instead of mopin about with what was and what ought to be, we've got to make it be. No good tryin to explain to the likes of Sebbie or Felissy Brindle. It's you and me and young Tony'll make it and Mum Collins god bless her for a scandalous bag of dripping. There was a time when we took to the hills with our guns you see, and that taught the bastards.

– Calm down, said Annie/Vivien. You're getting carried away.

And yes he was subsiding, deflating, hideously, a shrivelled balloon with the air escaping, his real moments abandoned to a different occasion. What was happening? He could no longer distinguish between a Remembering and ordinary life, or could it be the future? and was it still himself or was it Bertha the hound living this nameless airless alarm? Who was the man hammering, up there on a ladder hammering nails into timber, building, putting battens on a roof looking out over the valley like a sweet breath of childhood, and then climbing down, backwards, shakily, feeling the urgent need to lie down somewhere solid and safe. Yet seeing the body from outside, seeing it, himself? come climbing down. Being inside the feeling, yet outside the sufferer. Uncle lay in bed twisting against this vision of fate, against recognition, against the omen of the old man building afresh, the old man lying gratefully on a bare floor. But no, not a man . . . a dog and in the grass, yes Bertha out in the sunshine lying there with head alert. She lies, ears pricked. Suddenly her head goes up, the long elegant nose pointing to the sky where a hawk circles far above and is gone. She turns her attention to her paws which she licks a few times for the sake of routine. A tiny whistling sound. And her head snaps up again, ears as far forward as they'll go, the muscles bunching in her haunches ready to give chase, her mouth tightening and the ghost of a growl rumbling through her. At another noise, this time from behind, one ear switches to the job of interpreting it while her attention remains undiverted. Something's about to happen. The growl becomes almost like a song, evil is in the sunny air. The stupid wrens dart and dance their bright blue patterns and the yellow robin methodically obeys the dictates of his voracious appetite. But something is seriously wrong. Bertha is now standing. Life is out of kilter. The evil has no direction yet. She puffs little exploratory breaths through her nose, scenting, her tail rises stiff and angry. No hawk could interest her now, receiving a telepathic message through her skin as she is. Eyes, ears, nose, all at a pitch of awareness. Her hackles stand right along her spine and in a clump down near the tail. A yodelling cry breaks from her and she stands immobile. She is beginning to know and ready to understand. Birds twitter in and out of the bushes. Insects drone contented with business in the warmth. The hawk resumes that same circle in the high air as if it had been marked out by his repeated passage. Flies promenade the dog's flank while a few fleas make brief appearances before vanishing industriously back in among the warm fur.

She knows.

– We've got to fight, Uncle muttered thickly.

– Calm down, said Annie/Vivien. You're getting carried away.

– It's up to us now, said Uncle with a flash of understanding that the moment had come, the land could be truly claimed as their own, that at last they belonged and if they didn't defend the mountain, nobody would.

– It's up to you to rest, she insisted.

– Listen. We've still got our guns and there's water at London. Help me out of this bed for christsake Bill me boy. We're goin to give that little lot a stickybeaks some fun to remember. Can't lose. It's in the bag.

– Uncle, said Bill Swan like a priest, taking hold of his hand to restrain him, and looking at it as if it were no longer part of anybody. Uncle, you've been here for two weeks.

By Thursday Uncle tottered about, learning his first steps, getting used to his walkingsticks and planning for the morning. The morning had become a matter of urgency because of what he had been told and what he had seen. Quite a lot of things appeared to have happened while he dozed and drifted on that well-remembered bed. For a start a meeting had been called, a meeting with the government men, the Milliners, O'Wheelers and the Hallorans. This ought to be stopped. Sebastian should stop it, because once you meet with them you're on their ground and there's no beating them.

334

Uncle practised with his walkingsticks, earnest as an athlete in training. Two weeks lost: it was a tactical calamity. In the morning he'd have to be able to walk down the hill to the store, it must be done. Then there was the domestic matter of a quarrel: this was hard to believe but young Bill had fallen out with Tony McTaggart . . . and the two of them close as twins since they were toddlers. And what the hell for! However, you were told to pull your head in and mind your own interfering business. The thing was final, Bill Swan and his mate were at war, nothing less. And this was the very time they needed to stick together for the sake of Whitey's. The last young people of the town were repeating ancient history, as if nothing could reconcile them.

Picking hairs from his nostrils and sneezing as a result, Uncle decided to confine himself for the present to his program of physical reclaim. Just that. He'd know what to think and what to say when he got there and heard the full story from Sebbie's own lips. Meanwhile it was a bit of steel in the wrists he needed. A long time since the polo field at Jahore, ay? Or was that him? Getting a bit muddled by luxury.

– It's not you I'm crooked on, he assured Vivien when she appeared hurt. It's my stupid self for gettin too old to be any use. I've got to do somethin because I know what's right. And he watched her as she painted the windowframes green. Nice dob a colour, that, he remarked. Can't recall anyone paintin anythin in these parts since George had a go at the milkshed, about when them nongs went off to be heroic in the last shindig in 1939, all about nothing.

– I wouldn't call *that* about nothing, she retorted, stung, the memories of being bombed still fresh.

– Of course it was. Same people is still runnin the world right now, bar a couple of them. Isn't that right? All they did was kill off millions who done nothin and got nothin out of it. That's how I see it. Clearin away the surplus in a manner a speakin, like the bloody plague, but into the bargain look what they did to the governments of the world, forced them to hand over their money to factory johnnies makin guns and aeroplanes, they was the ones with the whiphand. Winnin form. Now isn't that right? Looks that way to me. Course I'm only an old bushman sittin up on my little mountain like Jacky; and you've travelled the world. But it costs nothin to have an opinion. And if you've got no opinions where's your civilization? It's an unhealthy smell paint has these days, never used to be half so bad, as I remember. Then a course I'm deaf as a gate and they say that sharpens yer nose. Probably I'm growin more particular with age too.

Good heavens, she saw it: here was the whole town fighting against preservation of their buildings beyond their own use, while she was busy painting Aunty's house. Quietly she rolled her brush in newspaper, placed the lid on the paint tin and left them to rot. No wonder there was something in Senator Halloran's tone when he said at least there's somebody in Whitey's Fall painting.

Uncle was as good as his promise; the following morning he wheezed into the general store, each step a labour, waving aside Felicia's anxious attempts to prevent him barging straight through into Fido's den. This was no time for courtesies, he was exhausted and had to sit where he could talk in private. He made for the kitchen where he remembered it was. Two hens and a cockerel skidded on the lino in a desperate squawking attempt to escape out the back door. Sebastian, drifting in from the yard, his halo of white hair wispier than ever, his tunic vaster and more blurred at the edges, withdrew politely to let the fowls past. And then greeted his visitor.

– Sebbie we've got to stop them, Uncle declared as he crashed into a chair. Sweet reason won't stop them, that's for sure.

– And you mean that God has given it to us to have the necessary supplies?

– Well he certainly doesn't seem to have had me in mind, Uncle replied astutely.

– Do you remember how they came out to enlist us Uncle?

– Surely you wasn't old enough then?

– I was past thirty.

– Well now, how time plays tricks. Yes and we put on a good show too, thanks to ladies handicap events at the showground.

– This is a serious matter then.

– It's the life or death of all we stand for, Uncle replied promptly, banging the table with his hand and looking round in surprise at how unfamiliar this kitchen had become in the twenty-seven years since he was here last. Sebastian did not reply for a long time, but sat staring through the window from which he'd seen Mrs Ping's truck lurch out of sight, from which he'd seen fate as a blue car approaching round the curves, also Bill Swan's motorcycle slewing down a matter of minutes too late; and then because he hadn't moved, he'd been able to watch the shuttle bring back the same threads through the tapestry God was completing, the motorcycle and the car; the continuity homed in his mind, the end, the beginning; the purpose. He had persevered with sitting there till the very parliamentarian he'd once written to in anger intruded on his privacy wanting to telephone the Yalgoona police. We prefer not to enter into debate on the subject of our own lives, Sebastian Brinsmead Esq, he had written, rather we would ask that you extend us the courtesy of regarding the matter as closed ... no such courtesy had been extended, instead the senator came in person, not to listen but to persuade; these historical and aesthetic resources were apparently to be exploited despite any opposition.

– We were up on the hill behind the hotel, Sebastian said smiling serenely.

– They want to fill this place with trinket shops and them car-park things. If you're lucky, Uncle added slyly. You'll get a prime job considerin that beard of yours, real picture it is, that beard, the tourists'll want you in all their snaps, you'll be a regular favourite I'll guarantee.

– To be quite honest with you Uncle, we don't know what we might have in the shop. Things accumulate, you'll understand, over a long period.

– Explosives and ammunition, we need. When can yer let me know?

The Watch that Ends the Night

One

The brutal facts of the matter were these: Bill Swan and Tony McTaggart had argued in the bar of the Mountain, the word *she* was shouted on both sides, they'd then gone out the back according to custom and to save violating the Rememberings going on in there; Tony had knocked his enemy (his paragon) unconscious in the dirt and left him like that; Billy who found the shame insupportable prowled the street for days, a puppet of revenge. Those were the facts as everyone knew. Whitey's Fall was thrown into confusion, something deep and basic being threatened; the two last remaining of their young people were going to murder each other. Cain and Abel playing out their drama again, Romulus and Remus, old memories. The town felt itself dying, for the first time. Individuals lost their vigour, hands grew shaky, eyes dimmed, deafness became contagious, disused crutches and sticks were dusted and put into service, tractors and cars broke down with multiple minor faults, bits of iron began slipping off roofs, cats' teeth fell out, horses limped, dogs grew grey round the muzzle, the wind blew harder and dust crept into rooms where it had never been allowed to settle before. The old people felt themselves futilely old which was worse. Mr Ian McTaggart was ashamed of being one hundred and two, with the knowledge that

341

because of his great-grandson Tony he might not reach one hundred and three and could not guarantee the town would survive longer than himself; could not imagine the town had any chance once he was dead. Mrs McAloon as the oldest resident took root in her chair like some twisted parasitic vine and said here she would stay and wait for Redemption. They were brought up against it: the highway already intruding over the skyline, the machines audible all day, things would not go on for ever; and now these sole survivors of the plague of boy children were locked in a determination to kill off the tribe as gruesomely and publicly as possible.

A whole week after the fight people spoke in undertones and seldom visited the hotel. Rememberings seemed pointless if there was to be no future. Miss Brinsmead herself began to forget things. Mr Brinsmead, standing as ever in his shop against the wall, was no longer heard to chuckle at intuitions of God's purpose; Mum Collins suffered pangs of angina and closed her door against the morning tea circle; the great agglomeration of repair work at the welder's shed stood untouched, for Tony had taken himself off without a word. No one knew what Mr Ping was doing with his time, certainly not the jobs on hand. The only person who did see him actually decided to seek him out: Vivien believed that now at last her opportunity had come to do something for her Whitey's Fallers. As both an outsider and an intimate, her privilege stood clear in her mind. She would find Tony. She would explain. This much she knew, in some way she was to blame, that he and Billy had fought over her. It must be done frankly and neutrally, there must be the chance to talk, for him to release his pent-up frustration. Even to see the situation had a comic side to it. All she needed was to find him.

As it happened, he came to find her. Tormented with doubts and suppositions, he could think of no other solution to his misery.

One morning Billy went off to work for Uncle to cut away some of the vines and clear his yard. Tony arrived at the house, calling out from the gate, a huge awkward pale presence, refusing to go indoors to Billy's sewer of love and what else. Vivien proposed a walk then, put on her shoes and followed him. One behind the other they were refugees hurrying through the paddocks across illegal boundaries till they could no longer be seen from the town. The way they walked, that jointless action, the way they kept looking back over their shoulders, declared their guilt and they knew it.

– Who owns this place? she asked as he held the strands of barbed wire apart for her to climb through a fence.

– Pings. This one was Alice's paddock.

Foreboding filled her. The warm day, the dappled sky a flat slab of blue marble with the mountain a plain blue fault in it, the dusty grass, the stiff wind driving her on in case her resolve might weaken, none of it reassured her. Her instincts clamoured to warn her she was making a mistake.

– Mrs Ping, she said with horror, afraid of treading on a hand.

– One of the best, he nodded.

– And you work for Mr Ping don't you? she asked seeing herself as she had run into the workshop one morning shouting that the woman was in danger in her truck. And later, her hands hot with shapes of Bill Swan, death in her lungs, she'd stood while Mr Ping asked who says my wife didn't know?

– He's alright but he doesn't like us, Tony confessed observing his boots crushing the windswept grass. Calls us cattle. I hear him in there. Then, how're the cattle? he asks me every morning the same when I come in to work. And you hear the ladies at Mum Collins's having a laugh. Hear that? he says, it's milking time again!

Vivien thought of herself laughing at that morning tea club. Would they never get anywhere through all this grass? She wanted to escape the place where Alice stood bellowing for help, poor Alice too old for bearing another calf. The consequences of fertility. They passed a metal bucket on its side, quite new and out of place. Even the wind seemed powerless to dispel the shapes of flight in paralysis.

Tony led the way out through another fence and back on to the track, towards a boxy brown building with a white cross nailed to the end wall. He was taking her where no one ever went. Here they could be certain of talking without interruption. In one of those abrupt changes of mood typical of the mountain, everything was restored to its customary beauty, the blood flowing again, the numbness gone, birds calling, the scent of warm grass billowing up. They had put the threat behind them and were received into a seductive delusion that all was pure and safe: Vivien reassured and refreshed, Tony buoyant at having lured her here for a dreamed-of assignation, for the words, the fantastic sentimental words he had rehearsed. Wasn't this a victory already, a victory over Bill?

– The road is what people want, he said, making use of the alternative conversation to the weather.

– The people of Whitey's? she asked in disbelief.

– No, all the other people. They want it. (He needed to explain that they didn't have to know why they wanted it, nor did they have any choice in what they could want. But he had no words for his knowledge. A road was the thing, like God might be the thing, or starting a war. People went mad at the thought of a road, that was all, they killed each other on roads, sacrificed home and safety to roads, trees and gardens had to go, river banks, hills had to be sliced in half, if you only went as far as Yalgoona you could see that for yourself, rabbit warrens and wombat holes had to be bulldozed under, money needed for feeding the sick and aged had to be taken for roads, *given* for roads and willingly. This he understood and, naturally, he meant her to understand. How could any more be said? And why didn't she cotton on to this for herself? But then she was not just a city woman but a pom, the kind of person who has to put things down on paper before she can see what they mean. Yet he wanted her to see, if only so she'd have to respect him for knowing something unknown to her. Clumsiness was his downfall. Billy at least had the words, yes Billy could talk himself out of the grave. So Tony knew, even as he sorted through his recollected lessons for words, as he listened now for Mrs Ping's weary repetitions, what he longed to express was perhaps an idea Vivien couldn't understand, because she didn't already know it, feel it. Yes he knew, with his deep desire not to be exceptional. He wanted to explain, but this was the kind of thing that never did get explained. Apart from which, she robbed him of energy simply by being there with him, by having come, enjoying it, the two of them alone. His clumsiness came to his aid, he could hide behind that, play the dumb country idiot, his helpless failure to explain could be passed off without betraying its complex causes.)

They were standing at the porch of the disused church watching wasps clustered round a couple of nests under the guttering. The insects filled the quiet morning with tremendous activity, sounding tuneful as a mouth organ. Tony and Vivien stepped forward together. They were in a vestibule of blotchy red walls where ecclesiastical lilies and trefoils had been stencilled, crude as graffiti.

– How cool it is, she said giving her short curly hair a shake.

Yes and it smelt of the mountain, it had been empty so long, this tiny chamber filled with wasp-song. Vivien realized she was a fool.

– Straw, said Tony McTaggart digging the toe of his boot in some straw rotting beside the doorway. Rather this than trying to explain to her what she couldn't understand about Hughie Milliner and the road workmen.

They didn't look at each other, some delicacy prevented this happening, entering the little timber church itself, glancing about them like the captives of headhunters being shown the altar where they would be stars of their last performance. Yes this was a case of something close to panic. The dark red walls, old caked blood, the white ceiling dirty with a grime unknown in civilized parts, the apse a corrugated iron lean-to painted pale blue, its roofing speckled with stars; and where the altar had been lay a dump of decaying lino.

– Lino, he said nodding his shaggy head so that her attention was drawn to his neck which might be as big round as her waist only that this was a ridiculous idea. She saw how immense he was and how terrible he could be if it weren't for those shy boy's eyes and the nervous tremble of his lips, also the softening of hairs, silky on his arms, tangled and coarse on his chest. She recognized his patience and tolerance, his perpetual yearning, the great spirit that had driven his body into an exile of uncertainty.

Around the arch of the apse HOLY HOLY HOLY had been painted in gold gothic letters of not quite equal size; and this made Vivien love the place as people had loved it before they abandoned it. The two of them stepped across gaps in the flooring, still hearing the wasps droning their hymnal from monastery cells they'd built under the guttering. What Tony could not explain was that people *wanted* a road, that a road was a kind of sacred object which you didn't have to decide about or justify; known to be what man must make. Her ignorance of this was obvious. She thought you could argue about it and reason with it, she treated Senator Halloran and Hughie Milliner as if they might be persuaded to her point of view, as if they might see Whitey's Fall as an exception and not build the road after all. It was impossible for them not to build the road. You might as well ask them to justify sleeping, you might reason that they spend a third of their life in bed which could be better used. For himself, he knew why they built the road. He hated and feared it but he did know why they had to build it. Yet she, with all her learning and her travel, she could not seem to understand this. Despite her softness and tact, she was too rigid and inflexible in her beliefs to know what they were doing. Uncle knew, muttering about gelignite and violence: he knew. But she with her talk of committees, petitions, delegations and letters to the editor, showed no comprehension whatever, the darling lady. So small she appeared to him, yet so bursting with fire and ideas. For a stolen second he glanced down at the top of her head and a possessive feeling flowed through him as honey. Somewhere barricaded inside him a vibration was triggered: with a sensation of leaping he recognized it, he'd been through this experience once before. The vibration hummed to the pitch of the wasps busy with construction and storage. Outside the windows Tony could see lush paddocks, but Vivien wasn't tall enough, all she saw were treetops and, draped across the high sill, a pair of disintegrating trousers. The obscenity of the trousers raised fury in her, uncaring for safety she strode across the gapped floor and threw the trousers out, but they wouldn't go, snagged on rusty nails they clung there so she had to tear and rip them free, she had to hold them disgusted though she felt, and make an exhibition of how enormous they were. At last she flung them clear and turned red-faced to her companion, who was thinking ludicrously they might well have fitted him.

– People! she swore, her voice for the first time raised above a murmur.

He nodded, hoping to distract her from what had till now been hidden by those trousers: a heart daubed on the wall with an arrow through it, an arrow with a penis head, and the legend *Bubbles loves me*. He would like to protect her from that.

– It used to be a church, he said idiotically.

She went to where the pulpit once stood and faced him. She was serious but smiling, perhaps a little timid, and anxious to rid herself of all anger and fear.

– I love it, she said reviving the vibration in him. The bees love it too.

– Wasps, he whispered or didn't whisper.

– My great-aunt used to take me to church in England sometimes. Her favourite was the Palm Sunday sermon. She could cry over that. The church decked with sprigs of willow. And the lesson about how they strowed the pavement with palmleaves and Jesus entered Jerusalem. Aunt Annie would cry over that and say, look what they did to him when he got there though. She used to go to church in a big hat covered with real flowers on Palm Sunday and she'd have flowers pinned to her dress as well. It took ages to get her ready in the morning. But it meant more to her, for some reason, than Easter or Christmas. And to think it might all have started here in this church. I must write and tell her the news. Look, part of a hymnbook! Vivien stooped to reach down between the rotten boards, retrieving a few dog-eared pages between covers.

– I know these, she exclaimed joyfully, it seemed so important that she did. She began, taking her note from the wasps, crooning a phrase here and there as if to prove to herself she could remember.

The humming in Tony's chest took him unawares. In a flash it ballooned to a great painful lump, he fought back but it throbbed and grew with amazing rapidity, out of his control, he was a vessel, an instrument.

– *O God our help in ages past, our hope for years to come*, he sang.

Vivien stood transfixed, the heady sound filled the church, every note perfectly pitched.

– *Our shelter from the stormy blast, and our eternal home.* The ancient hymn young and jubilant. *A thousand ages in thy sight are like an evening gone*, this was a magnificent voice, a great voice, the power of it verging on the painful, *Short as the watch that ends the night, before the rising sun.* She felt humbled, ecstatic, in the presence of a talent she'd not suspected, having forgotten that part of Billy's story about the quest for the Golden Fleece. Yes, and it all meant something to her. *Time like an ever-rolling stream bears all its sons away*, he was grieving now for the departure of his friends, the exodus from Whitey's Fall of nearly all but the elders, *they fly forgotten as a dream dies at the opening day*, the ever-rolling stream, the one thing universally understood, forgotten dreams indeed, the search for security, the heartbreak, the futility, and him standing there, Tony McTaggart, wildly in love with this stranger who had come to stay, not knowing if he was a man or not, at nineteen already haunted by anxiety about himself, his powers and his functions. She was Bill's woman and this he knew. Even so she had come here with him and shared what had happened. She had received him, and it seemed she even respected him. To touch her would be a climax of intimacy. The hum of wasps worked in him as he wavered between action and accomplishment.

For a few minutes, his singing released Vivien from suffering the vague sinking of the blood which had become part of her life. His singing supported her. He had breathed life into the old church. His voice all the more surprising, not just because such a large man produced a tenor, but because the voice had no trace of the immaturity which still hung its awkward shapes about his person, its tatters of a stubborn boyhood. No, that voice came rich and full, had disarmed and overcome her, in a curious way she had been possessed by it, so when he finished she was the one who felt drained.

Jealousy was what Tony endured, an insane consuming jealousy of Bill Swan. At last it would have to be in the open. Whatever the price, he could no longer live without knowledge of himself. He stepped up to the altar-space where she now stood. He fumbled his arms around her. His warmth overpowered her. She accepted, perhaps. This was happening because there wasn't any other way. What could she do? She was not repelled. The landscape breathed in through the missing windows. Momentarily this giant man, his arms explorative, possessed her, his chest a hot wall where her head pressed. Yet she was rebelling, yes as his voice ceased to reverberate through her bones she resisted motionlessly, stemming her fascination with strangeness, her legacy from a people perpetually in love with the exotic. Her withdrawal, slight as the gesture was, communicated instantly. He released her. And his mouth which had hovered above her hair, drinking, remained dry and empty and untouched. If this had been all, his fury against Bill Swan would have been intense enough: but worse, he had revealed his weakness, betrayed his life's secret, the shame now known for the first time ... not just to this woman, but inescapably to himself. He loved her, yes, craved her, dared to touch, presumed to take her, but his body showed no sexual interest. When she yielded, too quickly for him, she pressed against his limp parts. Nothing; the miserable absence of purpose in his life. The memory of how stung he'd been by that stupid boast of Maggot's – You big useless bastards, you'll see, when you're married your wives'll sneak round to my place or Billy's for a decent fuck! And Billy, his one friend, was doing this to him. You could even want to be like the twins, at least they got it off together. Vivien caught an expression in his eye which she wished she hadn't seen. He is afraid of me, she knew it. Perhaps it was important that she had seen it. He needs me as Billy doesn't, for me he has risked everything, he is ashamed of himself. This gave her power, enough to create him for herself, the sort of power Billy never gave her. So she reached across the cold stream flowing between them, across the swiftly deepening crevass. Already an unknown darkness yawned beneath her gesture, she took him by the wrist and drew him, resisting, towards her.

– I admire you so much, she said. She would go through with it, she did not understand why, with a sinking recognition she knew she would not refuse him.

He surrendered. He allowed himself to be drawn, even felt her fingers trespassing, teasing, lifting, creating pools of delicious passive sensation in him. Was she to help him into manhood? Even though she was Billy's lady, sheila, whore. He wanted her. Now was the time, the test. She was going to do it for him. Hadn't he prayed? More than anything. Would he give up the rest for this? He would. But. But she. She was failing. The possible peak of surprise waned. She was failing and she guessed as much. Though, sooner and worse, he knew it too. Indeed it was he not she who failed, now more ignominiously than before. Her face still buried in his cushiony blond hairs she knew it. A dreadful unexpected sob tore ragged from his throat, so that he wanted to smash her head. He could murder her so easily and he would. Her impudent fingers withdrew, she was ashamed as she ought to be, recognizing her first implacable enemy, the first person to truly and calmly wish her suffering, dead.

– I admire you, she said.

His eyes were killing her. Hatred sobbed up through him again, his breath pouring hot and moist on her face. So she was determined not to stop till she'd finished him off, Billy's woman, Billy the boss, the little cock of the gang. Another cry barked out of him. She was working with her mouth, losses were happening, down on her knees on the rotting floorboards, horrified at what she had begun, desperately performing unnameable enticements so that his mind cried out in revulsion while his body still hoped for its own signs, poised ready for salvation despite everything, his anguished eyes turned to the gothic inscription HOLY HOLY HOLY, to the pierced heart *Bubbles loves me.* Not *I love Bubbles*, no, so much more cocksure than that. Help, help, he was keening silently, please help o god. The blood-dark walls trapped him, the Church of England suffocated him, stars were peeling from the apse, holes gaped at his feet, he was Thomas à Becket and this was the end, the window still festooned with ribbons and shreds of the dead trousers he might have been able to wear, wasps murderously insistent with their business of fertility. She had stopped. Gone. Run out. Left him with his jeans down round his ankles, his huge loins trembling, colossal legs burdened with lumps and mounds, rustling thick with monkey hairs, lost in the dead church. Nothing more humiliating could have happened, nor more complete, the heart itself squeezed painfully, nothing more pitiable or filthy than this, nothing more inexcusable. He tottered to the window, hobbled by clothes, and driving his fist at the heart on the wall, smashed clean through the red paint and grey timbers, shattering a hole large as a football.

What was left for him but to turn wild, sidle out into the scrub, rage and forage, live as an ogre, a legendary vengeful stealing kidnapping hunting animal?

Two

The occasion called for drastic action and so Miss Bertha McAloon roused herself. Was there to be no rest for the weary? she complained. Was there no respect left in the world for age? Apparently neither, for despite her talent, here she was, an old lady, ninety next birthday with perhaps only another fifteen or twenty years to live, nursing the lovely knowledge of a power inside her, dragged from her livingroom up to Wit's End, suffering the discomfort of young Peter's Land Rover with the wooden seats, to find herself being given lip by her only son George Swan and what's more catching that silly rabbit Rose winking and squinting at her from a hiding place to give some hint or other.

– Peter's brought me, she piped. Because I had to see for myself or I wouldn't credit I would not.

So saying, with the Irish speech still cherished by her family, out she got, down from the vehicle, shuffling through the dirt, she pushed aside George's fumbling attempts to observe the obligation of kissing her. She advanced determinedly, both hands securing her purse, the eternal mauve dress known to everyone snapping its hem in the wind.

– Keep off keep off, her tiny voice came out hard-edged in the effort to be heard. While I look for myself. Good morning Rose, what are you winking at me for? Speak up, I can't imagine why you're making faces behind George's back. Get out from under my feet George for goodness sake, you can see it's the old troubles I'm having, not that anybody cares a fig, as I've come to realize all too well.

When she stopped by the felled tallow-wood tree, her mauve dress appeared to have ideas of its own about continuing. Miss Bertha McAloon fought it grimly, she was not going to lose her balance in front of these geese, she was yes she was intending to to stop exactly here where that boy's crime lay for all to see. She also fought sweet memories of her first year married to Uncle all that wasted time ago when this tree was a sapling, which made matters so much the worse.

– And what did you do *that* for? she said as if to a tiresome child for the umpteenth time proving a disappointment to her hopes. I'd heard, she continued. But I didn't believe, I did not.

– Goodday George, Peter Buddall greeted his cousin gruffly then turned to his sister. How's life Rose?

– I'm alright Peter. And Patricia?

– She's good.

The informalities over, they turned to watch the old lady inspecting the fallen tree, which was her reason for coming.

– That was my tree, she declared. You know this I suppose George? That was my tree, said Miss McAloon who'd once been Mrs Arthur Swan and who now witnessed a further betrayal, an unexpected blow, a senseless insult. She couldn't bear to face them. Her tiny feet planted securely in the dust she would keep her back to them forever, her little piping voice warding them off with its repetitious plaint – I had that tree from when I was young it's like watching a finger cut off, it is. Actually she was thinking bitterly of her talent. If she'd been truthful with herself she might have found she didn't care quite so much about the tree, the thing was that the house had been hers and she'd given it to George. So they ought to keep thanking her and everything they changed or damaged reminded her of those overdue thanks. She had to let him know, then, him and Rose too, that the tree shouldn't have been cut without consulting her first. And, by a familiar mnemonic this led to the wicked indifference all her relations showed towards her talent. Miss Bertha McAloon was a knitter. Not one of those mortals who produce simple and useful articles like cardigans and socks, but a knitter who would work with twelve needles and produce a seamless horse rug in double cablestitch, who had knitted the stage-curtains for the School of Arts, who had once knitted a red carpet thirty yards long for the ceremonial inauguration of His Royal Highness Prince Henry William Frederick Albert, Duke of Gloucester, Earl of Ulster and Baron Culloden, K.G., K.T., K.P., P.C., G.C.B., G.C., V.O., as Governor-General of Australia; only to have her patriotic gesture spurned, the huge crate returned by departmental lorry with a covering note to the effect that the Commonwealth of Australia and the Australian People already possessed a serviceable red carpet for the reception of the Prince, a carpet manufactured by Messrs Axminster of Axminster, Devonshire, United Kingdom of Great Britain and Northern Ireland. This same Miss McAloon it was, too proud to yield to such rebuffs, who then commenced her great work, dedicated her life to a vision, who eventually purchased the Buddalls' barn which was solid as Ayers Rock and big enough for the carpet to be shown full-length, who divested herself of all impediments to her vocation (husband, son, household duties) and began the real work of knitting; knitting partitions for the barn, rooms of wool; she created knitted ceilings, coffered, domed and pitched ceilings to suspend from the rafters, whole walls she knitted, with ribbing round the doorways and windows. She breathed the air of wool and of the immense weight of naphthalene mothballs she hung among it. She repaired and embellished the rooms, even knitting pictures of the outside world to sew on here and there as reminders, a window, with the exact scene outside rendered in four-ply and glorious full colour; and because of her loneliness in the service of this talent she knitted lifesize bodies of people and sat them on chairs so that she always had company and somebody could watch her progress while space in the building gradually dwindled to cubbyholes in the musty cells of plain and purl. The wool wound once round the little finger of her right hand, her needles flicking and clittering, she was lost to the tragedies and uncertainties of life in the community. Ah yes, she'd go down to the Mountain Hotel for the occasional Remembering, largely for the sake of Jasper and his dear wife Sophie who was her sole friend, her sister-in-law, and certainly the only one to appreciate what she was doing. But Peter Buddall had turned out alright as he grew, and he brought her most things she needed. Peter who she now requested to join her in deploring the murder of a friendly tree and one which, indeed, had been hers and reared by her in a manner of speaking. But he sat where he was in the Land Rover, glumly acknowledging questions put to him by his sister Rose, while he let Old Loony McAloon talk herself silly.

– Why couldn't you have sent young Billy down to ask me? Miss McAloon returned to the attack on her son. He never comes to visit his grandmother. I could be dead for all he cares. And for all you care too, my boy. You're not grown so high and mighty you won't stand for a dressing-down by your own mother. She could hear for herself how shrill her voice sounded away from its woollen home. They contemplated the wreckage of the tallow, even its leaves now shrivelled.

– I felt sorry for that tree, said Rose bravely.

– Shut your silly face, her brother told her from behind the wheel.

Beyond them the mountain had become a frail eggshell, presented itself as discouraging, drawing about it a thinner air than usual. Bertha stroked her moustache and kicked the dust with her tiny boot.

– My father, she mused. My father was a fine figure of a man so he was. I had the brains of the family of course. But he was a fine figure. For a moment she glimpsed, through shutters of understanding, a nightmare of how meaningless the human experience is. There she stood in her nervous mauve, with the things she knew. What a bother the endless everything became once you went out visiting. Yet it couldn't be denied, looking at it, that the air was somehow simplified with that tree cut down. Miss McAloon felt tired. Tiredness came upon her sudden as cloud-shadow: one moment warm and capable, the next a coldness passed its crescent blade through her and she needed a chair. Home called. Home, with its beautiful easy familiarity, the restful shadows the lovely touch to the fingertips, the fibres seeming to breathe with you as you went.

– Are you going to come home? Peter demanded brusquely of his aunt, having observed a telltale change of mood.

– What could be more delightful? she answered her vision in those mincing tones which had so grated on Uncle's nerves when they lived together.

– Won't you have a cup of tea? Rose asked, appearing to her mother-in-law to zoom out of obscurity and whiz past, threatening collision. It was the sort of question that took you a few minutes to cope with. Things happened this way for Bertha McAloon, events like droplets of icy water, her own progress through space appearing endowed with painfully sharp definition; a body responding sensitively to whatever came to her from the immense void out there, a sole figure on the comfortless steppe occasionally assisted by a word, a crow, a chance enemy rushing at her and veering past or, seen on the horizon, some longed-for angel beckoning but gone at her first step in that direction. So although she knew she now stood close enough to touch the fallen tallow-tree, to her own view it lay separated from her by long perspectives. Sometimes when knitting she could believe the horizon itself unravelled to become her wool, that it was being drawn into her personal web, yes they were the moments when all doubt left her and her talent took her into itself and afterwards she would gaze astounded at what she had done, admiring it, loving it, wistful with the apprehension that she might never do so well again. Did something have to be said to Rose?

– No, no tea, Peter Buddall answered for her and for the demands of his own schedule. He started the motor.

– At least I've seen it, what I thought I'd never see, and my own son did it, no need to wonder who's the guilty one.

She climbed in, a tremble of mauve and a talent. Nobody made anything easy for her.

– Whatever did you do that for George? I can't imagine what gets into you. It was *my* tree I suppose you know. Your father robbed me of just about everything else I had. Only the tree.

I wish, she thought, I hadn't given them the house. She remembered waking on that day Arthur walked out, remembered looking at the mountain and watching it go wrong. With intuitive grief she imagined she could see a ravine no one had ever discovered before. And now, yes, the dead tree also left a gap in her stomach, a reminder of her hunger for thanks, after all whatever Rose and George had she'd given them, and would anything be left now the way that boy of theirs was going?

– If you'd only grown taller, Miss McAloon aimed her deadly dart at her son with practised accuracy. Then you'd have been kinder to your mother. That's what I've always said. She settled back in the passenger seat.

Peter let in the clutch, backing sharply. Rose and George looked at their benefactress through the flat glass of the windscreen, seeing her in an oblong frame like an exhibit, a work of art, a dried arrangement, careering backwards ... dwindling. The Land Rover swung round recklessly and sped off, bearing with it plans for a knitted tree if such a thing could be imagined.

– Bloody stickybeaking old bat, growled George. He collected a loose gob of spit and squirted it out as if now cleansed of guilt for not satisfying whatever need his mother was continually parading and reminding him about.

Three

At last Vivien had a reply from Aunt Annie, a rambling letter full of news about the peonies this season and how she'd just discovered they originated in Japan would you believe, about Mrs Cox and Mrs Pye down the road, about the new vicar and how he plasters his hair forward over his bald patch as if that didn't give him away, and what's the matter with a bald patch she'd like to know, when it was known to give men a more mature and thoughtful appearance which heaven knows most of them could do with, about a brief meeting with Mr Rosenbloom in the baker's and how he had bought wholemeal bread whilst she bought the thinnest sliced milk loaf of course and how Mr Rosenbloom had heard from his long-lost sister a doctor or something who'd visited last Wednesday and behaved in a most peculiar manner towards Aunty, so familiar though they'd never had the pleasure, taking her hand and weeping, how this lady doctor had thanked her from the bottom of her heart from time to time and ended with the offer of a holiday in Berlin should Aunty feel inclined *with all the luxuries guaranteed*. As Aunty said, when you get to the age of ninety you don't think much more of foreign holidays than you do of all-night parties. I laughed right in her face poor thing, Aunty wrote, but who could help it? And what

358

of Arthur Swan, she enquired, was he still coming round offering his advice on how to run the world? Give the darling old ratbag a tweak on the ear because I'm thinking about him, she wrote. Oh God, Vivien love, what fools we can be and no mistake. I'm so very happy that you like my house and I cannot tell you what it means to me that you intend to settle there. It's like waiting for someone without knowing it; and then suddenly there they are and you find you've been waiting. I feel very much at rest, thank you. And I've begun all sorts of tidying up I've been meaning to do for years. So now I have a little surprise dear, I was cleaning out my treasure trunk, 'Aunty's Dump', do you remember it? when I found a bunch of letters I'd quite forgotten. Among them I discovered this one from your dear mother which I thought you might like to have as a memento.

It made Vivien's hand tingle. She tested the deckle-edged paper, it communicated strangeness, she was too nervous to open it. From so long ago. Herself afraid. So she tucked it safely in her purse. Straight away taking it out again, she couldn't bear that. She opened it with a reckless impulsive gesture: at one glance Vivien knew what she most needed to know. Her mother could write, her mother was, or had been, a real person. This was the most definite thing about her, this letter.

She stood and savoured an impression of the style, the handwriting. Her eyes were ready to help. She was still the little girl telling lies about her mother because she didn't have one: her mother the aircraft pilot who died in a crash, her mother the famous pianist killed while on a concert tour, her mother the explorer kidnapped by bandits in the Sahara Desert and never heard of again, or lost in the Amazon jungle, her mother who had murdered a baby and was living out a life of shame secretly in prison, her mother the British spy and the government not daring to leak where she had been captured for fear of letting out State Secrets, or more simply her mother who had eloped shamefully for the sake of love.

This was the first time she had ever seen her mother's handwriting. Vivien was over the initial shock, the basic conundrum solved ... yes, her mother did have writing of her own. How ludicrous to be letting the tears run in public. You have to pull yourself together. It's only a letter. The letter must say something. Who knows what? Wasting time, crying. Vivien took fright at the infinite space in her hand, the discovery she would make the moment she read the first words, fate taking an unasked part in her life, her vessel hurtling forward into nothing. Or falling? That dreadful Brinsmead woman. Was this the straw? the drowning person's lifebelt, a reprieve, a turning point, could she expect to remain the same once she'd read it? Might this scrap of paper hold her up?

Previously, all she had of her mother was the wedding photograph; father looking unlike himself, sleek as a plaster dummy, his arm linked through the plump arm of a rather insipid girl with her bridal veil pulled too low across her forehead, a girl with teeth and nostrils, wearing pearls of a kind.

The handwriting was there in front of Vivien, bold fluent writing, no doubt about that, and fast. The signs were clear, the woman who wrote this wrote often and well. Elegant capital *P*s and *G*s were balanced by the dashing squareness of the capital *T*s. The blunt tails of the *y*s and *q*s given quality by her Greek *e*s. Most of all, the flow across the page, letters of her personality.

With relief Vivien admitted that her real and unspoken guesses (of shame and idiocy and squalor) had been wrong, for here was the evidence: her mother had been educated, she wrote positively stylishly. The occasional word lodged in Vivien's mind from a cursory look at the whole page ... incredible, elocution, monster, Gregory, straightforward, lovely. The rest was calligraphy, character, history, a voice. What did she use this voice to say to Aunty? What words had she sent to her relative by marriage? And incidentally to her unknown daughter, the daughter she must have been pregnant with at the time of writing? Only one fragment survived as Vivien read the harmless trivia: *we're positive the baby is going to be a boy. Gregory said he will take an over-dose of sleeping pills if it's a girl instead of a little ally for him. How we laughed! ... love Esther.* She didn't mind. No she didn't mind. Esther was forgiven and so was Annie. Gregory, Daddy that is, presented another problem. She'd need to think. Daddy who did,

360

in fact, take an overdose of sleeping tablets twelve years later.

– Thank you, she spoke. Yes, just as Aunty had once told her straight out that Daddy was dead so she could bear it and be done, now she had sent on this letter as soon as she found it among her papers. What would Esther think of a daughter who lived with a man sixteen years her junior? What would Aunty think of her on her knees in Aunty's own church lipping at the genitals of an impotent giant bearing her name McTaggart and to whom she was also Great-aunt Annie? Vivien glanced up past the hotel to the little slaughterhouse where a group of crows held the grass captive, all eyes and beaks. I shall write to Aunty and ask her outright what my mother died from. I shall tell her I am Bill Swan's mistress too. But at this moment Aunt Annie seemed curiously vague, her motives unaccountable, her presence weakened.

So Vivien stood on the powdery road, burdened yet elated with new knowledge. The ever-present wind, sweeping her hair over to one side, folding her skirt against her legs, tugged at the letter. So she continued, her most private thoughts naked to the world. Rainless clouds swooped close down to the mountain. And she was being watched too, you may be sure. Not only by decrepit ladies spying from creeper-infested verandahs, but openly by Mr Rupert Ping, outside his workshop, practising the dainty habit of moving from foot to foot on the spot, a featherweight boxer. Those clouds swept out of sight so fast you knew it was the world turning and the clouds themselves motionless, the headlong rush of the mountain into your life. Mr Ping stared unblinkingly at her, attracting her attention, no question about that, the long scar down his cheek making him appear to be smiling but he wasn't. Vivien felt she needed somewhere to sit quietly to cry or gloat over her new possession, the most unexpected gift, a mother. But she obeyed his unspoken will: put the letter away, folding it inside Aunty's letter, slipping it in the envelope then shutting it securely in her purse. Mr Ping's scar smiled; she was just the person to appreciate what he had to show.

Vivien knew this interview with the Chinaman would be about

the disappearance of Tony who worked for him. The guilty are always a step ahead, and how guilty she was, Tony not seen since their fiasco in the church. The welder unable to cope with the work at his age and the apprentice never there. I was the one who sent him wild, she admitted, preparing herself for judgment among the workshop tools. She walked towards that metal cave, the dry day puffed around her shoes. The clouds raced or the world raced. She felt dizzy. That letter in her purse was a lifebelt. She would be safe, eventually she would.

Rupert Ping led her inside. Vivien was immediately impressed by the suggestion of a crypt, symbols and emblems on the walls; crosses stars moons, the crucible of oil, bottles without labels, bottles of light. The floor of the workshop congested with broken-down machines. The air's heavy metallic smell imposed utter silence. The realities outside no longer existed. She thought of herself and Tony in the abandoned church. Here was its negative, its living half of meanings and functions. But in the apse of this place the altar had not been dismantled to make room for a heap of rotting linoleum. By contrast, she stood hypnotized by what her guide showed her: an altar, yes, the great steel column of the hoist, and on top of it a cow standing terrifyingly still. Unearthly and sinister, this cow called to mind things familiar, nightmares of falling naked and memories of being alone. The cow gazed out over Vivien's head with huge glassy eyes. Nose varnished, teats ripe with sawdust, legs steady as stone, this was Dame Nellie Melba about to launch into *The Holy City*. She disdained to acknowledge the audience, up there awaiting her cue, attuned to that adoring hush, heavenly intimations already in the ears, the note about to be uttered.

Vivien's reaction falling short of expectation, Ping's whole attention was on her, gathering clues. He raised his fine bare arm, young enough for a man of thirty though creased with herring-bone scabs, pointing up to the cow on the vehicle hoist.

– That's Alice, he introduced them.

– Alice! shrieked Vivien, the word yapping in echoes along the iron walls.

While Alice remembered bellowing for help, the calf was killing her, and even her loved mistress with the gentle hands roared away when she was needed most.

Instead of the expected, instead of seeing the point, Viv turned her back and ran. She clattered on stilts out across the huge concrete floor, the oily air resisting her tight lungs, her breasts an impediment, the earth turning turning the opposite way so she must run faster to move at all. Fresh in her mind the smashed truck, its one wheel meditatively rotating while Bill intoned curious syllables *wreck wreck queer Alice Iris* and his face still dark from the strain of tilting the truck to allow her one glimpse of the corpse's arm jutting from a pulp of meat, a twisted head of neatly combed hair. Also an older memory of her own mother staring her not quite in the face, eyes huge with indifference. It was gone, illusory, untrue. Vivien ran from the horror of Alice and Mercy Ping's husband, from the voice of a murderer, the taxidermist's fastidiousness, the affront to her animal-loving British sense of what is proper.

Could he hear her give-away panting? She blundered into the blinding day, driven by panic, straight out yes to the road knowing there could be only one sanctuary, Miss Brinsmead's shop; there she'd be safe with Miss Brinsmead, if only if only. And of course Miss Brinsmead, being a lover, knew when this moment arrived. Standing with her back bravely to the cat and its narrowed eyes, her hand on the date, refuting the shop's complaints, defying that gossiping crowd of frocks, she prepared herself for an emotional onslaught.

– Someone wants me, she said to her brother. I'll leave the shop to you.

He was surprised into taking her place. So she bustled out patting her wire entanglement of hair. *If only if only*, she heard Vivien longing for her protection. She ran across the road. A terrified chicken sprinting in front of her dodged aside at the shed door as Vivien lunged, sightless with sunshine, into her saviour's arms. Felicia Brinsmead bore her up joyfully, triumph in her heart and her flesh young again; why should she care if the street was filled with watching judges, mouldy lumps of stone on verandahs

363

cracking open their eyes, trees gesticulating, the hundred doors of the Mountain Hotel edging open so the faces of the dead could spy out accusing her. Fido had prepared her for worse than this. She nursed her lovely woman. The sky tugged stiff as blue canvas in the wind.

Events changed direction, the atmosphere changed, the mountain itself ripened a shade darker.

Now came Sebastian's turn to hear the imperative call of love. He heaped iron weights from the scales on top of the newspapers for safety's sake and marched to the rescue, past lines of rubber boots at attention. He stepped outside, his pace quickening with agitation, the doors clashing behind him. The town was alive with its owners all answering the summons, even the matriarch McAloon being carried out on her porch in the cocoon of her private smell and setting herself up with a brass telescope. Grotesquely ugly with their fatty noses and sticking out ears, the onlookers sensed the unexpected. And sure enough the saint burst through those PROVISIONS HABERDASHERY BOOTS & SHOES doors, his halo awry and rage actual rage transfiguring his face, a thick roar emerging from his throat, jealousy shaking him free of his bland contemplation of God's mysteries, the sublime tapestry in tatters. He thought this affair of hers had been dead. But no. So he was Oliver Cromwell, bristling with principles. For half a century the fear had lurked in him that it would come to this, despite all appearances, that one day the scandal of his sister's affair with Rupert Ping would be common gossip. Grateful to see Vivien Lang restraining her before she had a chance to make a total fool of herself, he touched her as he passed to thank her. And now he was running, a bull elephant, slow to gather speed, into the shed where he had never been before. Ping had to be stopped. There must be an end to his sending out allurements and inducing infidelity. Witnesses were swept up by his bellow and carried in behind him, drawn on the wind he created.

– Ping, he called on his enemy.

The audience assembled itself in that dim place, the show had begun. No one had ever heard Sebastian Brinsmead address

Rupert Ping by name before, their mutual hatred was known to be too deep. The studio orchestra raced in full flight to a climax and stopped dead.

– This is idolatry, Sebastian whispered with respect. It's disgusting. We won't have such things in a Christian town.

The congregation gazed at the theatrical cow high on her hoist: creased neck, sharp bony structure of haunches and great pendulous shapes hung in the skin sack, her brow wrinkled, a wise woman's expression. So Alice contemplated the same truth as before, just a bit above their heads, her varnished nose in the air, eyes glassy with revelations, she balanced miraculously, a thing of beauty.

– She's dead, Mr Ping excused himself.

Ian McTaggart remembered a time long ago with a cow on an altar and what began with laughter and dancing ended with ... surely not ... murdering his brother and two neighbours. Could that be right? The mind plays such damn tricks; the night of sticky hands and gagging nausea. Then dawn and the shores of a lake in the desert, a scattering of red flowers, men down on their knees eating the stones with gratitude.

Only Uncle could break the mood of righteous indignation. Sebastian, deflated, lost purpose: had he misunderstood Felicia yet again?

– You came to live among us when we was gold prospectin Rupie, Uncle said. When Merce was as pretty as a doll. An now we've give up the idea of findin a fortune for a couple of hours work, and Mercy dead too, are yer tryin to tell us somethin old son? Is that it? Have we slipped back into cattle folk? You're givin us a message, am I right?

– I reckon we seen enough, Mum Collins declared almost as upset as if it was her own Myrtle on the hoist. Heathen practices, I call it. Uncle you're soft in the head! She elbowed her way out and relatives followed her example, which meant just about everybody eventually. Fifty years they'd waited for this row, for Sebastian to have it out with Ping, for a brother's jealousy to be given its head. They left reluctantly, disappointed yet again.

Only Felicia had resisted the pull of what was going on, smiling abstractedly, her arms about Vivien, her rancid bundle of hair at a tender angle. But it was true that her mind was not wholly on the job of comforting this desirable person. There was some future which she ought to foretell, forestall; the message was vague but urgent, connections not fitting together, her immediate pleasure putting her off her stroke as a seer. And now it was too late. Bessie Collins flouncing out of the workshop with a herd of goats at her heels. And then Uncle putting an end to contemplation by standing in the middle of the street, waving one walkingstick, shaky from his fortnight in bed, hanging on to his ally Sebastian and shouting gamely.

– Tomorrer we meet. There's a meetin. Sebbie an me has decided on a meetin.

Felicia heard. But she was still clutching the warm shell of love, wrestling with shapeless premonitions, murmuring that there was still one sign to come, Vivien, though I can't foresee it however I try. She stood under the gallop of that sky in the shadow of the mountain now switching from green to grey, chilled by the passive body of her beloved young stranger, still murmuring, her broad face and the helpless bags of her figure, the nodding coagulation of hair, emitting the staleness of the unwashed, unable to stop falling, more yet to come, a vision swam clearly into mind, of herself with Sebastian in Venice: him wandering aimlessly dignified inspecting ancient stone carvings, while she, swearing she would never travel again, stood electrified by a sign, a portent, a notice nailed to the door of the Basilica Santa Maria della Salute *BEWARE, FALLING ANGELS.*

Vivien recollected her manners and patted the old lady, accepting her duty as comforter, forgetting altogether that it was she who had sought comfort, the macabre insight into Mr Ping's obsessions less threatening now. She helped Felicia home, escorting her right into the shop, though the olives had a few tart things to say about that on behalf of the League of Decency.

Meanwhile, Vivien's purse lay where she dropped it in the gutter, heavy with the presence of an unknown mother, not noticed by anybody except the punctilious Rupert Ping stationed in his doorway once more.

Four

Miss Bertha McAloon discovered to her surprise that Senator Halloran had been on his way to visit her at the time of his misfortune. His flat tyres delayed him for a day, but he still honoured his obligations. Whilst she distrusted him, she wasn't the woman to deny herself a taste of refined company. Actually it turned out to be the refined company of two men, not one, plus the dog Ocker who had been recaptured, because the Crafts Consultant of the Australian Historic and Aesthetic Resources Commission had been scouting in the area. The introductions were formal: Miss McAloon Mr Simon Harper-Richards, Simon Miss McAloon, how d'y do, how do you do, good morning or is it past midday time does fly, really, doesn't it, we've come on the suggestion of your neighbour Mr George Swan, my son he is, your *son* I see Miss McAloon, and what would George be meddling in my affairs for, simply co-operating in our search for notable buildings in the district he assured us your own house is unique inside and not to be missed, well it's tidy I'll say that for it and I'm sure it won't do any good coming in but if you must and see for yourself Senator Mr Simon ...

(I'm silly and I know it, silly and bad too, George'll cop it from me, only yesterday this bloke went siding with the highway folk,

367

whoever saw Sebbie so carried away looked like he'd have a stroke and good on him I say, smashing our mountain about, the only one we've got, I ought be to sending these pansies about their business with a flea in their ear by rights, but then there's *my* rights and it's about time, with the interest of them in power, who knows but they mightn't laugh, they might see, I'm not that silly I'm afraid to look opportunity in the face and give him the wink.)

– Come in then. You have to step on this side, the other's gone rotten on me.

(No going back now, O glory woman you're making a fool of yourself sure enough, but it'll be one in the eye for all them back there, Arthur and all, the art man didn't go to their places I notice, so it must be he's heard about my talent, it must be he's an expert on knitting, well I've got a thing or two to show, what a dill to let them in, such threads and tatters, look at those hideous clumps of wool, but it's all *fallen to bits* since I went out, a dirty old spider-web, not even proper walls now and I never noticed, nor the carpet gone except round the edges, and the stink of naphthalene it's a wonder I haven't gassed myself or maybe it's what keeps me young probably, I could cry I'm so ashamed, but I deserve it, haven't I told myself a thousand times the vanity'll be my downfall and so it stupid-well is, go on you pansies, let your eyes pop out, laugh yourselves silly at my expense, I'll get young George for this, it's because I ticked him off about cutting down my tree, that's what it is, I'll pay him back you see if I don't, that's right Simon Whateveryournameis stick your froggy fingers through the moth holes, ever heard of a moth, well *you* try to keep them down and you try reaching up there to mend it if you're my height, no I wouldn't stand on a table to save Isaiah from temptation, oh I could cry I feel so angry, fat lot of good you'd be in bed I don't suppose you've got anything between your legs bigger than my little finger anyhow and enough hairs to make a decent set of eyelashes, it makes me so angry, and at my age I shouldn't have to put up with it, I deserve better, haven't you noseyparkers got more to do with your time, I wish I'd had the chance to straighten my hair at least.)

– Miss McAloon! Miss McAloon! this is ... stupendous. I have never ... Frank just *look* at it, oh Miss McAloon ...

(What's this he's raving he's laughing at me now and him no more than a kid in long pants, no not laughing, can it be, he's going a bit far isn't he, just a lump of old knitting, though I must admit a good job, or was when I did it.)

– Please Miss McAloon may I bring my camera in and take some pictures? They'll never believe at the Commission. You'll be famous I promise you.

– I suppose yes if you really want to Mr Simon ... I used to click the button on occasion myself with the Kodak, especially when there were decorated cycles, or the picnic races, or my dear little sister Edith in her wheel chair, but that was a long time ago now, to be sure.

– We're most grateful to you Miss McAloon. This will mean so much to Mr Harper-Richards.

– Of course you've caught me unprepared.

– It's very kind of you. Now Simon, do you want us out of the way? Miss McAloon to be in the pictures, of course, over here Miss McAloon, should she smile Simon or be serious? whatever you feel Miss McAloon, I'll make myself scarce then, so I don't get in the way, give me a call when you're finished will you? I'll be out in the car with Ocker.

(He's touching my knitting, putting his fingers all over it, what would a fellow like that do for a job with those soft hands? He could put them on me if he likes, just for the trial to see what they're like.)

– Your house is one of the marvels of homecraft. And so won-derfully preserved. We'd need to restore it of course. Might be tricky. This doorway is a masterpiece, a masterpiece; what's that stitch called? Just point towards it please and perhaps a little smile this time thank you.

– Ribbing.

(That was done when I was so unhappy, I hate that door it's such an unhappy door I'll never forgive Arthur in all my days I'll never forgive, I never will for wasting my life.)

– You know I'd be inclined to suggest a buckram backing for

the passageway, the walls have been too heavy haven't they, for the wool, sewn-on buckram backing might answer the problem, but what's on the other side may I see? Thank you. A monumental wall, really, purely in concept it's unique, unparalleled, I assure you I see craftwork all over Australia, weaving and tapestry and so forth, but never such knitting. Ah! Ah! Miss McAloon, this ceiling! Ah what a ... the ceiling my dear lady is a masterpiece, it's like the roof of a mosque, were you ever in the east? it's like the Alhambra.

– You can't get much further east than this, she laughed bitterly. Or you'd be in the sea.

(Three years it took me, that ceiling, and what a waste, I must have been out of my mind to think of it, I wish he'd go away, what did I let them in for, I'll bet Arthur put them up to this, prying with their camera, all these years he's dearly longed to see inside where I live and set foot in my house, he knows I've got a secret I won't show him, this'll be Arthur's doing. I thought George wasn't up to it.)

– How is the ceiling hung?

– Off of the rafters.

– The arches are beautiful, exquisite. It's a lovely lovely house. No amount of cost would be too great to preserve this. It's priceless. Like nothing else ever thought of.

(Now everybody can see in to what I've been doing and how they'll laugh, that window's the death of Grannie, and the ceiling's what I did without when Arthur went and all those gossips waiting for me to put a foot wrong, which I never would do, not even in a pink fit, oh the dirty smelly place and these city folk tramping in, they're having me on, the big joke in the photographs.)

– We'll mount these photographs and make an exhibition of them if they turn out well enough to do justice to your talent. You'll make a fortune from tourists.

(Tourists poking their noses in, I'd sooner be a clown and dressed up, what have I let myself in for, well they won't come, and I'll tip you out on your ear too young man.)

– Miss ... Words fail me. Miss McAloon dear, the *pictures*. The knitted pictures.

– That's only what you'd see if you could look outside. They're kind of windows.

– Mind-blowing. Please, please come and stand by this one.

(That's a picture of how lonely a mad old lady can be, you think it's just a view of the mountain, it's a great heap of loneliness, that mountain is, it's all my mad hopes, I've cried more tears than you'd imagine Mr Pansy-Pansy.)

– The people here, these sculptural figures in the chairs, might I enquire if they're *of* anyone? Known to you?

–Oh yes as it happens. This is the Maharaja of the Hindoos and this here is Queen Victoria for when I want a stand-up argument. I've got to have somebody to talk to. Or it'd be madness I'd face. So if nobody comes ... And Florence Nightingale over there by my bedside. I was a nurse myself you know and when I was only fifteen I went to Yalgoona Hospital and two weeks afterwards they called me in to say would you like to go to Melbourne to see the Duke of York declare Australia a nation if we pay the fare. They did and so I went, I was the youngest person there, I believe, as an official guest representing the nurses of New South Wales and all because I was the youngest nurse in the State, they found out. So I saw it all, the whole ceremony. I've still got it up here in my head. I can still see it, every detail as if it was today.

– Fascinating. You must tell this to Senator Halloran it sounds like his kind of stuff, he'll have you on tape.

(On toast, eat, chomp, spit, chew, disgusting juices, I'm so ashamed I've been the biggest fool you could ever imagine.)

– This is interesting. What's this? Is it unfinished? Is it just begun, something new? This round end like a wheel with spokes and rings, like the beginnings of a log lying down. What is it Miss McAloon?

(The grief of my heart, that is, the last weeks of my forty years in the desert, my secret, the thing I'm going to drag around after me, poison, I hate you for that.)

– But my dear, there are *moths* in it already. Look, when I poke it, they're tunnelling in. But everywhere else you've put naphthalene ...

– I'm leaving it.

– But the grubs: it must be saved. They'll eat it out.

– That tallow-tree is the only new thing I've begun to knit. See who can work the fastest, me or the moth. They cut down my old tree, you see.

– And so you began knitting another one? We must save it. The concept. A fallen tree. A knitted tree. A triumph of the imagination. Priceless.

(That lump of sobbing in place of a life, in place of the years of happiness I hoped to have, let the moth eat it, the rot inside here, my heart.)

Who has done this. To me? Who?

– Please, please, Miss McAloon you mustn't cry. You'll be famous I promise you that. What more can you want?

– They always said they'd have revenge, they said I was too proud and so I was. Look what you've done to me. Now out you go on your ear Mr Pansy. If you think I'm crying you've got the wrong idea entirely, that you have. And if you come back here I shall pull the pants off you, because if you're not any good for that you're not any good for anything else, I'm thinking.

Five

Fido applied his watering eye to the torture of that draughty peephole. He was awake, though it must be past midnight. Lately he'd developed the habit of sleeping for part of the afternoon. Then at night when his parents were asleep he could wander through the dilapidated passageways of the house and shop, his own master. Better than that one horrible muck-up when he had taken the risk in daylight and found the town deserted. No, at night he was able to go out into the garden, wondering why he'd never dared do this before, so safe, so simple, drunk on sweet cool air, lying awhile in the long grass, breathing. This was full moonlight so brilliant you could even see colours, the sky blue, the grass green, the leaves black with silvered edges. Listened as crickets chirruped from one end of the yard to the other. He could see nothing unusual out there tonight either, the place alive and still, even the wind seeming to have dropped a little. He eased his door ajar. He was away, flitting along the corridor to the kitchen, through the back door which had stood open long enough for the hinges to disintegrate. His soft bare feet in the grass, shivers of erotic pleasure so his scalp crawled, his skin tingled. Was this freedom then? Uncle Sebastian turned angry today for the first time ever. Fido was proud of this, informed his diary of how the old man looked in a rage, the loudness of his voice, the flurry of air that followed him, the ponderous thud thud of his boots because his hips were so seized up, how peeping from the shop window he'd seen his mother cry and Uncle Sebastian barging across the road into the repair shed, how his hair had been like white fire. Yes, Fido actually told his diary a proper secret this time: I love him. And the diary now bore this knowledge forever until it might be burned. He lay down in the long grass as before, allowing damp tufts to stroke his cheeks. I love you, he said to the grass, the garden, the crumbling brick chimney solemn as a human face. He forgot the pain in his eye, that bloodshot eye, but he could not forget the ache he felt for company, so even while luxuriating in the feel of night-time and the sounds, he was saddened by loneliness. In his head right then and there he wrote an ode to it which began:

> *lonely only me and the grass is grieving*
> *lonely for the friends I might have had*
> *except that everyone is gone or leaving.*

It wasn't what he'd meant to do, nor how he meant to feel, but you couldn't help it. Unexpectedly he realized the time had come for murdering his parents. Yes, he'd dreamed of this for so long. And now his twelfth birthday had passed without anybody celebrating it, he was almost a man and could handle what must be done. The only thing he couldn't handle was this imprisonment. Run away? They'd be on the phone to the police, his life wouldn't be worthwhile. Anyhow, hadn't he planned for two and a half years to murder them? After the mountain, which must be blown up first, he'd attend to his parents. Unless they could arrange to be blown up with the mountain. He'd planned and planned it, almost enough dynamite lay stacked away, accumulated over the years. But now today, when least expected, all the weapons and explosives hidden in crates under his shelves had gone, vanished. Had he been tricked? Or on the toilet? He supposed they must have been stolen while he was asleep. It set back his plan for the mountain. If he'd known how to use them he'd have done the job long before this. If only somebody had taught him how to make an explosion big enough to blow the mountain to smithereens he'd have done so. It might not take all that much, especially if gelignite was more powerful than dynamite. But was it? And would it need to be buried? How did you use a detonator? These were essential questions.

And now Fido dreamed he was being given a demonstration. Miraculously, when it was too late, someone was showing him, he did seem to be watching, learning. And he was of course. Half asleep and shivering, shaking with cold, he was gazing into a pool of yellow torchlight and seeing the detonator bound to the gelignite, being crimped to a fuse.

He crept closer, crouching near the man behind the old shed, the man showing him what he wanted to know, working clearly item by item, steadily completing each stage, his fingers defining their exemplary logic. In that circle of dull golden light familiar objects began to fall into place, you could see how they related. Fido crept closer, breathing beside the man, sharing his skill, the very master he needed most. Yes, you had recognized Bill Swan the Burgher of Calais (let me introduce myself as a prodigy) bowed in anguish, so that you could creep close without fear.

As indeed Bill was farewelling la dolce vita, confirming his vows finally against the values of Hollywood and its successors.

– And who the hell are you? he whispered controlling his shock, blinding the child with his torchbeam, a child he had never seen before.

– I'm Fido thank you, said Fido eager to be friends. And I've been watching you because you're going to blow that up and kill everybody in the shop.

– Shut up you little bugger, I'm not.

– Then what else is there to blow up? demanded the child. I know, I've been living in that back room and watching for somebody to come to the shed.

This made everything impossible of course, you couldn't silence the kid whoever he was, you couldn't go ahead and demolish the place because they'd know who did it, you should have taken Uncle's advice and done the job boldly in daylight with Uncle as decoy.

– I could punch your fucking teeth down your throat, Bill snarled, which wasn't the sort of thing Fido expected anyone to say.

– What's in the shed? asked Fido, learning about the problems of communication and feeling small as a figure in a landscape painting. But the man had already gathered his gear and was sneaking out of the garden, moving unhurriedly, unstoppably, making a getaway. The lifelong needs Fido felt, the desperation to be rid of that mountain watching him all day, took possession of him in one delirious flood of energy. Without thought he sprang into action, darted in front of the criminal and snatched the prepared charge from his hands, enough to start his own explosion at least, the movement so swift and unexpected the gel-ignite was gone before Billy could hang on to it. With that unknown boy running up through the long grass towards the house, seeming to know where he was going. Next moment his body came hurtling back at Billy, tossed doll-like through the air by a flash of light into a high-pitched silence; his sight blotted out and his shocked ears singing, half-blind and half-deaf, and knocked backwards by the blast, Bill saw that body hurtling through the air and landing as a sad little heap in the weeds. He crawled and wallowed through wet growth, his brain propelling his numb body, act act act, hands grappling with the mulch, must get there, over there, the boy in the dream, the thing he thought had happened. When the lights came on and he could see the house still standing, he expected the calling voices to be Uncle and Vivien, struggled to get up, lurched forward, pitched face-down in something soft, warm, comforting, repellant. This was when the screaming began. He was looking up and wiping his eyes, the poor hurt child, was it himself screaming, no, that screaming was coming from a wild figure struggling against nothing but the night sky, interrupted with hideous retching and vomiting, wavering bright lights. Some awful limp heavy thing flung its weight across him so he couldn't breathe. There were blades of grass near his eyes, he could see perfectly their moonlit cutting-edges, as if magnified. But all else blotted from his consciousness by a particular stench; a stench he had known once before and enough to frighten him got in at his entrails and screwed them tight. Sobs and whispers, creeping and sucking noises. More lights. Something serious happening. The night itself trickling down into the soil. But he breathed poisoned air, breathing, the lung-cutting chemical smoke now mercifully ate away all other sensation.

Sebastian Brinsmead looked at what he couldn't bear to believe, the fragments of a jigsaw he ought to be able to bring together, jagged pieces presenting themselves for acceptance and comprehension: the night bursting into flames, the slam of a heaven-sized door, that face clotted with blood searching between the torchbeams for his own eyes, that drunken face in its sickening mask, running, his knees and hips an agonizing reluctance to bend, his barefoot hobbling haste along the passage, sounding loud as boots through their house of no mirrors, wooden elbows thumping on corners as he staggered, smoke already blocking the back door, Felicia's bundle of hair bobbing out into the night ahead, sitting up in bed not believing and the heart pounding unbearably, a shattered chicken corpse thrown against the porch, the ragged meat hole, a pig's scream coming from Felicia, himself grappling with her, holding her to him in a parody of affection, hugging her hysterical struggles, pain lancing at him through all his senses, that sweet face in the grass with mouth open, moon-touched trees tossing and feathering, the blood-mask person falling back, with Felicia free and on top of him, her swimming over his liquid form to her son her angel, he himself Sebastian locked upright even now, locked inside himself still, prisoner in the high tower, a dinner of pearls for a starving man, feathers hanging from his feet, a porcelain doorknob white like bone in his hand, the ragged meat hole, Felicia's words indoors *It's the war!* as if she recognized it, as if it had come at last and joyfully, as if it made sense of many puzzles, neighbours banging gates and shouting, himself coughing a horrible thick cough which might choke him, the reek of putrifying food in bile, running stumbling walking feet, stifling gelignite fumes, the thud and rattle of earth thrown up against the wall, that face rising from the slime and speaking *The Golden Fleece*; a boy's arm reaching wide, the small hand palm-upwards in grass asking for something.

People stood back as people will. When they knew how little could be done they formed a ring till morning. The trembling torches paled in a steady dawn; the ancient residents whose eyes had seen everything stood waiting to find out what this was about, a dead boy in the garden, half his chest blown away, Bill Swan plastered with blood, Felicia Brinsmead lying beside the child and no more tears left in her, Sebastian her brother rigid still inside the prison of his flesh, and a large hole blasted in the ground. Thus at dawn the living elders contemplated that dead child whom no one recognized, instinct (and perhaps experience) telling them this tragedy would touch them more intimately than they knew. Above the town the mountain rose pale and luminous beneath a thick band of green light pressed down on it by rainclouds. A trace of misty blue light hid along the cream gullies; the crag with tall twin boulders like betrothed figures stood out in bold relief, lichened, pale copper green. Across the countryside a crow called its complaining tremolo.

Jasper Schramm opened up the public bar, there being only one place now for ceremonies. A stale aroma of smoke and sour hops flavoured the sharp mountain air, deliciously nostalgic. Woolly curtains swayed in and out of the open windows, sluggish as if wet. The dun lino gleamed with grease. The bar was a porcupine of inverted stool-legs. As you stood there respectfully, the boy lay on a table, washed and wrapped warmly in a blanket. Sad blanket. The bleeding had stopped. The sun was about to rise. You could see now how beautiful the child was, tall and fair with handsome features and a fine skin, he lay angel-like and translucent. So far nobody had spoken a single word. Then Ian McTaggart, whose right it was to preside as head of the collective families, hobbled in, soft-footed, once all who were needed had assembled. Felicia looked out of the window at the first sunlight to slip down off the mountain among the buildings, she watched it streaming in under that vast raincloud, the land sponging up warmth, she could see across the road over houseroofs to the paddocks which appeared to hang vertically as a green backcloth pinned up by studs fashioned in the form of cows. She was ready. She marshalled the courage of all she knew. She faced her relations, both friends and enemies. And spoke.

– This is my son Fidelis d'Oro Brinsmead. She drew the tremendous silence into herself, needing every ounce of strength to control her voice so she could address the corpse, publicly, at long last.

– Mummy loves ... she whispered now crouching beside the body. The word *mummy* striking her hearers as grotesquely inappropriate. Her face fell shapeless as she blubbered, having no rehearsed expression for this, her burden of hair lolling sideways, forgotten. She was helpless now because she'd been caught in the shocking present.

The town stood in judgment of her. The prisoner in Sebastian's tunic fought to escape with his secret, fought the ancient war to establish civilization by suppressing individual needs, and his sister's sobbing made clear that she was waiting for him to complete her confession, that she at least could face whatever punishment might come, the worst already having happened. Flies zoomed in to reconnoitre, sticking first to this face then that, unable to tell the living from the dead.

– He's twelve, she whispered remembering with pain how she'd tried to make him forget his birthday in case he should ask for a party and they'd have to go through all that anguish again.

The child lay dead.

Only Vivien recognized the face. Vivien, sick with worry about Bill, knew she had seen the boy once peering from under the holland blind when she banged on the shop door while the Chinese lady struggled with her truck on hairpin bends. The boy had watched her and then dropped the blind back into place. She touched Billy's arm to give him courage, knowing how he felt such a stranger to death. He was still dazed and partly deaf from the explosion.

Out through the hotel window the mourners could see, where the forest nosed down among the paddocks, a ribbon of smoke rising. They knew what it meant: Tony McTaggart, out in the bush, was boiling his billy for breakfast, also being sure to let them know he was alright so no one would send a search party for another lost son.

– I went to blow up the goldmine, Bill Swan confessed in neutral, solitary piano notes, scrubbing his hand over his washed cheeks. It's marked in Mr Kel McAloon's notebook. Under their shed. Then I caught that boy watching me. So I had to give up. Went down by the broken fence to go home. But he ran round in front of me. He snatched it right out of my hand. I couldn't help it. I saw him running up towards the ... Billy found himself looking into a mother's eyes, deep in, to where a frightened girl suffered something uncontrollable, so he held back the word house, knowing house to be a murderous word, also that he had said enough, that he must never tell them the boy ran towards the house. Supposing her son had wanted to kill her, she'd never hear it from Bill Swan. The morning cushioned on paddocks leaned in at the window. The witness nursed his bruised lip while the giant bellows of silence wheezed, he felt shameful tears rise, he was suffocating inside the hangman's hood.

The citizens watched the child and the child's mother, enbalming unasked questions in ceremonial tact.

As yet nobody knew that the blast, having shaken the general store like an earthquake, caused the towers of newspapers to collapse softly in overlapping fans of headlines. Suppressed evils began to plump up and slide into the open. The chorus of sou'wester-clad fishermen gaped from sardine tins at the *Sydney Morning Herald* receiving a letter on the high cost of babies. The convolvulus heard, purple with strain, of a Chicago man tortured and nailed up on a crude cross for Easter 1945. A veiny balloon rolled out with its knowledge of Japanese war atrocities and their solution: the Emperor Hirohito being taxed a billion yen on war profits. The Protestant chickens in their frozen purity puffed rock hard with indignation while the Pope took time off from the second world war to telegraph Generalissimo Franco 'Thanks to God for Spain's desired Catholic victory'. An unknown cyclist was killed again by a car at Hunter's Hill. Ugly and persistent, these ideas, set free from Felicia's restraining hand, insinuated them-

380

selves into public places exactly as Sebastian had feared. Squeezed through improbable cracks in their bid for the open, the world. Trouser-presses declared themselves blameless that the editor of an anti-Nazi magazine in the USA was emerging, once more, stripped, beaten and painted with swastikas. The potatoes accepted that Les Darcy's nephew should be wooed with national attention for victoriously beating another schoolboy. The Dean of Canterbury suggested to the hanging flitch of bacon that part of our Empty North ought to be given to the Japanese. With equal impartiality the bacon also considered Prime Minister Bruce's reply that the Dean must be ignorant of climatic conditions. Then the first of the slimy crew found its way to the doors which had been jolted loose (today there was no guardian of virtue to force them shut and shoot the rusty bolts): the *Financial Times* thanking the people for their sacrifices during the great Depression. And it was out. Already proliferating like a burst pinecone, spores taking flight on the Whitey's Fall wind. And right after it went Mr Non-Unionist explaining that 1930 was a year of plentiful work for men willing to undersell one another and put their backs into it. The jury of spirit kettles heard Robert Augustus Webber declared an habitual criminal. Both the cause of rheumatism, once more pronounced a mystery, and a Royal Commissioner appointed to investigate cold-blooded murder by police of Aboriginals in the Forrest River district crawled from the very year Felicia and Sebastian turned their shack into a shop. And then a dark ripe plum slithered free despite the begging hands of rubber gloves, out past the ghostly mirrors of tin and into the bright sunshine: the Reverend Gossip recommending the life beyond.

The cat among the eucalyptus drops, with his retinue of dead mice, bristled at the upset of his orderly world.

– The Golden Fleece is not in my yard, said Sebastian. It is everywhere under us. That shed only covered the first place we'd touched it.

Now Felicia's tears broke free in paroxysms, Sebastian was side-tracking the issue, refusing to sacrifice himself to join her. She was alone in the privilege of her grief. The people waited respectfully, granting her this privilege: crones propped up with sticks, wax models in wheelchairs, the world's oldest village idiot. They gathered to allow her her portion of grief and to pay their respects to the unknown Fido who was leaving behind his diary, his odes to loneliness, his loveletters ready to be slipped in among someone's groceries, also his inventions, meccano models for escape devices.

– When I was a boy, said Mr Ping surprisingly. Our Chinese name for Australia meant the New Gold Mountain.

The spirit passed out of Sebastian. He could never recapture the mystic peace he'd enjoyed all these years; the sure sense of an interwoven purpose, God's tapestry. Naturally he considered this in itself might be for a purpose and further proof of the divinity he could no longer witness. But consolation wasn't what he wanted, his expulsion from this state of grace hurt him inconsolably. Even his hateful devil-ridden sister might begin treating him gently, which is to say with pity. Ping's daring to speak now when he himself remained dumb inflamed the mortal wound of yesterday: jealousy. He hadn't the power to shake it off. His peace of mind as well as his outward tranquillity left him. What was worse, fears suppressed for years loomed into the forefront of his consciousness ... the instinct for self-destruction tempted him. This one gift from his ancestors persisted in speaking to the blood. Deep in the soft tissues of his bones seeped the timeless intoxication, the call to oblivion, the way out of the labyrinth, a hole slashed in the suffocating tapestry of God's infinite patience, escape from the appalling prospect of everlasting life. Suicide was one act that nobody else could commit for him, an ancient rite forever modern. Yes, the lure of release from being burdened with a whole people, his saint's cross. Saints make sure they are martyred; most couldn't stand the strain of their calling one day longer.

Fido lay dead. Sebastian's old enemy the licence inspector Kel McAloon who had hounded him for the location of the Golden Fleece, who had been obsessed with snooping for it through his drunken years, had achieved revenge by a simple cross in a notebook. In one respect Sebastian had been proved right; without the enigma of the Golden Fleece, Whitey's Fall would surely have been abandoned half a century ago. He had granted the people time to finish creating the mountain and grow to be part of it. A half-century of power for Felicia whose role was to show them the hell they'd come from. That's what her Rememberings demonstrated, so you could rise above the past by mustering its horrors in the placid present and shaping the future.

When he spoke of this to Vivien Lang in the street as they left the ceremonial laying-out of Fidelis d'Oro Brinsmead, she cried out in repugnance at the idea.

– You mean to say everybody has neglected their houses just because they don't care while they're waiting to find the Golden Fleece?

– Oh no, he retorted with a flash of his young anger. You jump to such secular conclusions.

Sebastian established his loneliness again and thought once more of taking his own life, drifted into a seductive daydream. But he feared Felicia, who floated through her underwater flowergarden of luscious poisons, bringing him wet blossoms, waterlogged remains, and the rainbow shimmers where her hands finned, the forms of her beauty and her fetid age mesmerizing him. He was afraid to drown, because she'd be there to nurse him tenderly to her purposes. And if he swallowed poison, she'd be with him, being a master of poisons, if he hung himself in the lavatory at the Mountain Hotel by his father's self-same belt, she'd be hanging beside him in his last moments with her stifling kindness and her understanding of the moment to come; even if he died of old age, hadn't she been there before? if he died in bed he would be admitting her to his bed again. And now by the most unforeseen blow his treasured captive, his pride, his dear son and nephew, dead in the act of finding out who had solved the secret of the goldmine. The anger remained boiling in him. The body had been arranged ready for tomorrow's funeral. The condolences of lifelong neighbours inflamed his fury. As a prisoner he drove his stiff prison up and down the street, not willing to go home. He stalked about the township wearing tatters of celestial threads, betrayed by his moral paralysis, his denial of his son, incensed by the distant earth-moving equipment thundering up at the highway laying bare the great wound of gold, grief filling him with energy, goading him again with the delights of death. So Sebastian called out. In his huge voice he shouted, challenging the people to bring their firearms and Fido's heap of ammunition (which had been entrusted to Uncle yesterday) and answer violence with violence.

– Who will be meek? he roared to the crowd. You can see from here the highway's already across the saddle. Feel the earth shaking. They're blasting away the face of our mountain. So we sit back tamely, do we, and let them come here bringing velvet cushions and iron cages for us, the comfort of imprisonment in our own homes, locked in by the stupid kindly curiosity of sightseers, not daring to show our faces for fear of being photographed, for fear of being stared at and talked to by tourists? Are we to shut ourselves indoors because we don't recognize the outside of our own homes for the new paint and new fittings, for the blue plaques saying we live here, the tombstones of our own reputations? We are going to fight. Fight!

Wind tore and tugged at his tunic. Wind combed back his wispy hair till nothing of the halo remained and his skull was encased instead in a silver-white helmet, his pale cheeks red with anger and effort.

Uncle stared disbelievingly at the transformed Sebastian, then waved his walkingsticks in triumph. The fight was on. The whole town knew it. Their blood was up. It was a call they had all waited for. The moment they stood silently together fascinated by that vast seam of gold up at the highway cutting, they knew they were free of the power that once drew them, and that it was a freedom like all others which they'd have to fight for.

The guerrillas tottered back home on crutches, in braces and on wheels.

Six

Tony McTaggart awoke stiff with the damp and alert to danger, the twilight before dawn being filled with alien presences, the forest creeping quietly round him. He could sleep no more. He massaged his face with both hands to bring it to life. How filthy, sweaty and cold he was. He began to see, down below him, the foundations of a village and realized this was why he'd had that feeling of familiarity when night came on, he knew the place, a cluster of foundations looking like some mysterious alphabet laid out on the cleared ground. Night being leeched away along the horizon, the first birds called, tiny orange pardelotes jewelled the tree above him, casting up their three notes: topaz, emerald, sapphire. He could not shake off the fear which had been in him; fear leading to his decision that he would not live in the forest surrounded by watching faces, undergrowth alive with human presences. He must come out in the open. He squatted crooning while his thoughts reconnoitred the idea of building a shack down there where his ancestors had lived. For six days or was it eight years his mind had been coming back to one thought: while they worked side by side, Mr Ping had told him of Indian places, shrines, like temples to look at from the outside, but solid rock right through, no spaces inside. It was a conundrum.

With his own rifle, stolen from his father's house, he shot a rabbit dead-eye through the head and listened to the detonation of that shot magnified, punching holes in the forest. He felt better. There were plenty of plums on the tangled old trees down there. Tony took up the rest of his earthly possessions, which is to say his steel toolkit, and picked his way down the slope to his new home.

No one at Whitey's had seen a building being built for seventy years. That was a fact. Seventy years was about half a century before his time, so there were some things he'd have to find out for himself. You knew the kind of frame a house must have though, which was a start. Easy to cut young timber here. So it was that Tony McTaggart went down among the foundations to choose a site, cursing himself and his friends for having demolished old Whitey's house which would have been perfect. He cut four saplings. He found on old coin, a shilling, half-buried in the soil. Then he washed in the creek, the pure creek, took off his clothes for the first time since the church. And bathed. Stood in the water for the feel of it. He was thinner and his body's energies had reverted to growing hair, his hairiness having become prodigious. He washed, lay in the creek where men once worked their slavery and greed, he lay recalling times as a boy, the pony races, the whole world as the world had been in those days, not something you questioned or worried about. The years separated him out from his fellows, held him back from their self-confidence and even their religious experience. One thing only was left to him, the vanity of being the strongest among them, until this too was taken away by young Lance and in front of everybody. Lying in the creek, Tony felt the dreadful past begin to slip away from him. He traced the beginning of the creek right up into the clouds and its ending too.

The streaming water combed through his hairs, those abundant hairs, blond hairs swayed longitudinally down his body emphasizing the shapes of his torso and limbs so that he became a butcher's drawing to be carved, muscle by edible muscle, falling apart at the touch of blades too sharp to hurt, gently and easily being opened out, a pod, yielding himself and his seed to the knives of water, he became a branch of leaves, a flight of birds held together by the instinct of form. It was wind not water, fire not wind, the rush of time passing through him. The placenta once called Self at long last peeled away.

He was nobody. He lost the sense of lying on flat stones, the creekbed sank away drawing him down yet his nose remained above the surface, his body deepened, shortening till he was a shape he'd never been before. He was a ribbon of pale light lying along the current, snaking a flag of weed, so thin his sides swayed, long graceful shapes. His head a stone and heavy enough to withstand a million years of this, the water pouring into his whirlpool ears and washing out his clean eyes, swirling down the gutter of his mouth.

Nobody stood up from the water, his grey-chilled flesh sheathed in silver light, stood in the magnificence of his strength and began life, eating the food he'd gathered. But though he went back to look at the cornerposts he'd cut for his shelter, he did not set them up, he did not remember what they were for, they meant nothing any more. They simply were. The tools in his unopenable box became a memory of shapes of light. But he took up the coin recognizing it as the moon, placed it on his tongue to hide it. He went to a place where two trees had grown together, branches tangling, and there Nobody wooed the living creepers to weave themselves together. He left a hole to crawl in by, and he crawled in. He sat in the dim warmth of his brothers and sisters and sang. Then he listened. Sure enough he could hear the song coming back faintly. The mountain singing. He had to press his ear to the soil to hear it but it was there alright, richer for the harmonies the mountain gave it. He lay where he was, singing and listening. No need to search any more.

So Nobody came to live in this place where Tony McTaggart and his five friends had camped one night on their quest for the Golden Fleece when Tony had faced the moon as an enemy till it became a vision of the sun and he stared into it (wasn't he the apprentice of Ping?) so that his head sang with light. But now nothing was the same. A tent of leaves stood dark as an antheap under the trees, gnats gathering round for the warmth of a living body. Sucked plumstones and rabbit bones lay outside in a tidy heap awaiting burial perhaps. The creek muttered. Ancient as prehistoric remains, the vestiges of settlement sank in the ground. Only the rotting sulky with its upraised shafts appeared insectlike and alert on behalf of everything else. And so Nobody slept, woke, watched flowers open to the sun, shrimps close to the moon, frogs establishing nocturnal colonies, he breathed as the mountain itself breathed, transparent, unthinking, concealing the treasure within.

Seven

Now listen here Miss Felicia, said George Santayana, those who cannot remember the past are condemned to repeat it.

No wonder then, she explained through the years, that the newspapers keep people ignorant. The rich don't want us to learn. Whatever hat they wear, they want nothing to do with issues of the spirit. Today they're the oil lobby, tomorrow the armaments lobby, the pharmaceuticals lobby or the lethal minerals lobby, all of whom recognize the spirit as their enemy and its history as subversion.

Suppose while you are reading this ... suppose you had been aware of what was going on ... suppose you'd actually visited Whitey's Fall as the sole guest at the Mountain Hotel flinging open your upstairs window for the morning to claim you, you would have understood the issues as the senator did not. Think of yourself at the washstand sluicing water from a huge china jug into its rose-painted basin with the scalloped rim, cleansing your hands, the flesh under the nails white with cold, then towelling your face and neck, pausing to hear the roosters crowing, magpies ornamenting the countryside with their loops of song, cats and dogs being put out or let in, an old lady over in the gully calling to her cow Myrtle oh Myrtle, Mrs Sophie Schramm bustling in the kitchen below chivvying pans in readiness for the breakfast of fried ham and tomatoes, a bronchitic cough travelling the two miles from Robbie McTaggart's farm, the cajoling name Myrtle Myrtle filling the place with accents of love. Yes, you would surely have fathomed the issues as the roadbuilders did not, doing their jobs rather than think. Sebastian Brinsmead believed that being human is no accident of birth. If one says I'm doing what I'm told, I wouldn't be throwing you out if I had any choice, I've got enough worries of my own, there's always somebody worse off, you'll have to complain to those in the know ... this is to put humanness, the whole race, in peril. How quickly tribes die out, industries collapse, economies founder, freedoms are snatched the instant we relax our grip on them, whole empires dissolve. Only one man or woman at a critical time saying *no* might have prevented Hitler.

The people of Whitey's Fall were ready to resist. The parley had failed, the invaders remained ignorant that things could accumulate meaning beyond their exchange value. And with such total faith in money, oh boy did they have a shock coming to them. That night the old courage woke in your veins, the thrilling moment of change.

Shapes, black shadows on black, were collecting at the patch of common ground beside the Mountain Hotel. Three o'clock: the hour still hugged you with that thick darkness Jehovah sent as a curse on the lawful and orderly Egyptians. The night, perfect as night, could only have been worse from the people's point of view if it had been raining as well. Uncle remained philosophical, sat in the dust accepting Vivien Lang's ministrations.

– You couldn't think there was any end to a night like this, now could you? Not a star. Anyway they tell us some of them stars is dead already, did you know that, their light takes so long to reach us here. I wish I could believe it, it'd sort of round things out, because so are some of us who're watchin them.

– Dear Uncle, she whispered in her cold modulated voice and you could hear her kiss him lightly.

– Annie would've made me soft if she'd have had me to marry. Shapes and sounds were drawn to that place, old secretive dangerous shapes, hushed voices, greetings, the clink of solid metal, the squeak of rusty wheels, things trundled and dragged, the night full of purpose.

– How could you have known they'd all come like this? Vivien asked discreetly.

– We're the ones who went through the bushfire. I reckon the day we watched them company miners from the End light off down to the coast with their tails between their legs, that day we stuck together. We've never forgotten that. We got our disagreements, us fellas, but we think the same. It's natural everyone has come. Every stick of the town is a reminder we're family.

They were puffing in a close group and touching, rustling together their dry vegetation and uttering affirmative syllables. Like most elderly people, they were more at home in the dark than the young. Uncle waited for half an hour to settle. The gathering was complete.

– We never thought we'd come to this, I shouldn't wonder, he said. Is there anyone against goin ahead with it? I'll take it upon meself to state a fact. Up there them machines have dug up more than dirt, are you with me? A shove is as good as a wink. Down the bottom of their cut they've scraped the surface a the gold.

The night held its breath.

– This mountain's solid through and through like we've always said, millions of tonnes of it. Colour just a bit too deep for the miner to get his hands properly into her. No accident, that. We remember what our lives has been with hard work, it's given a meanin for our mob. Well there's two things could happen now as I understand it, eether them fellas dig further till they finally wake up, or else they get stopped and meself I'm all for stoppin them. If yous fall in when I head off, you're with me.

He waited politely for any dissidents to creep away home, heads heavy with plans to stake the first claim up there. But not one person moved.

– Tough luck havin no moon, Uncle continued hoarsely a while later. Still we know our way, we'll give it a go. Take it easy is my advice, no use rushin and exhaustin ourselves. The first to arrive gets dug in and ready. Others come up behind when they can make it. If yer can't carry yer gear, Billy'll push it up in the cart. Right mate?

– Right, Bill agreed.

– Them up there, Uncle addressed the blanket of night. Has got a bit of a shock comin. Tomorrer'll be the funeral of our sister Felissy's young feller. That buryin is goin to be here at Whitey's, come what may, and us with our minds at rest about the future. That's a promise, Felissy. Whitey's is ours for dyin and livin. They've got to cotton on to that. Now for the ladies, this is the plan. Mum, your job's to take over from Felissy on account a her tragedy. Barricades has to be ready by dawn so's they can't sneak up and take us in the back. There's no time to be lost when you're dealin with these cunnin bastards.

– She'll be jake Uncle, Mum Collins answered briskly. We've got a hundred and forty-two chairs ready outside the hall right this minute. That'll make a barricade to keep out a tank. In addition to which if they try it on, they'll still have me to deal with.

– God help them then! Give me yer hand darlin.

Plainly the time had come; the sky would not clear, no help could be expected from the moon tonight. They began to disperse as the men moved off up the hill. The women regrouped at the School of Arts to organize their barricade. Within minutes the space beside the hotel was deserted, tiny night noises reasserting their usual rhythms, while indoors Fido lay in his own blackness.

But the cloud did break eventually. Sightlessness evaporated, the lanterns dwindled, a rift of stars flashed, delicately fringeing the verges of scrub. You could see the whole company now, the gentle pace almost a dance, the wavering interplay of figures, the relief of sight touching the clan with energy. Shadows slipped out of the forest to join them, hermit prospectors with weapons slung carelessly on their shoulders, bandicoots and a sociable wombat. A frogmouth flew up ahead on its owl's wings. The stars travelled with them. Trees floated like sponges in the cool tidal wind; the mountain itself a swimmer's head of curly hair, face tipped to this side for breath or to speak to you.

When the first of the insurrectionists arrived at the promontory jutting into a roadstead of newly formed mist, they made their way right out to the point and sat there. This was their objective. The drama could begin. Immediately below, wheel-deep in cloud, floated the drowned barges of road-making machines, fabulous with a freight of tyranny.

Sebastian and Uncle supervised the disposition of the troops. In bright moonlight the ancient forms lugged their firearms and supplies to vantage points. Billy, hissing and panting as the heavy cart strained to get away from him and dug its wheels into every available rut, took time out to search for a glimpse of Vivien down at the far end of the procession, hunched exhausted over the handlebars of Mr Ian McTaggart's wheelchair as Mr McTaggart himself clambered out to walk the last stretch as he imagined he could. Changes came over the land in this light, sudden blots of mist or shadow, an army of bayonet blades on the slope gone as soon as seen. Sounds of creatures extinct for a million years crying out again in the earth's memory.

Bill Swan handed out blankets in which the oldtimers wrapped themselves against the cold as they crouched waiting. Vivien, refreshed by success, pranced round, tiresomely brisk and matter-of-fact, obliging people to accept hot tea from thermos flasks and vintage 1947 biscuits donated by Felicia. A rind of light emerged round the outline of trees on the horizon. You could taste the dawn on your tongue. Somebody snored already. The twenty-fifth hour of Fido's death. Billy still felt blood crusting on his face.

Up front Sebastian's helmet of hair gleamed silver and tight as grief. Who knows what memories of Fido's loneliness and complaining imprisonment were revealing their pale underbellies to his net of guilt, what precious moments of laughter on that young Botticelli face? The acid of betrayal coursed through the saint as he recognized his holy tapestry as an excuse for inaction, a kind of tolerance which amounted to oppression.

Bill unloaded ammunition from the cart into a pram for the sake of its lightweight manoeuvrability.

The whisper went round that Jack Collins had collapsed and dropped out somewhere along the ridge, back there among the boulders. It was marvellous that he had made it so far, being a man locked up in his lumbago. Vivien was dispatched to find him. The sky dissolved to liquid light, washing out the last stars. One frog down below by the new highway announced its intention of seeking company. The blanketed figures began to shift and shuffle, stretching weary limbs, unloading spare gloves and cartridges, numbly crushing the sandwiches in their pockets. They improved their positions from a military point of view, sighting on the enemy machines, unlikely up there as a coven of Ku Klux Klansmen.

This was the battlefield: the defenders concealed on the height, the invaders exposed beneath. If the government men wanted trouble they'd get it. They had been given time; another day and they'd possibly have the clearing completed beyond the cut, then gelignite would be little use against them, they'd be through the gap, out of reach of ambush, there'd be no stopping them. From the promontory you could survey the whole area; the natural saddle had been further hollowed out to form a cutting and so the bed of the highway lay deeper beneath their vantage point than anyone expected, its broad flat surface curved away out of sight to the west. Looking due north across the cutting you could even make out the smudge of Yalgoona set among its marshy paddocks. Back the way you'd come, the roofs of Whitey's Fall nestled in against the mountain flank more than a mile away and, as Sebastian passed round the binoculars, the ladies could be watched busy fortifying their barricade, plying each other with delicacies and scanning the skyline already expecting explosions and gunfire.

– Reminds me, said Clarrie Lang who was young Lance's grandfather. Of last time we took to this hill, them girls ran picnic races for us. You remember Ian?

Ian McTaggart remembered but he said nothing. His fingers plucked irritably at his blanket. Dawn was his time for listening to his garden.

– I could do with that jacket Bertha knitted me once, he grumbled eventually. She was pretty when she was young, he added inconsequentially. For a few years she was.

The traces of mist along the gullies began to dry in the sun. A man down there started whistling a popular song. The enemy. He came in sight strolling along the huge bare roadway, stopped and pissed, contemplating the piss, interrupting his tune while he did so, taking it up again when he had finished and shaken the drops off. The grandfathers and great-grandfathers exchanged looks. As one, they felt the urge to move closer to the edge, rising in unison and bobbing up, stepping in time, taking cover and re-emerging: much like a Japanese ritual. They settled right on the brink of the cliff. No need to puzzle over tactics, or question that the pissing man was trespassing. Long since, the community had attained that organic phase where a retraction in one arm of the sea-anemone triggers a general spasm. They were creators of a town, and a way of living in it (or at least with it) that began as complete identity with the mountain ... after all, they were the ones who, against all odds and for half a century of failure, refused to move elsewhere. Time to load the weapons. Anxiety imprinted their wrinkles, dimmed their questioning eyes. The labourer sauntered back out of sight, having noticed nothing, to where his mates lay sleeping or waking. Not long to wait. Basher Collins clipped a magazine of rounds into his well-oiled .22 and then helped the older men with breech-loaded shotguns. Uncle opened a case of miscellaneous ammunition. Sebastian and Billy worked together, as the plan was, preparing gelignite charges, aware of the terrible irony in this partnership.

– Have you only got pointed bullets there Uncle? whispered Mr Ian McTaggart. There's no art aiming with pointed bullets, he grumbled. Any fool can line up a target and fire. He held out his ancient Männlicher for admiration till his arms shook. I've got me own bullets for her anyhow, reliable round-headers: he had laid in his supply during the year 1916 on the understanding that the Mexican uprising might well have repercussions in New South Wales.

– You'll handle em, Uncle agreed placidly. He unwrapped his own weapon bound in oilcloth and displayed with satisfaction the double-barrelled big-game gun, one barrel rifled and the other smoothbore. Elephants is gettin out of hand, he joked un-smilingly.

Sebastian signalled to Billy and the two of them crept away, conspirators, down one side of the gully, instantly vanishing to a quiver of leaves. Hard as you might listen there was only the clan memory of four oceans in your ears. They were gone into a long absence. Below, those empty road-machines froze to the ground; monstrous scoops and graders, and even more monstrous rollers and crushers. Uncle, absorbed into the panorama beyond, sat brooding on Hughie Milliner's patronizing way with the big questions when you knew he'd spent his life on the respective virtues of two brands of chemical beer, his impatience with old age and country slowness. He spoke to me, Uncle remembered, like I speak to little Merv or Fred. Also Senator Bigwig insulted you with benefits you were too stupid to see for yourself. This wasn't a game, the life of Whitey's Fall hung in the scales, but a straightforward last-ditch case of us or them. They weren't giving us any rights at all, not even the right to an opinion. They were moving in under cover of smooth talk, destroying the place past recognition.

Uncle's uncle, Robbie McTaggart, loading his weapon, was having trouble finding the breech, half-blind as he was. He kept missing the hole and dropping the cartridge, then he'd have to put down the gun and run his face over the suspect area like an insensitive Geiger-counter till he located the damned thing and the fumbling process could begin again. His stiff fingers trembled, clacking together. He's only ten years older than me, Uncle thought irritably. Then at last the cartridge went home, the gun was ready and God help anybody who got in his way, though he immediately lost track of what he was doing or why he was here and gazed about abstractedly much as he might at home in bed where he ought to be.

Sunshine streamed warmly over them, it was a lovely balmy day full of birds and lively insects. The men down on the highway site could be heard joking while they munched breakfast. Somebody threw a tin plate on the ground by the sound of things, rewarded with shouts of appreciative laughter. You had to remind yourself they were the enemy, that Milliner had already rejected the peace offer. You couldn't trifle with a fellow like him. You only had to remember the workmen calling Mum Collins Grandma and asking to buy a drink of milk from her cow, the senator spreading his useless white hands appealing for reason. No, he was appealing for surrender. There was nothing original about the meek and mild technique of conquest. Who were these workmen anyhow? You couldn't imagine them settling down and belonging in one place, they were mercenaries. There was that restless look in their faces to tell you any place was much of a muchness to them; the sort of fellows to find trees a nuisance, the mountain itself a nuisance. Hark at them now. Didn't they notice that dark streak along the foot of the rockwall they'd been shaving away, or guess what it meant? Were they bundling off the black gold with the rest of their rubbish? While they laughed over breakfast had they noticed the wind shifted a couple of degrees to the north? You couldn't afford to be sentimental with this class of person, on a Sunday they'd turn into tourists, no trouble. Just because they spoke the same language meant nothing. Look at the Irish on television, Protestant against Catholic, not even schoolchildren were safe.

Meanwhile Bernie Collins had taken over the job of wheeling the arsenal pram, checking that everybody was fitted out. This distribution of ammunition developed into a complicated hushed dialogue about bore sizes and bullet design, about smokeless bullets and the ordinary smoky kind, about flanges and rims; but eventually each man was equipped more or less to his satisfaction. Uncle stood up to take charge of the pram again. Then he set about directing the emplacement of his gerontocratic troops. Meanwhile Vivien found herself a position under a treefern to establish her little first-aid station and canteen, for who could tell what opposition they might provoke and how long they might have to hold their line. She was already feeling capable and useful as a result of rescuing Jack Collins in good enough condition for him to rejoin them at least to act as reloader when needed. Yet she was thinking it's a pity she wasn't a trained nurse like Aunt Annie. Aunt Annie who knew about emptiness, nursing injured soldiers in a bombed-out village where neither allies nor enemy belonged. What if none of us has the right? she thought. She wondered if there had ever been a tribe of local Aborigines.

Wally Buddall using the binoculars picked out his wife Mary remotely but vigorously flapping a sheet from the hotel balcony which was the agreed signal that the ladies were ready for anything, thus establishing workable lines of communication. He reported this to Uncle who slapped his pink toothless gums together with grim satisfaction, having had to ask for the information to be repeated on account of his deafness on that side.

The enemy were in sight.

Eleven workmen came wandering along the culvert below, still talking and picking their teeth, amiably unsuspecting, oblivious of the trap they were walking into. A twelfth, unseen by the Whitey's Fallers, strolled close in against the cliff choosing a private enough spot to piss, being a rather shy youth.

Uncle began to grow agitated, Billy and Sebastian weren't back yet, there was no reason why they should take so long. Without them nothing could happen, the whole campaign hinged on them and their explosives. By jesus we could a done with Tony McTaggart today, he muttered, we miss the big fellow. Where the hell were they? They'd had all the time in the world since dawn, after all. Their blast was to block the road and close off the eastern end nearest to town. God help them if something had gone wrong. What if Sebbie couldn't manage the climb, what if he'd fallen? The rest of Uncle's troops took off their reading glasses, put on long-sight glasses, plugged in their earphones, popped their loose false teeth in safe pockets, settled their walkingsticks and crutches firmly, then they slipped off the safety-catches of those weapons modern enough for such equipment. Way below, the enemy appeared in excellent spirits as well as appallingly young and strong. But you were up here and that was an unbeatable advantage. All it needed was Sebbie and the boy to come back, their mission successful, for the order to be given. Instead of which the rustling of bushes (yes, at last at last) turned out to be a strangely garbed scarecrow arriving, a stick-insect of a fellow, the sort of old man who wouldn't be advised to sit too close to a naked flame for fear of going up in smoke (no, who the hell), he was wearing a green jerkin pinned together with echidna spines, a broad hat from beneath the brim of which his eyes darted about furtively, shyly, a keeper of secrets. The scarecrow, bent double under the weight of a wooden box, now placed this with reverent care before Uncle, whispering an invitation for him to inspect its contents.

– Who are you? demanded the General in an undertone, furious about his grandson.

– Eggie.

– Come on Uncle young feller, what the hell are we waiting for? grumbled one centenarian burping and farting freely to relieve the pain of a disturbed digestion.

– Eggie Schramm! but I never knew . . . the General croaked in astonishment, now really worried about his grandson, while Gottfried Egmont Schramm, prospector, brother of Jasper and thought dead on the mountain long before this, presented his face for recognition, a face deeply pitted and with grime seamed in, then stopped to scratch in his wooden box like a scrawny rooster.

– That's my mortar, he explained once he'd taken out its parts and settled himself to the gratifying task of assembling the mechanism. If it worked, which seemed increasingly unlikely the more you saw of it, this would mean the precious addition of artillery.

The eleven workmen below began dispersing, ready to climb into machines heavy as tanks. This was a disaster, the strategic moment to strike already slipping away. There were only seconds left. You could have had the lot in a group, unprotected, even though Hugh Milliner didn't seem to be among them as hoped.

– Where the hell . . . Uncle let the words grate out of him. This was the one failure he'd never even considered, the cavities of his body filling fast with dust.

– I call it the Gottfried bomb-lob and you'll see Uncle, Eggie began getting his words out more fluently now.

– They should be back, they should . . .

– Here is the bomb.

– That one? Uncle found himself surprised into paying attention for the bomb was unmistakably a jam tin. He now looked closer at the mortar itself, set up on a hunk of wood, the barrel

a length of wide lead pipe of the old pattern. Ridiculous. Un-
forgivable.

– Uncle … Uncle … Uncle? came the whispers from all
round as cramps and arthritis developed among his puzzled
troops, eyes began watering with strain, prostates protesting,
frayed threads of their clothing reaching for earth where they
could take root. He must come to a military decision. The assault
pioneers had let him down. No room for worry on their behalf.
They knew they had to look after themselves. The battle must
begin; the moment to strike had already been missed.

– How do you find its range? Uncle demanded speaking right
into the inventor's ear.

– You've got to feel it mate. I've got the feel.

– Fire when you're ready then Eggie. Try to knock out a bulldozer or two. Fire!

Uncle gave the general command, even though most of the
enemy had already passed by unharmed and were now somewhat
protected in the cabs of their vehicles. A couple of .22s went off
immediately, plus a large-bore shotgun. Hundreds of birds, flying
in interlocking straight lines, whizzed this way and that across the
cutting in danger of intercepting the bullets, and then hid palpi-
tating among the trees. There was an immediate casualty in the
person of the veteran who fired the shotgun and now found himself flat on his back with a dislocated shoulder; Vivien Lang
already crawling to his aid bearing bandages for a sling, an aspirin
and a cup of water. The shots had a dramatic effect on the enemy.
Two bullets were apparently still on their way to North America,
but the other hit the facing rockwall not twenty feet from a gravel
truck. There were shouts of amazement, anger, alarm. Faces
peered up out of the vehicle windows. Bang, blang, a couple more
let fly with a puff of rust. Egmont Schramm was employed deftly
stuffing a paper twist of gunpowder into the barrel of his mortar,
poking it down with a stick, sliding the jam tin bomb on top, pushing the fuse into a hole he'd made for it. He sucked his skin lips
with appetite, striking a match and lighting her up. Way down
there from the direction of breakfast, Hughie Milliner came

sprinting along the unfinished highway, shielding his eyes as he scanned the clifftop his men were pointing to. Pong! went the mortar and its silver bomb shot out, sailed high over the road, lobbing far into the forest the other side, where it simply disappeared among the leaves, dead and lost, falling too small to be heard. They waited, hoping for a delayed reaction. But nothing happened.

– Powder's too good, the inventor swore.

At this point half a dozen museum pieces consented to fire, they clunked and pokked and slammed. Truth dawned on the enemy.

– Jesus Christ, came a voice rising clearly from down there as a couple of bullets bounced on the road. The huge machines roared into life and the first of them began moving just as Billy Swan scrambled into view sweating, bleeding and dusty.

– Where the hell . . . Uncle roared, no longer able to restrain his voice.

– I was ready fucking ages ago, Billy shouted back pushing aside thick scarlet clouds and digging his feet in flesh. I don't know what happened to Mr Brinsmead. He was supposed to give me a signal.

They stared wildly at one another, the implications becoming a live charge leaping from one to the other, black suns floating between them.

– This yellow chap's the smoke bomb if I'm not mistaken, Egmont drawled fingering another canister lovingly, not willing to part with it.

– Aim anywhere, Uncle told him in despair, at the same time watching Mr Robbie McTaggart juggling with his .303. Hopeless. Billy give him a hand, Uncle ordered.

But old Robbie would have none of that, half-blind as he was, one-hundred-and-one and on his first visit to the mountain for seventeen years, Queen Elizabeth's congratulatory telegram in his breast pocket, he was still full of the pride of having once been a marksman entitled to wear the crossed rifles badge, he'd yield to no whippersnapper advice, not him, considering. The rifle in place, he fired. And a shocked crow watching him from the safety of the branches burst to a shell of feathers without even a squawk, while the marksman peered attentively into his myopic haze for evidence of any mortal wound he might have inflicted. Uncle himself now fired the rifle barrel of his elephant gun and the bullet rang against the scoop of a digging machine, ricochetting back towards the cliff to their left and burying itself, to the accompaniment of a yelp of pain, in the thigh of the twelfth man, the unseen workman who, having had his piss interrupted by gunfire, decided to climb up out of harm's way or else, on more honourable reflection, to surprise the attackers. Hughie Milliner had scrambled in beside the driver of a grader and this machine now swung its long body in a neat semicircle, leading the way back up the saddle to safety. Four more tanklike giants lumbered after it with a stupendous rumble of motors. Pong! went the home-made mortar and its yellow bomb flew out lopsidedly, spinning with a sound like one of the Roman gods practising trilled r's up that way. Out it spun in a curve while a couple more shots came close enough to the mark to actually hit the mountainside.

– They're bloody mad, a man howled down there in the trap.

Away beyond the convoy of earth-moving equipment spun the yellow bomb, lobbing right in their path where it exploded with a magnificent ball of smoke, smoke spread dense and black, bringing the vehicles to a halt. Black to grey to blue to a sumptuous clayey yellow the smoke billowed filling that end of the cutting. The vehicles backed, slewed round and charged off, panic-stricken, in the opposite direction, running the gauntlet of gunfire, down towards the unfinished part of the project. The colossal machinery no longer threatening, now plainly tail between legs, Uncle let out a ferocious cry of joy. The battle was really on. He scented the air calling on ancient lusts. Though curiously enough, if you were to believe your nose, the smoke needn't exist, the breeze still smelt fragrant and fresh with wildflowers.

One of the senior Collinses, the one with both good eyes, was on lookout with the fieldglasses, watching for developments in Whitey's Fall. And sure enough the ladies were stirred up like a wasp nest over something; he didn't have to wait long to see what. Three cars swung round the bend into view, one of them white and one red, plus a blue Ford; trailing their plumes of dust they swept up to the barrier. Doors opened simultaneously giving the scene a Charlie Chaplin effect and out poured a gang of uniformed men. The ladies set about waving their arms. Their newest hats, which they'd thought to wear as a mark of respect for this special occasion, waggled expressively. One of the uniforms shook the barricade of chairs but had the misfortune to choose Miss Bertha McAloon's section, so that already she was pumping something at him, her elbow a piston, and his arm went up to shield his eyes from her insecticide spray. The chief uniform by all appearances, slower than the rest, confronted Mum Collins and by the developing sag of his shoulders, the deflation of his whole bearing, found he was hearing more than he bargained for. From the blue car came the unmistakable figure of Senator Frank Halloran with his black dog cavorting round him recognizing a joyful occasion; Senator Halloran, friend of the people and patron of Aesthetics, now approaching hurriedly in odd bouncing steps. The ladies were busy, gathering around something on the ground, stooping down, they were up again, now their arms drawn back, yes they were hurling things, traditional eggs and vegetables, yes at the officials. This produced an effect. The uniforms, cowering, were driven back, routed, no question about that; they were in retreat.

One hand on the pram-arsenal, one clutching his walkingstick, Uncle, knowing nothing of this yet, was nevertheless jubilant at how his own campaign had developed. He nodded to his troops while they squinted and peered through their spectacles.

– Keep at them! he ordered. Of course he was out for blood, it was the meanings of his life he fought for, and there's no more desperate cause, as shown by the history of the world and its religious wars. Keep on to them!

At this, Grandpa Buddall's shotgun jammed and the bad-tempered old coot threw it to one side where, unfortunately, it hit Uncle's walkingstick, which was knocked right out from under him so that not only did he lose his balance but he lost hold of his arsenal. The pram crept out of reach, rolling slowly at first and then faster till it bucketted down the slope. On rolled the pram, dipping, a ship at sea bearing its cargo of dynamite and ammunition. Billy yelled a warning to Sebastian Brinsmead who at this moment appeared, struggling up over the stony ground, mastering the stiffness of his joints, an expression of triumph in his eyes. He was helpless to dodge the loaded pram, so he clung where he was, facing it; the baby-carriage charging at him, jolting along at a spanking pace, Fido's store of dynamite aimed with deadly accuracy.

– Sebbie! they cried to the man who had discovered anger. They held their breath as the arsenal rushed past within inches of his shoulder, out over the cutting. At the precise moment the pram was seen to launch into space, a tremendous crash came from below, followed by the roar of shifting rock. The road machines behaved frantically, whining, caught up in the complicated avoidance of collisions with each other, scrambling among themselves to escape the sheet of rock which swung out from the cliff, folded, and crumbled, cascading down in their path. The earth itself shuddered. As if to confirm the closure of the roadway, another multiple explosion marked the final restingplace of the pram, with numerous small crackles and bangs following. Uncle was on his feet again, nursing his bruises and literally hopping up and down with energy.

– Get the bastards, he ordered as Milliner's government drove out through the clearing smoke towards safety along the hundred miles of highway they'd already made. Then it occurred to him that he had witnessed the treachery of his kin, that there were men around him who hunted and shot their own dinners every day of the year, whose weapons glowed with a faint sheen of oil and loving care. So how was it nobody down there had been hit? They were shooting wide, the bastards, too stupid to see the facts, the enemy as enemy, too gentle to recognize death in more ways than the obvious.

– This isn't a bloody game, Uncle roared furiously, a murderous vengeance in him. He fired the elephant-killer, you could hear the huge bullet take to air before it smashed through the glass cab of the grader, you could hear the old man sigh – That's what I meant to do. But you couldn't tell if anybody had been hit. The machines gathered speed making thunderous progress out of harm's way, the smoke from Egmont's mortar bomb having taken wing for Canberra. Billy was shouting jubilantly (though his memory flashed up the scene of himself at Mr Whitey's ruined house hurling a rock and the senselessly flattened face of a verdigrised clock). Beauty! he shouted.

No one was left to shoot at, the only person in the cutting being that youth hiding against the cliff, clutching his bleeding thigh, and they didn't know about him, nor that he had been wounded. Uncle looked grim and shaken when he faced his men, surprised to discover some of them lying stunned on the grass and Vivien busy with a cold sponge and spirits.

– Now they know we mean business Sebbie, he growled, his anger ebbing. What have I got to lose? he asked. Bastards wouldn't listen when they had the chance. I'm too old for peace at their price. A single tear of tiredness gathered to rest, heavy in the corner of his eye. His body a cave of ice that crazes with cracks ... no warning, a sudden freezing shower of irreplaceable shards, his gut rattling loud as a crate of milkbottles ... he stood upright and took the yoke of the world's survivors on his shoulders. The barrel of the elephant gun scorched his hand. His huge ears had grown to solid flesh at the blast.

– Get a load of this Uncle, the lookout called four times to get through. He passed the binoculars across. There's no doubt about them ladies of ours.

Uncle adjusted the focus and saw for himself the confrontation at Whitey's Fall, the cars full of officialdom, their doors slammed shut; and the wives, mothers, daughters and aunts of his troops defiantly bunched together, hands on hips, elbows clashing, a conference of hats. Distant car horns could be heard. A folded sheet began flapping from the balcony of the hotel.

– Mary says they're holding out, Uncle reported. No worries. At that moment he felt terribly sorry for the women still carrying on, not knowing the real battle had finished. Yet he felt somehow apprehensive about his victory. The fear remained that if he took the binoculars away from his eyes he'd find he was weeping. He saw the side door of the pub swing open and a solitary figure run out into the street then stop, momentarily lost, standing alone looking down towards the barricades. Poor Felissy, he said, there's so much we don't know, there's a lot we're better not to ask. The cruel silly woman, too clever to love her own boy. Education is a terrible thing, he concluded. And travel never did nobody any good that I ever heard neether. He lowered the glasses and sure enough he was weeping.

– Billy, he commanded. You go down and see what can be done back home. No need for that barricade now. Viv can stay here for the ones who're shaken up. Who's for the journey back? We won, outright. Now perhaps they'll listen to what we say.

The barricade was being dismantled, individual chairs restored to their domestic function. The uniforms (a policeman, two forest rangers and the Yalgoona Volunteer Fire Brigade) were sweating downhill into Whitey's Fall in single file, bearing stretchers on which lay the stunned and exhausted old men brought back from the battlefield, released from Vivien Lang's amateur care. The ladies clucked and crooned over their victorious menfolk. Senator Halloran, exuding cleanliness like a poison gas, confronted two ancient smelly wrecks barely recognizable as Sebastian Brinsmead and Uncle Arthur Swan. His hands squelched together disapprovingly as he complained to them that, had they only curbed their tempers and waited for his arrival, he could have spared them the trouble of turning criminal.

– And what about the moral question? the senator challenged them passionately. Terrorizing the innocent?

– All questions of morality finally mean only one thing, Sebastian informed the wind. War.

Frank Halloran grimaced dismissively. He opened his briefcase.

– I've brought a letter I'd like you to read. It's from the Minister himself, as you'll see, authorizing me to appoint members of your own community to sit on a committee. The committee to be set up immediately will discuss the entire regional scheme, the highway, the facilities, finance, services, everything; and you'll have your chance to put your view in a lawful and peaceful manner, he gave his verdict on their guilt and added with satisfaction, nothing could be fairer than that I'm sure you'll agree.

So now the proposals were passing between them: representatives of Whitey's Fall to include the 'two community spokesmen Mr Sebastian Brinsmead and Mr George Swan' and three others to be appointed; also one representative each from the Australian Historical and Aesthetic Resources Commission, the Department of Main Roads, the Ministry of Tourism, the Department of Justice, and the House Committee on Land Titles; this meeting to be chaired by an independent and disinterested citizen, to be a retired magistrate whom the Chief Magistrate's office would name in due course.

– Oh I blame myself, the senator muttered recalling the day he lost his dog and went back to Vivien Lang's house dripping wet, in time to surprise the Swan boy crowing I've got the gelignite and I'm going to blow it up. The police should have been called then and there.

The two-way radio now began gabbling its travesty of Hugh Milliner's voice and one of the rangers was droning back various calming sentiments, plus assurances that law and order had already been restored and medical attention was on its way to treat his wounded workman. This was the sort of anticlimax nobody expected, the uniforms wandering round on their weekend off as if they weren't spattered with congealed egg. Senator Halloran taking charge spoke as the leader who'd won the battle. Foreman Milliner's voice on the radio assessed the damage at two days' extra clearing work for the machines.

– What does it mean? whispered Mrs Collins as if finding her house locked.

The terrible exhaustion of attempting murder now shown to have been futile, Uncle gazed back at the mountain, back where he'd come from. He offered no answer. He'd become a boy inside an old walnut shell.

Eight

Fido lay waxen in his coffin while his wax mother hunched over an open book. She might always have been there, not daring to move, her pendulous body ready to fall apart into fatty pieces, the fusing flame of an ordeal too recently survived, her soft grieving forms held together only by her dress. Though in fact she went outside once; hearing shouts and feeling the ground tremble at the impact of an explosion, a gasp of dread filling her body which was found to be a nest of bats whistling and whirling madly with the shock of a boy thrown into the garden again, his side blown away. So, leaving him dead as he was, Felicia ran out into nothing. An empty street where her painful heartbeat suffocated in solid air. She saw, uncomprehendingly, the road blocked off with chairs, ladies shouting so you couldn't recognize their voices for the words, and cars full of men facing them, facing her. She stood alone reliving yesterday's horror, unaware of the tidal dust tearing a door open and slamming it flat back against a wall, nor hearing the regular moans of a loose sheet of roofing metal, nor appreciating the supple television antennae bowing to the blast as resilient as saplings. Lost boys' faces and voices played in the street, but her own son was never among them. She must not be distracted. To protect her grief she strutted back inside the lopsided Mountain, intent on keeping her balance and reaching God for Fido's sake. Once safely through the door with its frosted glass PARLOUR and settled in her chair beside the last angel, she took up his diary and turned the page. Presently her veins began to set. Words swam in a glassy frame of tears, only her lips retained the power of life, trembling so violently her whole mouth became helpless to express anything.

I've been spying into the shop like I do and whispering how miserable I am so somebody might hear and come to my rescue. Today I began specially saying the date because it's against my mother's rules and regulations and it is my birthday. I have been getting excited and at last it is here but nobody says anything. If you're wondering what I've got to cry about, it's because I'm waiting for my mother and my uncle to say Happy Birthday Fido. I'm twelve and I might as well be nothing. No one remembered how old I am but me. I'm so ...

Felicia habitually told those who asked her, of course I can tell what's about to happen, it has all happened so many lives before, but this had not and took her wholly by surprise. Oh yes, there were premonitions, the character not yet fully armed against hurt. She tried to protect poor Fido, pretending the year was not yet a year. Felicia turned the pages.

MOST SECRET. Maybe I have got enough dynamite to blow up the mountain so I'll never see it watching me again.
Signed Fido.

Another time she might have laughed. But now it simply made no sense. She shut the diary as any mother would, seeing the irony of the dead youth among the aged, accepted by them. Alive, Fido would be a scandal, yes she knew. The cruelty of man is unchanging. As Felicia put down the diary she recalled noticing somebody else out there in the street, standing apart from the barricade; Rupie Ping in his doorway, Rupie who had never been to school and grew to marry a schoolteacher, ah she knew his history, how he'd been brought from China at nine to perform in Melbourne and Ballarat where, suddenly possessed by a vision, he had begun walking away from the perfectibility of movement, out of his appointed place in life, exchanging the stylized order of art for a chaos of pedestrian experience, and for ten years walking till he discovered Whitey's Fall in the heartland of the barbarians. Rupie was a man of the world by the time he reached Fido's age. Who could imagine Fido making his way up to Wit's End, let alone across the State? I'm so unhappy, he had written. She gazed at the boy's face for longer than she'd dared when he was alive and awake; she gazed struggling to imagine how his mouth might have spoken these words, how his pale hand held the pen to write them. What if, like Rupert Ping, he had simply walked away from her? The treacherous thought presented itself that at least this could never happen now. But her grief flowered, too intense to be affected by whimsies. She realized his hands ought to be crossed on his chest for the reason that this is how dead bodies are always arranged in their coffins.

Felicia took hold of the lifeless hands and pulled them so they'd meet, the resistance of the flesh more dreadful than anything she had known. Once, nailing rubber strips from car tyres across the bed base when the springs rusted through, with Sebastian gravely hammering at the other end, the rubber wobbled heavy against her will, exactly as these young arms wobbled now. They would not stay, but slithered with ugly persistence across his belly. Couldn't he see she had suffered all she was able to bear? Defying her still. Morning glinted on his tentative moustache, hints of what was to come. The fine gold hairs, barely visible in direct light, unnaturally prominent in these slanting rays of stale beer. She saw him as a young man. Who knows what it cost her, but she faced the vision, the recognition of lost hopes. Had he ever seen himself like that? Had he felt the stirrings of manhood in him? She resented the thought. Fido as a man would not be her Fido. And how had his little sex thing grown? She thought of him as a small boy: all these betrayals. It was so long since they'd been free with one another. She had never, of course, wanted him to be born, her pregnancy an extravagance of fears: mongoloid, malformed, idiot, siamese twin. She remembered undressing her mistress who married the unfortunate King George III and how a servant opened the curtains on the far side of the bed and she had glimpsed his majesty naked, his white chest shapeless as a boy's, his soft hibernating arms, rebellious hairs disfiguring him in ugly clumps. No, her Fido would have grown like his father, a splendid figure of a man. But she had been tempted to throw the baby out of a train window because she was sixty-one and grotesquely mocked by her fertility. Once she found a Russian widow willing to adopt him but, with all the papers signed, she snatched him back and abused the poor woman for a kidnapper. Twelve years this boy had ruled her life. Everything she did had to accommodate the secret. She fretted for him and his imprisonment yet she always came back to Whitey's Fall, she always brought him home with relief and shut him in, as once she would have liked to shut Sebastian in when she feared he was casting eyes, especially on a certain farmer's wife in Quebec Province. She feared the farmer's wife as she'd never feared any woman before, not even the young *répétiteuse* of the Paris Opera whose legs he'd so salaciously lusted after in 1952. He wrote the farmer's wife a poem if you please, which Felicia found and committed to memory

A pure white stitch in the tapestry
Your soul the highlight of God's own eye
Let nations burn themselves in rose
Green and gold – without your thread
My dear their histories decompose.

Yet now she respected Sebastian for it. With the death of Fido she knew what it meant. Fido's pure thread might indeed stand out in the universal design. And the decomposition of histories was precisely what she felt in herself. Fido's dead body leeching her of power. She would not be herself again.

At this moment she knew.

She had stopped falling. Felicia Brinsmead, the child's mother and aunt, old enough to be his grandmother, his great-grandmother even. She observed her own arms with surprise, the puffy flesh; her legs so sturdy; the homely largeness of her breasts. The person she recognized was a mother, a countrywoman and a mother. Already she couldn't quite recall what she'd been suffering. Fidelis, she said, the name coming to life at last. She reminded herself of the way he dipped his buttery knife in the honey, how he longed to practise his whistling out loud, how he bared his lower teeth when angry, how he ducked his head to meet the fork while eating rather than trouble to lift his forearm from the table, how he drummed his fingers to the point of maddening her, how he smashed her Spode teaset one piece per week with innocent churlishness, how wildly he kissed her as if possessing this flesh at least. She made another attempt to arrange his hands decorously. Your wicked father! she wailed. Oh she had no illusions. God help those who had. There's no doubt she wanted Fido to be normal, Fido who'd given her almost what she craved. And with his flowing blond hair in a curious way he looked wholly in keeping with his glamorous generation out there in the world where he never went. Miss Brinsmead looked up; somebody watching. And yes, in the doorway stood her own cat, hypnotizing her, reducing her to a calculated slit in his eye. Rastus was here to demand loyalty. He advanced as only cats can, seeming not to have noticed the floor. And before she could stop him he launched himself into the air, landing softly, with an elegant switch of his tail, on the rim of the coffin. Faintly perfumed with eucalyptus, fresh from his bed of sweets, he stepped down on to Fido's feet. The cat advanced one plush exploratory step at a time, whiskers humming with surprises. He showed no sign of recognizing Fido. He advanced towards Felicia, treading lightly, unfeelingly on the dead boy. With one forepaw on the mouth, one on the eyebrow, he stopped to count to ten for the benefit of who might be watching. Miss Brinsmead woke up. She screeched and swept the cat off, sending him flying out over the side of the coffin to where he twisted mid-air as an acrobat and landed on his feet none the worse for a chance to show his skill, leaving behind a tiny bloodless scratch among the hairs on the corpse's upper lip. Rastus wafted up on the windowsill; he was a framed model of a cat, putting on his sphinx eyes and square

412

jowls, he was gone, the heavy curtains swung mustily in the open frame. Miss Brinsmead gasping for breath now noticed a picture beside the window, a print of an old painting, and beside the print a notice MEN CAN ONLY USE THE PARLOUR IN THE COMPANY OF LADIES. This did surprise her. And it had hung there so long unread.

She looked at the print too. She went right up to it and noted the caption *Birth of the Virgin S.Maria Novella at Florence*. Then she granted her eyes respite from watching her dead son, permitted them to take her right into the illusion of the painting, that cool ornate chamber, in among the women with their expressions of self-assured innocence, the pouring of water into a cold brass pot, the laced bosoms and coiffed heads, the propriety and seemliness of standing round not looking at the miraculous baby, except for her seated mother. Yes, among those solemn figures (the young ones conscious of their beauty, the old ones of their wisdom), the mother and her child quietly laughed into each other's eyes. Observing them like that and knowing they were destined to be the grandmother and the mother of Jesus, Miss Brinsmead's sadness was infinite.

When the neighbours came they knocked at the hotel door, filed in and stood about not looking at the corpse yet paying their respects. Only Felicia looked at him and would not raise her eyes. The parlour filled with summer perfumes. Just about everybody attended, the old and the very old, Swans, Buddalls, McAloons, McTaggarts, Langs, and Collinses. Also those without issue: the Schramms. Then the town elder, Mr Ian McTaggart, shaky from the early morning battle, made his way in. His weary eyes looked up at the curtain rail, seeing perhaps the vision of a garden of circles, of endless bounty. Though a man of few words, it was his privilege and duty to speak for them all.

– This is the last child of Whitey's Fall, he said. This youngster we never knew. We want to give you a good send-off, fellow, because we're old, he said empty of pride. And it makes us sad in our hearts to see you like this.

Sebastian let out a sob as terrible as his anger had been the day before. That one sob filled the room with all it meant. Mum

413

Collins felt for Sebastian's hand, realizing the strangeness of the occasion, that she had never touched him before, not since he had become a man.

– We would like to have known you, Mr McTaggart went on severely, addressing the corpse on behalf of them all. I spoke at your grandfather's burying, poor man who hung himself.

He left a pause while he wheezed for the strength to continue. When he did speak again, it was to dream out loud.

– If you leave a stack of bricks on a flat place long enough, they'll fall over. That's a mystery. Nobody can tell me why. Like when a sea eagle comes in from the coast all this way, he shouldn't have come so far but you're glad to see him. Think about that. We could have done with a mascot this morning, the dreamer had forgotten the nature of the occasion.

He lurched forward to the coffin. He witnessed death, a weather-worn mossy stone head looking in for a long time.

– He's a fine lad Felicia my dear, he complimented her. How wicked we are, he added to encompass them all (us all).

– Yes, she whispered.

The mourners moved closer to examine the boy's face for likenesses.

– Well mother, Mr McTaggart concluded thus making her relationship legitimate. If you're ready we'll take him now and put him away.

She nodded.

– I brought some flowers, Olive McAloon offered.

So had they all. The summer perfumes advanced to suffocate Miss Brinsmead. They arranged the flowers in the coffin, patted rustling chrysanthemum petals into place, bedding carnations and honeysuckle deeply in every available cranny around the child. Then came the ritual draping across the coffin of a string of metallic tassles, last relic of the old horse-drawn hearse from the town's heyday. He was ready. Bill Swan and his father took one end while the two Buddalls took the other, being the nearest match for shortness. They hoisted it on their shoulders. Jasper led the way carrying the lid to be nailed on when they reached the graveside, as the custom was. Across the bar-room they went, the coffin bucking and pitching while they failed to agree on a common step, the body softly thudding, the heap of flowers heaving to the shape of a boy, blossoms tumbling out as Fido let tributes drop. Rose Swan, Billy's mother, picked them up because she had, perhaps, lost her own son.

Sebastian could not be expected to realize Felicia, for once, did not understand what anything meant, had no notion what he was doing for her. He stood miserably among his customers, sacrificing himself to his sister's greater need. The town was allowing her the privilege of sharing her grief; she needed to, God knows she had been through enough. He would destroy this for her if he demanded the same right for himself. In his view, the people thought her strange and cruel to keep the child hidden, contributed their flowers with tightlipped disapproval, but did not regard her as an unnatural parent, not in her sorrow. He need only speak the truth, claim his darling son, to destroy what she had, the communion at this moment, to make Fido an object of revulsion. Forgive me, Fido, he prayed as a nonentity. He had expressed what he felt early that morning when his charge of gelignite blasted away a slab of cliff to crash across the mouth of the highway. He and Bill Swan had prepared the charge and placed it carefully: in that moment coming close together they moved to the same rhythm, expunging the same memory. So close were they that when he decided to stay with the charge and be killed by it as his son had been killed already, Billy said nothing, asked nothing, understood but did not judge him. Suicide is not often witnessed, still more rarely is it tolerated. Bill, however, turned his back and set off for safety alone; to become a murderer twice. Yes, as Sebastian Brinsmead watched the coffin rock out through the door, he acknowledged that fate was dignified by a certain justice. The corpse had just time to nudge out a head of hydrangea for him. He saw it was for him. He watched the feet trample around it, his son's token, a blue pad of flowers, a hemisphere of space on the floor. Sebastian approached it eagerly, but Rose Swan was there first and gathered it among her anonymous blooms. A voice was speaking to him, he realized, Miles McTaggart, Miles whom he'd nearly forgotten except sixty years back as the fastest boy runner he'd ever seen.

– We dug his grave beside Kel McAloon, said Miles kindly. We thought you wouldn't want the boy next to your father, he added by way of explanation. Him with the sin of taking his own life.

Nine

You see, said Mr Ping facing himself in the mirror. I can still do everything.

Look at the scars, said the man inside him.

Look at me, said Mr Ping instead. And he stood on his hands. He had a feeling he could no longer stand on one hand as he used to, so he didn't risk that.

You never seem to take my advice. You still pretend you're young. I thought we'd cured that.

It was different when there was blood, said Mr Ping lying belly-down on the floor.

Yet you know it's impossible.

Youth? Actual youth? Maybe it's not youth I want after all.

You mean it could be something you missed?

Why not? If other people have it. Perhaps I want to stay young so something can happen.

Happiness, suggested the man inside him.

Why shouldn't I? Mr Ping began a routine of push-ups. His face bobbed in and out of the mirror's range. Silence in the cool bathroom. But the moment he stood, the voice was at him again.

What's the point of keeping in training?

Watch this, said Mr Ping leaning backwards, hands above his

head, far back, arching right over till his palms rested on the floor. Then he somersaulted towards the door and came back to the mirror with a vain shake of his shoulders. Sixty-eight and I can still do that, he pointed out. The man inside him was struck dumb. So he reached for his trousers and pulled them on, slipped his arms into a shirt (he'd prepared the one with the pockets for today). I've got an idea, he said watching his fingers at work on the shirt buttons, refusing to look himself in the face. Then he took his boots which he seldom wore and threaded a single long lace through both so he could sling them round his neck. I can still do everything I used to do, he told the mirror. So why not? He went out to fetch his jacket. On top of the jacket lay an unfamiliar ladies' purse. Of course, yes, he remembered the other day. The failure of Alice. That Lang girl viewing his beautiful beast. He had forgotten how the job began with his savaging of Mercy's beloved pet; but restoring a dream was fresh in his mind. In the end he watched with the locals as if he were not related to the cow. Mr Ping opened the purse he had picked up in the gutter. Inside he found two letters. One of them began: Vivien my duck, you should just see what a picture my peonies are this year, something wonderful will happen if you believe in signs, how green Mrs Cox and Mrs Pye, whom you will remember I dare say, go when they pass my gate, I could clap my hands, they have made my life a misery with their tittletattle, you wouldn't believe ... Mr Ping was not interested. He unfolded the other letter: Dearest Auntie Anne, nothing has happened yet ... Mr Ping laughed a silent laugh. He felt purged and hopeful, anything possible, the world invited him. He could tolerate triviality. Also he had an inspiration. He replaced the letters in the purse, he would be passing her way.

That was how he invented the act of disinterested kindness.

He'd call, though he had no need to do so, and leave the purse for her to find when she came home from the funeral. Everybody was at the funeral except himself. He'd place it on the verandah. He could see nothing against that. He turned along the Lang track with this irreproachable intention, pushed open the gate and walked in up the steps without hesitation. It never occurred to him that she might be afraid Felicia's nightmare could prove contagious.

– My purse! declared a voice, startling him. How kind of you Mr Ping. I was so very upset yesterday.

She didn't like him, he could tell. Yet she invited him to have a cup of tea with her, which he declined.

– Are you going to stop in this town? he asked, surprised at the way she clutched the purse with its gossipy letters.

– That's how things seem to be turning out.

– What did you do for a crust?

– I was a schoolteacher, she answered.

– There's no kids to teach here.

– There might be.

– My wife was a schoolteacher, he drawled in the broad Australian accent he'd cultivated, his virtuoso defence. Till no one wanted her any more.

She did not comment on this. Instead she retired inside to put her purse somewhere safe, then came back with the air of a new woman. Mr Ping was already surrendering to the flow of events, his mind agilely resolving difficulties as they arose, he found that without any plan a sequence of action was shaping itself towards a definite conclusion. Everything depended on moving as opportunity presented itself. With an ironic twist of his mouth he recalled Felicia once telling him I do not accept what you accept, that is all, I do not accept the world you accept. But what did he accept? What was his world?

– Miss Lang, he said. If you want to thank me, you can come down the street to the workshop.

Unwilling as she was, she agreed to go. Dreaded the workshop, the complex presence of that stuffed cow. They walked together. She braved the threat of what she already knew: not just Mrs Ping's dead hand in the grass but this man who was her husband refusing to help save her, also the proprietorial tone Mr Ping used when referring to Miss Brinsmead. These accusations stuck burrs in her mind on the way, neither of them attempting to be companionable. Yet he was so mild and courteous.

He did not ask her into the workshop, so she needn't have

feared Alice on the vehicle hoist. He was only in there a minute before he came out again and began padlocking the two doors. Vivien glanced across the fields to the cemetery where a group of black figures, a mourning conference of scarecrows and crows, stood in a close circle. She should go and join them.

– Now, said Mr Ping. I'm going away. These keys are for the workshop and that one for the house.

She held them warm in her palm, messengers of his body heat. She remembered Auntie giving her the keys to her own house, and to the labyrinth.

– I'm new, she objected.

He was already leading the way in the direction of the waterfall. They reached the head of the winding road where Mrs Ping had driven to her death and now rose with the rest of the dust on the wind.

– There's one thing, he said. You might have to go away.

– No I shan't go, she answered after a while, fixing her decision.

– But you are in love with Bill Swan?

– . . .

– People with young children move away.

– What will you do? she asked, evading his argument.

– I shall work as an acrobat, the old Chinese replied promptly. I know the trade. I'm not happy here. Mercy, she belonged on the mountain, but I was never happy in prison, Miss Lang, I was taken from my home a long time ago, a small boy. My name in Shanghai was Lu P'an Ping. Why did Australians call me Rupert? It's a mystery.

He turned his face toward her for the first time, requiring her to meet his eyes. She controlled her distaste; among the crazed wrinkles, neat scars down the cheeks and across the brow gave him the appearance of having been carved up, stuffed, and stuck back together. His fine white hair had been cropped short.

– I can come back here and you will have my keys, he said simply.

Vivien stood in her own thoughts, believing for the first time that her mother's name was Esther; accepting that her father had threatened to take an overdose of sleeping pills if she, Vivien, turned out to be a girl, *how we laughed*, and the precious evidence in her purse safely at home. She watched Mr Ping walk away, his jacket slung jauntily over his shoulder, boots dangling round his neck, looking down to where his wife's truck rusted, his neat bare feet scarcely raising any dust. Now he was far enough away, you could swear he was a youth, so slight and springy his figure appeared. As if the future lay before him. The faint sound of his voice singing in a foreign mode.

She clinked the keys already warm with her own warmth.

Ten

Uncle had a good long look at his house. He stood out in the street and took it all in for the first time in many a long year. His hound Bertha came and stood beside him, watching also, every so often turning on him her sensitive mechanisms for divining his mood. Then he started laughing. The more he looked the more he laughed. Bertha indulgently smiled. He was coughing and laughing at the one time, spitting out gobs of phlegm, his face a great raspberry, his eyes bright with tears. The dog caught on to the spirit of the thing and barked, she joined in happily, dancing round him on elastic paws. How ridiculous it was, this house, hut, everything slapdash, nothing finished, not even the guttering along the front, half a windowframe flaking its original blue paint and the other half disintegrating with dry rot, the whole place leaning against its chimney which had been added as an afterthought one winter, gaps in the walls patched with tin, roofline bowed, the verandah sagging, front steps fallen away, kitchen on a tilt because of the roots of that damn native fig, the fig itself harbouring the whole mosquito population of the shire into the bargain. But what kept Uncle laughing till it hurt, and so that neighbours came out to see, was the plants: grass sprouting here and there up the brickwork chimney, the choko appearing with a basketful of unharvestable fruit from a gap in the roof though god knows where its roots were, the mountainous tangle of living things, creepers and morning glory heaped by the ton over the whole building, stinging nettles among verandah chairs and blackberries in the outdoor bathhouse, his water tank buried under a thicket of lantana, and proliferating grasses tall as a man growing up inside the front room windows, prisoners clawing at the glass.

Billy's head poked out from among the morning glory.

– What's up, Uncle?

– You look so bloody silly, Uncle laughed, with your head poked out.

– Well I'm doing what I can for you, Bill's face retorted irritably, a flower among flowers.

Uncle laughed all the more. Lately there had been too much sorrow and worry to be healthy. This was a joke he'd been waiting for, you only see the funny side once.

The hound barked ecstatically trying to get inside the laughter. Then Uncle's neighbours began joining in. They stood in the dusty street, hands on hips, and laughed at their own old wrecks. Look at this! and just get a load of mine will you! More people gathered, pointing and sharing what they saw, their threadbare voices young with laughter. It was the joke of a lifetime.

Eleven

Mr and Miss Brinsmead sat in their kitchen, not having spoken, the house and the shop fomented warm silences and consolidated the rightness of things which do not move, the dust putting a finish, a bloom, on everything as it was. Only the kitchen and the bedroom still suffered change and use; Fido's den had given up singing to itself and already crumbled though no one bothered to see, and the shop shut yesterday. They were dressed in their travelling clothes, ready except for their bare feet. But this was not to be another journey abroad with the gold mountain in their wallets. Felicia had lost her bright questioning, her contemptuous toss of the head to set her hair-bag nodding. Sebastian too appeared altered now he must live with the way she hated him for his gift to her, the grief he longed for for himself; he'd grown softer and pinker, with that surprised air of a person who has lost a lifelong protection. She fed him, he fed the chickens, she untwisted his braces when he couldn't cope, she passed her a letter from Senator Frank Halloran which she had already seen but might wish to read again.

Dear Mr Brinsmead,

I'm pleased that we can finally agree on the date for convening our committee and the personnel to sit on it. The sooner this deadlock is solved the better. As you must be aware, every day the highway project is delayed costs the taxpayer thousands of dollars for the idle plant alone, not to mention the cost of uncertainty to yourselves.

The committee will be invested with a broad brief and, as the attached agenda exemplifies, is expected to discuss the whole range of issues associated with the Government's plan for the region as this affects Whitey's Fall and its development.

The committee's first sitting, which should resolve the main issue of the highway and its proposed route through the township, will commence at Whitey's Fall School of Arts at 10.30am, as agreed. Local personnel will be as set out here: Mr Sebastian Brinsmead, Miss Felicia Brinsmead, Mrs Bessie Collins, Mr Jasper Schramm, Mr George Swan.

I look forward to your co-operation and trust that the discussion will prove fruitful and cordial.

Yours sincerely,
The Hon. F. T. Halloran

Felicia received the letter in her hand but declined to re-read it, renewing her knowledge by the feel of the paper.

– We shall begin in half an hour, Sebastian said.

For this one moment his sister heard in his tone the hoot of a Sydney steamer and her footsteps together with his drumming the boards of the old pier, the excited voices of travellers and sea-gulls, heavy objects being moved around … also she heard a thrush calling from an ashtree and saw the ring of flowers she made to hang round his neck while behind him priests advanced in their black habits escorting two prisoners, one of whom called *the sea, the sea.*

Sebastian used the silence to inspect his knees where his best trousers stretched shiny; to contemplate also his bare toes, long, white and dirty; to check the two pairs of shoes put ready near the stove. Then he gazed out of the window at that fateful gravel road down the mountain. A fowl strutted, queening it round the kitchen, the ceaseless wind outside tearing at gutters and loose windowframes. To his astonishment Sebastian was assailed by nostalgia, yes for somewhere, for a paved square surrounded by stone buildings, sun-warmed columns, trembling slatted shutters, drains, voices speaking Greek or was it Italian? himself holding little Fido's hand, pointing out flowers in urns and the British flag fluttering in a breeze perfumed by oranges. Where? But the scent was gone, his eyes saw only a dirt road with yellow dust lifting. He heard the clicking of hen's feet. He did not go outside: why should he look at that great hole ripped in the yard? or the last living tallow tree in the district?

– Soon we shall be needed, he said.

His sister stood at the door, one foot in the sunshine, listening not to him but to the mountain where the roadmakers awaited permission to push their bulldozers through the rubble of gold and clear aside all trace of a battle best forgotten. She had withdrawn the privileges of sympathy from her brother and husband, the betrayer of her child. Last year, bushfires fumed along those forested slopes all summer, smoke smoothed the rocky mass thin as a paper cut-out; and the setting sun a dull white disc going yellow, eventually dried out to the brown blood of old wars; the foothills and boulders blue, the grass grey until evening when the mountain became soft smoky wool with loose threads left dangling from the tapestry for the white trunks of trees ... she had seen the wooded islands of Greece stripped of their timber and left stark and waterless so that a race of philosophers and wrestlers could enjoy the satisfaction of clearing the sky itself of clouds and creating a man-made climate, however barren.

Sebastian grunted as he slipped his shoes on without socks, as he folded his crackling body to grasp the laces, getting too old.

Agenda and reports, briefings on the reports, a seat on the committee, the Department's approval, what could be more important to the conscientious Canberra man? The seductive idea of committees: decision without individual responsibility. Civilization itself. Give us our daily bread of problems, for ours is the power and the glory. We'll set up a Royal Commission with principles, guidelines, a policy-co-ordinating sub-committee, a tabulated breakdown of the budget, estimates, a system of assessment, ministerial advice, an establishment, sub-let consultations, implemented advice, a digest of documents, research addenda, a précis of findings by previous commissions of enquiry and so forth. Hand it to us: you do nothing, we'll do it for you, just don't cause trouble, we'll get to the bottom of any scandalous affair for you, and if we need to use the High Court the High Court it'll be, we'll know what to do when it's on the agenda, that's what keeps the Public Service incorruptible. The point is, who will sit next to the Chairman? who's senior to whom? are we being flown first class or economy? will the Commonwealth Car meet us in my name or his or hers? did somebody say there'd be a member of parliament with us? a senator? well a senator will do, what's his first name? does he play golf? no chance he's a queer I suppose? how shall I know what clothes to choose? you can do a lot of damage to your cause by the mildest hint of eccentricity or lack of it.

C.I.A. interference? just our cup of tea. A nice little case of planning for ports or harbours? yes well you need a statistician, a numbers man, a customs man, advice on the look of the thing, PR, hundreds of details could be botched if there aren't the right departmental committees at their back. What's this one: a ministerial enquiry into child-bashing? good, that's a lovely one, that'll last for years, no end to the children, parents always pushed further than they can cope, it'll take a thousand gallons of tea and a vat of scotch to straighten that one out, employment for paper and pen manufacturers, it's very productive, an enquiry like this, and of course the travel industry gains, you can't deal lightly with a serious matter like child-bashing, the Northern Territory child-bashers have every bit as much right to be heard as their brothers and sisters in Canberra, these things have to be understood before they can be acted upon, we shall need to go everywhere, and stay, no excuse for haste, unpardonable, the safety of children being at stake, whole lives ruined, future of the national character etcetera, you have to be patient if you want kids to talk at all, let alone talk freely, and against their parents, trust us we'll get the full story, we'll flinch at nothing being independent and with no axe to grind, it'll take a few years perhaps, but let's be realistic, in the end we'll get it ... as long as you're sure I'm on the list, there hasn't been a squeak out of Wilson you say? and Marjorie Longhurst thinks she ought to be on everything to do with children because she once had one. As long as you're sure. We'll do a wonderful job, such a heart-rending issue, will I be travelling first class? and are you giving me teeth enough to make our presence felt? Another one coming up? But then it's a case of priorities. What is it? Enquiry into regional development, local complaints demanding re-routing of highway? What's the story? Is it important? Is it news? Would there be travel? New South Wales country district: forget it. Not me, I take it the road isn't begun yet? Half finished! Then what is there to do? A complaint, a local ... thank you for the coffee Miss Appleby, is it stirred? biscuit? bless you ... but that's ridiculous, it'll be finished in no time, why mention it to me? Complications with the Aesthetic and Historical Resources people? that's more promising, a sort of green-ban perhaps, could be some mileage in that, I've got the picture, they want to save the place from the DMR, right? That could spin out, well I *might* be interested. But the bashed babies sound more in my line, with my training you see, far more challenging. Do you think it might backfire? I realize the problem with civil liberties, private lives and, yes, I do. Might the main road thing last? Which departments are fighting? All of us against no one but them! Why don't we just build it? Who are they? You can't be serious Martin. Such a waste of my ... who? But Martin that's ridiculous. And there's this child-bashing. We've worked together how many years now? You know I'm an old hand at these enquiries, they won't put anything across me. It'd be a waste. *Drive* there! Oh my God what next. I think I might be ill in any case. Spot of the old bother you know. Hate to let you down with your cowcocky committee but if health won't permit ... a who? Senator who did you say? *Is* he! He's the one who's investigating the Public Service surely. I begin to see. And isn't he also the one named for that overseas investment survey? I know I did and I still do. I can guess how you feel about the Public Service one. He does look like being one of those thorns in the side. The overseas thing is really a national priority though. Bound to take ages, it's so very wide-ranging and the implications ... Might it necessitate a trip to Tokyo then? *And* New York. Martin, I do see that we have to consider responsibilities. We've known each other a long time, Wesley College ha ha and so on. Why should I let you down just because of a nervous complaint? What if I do come out in hives? This one is only for a day or two I suppose. Well then! Halloran isn't it, Frank Halloran? Of course I met him a year ago you know, nice fellow. I've got it all written down in my book. There's even a memo if I'm not mistaken. Yes at the Asian Trade Fair. We got on. Pleasant man. Should clear up this highway thing in a day. As long as there's a car. Of course I don't object to a long car trip. If there's no air service how can it be helped anyway? No, you can only do what you can do. I'm most grateful anyway. I suppose we'll be sharing cars? Once you can give me definite word I might phone Frank Halloran, he'd be glad to travel with someone he knows I expect. In any case I'll phone right away I think, groundwork, tentative suggestion at least. And these local issues may seem small but they strike at the heart of democracy. People in Canberra don't know enough of the grassroots issues. It'll be an education, I'd be delighted. You'll certainly need to be thinking about that overseas investment business, political hot potato. And I shan't forget your interest in the other thing, the Public Service thing, Martin. Martin, Mavis and I were hoping, perhaps, you and Valerie might be free for dinner some time next week. Interesting couple from the Canadian High Commission coming over. Oh and I hope you'll find someone to hold up our end at the child-bashing business.

Mum Collins took a scorched felt pad in her hand and shifted the kettle to the cooler side of the stove, she opened the firebox and shoved in a couple more chunks of wood and slammed it shut, then she heaved her washing water over the heat. She wiped the backs of her hands on her hips and the palms down her apron front, pretending she was full of satisfaction with the world, but that was her way. The clock on the mantel kept getting a look from her and four times she went out into the yard for a confidential chat with Myrtle the housecow. She had some tricky questions for Myrtle too, such as: How'll I be if they give me something that's got to be read off the paper? This was the sort of thing Myrtle had never thought of. And if I come right out and say don't pass me nothing that's got to be read, what then? I wouldn't shame the folks, not for anything. It's a quandary right enough and no mistake. I'll sit meself down next to Sebbie, that's the ticket! He knows I don't read and all. She looked again at the clock and said oh my God there won't be time for washing the clothes. Bustling about in a mixture of nervousness and satisfaction, she switched the pots round on the stove and gave the ash-rack a good jolting so the ashes fell down as a red waterfall into the pan, wondering whether Jas Schramm got out of his bed sober and decent enough for a meeting.

Up at the Mountain, Jasper was already tired, having been awake all night with the same worry, through a trial of jumping nerves and nausea to emerge calm in the morning. Locked in the parlour by his own arrangement, he had put his face on the floor, for coolness, breathing the air which had hung so heavy round the dead boy. Shamed that the senator probably welcomed his name on the committee list because of his drinking, that he was expected to let everybody down, and most of all that they had forgiven him in advance. So he set out to remake Jasper Schramm, nerve by nerve he extracted the old fresh body from the new ruined one, each usable memory torn from the enemy, at three o'clock he took off his clothes and stood revealed in his baggy disgusting flesh, shivering with self-knowledge. Then he put on his feud with Egmont and saw himself in the wrong, acknowledged his family's mothertongue, he accepted the humility of a man who inherits all he owns and watches it squalidly dwindle, he put on his wife's kindness, he dressed himself in the habit of a man who has no respect for his work, with his shoes his petty misdemeanours were tied to his feet, with his cardigan he fitted himself into the years of inaction. At dawn, standing ready in front of the window, Jasper Schramm was touched by the understanding that he had created something, even when he thought he was doing nothing. Yes, the hotel had become what no hotel could expect to be. The agonizing protection of his own privacy in public had made it a place where no one else need fear intrusion either. Without him, Remembering would never have been possible.

His eye strayed to the picture beside him. He recalled it in his bedroom when he was a boy, his mother fixed it there, a hammer in her funny plump hand and a nail between her lips the way she held pins when dressmaking, and her asking where, through clenched teeth, and him saying he didn't want it at all because it was full of ladies and nobody else. She pleased herself in the end. *Domenico Ghirlandaio: The Birth of the Virgin.* He gazed into the cool ornate chamber so meticulously portrayed, the irresistible illusion of air, the calmness of those women in the presence of the mother of the mother of God. An age of saints, because you couldn't tell this mother from any other. Everything in good order and ready, the room telling its tale of the years of preparation. Mr Schramm heard the key in the lock. His wife came in, her figure upright with disillusion and stoicism. Appraising what she saw, she was proud of him. Morning light trembled in her tears for a second as she handed him his breakfast tray. He was a guest in his own hotel, as she poured the hot brass-coloured tea. Words wouldn't come, not even a greeting. Framed by the room's perspective, they looked into each other's thoughts.

Once his wife had left and set out for her morning chat to Mary Buddall, and Jasper had watched from the window the unbearable loneliness of that one woman's back in the empty dust of the world, he struggled into the suit she had prepared for him. And ceremonially closed the Mountain, the upstairs first, each shutter and each window, then the downstairs beginning with the kitchen. He got pretty shaky. Perhaps one nip of whisky would steady him. After all, it would be fatal if the government men thought him nervous. He pulled the curtains closed, bolted the public bar, wiped the rust from his fingers. Surely just one nip wouldn't hurt? The bottle was over there. Wouldn't take a moment. He wavered among the upturned stool-legs. A small heap of dust and cigarette butts remained in the middle of the floor from when the cleaning was interrupted. He took a dustpan and cleaned it up. To occupy his hands, he carried the dust out to the bin and then replaced the dustpan in the closet where it belonged. He would not go back behind the bar again; the dear battered fittings, the stale smell, the magniloquent proportions of this room with its vulgar rococo mouldings, important mirrors, knick-knacks left by visitors, trembled with familiar music, the champion trout stuffed and varnished in a glass case, the black tankards hanging by hooks, the dead television with its smoked face, the half-empty whisky bottle standing fugitive among clean glasses, wooed him with a soft old lullaby. Jasper Schramm marched into the office shutting the past behind him, took a sheet of the notepaper his father designed in 1934 with *The Mountain Hotel, Gem of the Goldfields* printed across the top and *acknowledged for excellence by world celebrities* in smaller lettering at the bottom. He licked the point of his Biro and wrote in a loopy hand:

THE MOUNTAIN WILL BE CLOSED
OWING TO THE CONDUCT OF A
MEETING WITH THE GOVERNMENT.

As an afterthought he signed his full name Volker Hermann von Jaspers Schramm. The notice pinned outside, the door securely shut, he left. He did not look back. He did not hear the Rememberings clash in a tide as deafening as Waterloo. In his white shirt, black suit and black tie, he was decked out smart as a funeral, his hair bank-manager grey. The government cars, already arriving, nosing into the grassed footpath outside the School of Arts, made it impossible for him to go back.

Twelve

The School of Arts, perched on its tall spindly piles, quivered alive. Wind pushed and worried it, loose roofing gave out the periodic bassoon note, grey timbers grumbled together, nails complained in their sockets, the trellis swayed, grit rained against one wall. Inside, it was a drum. You could look through cracks in the floor, far down to the sunlit dust below. A few bars of light struck in through the gapped wall, probing among the figures seated round a trestle table, a table famous since the 1924 Country Districts Division Five Ping Pong Championships. All day the people sat suspended in a solution of motes, heard summaries and reports presented by departmental representatives, and no further discussion arising. The delegates waited, inert in the living building.

First you should take account of the chairman, a man pledged to impartiality, a man who wished to appear younger than he was, a figure of studied rectitude. Self-conscious about the placement of papery hands, the composure of lips, he had something private to hide. His hair, suspiciously dark, clung flat to the skull, he wore rings on four of his fingers, he had not quite grown accustomed to his false teeth. A magistrate, so formalities presented no difficulty. He didn't look at anybody, either he hypnotized his papers or the circular fretwork vent set above the main doors which were rusted shut at their bolts and hinges.

On his left sat an officer of the Ministry of Tourism, serving as minutes secretary, presenting a façade of youthful eagerness, pen poised, a few headings sketched out on his pad, his clear eyes reflecting the room, his left hand dainty as a girl's played the bass of the *Appassionata*, his suit coat hung open in the Italian manner. His fair hair, brushed up to the natural look, might well pass for natural out horse-riding on a breezy day. He would get on and the evidence was before him. Privately you might guess he was a sexual teaser destined to become respectably suburban, father of two and patron of pornography.

Looking now to the north-east corner of the table we find a tall lady, one shank grown meditatively round the leg of her chair in wishful memory of childhood breakfasts, the other stretched a long way in front. She hadn't had her daily sunlamp treatment but that made no difference, her skin would take months of neglect to recover, having been so burnt and oiled. With striking artistry she had drawn the face of Nefertiti on her own face giving the curious effect of their not quite coinciding. She had the same long tender neck, the same unblinking expression, thinking back a couple of thousand years to when she could order as many throats slit as pleased her mood. There was a gleam in her eye, and whoever spoke first, she would speak next. She had an answer for everything since the world revolved about her and her career. Even in the dimness she glowed, her dress being an opulent cluster of scarlets and golds, the Australian Aesthetic and Historical Resources Commission knew what it was doing appointing her as spokesman (not for her the coy modernism of spokesperson, oh no).

Next to the lanky Nefertiti we find Mum Collins, transfigured. Her tufts of white hair stood up, more unkempt than ever and giving the impression of severe electric shock, her face with its furry moles and pads of flesh, her short neck and enormous bosom, her hands clasped like a petitioner, the chamois-leather fingers pinched cruelly by two plain gold rings, her everyday dress as it usually was, yet her eyes were in a blue fear, there was something untrustworthy on the table that reduced her confidence, sapped her self-esteem.

On Mum Collins's left sat an extremely discontented individual, a man whose sighs and figure expressed petulant irritation with his being there at all. He was perhaps forty-five, his face devoid of character yet with hair completely grey, he had been used up by something not worthy of him, his aspect was curiously sad, you can see he had once been dux of a private school by the random wrinkles proliferating on his boy's face, remembered shreds of information not meaning anything, and creating none of that sculptural quality which marks out a definite character, even a bad one. A fan of puckers at the corner of his mouth pursed his face disagreeably. His particular silence constituted an accusation. He ignored the form of meeting procedure with the virtuosity of a thousand rehearsals. When he did look up it was to reduce Senator Halloran to ash. Three other committee members sat between them on the south edge of the table. First a bald man who kept polishing his head with a handkerchief and slipping his glasses off then popping them back on or casting them on the table like dice, snatching them back to polish them, then polishing the head some more, then blowing his nose in the same handkerchief (a dry blow done for the form of the thing), then experimenting with his glasses perched on the very end of his nose, then thrusting them up like an oldtime aviator on his forehead; beside this bald man lolled an immensely worldly person, one of those large-boned chaps who have elected to be thought elegant, to have panache, a dotted cravat tied in a careless heap against his stringy throat and a matching handful of linen frothing from the breastpocket of his grey suit with the pale check, his white eyebrows and suntanned nose, his good-humoured gestures and kindly sentiments, his fatuous line of thought, his careless nonchalance, offering gallantries to Miss Felicia Brinsmead in her Paris silk with a dash of colour at the throat, her bland moony face fixed to an expression highly unsettling for anyone hoping to engage her in rational discussion, her hands spread flat as if the famous table were the counter of her shop.

Senator Halloran, modestly having choosen to be at the south-west corner of the table, periodically reached down to stroke his black dog curled under the chair (well, in the bush they don't mind informality), touched up his image as arbiter, the man of the moment, one foot in either camp and respect all round. The way he cracked his knuckles betrayed some intellectual activity but so far he had said nothing, local yellow dust burnished the shoulders of his dark jacket because he drove up with the car window open. He welcomed everybody by name when they first gathered.

The west side of the table was occupied by Jasper Schramm and Sebastian Brinsmead, respectability still sitting misshapenly on Jasper, his nose pendulous, and flapping earlobes worn as if they could be taken off at bedtime. He kept his eyes down for fear of being humiliated by curious glances from those he loved. His elbow touched Sebastian's elbow. Sebastian, tightly buttoned in his jacket, locks of white hair drifting free behind his ears, the fine white beard spread on his massive chest, every particular of his face settled by some perfectly defined characteristic, the founder of a stable society, a Moses. But he was neither at ease nor conscious of his dignity, he had not yet trusted himself to acknowledge the man between himself and the chairman, the last member of the committee, Mr George Swan, Judas, Quisling Swan the stocky redneck, bitterness and moralism endowing him with a quality of vigour no one else had.

So they deliberated while wind worried and pushed at the building. A bird fluttered in the ceiling. A few spokes of solid gold sunshine sliced the teeming air, the hall drumming sensuously. The committee was waiting, the chairman having delivered his preamble and his summary. The minutes secretary finished the left hand of the *Appassionata* and held his pen poised to add a couple of noughts to his salary. All that was needed was somebody to speak, for reason to take its course.

Thirteen

Mrs Rose Swan stayed at home meekly working at her chores, the dear little person, mulling over insignificant griefs, sewing at the window where you used to see the tallow-wood tree in the perpetual wind. She assured herself this was a great day for the town, what with the government meeting and George being chosen. Everything would be alright if only she kept quiet and let the men get on with it. But how could she help wondering what her husband was saying, fearful that he may not be clever enough to save making a fool of himself? A suppressed voice spoke of him contemptuously, but she wouldn't listen. Instead she took refuge in a dream of wealth to be brought by the highway, how she'd have this and that and all electric.

Suddenly, with the fluid rapidity of a bird flicking its tail and shooting off in an unplanned direction, the world about-faced. Life flipped over. And before you knew where you were, it whirled away on a new course, so that you giddily caught your breath and staggered to retain your balance. The afternoon television program which had been occupying a space somewhere back of centre in her mind, at about the level of her sewing (she was mending Billy's clothes for when he returned home) now loomed urgently to the foreground. An announcer interrupted the bland chatter, presenting himself solemnly before a backdrop of the nation's capital and read a newsflash. The newsflash stopped Rose Swan's blood.

– The Government of Australia has been dismissed by Vice-Regal decree, he told her. The Governor-General this afternoon dismissed the Prime Minister and his government and called on the Leader of the Opposition to assume responsibility for running the country in a caretaker capacity.

Rose Swan jumped to her feet, scattering the fragments of her littleness. She towered, she froze, she raged, she sparked with understanding.

– So we're still a colony then! she shouted at the announcer who, unaware that this was the first time she had shouted in forty-seven years, droned details that did not explain, could not explain, what was happening. He talked to an empty room. Mrs Swan had gone, her sewing a heap on the floor. She already knew too much to wait for the sedative of dispassionate reason, prismatic colours playing at the rim of her vision, such was her anger. Out in the paddock she headed south-west across country, the sun in her eyes. Must be at Whitey's Fall before the meeting finished. She'd walk the whole two miles if need be. No, she'd run. Little Rose pushed herself to trot. Unfamiliar. Was trotting. Feeling the unaccustomed discomfort, her breasts flopping, stomach jig-gling, thighs and cheeks. Small as she was she felt encumbered by fat. Lungs wheezed. But this had to be done. Mrs Swan was running, making a good go of it. A spirit woke in her. Something nobody could imagine in peacable Australia; the government overthrown by a single man who'd never been voted for, the Queen of England a sinister playing-card figure. Trumps. The Governor-General, to her astonishment, shown to be the joker in the pack. But Mrs Swan ran without fear. She was rediscover-ing herself, second wind coming nice and easy, her stride length-ening. Herself growing, pulsing, flying, head thrown back in the glorious wind. So long ago. And what did she know? Yes. Yes. She recognized this as a moment waited for. That's right. People don't always have to be told what to do. The idea had not shaped itself clearly, but she prepared for it. She ran through the grass along the windy skyline with *rejoice* in her heart, because at last we'd know what to do. It was the finish of the monarchy in Australia. It was civil war. And this would show the roadworkers were not the enemy, they'd be with us. George was right and Billy was right too; we can't be kicked around. If Queen Elizabeth wanted it this way, she'd get it in the neck. Ourselves on our own two feet. Independence. Rose Swan panted out the one word *us,* word of hope. *Us. Us. Us,* she hissed with each expelled breath. A rhythm of *us us us* and her great strides. Running strongly, she could last for ever. She was carried along, lifted up, not alone. No. There were others running with her. All over the country at this moment, perhaps thousands of them. Whole cities of people running to their kin, to gather and rise up for their rights. She ran. A lone woman on the great bare hillside, heading round the flank of the mountain towards town, her mind ripe with a single thought: this is what we've been waiting for.

Mr George Swan listened to the chairman outline the procedural assumptions behind the submission from the Australian Aesthetic and Historical Resources Commission which I shall now circulate for your perusal and consideration ladies and gentlemen. He heard Felicia Brinsmead giving her girlish cough. Already uncomfortable at catching the eye of the senator too frequently. Mr Swan wondered briefly what the senator thought of Miss McAloon his estranged mother and her house of knitted rooms, the choking mothball fumes. Well the old lady deserved to be taken down a peg, the way she marched about judging everything. Even the blasted tallow-wood had to be hers of course and not within his rights to cut down. He heard the submission read out; he was beginning to see something.

So the minutes secretary offered his considered opinion of the problem of getting the highway men (chuckle chuckle) back on the job with the least friction possible. So the Nefertiti lady in her glowing reds and golds registered an impassioned case for the unique village, this collective creation of primitive artists, this Australian cathedral as it were, to be painted, treated, propped, reinforced, sealed and made a monument to the genius of our nation. So Mr Brinsmead spoke icily of rights and privacy, astonishing the meeting with his presence and fluent command of foreign examples. So Senator Halloran placated every ruffling of feelings, every emergent dispute, stressed the national strategy of the planned highway and heard with disbelief Miss Brinsmead reply that the highway was trivial. So the bald man polished his head and blew his nose, experimented with his glasses on the tip of his nose while he bleated yes and yes yes to everything. So the debonair architect scattered kindly gestures about and offered a ritual courtesy of elegant compliments. So Jasper Schramm stood and could find no words, but would not sit, mystified that even this might be his proper contribution, held them all to silence, the doughy cheeks working, his mind stuck on the sobriety of some women in a painting of the moment the world changed. So this speechlessness made George Swan think. So Mum Collins shook her head and berated them for a mob of interfering mongrels to come disturbing decent people, so she called them son and sonny and youngfellamelad, my boy, my girl, poppet and you damn hussy. So the chairman pleaded for restraint, decorum, order and an end to argument. So Felicia Brinsmead addressed the nature of the past, taking words from their very mouths to use against them. But still nothing happened. The wind pushed at the building as usual, the roof clattered, a few dazzling bars of light pursued their sundial pace across the room. The dusty air pulsed about them. Reason had died and power took its place: only those without power or the desire for it had the least idea this happened. George Swan, with his vigorous narrow viewpoint, his energy and greed, became the central figure in the discussion. A picnic lunch was unpacked and served. Cups of afternoon tea stood in their rings of milky liquid, biscuit crumbs crunched among the papers. The chief document, a ministerial proposal awaiting the signatures of local residents, lay flimsy and treacherous in front of the chairman.

Then the most unexpected thing occurred: the wind dropped.

The mountain wind which had blown with absolute reliability since Whitey's Fall was built faltered and died altogether. The buildings, braced so long against its pressure, sighed into awkward attitudes, boards creaking painfully at the unknown, leaning to the east for knowledge, the stillness unearthly. The committee listened with apprehension, their senses stretched alert, waiting for reprieve, for a renewed rush of air, the known world.

The chairman spread his hands before him and examined them for clues to the mysteries of nature and the fickleness of humankind. A steady rain of silence immobilized the meeting. The mountain was to blame for everything, the place incomprehensible. Through the open door the warm air trickled out. Nefertiti shuddered. The trellis groaned feebly. Nothing is without its consequences; a cricket under the floor burst into song, which caused a balloon of tears to rise in Sebastian Brinsmead's chest for the Lord had cast off another thread, the tapestry perfect, intact, seamless and almost relinquished.

The eight men and three women looked deep into each other, wholly preoccupied with allegiances, passing their decision along so that yes became no became yes was reaffirmed as yes and yes again became no became yes became definitely no and absolutely no again. One vote left to be cast.

Mr George Swan, the perennial dealer, master of the card-pack, was still to speak; the government already had a five to four majority, so they were relaxing because this fellow was a pledged progressive, a yes voter. The seating arrangement now shown to have had some system. So the chairman's hands were washed of blame, the magistracy seen to be above manipulation even on a parliamentary scale. The workmen up at the road site felt a spirit of hope dispel their sluggish weeks. George Swan opened his dry Quisling lips, hearing what nobody else could hear: his wife's quiet words that night the motorcycle carried Billy away from home for good *You were wrong George.* It was an enigma, an admission of love. He heard it again as he felt her soft hand slip into his, this sensation altogether beyond his control. No, he said. Then he spoke it out loud No.

– No.

– Your father will be so proud, Mum Collins whispered across the table.

Senator Halloran's face flushed a difficult red above his white collar; angry, embarrassed at his nominee letting the side down, alarmed that the project might be further delayed, that he might be blamed for bungling, yet gratified at how right he had been about these impossible people, exasperated that he waived his right to speak in the debate, caught by the simple trap of leaving power in the hands of the one man completely unknown: the chairman. To risk so much. Wasn't it on the cards that the magistrate could actually be impartial and therefore unpredictable? Madness. What did anybody know about this lugubrious fellow except that the Chief Magistrate's Office sent him? The Chief Magistrate himself might not be above suspicion. Too late to check. Senator Halloran boiled with frustration.

The room quivered. The inside of a drum. That loose flap of roofing uttered a ghost of its bassoon note.

The chairman consulted his immobile knuckles, then complained wearily that this was not as he had hoped, however the will of those present being amply clear and beyond further argument, distasteful as it was to him personally to take action in a matter he'd hoped to leave to those more intimately involved, he found himself duty bound to offer his own judgment on the evidence as put forward, trusting this would not be inferred as proclaiming the present hearing exhaustive, he was bound to find in favour of the case representing most responsibly in his view the general benefit of the community at large, a benefit which included not only progress, admirable as progress was, but conservatism where the implementation of new ideas meant irreversible changes. He paused and helped himself to a sip of cold water from his glass to confirm the authenticity and dignity of this impartial decision. Then he croaked the word yes. The word the government was waiting to hear. This was what he had been sent for. And brought Frank Halloran alive again. No one could guess the government itself had fallen. No one could guess the horrors of subservience to follow, the rapacious dogs of international commerce tearing the carcase of the land apart, nor that for all the blunders these might have been the most enlightened years, nor that the people would lie down under the imperial heel. No

442

one knew that Mrs Swan was sweating it out across the paddocks bursting with joy and hope.

– Have you ever cut down a tree? George Swan asked the School of Arts. A tree you've known all your life? And taken full responsibility for cutting it down?

Tears streamed through the valleys of Mum Collins's experience, from all her generations the suffering and fortitude gave way, the virtues of courage and honesty swept up through her in successive waves to pour out. Without a word, for there are no words, she sat, her eyes ejecting the world as she knew it to be, the beauty of the mountain flowed down her cheeks, her kindly face itself a map of that mountain; birds too familiar to need names all made tears; tears washed out shy spiders together with the scent of horea and the deep blood of running-postman; out through the crevices where her great-hearted smile grew now welled the colourless amalgam of all colours, the perfumeless knowledge of all perfumes, the bitter taste of everything good being reduced to a thin salty solution.

Mum Collins's tears poured on to her dress and her large bare folded arms, down to the table top where (due to its unequal legs) they formed themselves into a runnel, the blind head of which stretched to a golden worm, wavered, seeking, sensing ... till it set out with that slowness which takes the watcher beyond time, advancing straight for the chairman, its brow gathering again. And again released. Still the tears flowed from the endless resources of Mum's huge body; from her thighs and her elbows the forces of grief gathered, from tributaries as remote as her heels and her palms the waters came, from her loins they flooded up into her head and ran glittering, splashing, spouting on her folded arms, out along the channel now established, pushing the head of the tearworm inexorably closer to the chairman. The blind head blazed in a single needle of sunlight that probed through the rotting wall, the tear-journey witnessed by all but Mum Collins herself, its dazzling sparkle flared in every eye among the hollow shapes, and so the head of the weeping of the generations of Whitey's Fall crept on in the darkness and touched the document laid out before them, under the flimsy paper the unseen tears spread fast as grassfire. Immediately the whole sheet lay wrinkling, stuck to the tabletop, consumed by a grey shadow that shaded away the close typing and undermined the firm signature of the Minister who still used a fountainpen and ink, dispersing his name to a feathering of blue till the ink filled out its own image and a bird formed where there had been an ultimatum a moment before, the wings of the bird blue distance itself breaking free through blank grey cloud. Beyond it, at the far edge of the document, the tears re-formed so that, spent and exhausted, they reached forward just far enough to touch one fingertip of the man who passed judgment on the town and its people. He gently withdrew his hand with a magnificent show of unconcern and plunged it into the hot recesses of his pocket, vainly hoping to wipe away that icy contact with the real world, its history and meanings. There and then Mum Collins died of grief.

Somewhere out the back, her housecow gave a single enquiring moo.

Felicia Brinsmead stood up, not meeting the eyes of her husband nor the sober eyes of Jasper Schramm next to him. Not looking at the representatives of government ministries and instrumentalities, not looking at the honourable senator, nor at the magistrate in the chair. She concentrated on that nowhere which is without perspective, without focus. Distantly her shop cried out from a dream of portents *miserable miserable*. In one hand she was found to be clutching a pair of scissors. There is something horrible about domestic scissors brought out like that. The departmental architect next to her ducked aside, his dandyish cravat fluttered, agitated, in terror that he might find those precious chrome tips next moment stuck in his throat. Miss Brinsmead saw space. She reached round behind her head, the accustomed fingers caressing her bundle of hard grey hair, handling the netting sack, taking its weight upon herself. She began hacking at the roots, jabbing furiously with those scissors, the long points wounding her scalp, snipping and cutting, missing, wrenching, while her mouth twisted in concentration, her face utterly free of its repertoire of masks, her breath leaping out in huge sobs, explosions of gas from some soft decay, the blades crunched against her gritty hair and squeaked with rancid body oils, the bundle gaped open till light touched the nape of her neck for the first time in living memory, spots of blood blotted ugly patterns on her hands and dripped into the hair, still she drove the scissors to her purpose and the white girlish neck miraculously unlined now arched vulnerable to air and its changes. The hair banged away at her back, a living thing fierce with the struggle to survive, to escape more pain. There. She had it free, clutching it and tearing out the last few threads by the root. For a second her hand and her lip shook. She was reverent with the hair as if it might be a kind of knowledge grown from her head. She cradled it in front of her, helpless to the world while everybody could see the one golden wisp still curling warmly at the end as if nothing had happened. She studied her hair, never like this before. Placed the bundle on the table before her; she was a sovereign, the ceremony of laying aside her imperial orb. Next she bent double, straining the seat backwards, and tugged at her shoes which she put neatly on the floor side by side out of sight. Having accomplished so much, Miss Brinsmead returned upright in her highbacked chair, resting her stubbly scabbed skull against the wood. She was Abraham Lincoln. She was Abraham. She settled her arms along the chair arms, her bare feet flat on the boards, her breathing controlled, the acid stink of dirty clothing pervaded the room, a clock ticked busily in the well of her throat. When next the chairman looked up out of his embarrassment and disgust, her dead eyes locked with his, and no escape, lids sagging and red, her mouth hinged open, tongue lolling out with trails of whitish saliva dangling from it. Otherwise she might still have been alive with accusations. Though dead, she was draining the chairman, extracting his willpower, a warm placenta of air peeled off from around him, finally slipped free and lost. The impression of his inside-out head flipped beyond reach and away. Him left naked to the unknown.

– So to the rest of the agenda, he said. Now perhaps we can get somewhere.

Discussions began on a catalogue of implications. The two

corpses nodded and slumped on their chairs, as others settled in for long negotiations. The bureaucrats called on their reserves of experience, their training in patience, their capacity to bear crushing weights of boredom.

George Swan ached with the need for action. He had already sat too long. Idleness got him in its vice and knotted him painfully tight. Writhing against good manners, he suffered one flash of his nightmare: Billy leaving Whitey's Fall forever, escaping the carefully laid ties of marriage and duty. Long after George Swan was dead of impatience, the committee waged a tactical war over *then* or *therefore* and *provisionally* as opposed to *in principle*.

Breathing the pure mountain air, the government administrators toiled at their appointed task, never dreaming their bodies might be undergoing a change, the blood clarifying, purged of anti-bodies. The longer they sat in familiar deadlock the purer their blood became: and the more vulnerable to infection. By the time they began framing sub-section (ix) of section (h) of the provisos of the guidelines for proceeding with the preservation of the village as a historic monument, protocolitis struck. The contagion took the youngest first, the most imaginative next, then those whose attention was not wholly focused on meeting procedure. One by one it paralysed them, their hearts and lungs hardened and stilled under the proliferating disease. Nefertiti, who had so often watched her cat stretch every muscle when it woke, felt her own feline body reverse the process, contracting. Last, she and the chairman saw in each other's face a flash of panic as they succumbed at the same moment. Sebastian and Jasper, who had waited for most of a century already, could outsit anybody and noticed nothing out of the ordinary. The only other survivor of the committee was the senator. The air still hummed with quiet formulas, when Mr Brinsmead pushed back his chair and attended to his wife, easing the scissors loose, he crossed her hands in her lap. He kissed her poor wounded head in a gesture he had longed to make public for fifty years. He cradled the sweetheart, her skull now so light with no longer having to carry about the whole of history, stroked the stubble where his tears dripped on her crusted scalp. Then he took her scissors more

446

firmly in his hand, held them as a dagger, and stuck the long pointed blades deep into Senator Frank Halloran's neck. With his great strength Saint Sebastian forced them into the flesh, in among the yielding folds and satisfactions till they were buried right down to the handle. The victim let out a terrified hiss of blood, his crepe soles contracting, squeaking against the floor. Jasper knew now why he had dressed suitably for a funeral; last night he had put off his life when he thought he was remaking it, the ceremony an absolution, his soul made ready for the crisis that now came.

When Sebastian Brinsmead straightened up to stand before his maker, red-handed and defiant, he was the only living person left in that building.

The hall, perhaps the mountain, lurched. A boom like an earthquake followed an immense yawning of the timbers. The trellis fell off, teacups scattering solid as billiard balls among feet and ankles, the floor itself wavered upward, tilted to become a giant oblong wing. The sky exploded into twenty-four stars of glass shooting darts at the dead people inside. Dust puffed about their shoes from cracks opening under them, the tree outside rushed upward slow as a moon rocket, its foliage sweeping out of sight; chairs flung askew on a single leg pirouetted their doll occupants against the fairground wall. Sebastian Brinsmead was thrown flat, his chest being crushed at a blow by a beam he once watched set in place to carry the roof. Above the doorway the circular vent cried to the empty town of flowers, a human shout of alarm and pain. The conference table tipped on end displayed its proclamation: a blue bird escaping through grey words. The great doors themselves (last opened thirty years ago for welcoming a local horse who ran seventh in the Melbourne Cup) swung inward. Not the view of Brinsmead's store. All a rush of blank sunlight arrested a moment by two yellow butterflies bobbing together, as if love and the world would go on as usual.

Little Rose Swan, become a giant, strode staggering up the last bank of grass, stooped to crawl between the wire strands of the fence, not caring that this time her dress snagged and a small V ripped open on her back. She had reached the road with her head full of the word she couldn't get hold of. Never had she been rich before. Music in her blood. So undeservedly the keeper of good news. She faced uphill along the dusty road, walking, using these final minutes to compose herself. Knowing she was awaited. They were longing for her without realizing it, poor things, dying in their desert, wandering on flat places, singular isolated figures, lost, now turning to hail her so gratefully, so humbly.

Within yards of the hall Mrs Swan composed her hands, took a measured breath of mountain air, trembling. She smoothed back her hair and, in doing so, found she had looked up . . . yes.

One Commonwealth Car driver stood tilting his cap back, shocked to inaction, while the other was down in the rubble doing what he could to release the only survivor, Senator Halloran's black dog Ocker.

BOOK SIX

Exodus

One

Mountain wind ruffles the clusters of flowers once more, makes friendly noises in the open houses, drives hot dust pleasantly against your shins; this wind with its summer heaviness inside your shirt, buffeting and caressing, remembering its past days stale with grit and the smell of rotting leaves, its cold winter days of remote sea, spring days loud with coupling birds. Silverbeet and rhubarb stand up strongly in vegetable gardens, their crisp leaves rubbing flesh on flesh, a community in agreement. The figs and plums which had once jutted green and hard, bitter with youth, now sag full of juice. Bougainvillaea and clematis weigh down the fences with colour and scent, they break the guttering loose. In every detail Whitey's Fall is familiar except for the absence of people, the people who should be in the street as old people generally are or in their doorways on the step or weeding the garden or snoozing or swatting flies. You can't avoid a sense of emptiness, the incongruous knowledge that this lived-in place with its handworn handtended character is uninhabited. The houses are grey bare wood as they always were, weatherboards overlapping in wavering lines, metal roofs rusted the colours of volcanic earth, yet they are powerful with the touch of humanity, saturated by use and habit. Without the people, you notice how strongly they smell of people, how they've got the ways of people stamped on them, as if they could go on living by themselves, as if they've been working towards this, drawing the life-energy from their occupants, those who built them, from the memories of tent encampments weathering storms and smoke, the peaks of canvas like whitecapped waves stiffly arranged around the Noah's Ark of the pub full of bestial couples, resisting the jealousies of mining company employees from the New Reef, and drawing energy from times even before this, when the gullies pulsed with steam engines and the handheld pans of pebbles, when the original rush of prospectors, single males, the first male plague, surprised the innocent countryside with complaints of a mountain there. No such mountain was known to the Koorie tribe who had long since passed in flight, dangerous shadows, leaving enough dead intruders to make known certain religious sentiments. The empty houses live by the energy of men and women who survived punishment for their crimes against the owners of hens and fob watches, their pilferings of petty cash in Cumberland, their sauciness towards the Kent magistracy, their failure to kiss the Bible in the name of King William IV or his debauched brother George IV, or for that matter his mad father chewing ermine for breakfast and calling on India the whore to come and be raped in the hope that he might this way learn to endure the humiliation of his blameless marital conduct. Life-energy still possesses the town, carried over without break from hand to breast, from woman to man to child, from relatives and strangers, passed on strongly from the foot soldiers of civil wars in Oxfordshire and Lanarkshire and the peasants who suffered them, from visionary bookmen and cunning astronomers, sailors with their astrolabes and folklore, from Sir John Falstaff himself, and the nameless ostlers who when the house of Ross went up in flames tried to save the servants while their master was saving his horses, from the farmer's wife who saw the heathen Vikings come and did not run back inside her mud embankment but took up a flail, strode right out there and defied them to chop up her children with their battle-axes, making them understand her foreign words so that at least one stayed his hand remembering his wife at home and his dogs like these dogs, and elsewhere the artisan falling from a ladder of angels he was carving on an Abbey front and later being represented near the top of the same stone ladder by his apprentices as the first face to shine in the light of heavenly peace, two rungs above the commissioning Bishop, and before this when Julius Caesar had risen from his bed in the staging camp at Gessoriacum to attend personally (as he made a point of doing always) to the administration of some plan for equipment, his lady of the night, having achieved only a respectable minimum of satisfaction with him, reached her hand over to where he'd slept and felt the coverings damp, to her disgust yes damp, and she thought of the puzzle of this dampness while he made ready to conquer Britain; the long generation of this energy was stored in the houses of Whitey's Fall, energy which reached back and abroad, profound and limitless as blood, limitless as water on the world's surface, flowing and receding, malleable but indestructible, held by the magnetism of earth, trembling at its upheavals, smoothing its harshness, floating through air, ascending as a breathable ocean, clashing to spark the light of lightning, drawing delicate groundplants up to flower and be visited by bees so that in time when their petals wilt and stain brown, shrink and moult, the calyx will harden round a knot of seeds, the seeds falling or lifted clear in wallaby fur or on woollen skirts, hiving an endless continuity of the empires of yellow and crimson seen blooming still along the housefronts and roadsides of Whitey's Fall, all the more eloquent for the sound of abandonment beginning to thicken round the place, for the lack of any sign that Vivien Lang looked at them this morning and cried out in her heart what shall I do? No sign of this. The plants themselves tell their own saga, geraniums among grevillea, honeysuckle behind the wattle; and especially in Mr McTaggart's circular garden with its bounty of five continents burgeoning in concentric circles, countless flowers quivering at the wind speaking their perfumes from gorgeous lips. But the ancient ugly mountainfolk are not there today to tend them with tough fingers and bring them water from the tanks. The houses stand silent, no sound comes from them. Even the big machines up at the highway site, have not been heard for weeks now, not grumbling distantly at their chores, they have fallen into disuse again. But this time the workmen are not camped at the side of their cutting boozing in idleness and playing poker. They have urgent business in the city concerning their private fortunes.

If you were to walk into town this moment you could hardly fail to be struck by the accumulated meanings of the gardens, the placement of the town on its mountainside, these steps, that roofline, the dry drinking fountain, the petrol bowser still to be worked by a hand pump, this doorway with the words Please Knock, and someone else's disintegrating Welcome mat. The meanings are known simply by your standing still long enough to let them speak.

It is as natural for you to stand in this place as for the wind to move. Among the houses, the hotel, the welder's workshop, the graveyard, wind has its business, bearing no trace of gasoline although minutes ago the street was full of vehicles choking on their own black fumes, lining up in a gala procession and heading for the disused showground, followed by carts, people on foot herding their cattle and goats, calling their dogs to heel, and Grandma Buddall with a felt hat pulled tight down over her ears for comfort, and mounted on her old cow. No trace left in the street except shifting ruts and a few steaming turds dropped by various beasts. The echo of Rememberings ghosting into bedrooms. No way of telling how Bill Swan, ready to lead off the procession in that big rattletrap of a Bedford heaped high with bedding and boxes, took Mr Ian McTaggart and his invalid wife Violet proudly tearless in the cab beside him, the same Bedford now standing at one end of the showground, facing a logging track which passes obliquely across the surveyed highway (that same track Bill and five other hooligans had come down, from their foolish scrounging for The Golden Fleece, bringing instead the news of Kel McAloon's death). The Bedford stands at the forest edge in green light, a sunken hulk with Billy out front, the bonnet up, and tools busy in the hot motor. The old people still in the cab open a packet of sandwiches and then sort out whose false teeth are whose from the bedside jar they've brought. They munch placidly at the food – You'd a thought, says the husband, we'd a had more sense at our age. His wife replies, past the difficulty she always has swallowing – Well it is a new chance though Pa, a fresh start and that. Her hundred-year-old eyes stained in the whites to ivory. – How's it coming along son? they call to give the young fellow heart and so he'll know not to worry about them. – It's coming along, he answers burning his hand on the manifold and wiping a moustache of grease across his lip, wishing like hell Tony was here to fix it and worrying momentarily about what might have happened to Tony, shrugging at the memory of coming round after being punched, the urge to hit out, to keep it going. He pulls the rubber fuelpipe off its nozzle, this has to be a blockage or he can't imagine what. Just now his own motorcycle emerges gingerly on to the showground, drumming at such low revs it sounds like a giant sewing-machine. Jack Collins, the only male Collins left with both eyes good, and him a man who never married though he's eighty-seven and despite being related to a pretty fertile branch of the population, is driving the bike. Clutched on to him from behind you can see two purple claws and nothing else till the bike draws level, but already you hear a high voice hammering sharp little nails of words, tacking them into the brain, not even interrupting herself when the bike slows beside the stalled truck, not even acknowledging young Bill Swan greeting them – If you was to have listened to me, the voice is saying delivering itself of a mouthful of nails, you'd have loaded them boxes around the other way and put the mattress on top instead of ... Mr Collins raises his eyes to heaven as he circles Billy, travelling at about ten miles per hour and having already suffered his cousin's lecture on the wages of recklessness, to park behind the truck. There! hardly a dribble of petrol getting through, that's been the problem alright; Bill forgets about Tony as he detaches the pipe completely and peers along it, blows along it, kneels down and slips one end over the valve of a tyre letting out a squirt of high-pressure air and laughing with the satisfaction of success, calling to the old people that it's fixed now and hearing their bread-filled voices drift back to him with the offer of a sandwich. The 1919 Reo lorry comes whining into the ring, good as new, the boxy bonnet trembling, the stub nose jolting woodenly down into a pot-hole and rising with the assurance of a tank, singing along steadily with its load of roof iron, rolls of wire and boxes of new nails, taking up its position behind the motorcycle. Then immediately following, a string of horsedrawn sulkies and carts arrives, squealing with disuse, big wheels aching out loud over the bumps, and Mrs Angela Collins leading them in her smart rig, calling to the Bedford, calling proud and dignified as you like – Will you need a tow mate when we're ready to go? Not since her three teenage children left for the city has she felt the sap in her like today, her rig jogs past for the sake of display and then returns to its place, the four passengers on improvised seats all facing backwards offer the crones in the Bedford gummy grins out of their nests of wild hair – Tarrah! they call and Ooroo! and Be seein ya! so that two horses pulling the following cart look up from their considered examination of Australia and shake their traces with a pleasant jingling, teeth muttering against the bits, the crates of food piled behind them sway, giving off delicious mixed odours from earthy vegetables and steaming roast chickens in wrappings. So the Whitey's Fallers are gathering ready for a journey. But even this will not cheer Dick Buddall and his wife Doreen neither of whom is old enough to remember London; they're leaving the things that make life worthwhile because they're needed by Doreen's mother Jessie McTaggart who married a second time and to another McTaggart so being made a McTaggart twice, and then only because Jessie's one you can't refuse. Up till last night they had no intention. They were ready to welcome the highway and the tourists, they were saying we shall be glad to see the end of the old struggles, and it'll be easy keeping the place neat without the dust off that road, city folks are polite, and soon everybody's kids'll be driving the easy way home to visit. But they began to look around with strangers' eyes at their decaying house; visitors a threatening idea and a judgment. They are going because old Jessie's going, they are promising themselves it's only seven miles so if they change their minds, well the house is there to return to. But the house dies with the front door shut for the first time in living memory, and

Marmalade miaouling till they bring her along (though she wet on them when she twigged). Billy glances back at them from under the dinted green bonnet and waves because he knows their doubts, then refits the tube carefully clipping it on, watching the petrol run cleanly into the glass filter, he clangs the bonnet shut just as his Uncle Wally appears driving the famous steam plough, a Queensland design, hissing and pooting and clanking its chains, the blade periodically ringing against a rock loud as a churchbell, and a galah swinging morosely in its wicker cage from the canopy-frame, a passenger on a home-made seat so swaddled against the dust she can't be recognized, and Uncle Wally, his bald head wrinkled as a peanutshell, soberly raising one paw from the nest of levers as he pulls up at the end of the line, the invalid Violet McTaggart leaning out of the Bedford's window flutters her fingers, Wally being her son's nephew by marriage and a nextdoor neighbour, the crumbs dropping from her lips to hang on her mister punch chin. Uncle begins marshalling the people on foot and their smelly mixed herd of domestic animals. Bill listens a moment to the plough shutting off steam, the confused puttering of tractors approaching behind, the horse noises and the cattle. He climbs back in, the Bedford ready to go when everyone has assembled.

– Looks like we made it in time, Uncle says cheerfully taking a count of heads. Like I said if the town's got to go down, *we're* goin to strike the blow, not Senator Nosey's government john-nies. The bastards want to take us on, well we'll see who comes out a this one. Once I saw Bessie Collins lyin in her blood and Felissy and them. I sent some gold samples to the newspapers plus a couple a front page facts.

Wind blows through the empty houses of Whitey's Fall, down the chimneys into warm livingrooms, it scurries out from cracks beneath beds just stripped of their blankets, jets stream in through keyholes unstopped when the keys were withdrawn, it puffs up joyous heads of dust where carpets used to keep it muffled down. Some houses left open as well as empty are a tur-moil of conflicting currents, papers float about seeking their

457

owners and authors. A drawer stands open in Mr Ian McTaggart's house and the wind fingers through a heap of unopened letters there, unsettling the government envelopes and casting grit among them, a handful of seed on barren ground. In the unroofed houses all is still and the wind invisible, having scoured out any movables long before this; but in the newly abandoned places everything flutters, curtains and furnishings brought alive by the retreat of the humans who put them there. In Granny Collins's roominghouse, the tattered calico ceilings, pulled free of their nails, float delicate silken banners while little winds begin eating at the walls, peeling back the wallpaper, lifting flaps, and then lifting the newspaper pasted underneath for insulation, brown newsprint with few photographs, all bought in the slow months of 1908 when the editorials welcomed the American Fleet as Australia's new protector, just about the last papers sold in Whitey's Fall. The wind was never so busy here as it is now. If no one else knows, the wind knows. They have gone. They won't be back.

More headlines are on their way to Whitey's Fall to be stacked outside the late Miss Brinsmead's door.

TWO

A helicopter appears in the sky to the north-east, the air already drumming for miles around. There is no one to watch but the old buildings; and though they mutter together they're past caring. Simultaneously a bus crawls round the first bend of the road at the foot of the mountain; the only place it can go is Whitey's Fall. A minute later a car, careening round the same bend too fast for safety, slews behind the bus in a hot fog of yellow dust, swinging from one side of the road to the other, vainly hoping for a way past. Now another car joins the queue, another and a dozen more. As the bus creeps up, it trails a seemingly endless string of miscellaneous vehicles. To the south those dark dots across the paddocks are people trotting in the one direction, hastening, stumbling, their sights fixed on the mountain. From the west, as yet unseen, hundreds of motorists drive flat out, and illegally, along the foundations of the virgin highway, while in the gutters mad cyclists pedal through the flying grit over the bodies and bent machines of their fallen colleagues, private aircraft skim above them looking for room to land on the road ahead, a hearse and an ambulance battle it out at breakneck speed to gain a single place in the convoy. A thousand miles south the cold fishermen are loading pickaxes and metal-detectors into utilities, shedding

the silver scales of their dawn labours; while three thousand miles
to the north New Guinea warriors begin dancing through the
jungle, their minds steaming full of luxury cruises to Iceland.

At six o'clock this morning the news hit the country. On the
radio and television, in every morning newspaper the sensation
filled the headlines: gold. Whitey's Fall is the most famous name
of the day. While in Fleet Street journalists are putting the finishing touches to their prophecies of doom, duly introduced by complaints against Aussie attention-grabbing, Wall Street is too
frantic with insider trading and the dollar already plunging below
the critical level of the last recession. Kremlin phones are ringing
with vodka-thick congratulations. Photographs of the mountain
and estimates of its yield (varying from 600 000 tonnes to
1 092 000 tonnes of pure assayable gold) are instantly commonplace, and no sooner cut out for pasting in children's exercise
books than too dated to keep. In Canberra the Prime Minister
who interrupted his nightly crisis to summon a ministerial breakfast now sits desert-eyed watching his hateful colleagues while
particles of grime float across his field of vision. The Minister
for Mines is personally aggrieved and the Treasurer wishes in
his panic that he had studied economics instead of animal hus-
bandry. Indeed the whole cabinet of farmers and solicitors rival
one another in emotive bafflement, with one exception, but she
being a woman is not consulted. The Defence Minister is already
shouting for increased funds to build up our armed forces against
possible invasion to grab the gold. The Minister for Industrial
Relations tables a document, explaining tearfully that it rep-
resents a collective capitulation by employer organizations offering ruinous terms to tempt the workers back to work and bribe
those who have not already set off for the diggings. The ministerial private secretaries, as a herd, jam a respectable Sydney
phone exchange with calls to the same number: a number where
Senator Halloran's widow has the instrument off the hook and
is making rapid progress into a nervous breakdown. Several satellites, on line from United States corporations, bombard world
television with actuality pictures of Whitey's Fall. Johannesburg
magnates are selling their shares in their own companies and

460

investing in Balinese hideaways, the Cairo Museum pays for an urgent advertising campaign. Retired bloodhounds are sniffing the air in Jerusalem, and Eskimo ivory carvers flog their stock of phallic knick-knacks while the going's good. Swissair announces ten supplementary jumbo flights a day to Darwin and Melbourne; a Brazilian cruise ship, flung into full astern, thunders to a halt and ploughs around one hundred and eighty degrees to charge with two thousand cheering weeping passengers for Sydney or bust. The exiled Grand Lama of Tibet packs a clean saffron robe ready to go home.

When the bus labours up the final stretch, leaving the scene of Mercy Ping's accident far behind, emerging into the main street with a gush of steam from its radiator and ruined pistons clanking, the traffic jam extends right down to the coastal plain and beyond the limits of human foresight. The driver pulls out of the way at Ping's welding works. And the cars behind, released from torture, shoot past, through the town and straight out the other side without a chance of ever getting back. So when the road ends and they are forced to stop, the whole chain stops and two thousand three hundred and fourteen vehicles apply their brakes for the last time: in the whole length of this primitive road there is not one place out of town where a car could turn. Ahead, the track ends in a gully and a giant mound of loose slag. The cars that have reached Whitey's Fall disgorge people, but the prospectors further down sit tight, unwilling to believe in God. Then they spot the planes overhead, the fossickers on horseback, tractors bristling with tools crossing the paddocks, the invasion of foot-sloggers: they abandon their safe bourgeois shells. The mountainside swarms with people in a ferocious rustling speechless war, people drunkenly singing their way to glory, and people methodically casting an eye over the terrain, people already consulting the rocks and chipping at them with textbooks open at page 57 and page 123. Official estimates of the expected yield leap to 2 236 000 tonnes.

Meanwhile, the bus door has opened releasing a cloud of incense that drops the driver to the ground: seen to be Rupert Ping, dressed in a blue silk costume, springing about with bells

461

jingling at his wrists and ankles. Following him come four scarlet figures somersaulting on the grass. The windows open and sprout a mushroom of limbs which unfold to a human scaffolding where a tiny person sings *ally-oop* and swallow-dives into the arms of a waiting giant.

Five minutes later, Mr Ping returns from Vivien's house, mystified. He weaves his way among the stopped cars. Not only wasn't she there with his keys, but neither was anyone else he knew. The School of Arts lies in a rubble of splintered ironbark. The locals have totally deserted the place. The troupe of acrobats gather round him for information, their ancient Chinese faces rosy with goodwill. Lu P'an Ping has given them a purpose and he is among friends at this town. The workshop doors burst open from inside and a horde of barbarians pours out armed with stolen tools which they carry off in triumph to the diggings. A band of the more imaginative are still inside; ripping Alice's cowskin apart, they sift through the sawdust stuffing for gold. People have already reached the highway site. The clash of arms rings in the distance, a puff of smoke blossoms in the sky causing a pair of eagles to elevate and continue their perpetual reconnaissance at a greater altitude. The first tent goes up and the next few, so already a street is marked out. Wives and children establish community relations while husbands stagger back to their territory with the huge lumps of gold pushed aside by the graders.

Rupert Ping watches Alice's horns being severed from her skull by pessimists who think they must grab what they can as the gold will be cleaned out from the higher slopes, and turns his back. He glances down the lane at the side in time to see the last straggling familiar figures, Whitey's Fallers escaping to the showground. Standing on his hands, he runs to catch them, the troupe all running on their hands behind him, legs joggling in the air like vegetable ears.

The showground is back to its heyday, milling with people and beasts. Uncle marshals the procession of relatives, then waves the vehicles on. He watches with grim satisfaction as a helicopter and a squadron of private aircraft roar in close overhead: they won't be told! The trek to London is to begin. Elderly citizens sweat at crankhandles. And just as the Bedford begins to roll forward through the high grass, what should come bowling past to lead the way but Mrs Ping's little truck and Mrs Ping driving it, cool as you like, the tin mudguards trembling with excitement and the lady herself with a neat high-and-mighty look about her and not even a bandage on her wrist, carrying in her head an orderly catalogue of the populations and principal products of the world's nations according to her 1930 encyclopedia.

– Well I'm blowed, says Uncle. It's the track to London we're takin, he shouts after her and shakes his head wonderingly. Winnin form!

Billy lets in the clutch and swings in line behind Mrs Ping. The patriarch McTaggart beside him cackles into a paperbag, the blue budgerigar still perched on his head. His wife has begun her routine of leaning out of the window, anticipating travel sickness. The Reo chugs into position following the jingling steam plough while puffs of the steam drift damply against its windscreen. Tractors and bikes and the horse-drawn carts take their places. The contingent who are to walk the livestock get to their feet and dust themselves for the journey, when what should they see but a circus! twenty boys in brilliant costumes, tumbling, hopping on stilts and running on their hands down from the town. The old folk clap with delight, the Chinese acrobats are here to entertain them.

– It's hard for the ones that died of the committee meetin, Uncle says. To miss a gala. We should pay our respects: Felissy, Mum, Seb, Jasper, yes and George. Bloody George. Come to think of it, they was all Whitey's Fallers, not one among them knew London. Born at Wit's End to a man. Funny thing that. It's the most people to have died on the mountain since the 1908 riot, if you count them others as well.

– They did what they could, Vivien agrees taking his hand.

He clucks with disapproval at this commonplace. In her shoes, Annie would have surprised him out of his maudlin reflections.

The walkers amble away on stiff hips, swinging the leg out wide in fine style. Accompanied by dogs and cats, they drive some independent-minded livestock among which is Grandma Buddall's cow with Grandma cock-a-hoop on its back. The people are in no hurry and have nothing to carry. The dogs do the rounding up, the principal problem being Mum Collins's Myrtle who is convinced she ought to be at home going about her usual routine. Uncle laughs at her each time she tries to make a break. The party is cheerful, flies cluster on their backs holding some kind of parliament, taking a ride. The acrobats are chanting gibberish to the accompaniment of gongs and cymbals.

– Jumpin side-winders! Uncle shouts. That blue one there is Rupie Ping.

And Mr Ping executes a double back somersault with pride at being recognized in front of his colleagues. The walkers crowd round to congratulate him on his return. Vivien confirms that she is a woman of mystery by taking his keys out of her bag and handing them to him. The dogs and cattle begin to catch on to the rhythm of the music and step in time, so that Grandma Collins has to belt her cow, ineffectually screaming that she'll fall off the drunken coot. Even Myrtle accepts captivity and trots ahead having a mumbled conversation with someone she loves, while Jessie swears she catches a hint of Mum's voice along the way. But there's more here than aimless cheerfulness; young Viv Lang being with them. For themselves they don't need reasons, doing what they have to do, but she has to be comforted and reassured. Do you recall how we used to speak of this creek Uncle? Stranger's Creek, it ends way down there twenty mile down in Dry River, that fellow does. I've been prospecting along this creek in my time, never did much good but, though I can still handle a dish of dirt, dolly out you know, or trace a lead, makes you laugh when you think what they're digging out now. Tisn't a sport any longer, it's bloody murder, that mob back there's only in it for the money, if you ask me. Vivien answers little, brooding on her problem: how is she to break her news to Bill Swan? No room for doubt, she is pregnant. His imagined reactions muffle their talk. She carries with her her big black umbrella which she has not yet learnt to live without, the fear of getting wet as persistent as her English accent. She thinks of Billy when once he

464

flashed past on his motorbike, head strapped in a helmet, face unshaven for weeks, ferocious and innocent as a crusader. The old people talk, they reassure her so she can belong too. Pick up a pebble Vivien and carry it in your hand, gives you contact with the land. My gracious these shoes of Angela's fit me like a glove, so comfortable you wouldn't believe. Where is Angie? Driving her milkcart while Vance drives her pa's six-wheeler, what a laugh. That six-wheeler was rusted right into the ground; I'll get her movidng if I have to pull her along myself she said. Are you sorry to be leaving your home when you've only just settled in? one of them asks Vivien and Vivien replies. She shakes her umbrella. The talk goes on. I can't help feelin at home on this road, makes you want to whistle on a sunny mornin like today. I can see the last time so clear in me head, Tom Whitey a young fella like meself at the time, full a beans an jumping about all idiotic an strutting round the sheilas, a blasted turkeycock with his feathers going an his face red. Who'd have thought it'd be Tom finding a nugget, him and Paddy McAloon, and getting a town named after him? He had a load to live with Tommy did, knowing his father was the barber at Melbourne jail and shaving the heads of dead prisoners fresh after being hung; that was his job so they could take a mould and make a plaster cast for their gallery, that's to say when they didn't cut the skull off to get at the brain and see what made them criminals. They should have tried a look in their own heads, if you ask me. I don't suppose there'd be much left of this old place up here. London? Bill tells me she's a ghost of stumps and foundations, only the streets left really. Give us a fresh start then, won't it? Just as well; I remember some pretty crook things went on there, did some of them meself, like nailing ears on the barn door with the rest of the blokes. Ears? yes, cut off of Abos and Chinks and the like: we was young larrikins. Nailed them up we did, like a warning I suppose, or more like trophies when you think about it. For sport. Yes, we come a long way since then. We was barbarians when we lived at London, we'd trample on anybody, full of courage and full of wickedness, that's what a big place does to you when there's gold around and you're fightin for it. It'll be happening right this

465

minute back at Whitey's, mark my words. You can't have a goldrush without you become barbarians, that's for sure. People gets hurt and you don't notice, you don't bloody well *want* to notice, you don't care, don't even recognize you're doing the hurting most of the time neether, I done some wild things meself. Now then, now then, you don't want to frighten Miss Lang with all that stuff you men. Don't I but! I got my eye on Miss Lang! What a thing to say, man of your years, you ought to be ashamed, as I'm sure you are, Mrs Rose Swan declares to make her peace with Billy's woman. Eggie here, who we haven't seen for I don't know how many ages, can behave like a gentleman, you ought to take a leaf from Eggie's book is what I say, wouldn't you agree Uncle? Vivien finds to her relief she is no longer worrying about what she'll say to Bill. The acrobats perform intricate juggling tricks on the run, polished dragons' eggs spinning through the sky.

Now this here's where some steps end, they go out to a look-out, I expect they'd still be there cut in the slope, Jacob's Ladder we used to call it though I'm sure I don't recall why we should of. Wasn't there anything at Whitey's Fall when you first went? Nothing. Some of us here can remember it, the beginnings when the real town was London and Whitey's was a harebrain idea called Main Ridge, gold was mined at Main Ridge and up the way at New Reef too, but nobody hardly living at the place except in a few tents, then Walter Schramm got the idea of taking the beer to the diggers instead of expecting them to come here to London for it, and that was the makings of Whitey's, a town founded around a pub, a real Australian story, afterwards came the churches and houses and the School of Arts, it was the death of London, our shacks left to fall down as they pleased. Oh yes, there's them among us as remember pretty much all of it though we'd a been real youngsters back that far. Yes, like the days of big family conferences with grandpa and old Pop, Auntie, Mum and Dad and us all sitting out on the verandah if you can picture it, dropping a word in here or there, and silence around us and us considering what was said and deciding. But we've grown apart as people's been getting fewer. Had to happen. Nothing to decide.

The more they talk the more they look forward to arriving in the London they knew, yes they knew the way it rested on the north-easterly slope of their mountain, knew it in autumn sleet when the panorama fined down to an engraved sheet of metal and the tired earth gave out erotic perfumes of decay, knew it wreathed in the pink and golden gumtips of spring, knew it on summer evenings when you moved among the luxuries of conversation from opposite sides of the street.

The umbrella droops and flops along, more evidently useless and hateful by the minute. Vivien thinks of the real London, that's how she thinks of it too: the real London. Luckily she isn't given room to speak till she has had time to reflect; they are talking about a place where everything mattered down to the most fleeting association, first occasions, the magical art of naming things, finding the risks, the tricks, the natural forces, the foreign spirit of the place to be placated, and absorbing all this into their own survival. Now she comes to reflect on it, who would care about her reminiscences of the Underground, Bisto advertisements and Guinness is Good for You, the houses of parliament or the black Daily Express, what would a bobby matter or Lyons Corner House or cold pork pies, or the lunch hour crowd in Green Park? None of these things means anything because she has not helped create them, she has known them only as a tourist might. The Real London, a place where everything has a fixed name, is simply another blockage in her mind she must clear away. They'd listen politely, but perhaps they wouldn't tell her any more of their history. Did anyone ever jump off the lookout, she asks instead. My word they did, one old lady pipes up, two of the blighters together, young scamps defying their families, but that was right back at the beginning and they weren't people you'd know, they eloped up here to the goldfield where they thought they'd be safe, but a week hadn't passed before her father come from Sydney with a shotgun and they lit out along to Jacob's Ladder and off of the cliff, just like that, Lovers' Leap we called it for a year or two, then it got to be known as the Lookout again because that seemed more local if you see what I mean. Them bastards back there, says Uncle turning round to curse Gomorrah, they'd pull down Westminster Abbey to find the Holy Ghost.

467

Three

CB radios all over the country are jammed with the news; the army gives an impressive display of mobility moving into sleepy Yalgoona to control the flood of prospectors three minutes and forty-five seconds before an unaccountable thunder rises from the earth announcing the mass migration of semi-trailers from all round the nation, driven by night to converge on the mountain, laden with merchandise destined for looting or decay in the roadblocks. Fortunes have already been made; in the first hours of the morning lives are being dedicated to the protection of instant wealth, people joyfully loading their rifles and mounting guard over their nuggets. Imaginative diggers exploring an old water-supply tunnel at the foot of the mountain chip at the rock and discover a wall of solid gold. Japanese magnates in private jets bringing the new Imperial order wait with unflinching patience for their first sight of the colony. Meanwhile the bluff of paper-money is being called, currencies throughout the world, hard and soft alike, slip down the bank exchange ladder. Gold has a heyday. Government accountants in Washington and Brussels predict the ruin of the free world. The Prime Minister of Great Britain in private session with the reigning monarch deliberates on the possible benefits to civilization of dropping a nuclear bomb on Whitey's Fall. The Chinese ambassador to Canberra calls on the Minister for Foreign Affairs to offer protection against military aggression. Private editions of *Das Kapital* go on sale by the million in sex shops and butchers. Torres Strait Islanders aboard a navy of canoes invade the continent from the north. Two journalists have already sketched the chapter headings of their instant history *The Mountain of Gold: socio-economic stalemate* and the ostentatious cheque for advance royalties is this moment being signed by the manager of a publishing firm more used to quibbling over single dollars with down-at-heel novelists. Television cameramen claim the usual exemption from common courtesy, clambering upon car tops and elbowing the injured aside for actuality shots of the new rich weeping over their trophies. The old prospectors who have dedicated a lifetime to the art of subsistence and their faith that the mountain will support them are already fleeing along the London track with their relations. Eggie Schramm has stacked the entire bottled supplies of the hotel, plus a few kegs, on to a resurrected dray which some indignant heifers are pulling in an amateur fashion. The only other dray that didn't fall to pieces at the suggestion of being lugged out of the undergrowth trundles along under the weight of the bizarre stock of Brinsmeads' store.

As Uncle watches this drayload shudder past and chuckles at the corsets on top lolling in straitlaced orgy, he is stopped by a nasty thought. A missing person. He leans on his walkingsticks to puzzle it out. Now who? Who has been left behind that the corsets remind him of?

– There's somebody isn't with us, he calls and Angela Collins cracks her whip so her smart milkcart bowls past with a flutter of glossy spokes.

– Have you forgotten Bertha then? her voice drifts back to him with mocking cheerfulness.

How could he forget Miss Bertha McAloon, his own wife during those miserable years?

– I wouldn't do this to Bertha, he cries out in distress. She belongs, the old bitch. He hobbles over to the remaining vehicles as fast as his walkingsticks and dead legs will allow. Is there anybody can go back for Bertha? he asks.

But Bertha has her own resources. She hasn't been floating in that dam all these years without learning something useful for an occasion. The moment she hears she is wanted she sets out from her barn with its knitted rooms and the knitted world of the mountain in knitted windows. She says goodbye and good riddance to her art and half a lonely life of subservience to an ideal. She lies down on her back and floats. Yes, through the liquid air, her mauve dress no longer angry, fluttering excitedly, lifting to the breeze and filling out to a kite. Using the Bertha McAloon style, that unique backstroke tending towards a sidestroke, she ferries herself around the obstacle of trees, up and over Peter Buddall's farmhouse and away across the valley. She doesn't care a fig for the world, not on your life. She's Amy Johnson come back from the dead, she's the feminist answer to St Thomas Didymus and D. D. Home, oh glory, she's the missing link and Cecil B. de Mille is handing her a part, wouldn't you know, for a million dollars to go on being herself. She swoops across the cemetery with its six new graves, cheekily saluting the entire Brinsmead family under fresh earth and not before time. Serve you right, Rubberlips Brinso. Who's laughing now? And the brat a spitting likeness of the Pope! Here's a kiss for you Bessie, though why you deserve it I'm sure I don't know, but you made a bonzer cup of tea I'll grant you that. And Jasper, you'll be preserved like the Pharoah in your own pickle long after the rest of us is worm-droppings I reckon. As for Georgie Porgie I used up my tears long ago, son. If you'd been a dracula I would have rather that. You never gave me my revenge when I needed it more than breath. At least I'm saved from poisoning you. We should be thankful for small mercies. She floats in the clayey air while an astonished helicopter splutters down to get a closer look at her. Here you are you dirty perv, she screams, lifting her skirt and flashing them a glimpse of what all men are after, gratified by the sudden elevation of the machine, she waves when she can spare a hand from ferrying herself along. Up over the McTaggart fences she goes gliding so close to the soil she could touch the grass of the old showground. And here is the rabble of her kin belting the daylights out of their sluggish cattle, plus Uncle what's more shading his eyes to stare at her as she swoops upward. Mind your business Arthur, she calls gleefully as she circles him, or I'll piss in your eye for sure. So you want me back do you? You think I'll come running? Well I shall let you know me terms when it suits meself. And off she floats, triumphant, mocking the clumsy horse carts, spearing through puffballs of steam from the Queensland plough, blowing a raspberry at that sneakthief Billy, pursing her lips on observing the wowser Mercy Ping back again after not long enough away, and arriving well ahead of them all at the halfway clearing where they'd be taking a break. She floats down steering herself for a soft landing, not sure how to do this without snapping a leg or a rib. She chooses the softest looking place and flops into a luxuriant cushion of stinging nettles. Jesus Christ! she swears in fury. This is no bloody joke! O god it's killing me. She scrambles out adding another grudge to her personal Domesday Book. However, she saved her back a nasty gravelrash and she has recovered her composure when, some hours later, her grandson eases the Bedford carefully over grassy mounds to park in position ready to lead the way again. Mrs Ping is nowhere to be seen. The other vehicles nose up over the crest and roll down on the flat to stand round shimmering with heat, mirages of themselves, the horse carts solid among them with the horses cropping. Miss Bertha McAloon, waiting to claim her ex-husband and give him hell, assumes command and marches among them with her stick-arms gesticulating, making an art of spreading the rugs, an art of placing the fire and hanging billycans over it. She's got it in her blood.

– How's it going grandma, Billy sings knowing that she'll hate this.

– I'll sort you out too! she promises. See if I don't.

Mr Ian McTaggart stands on the runningboard of the Bedford to make an announcement while Billy sounds the horn for attention.

– We made it this far, says the trembly old man. But there's them walkers still coming behind. We got to take account a them. You've had your turn as a passenger, so anybody here who's under ninety-five can have a try at walking when you've had your cup of tea and a bite. Yous can set off when you're ready and that'll leave seats for the worst cases of them behind to ride the rest of the way.

He is helped down, flushed with embarrassment at having to speak so long. Miss McAloon sniffs at the very idea of orders as she casts a handful of tea into the first boiling billy and hears the leaves hiss among frantic bubbles. Then the next and the next.

– Ready, she orders (like most artists unaware of her own sins). Take them off the heat and tap the sides to sink the leaves.

– I'm all shook up, complains her sister-in-law Olive. After being in that rattletrap steam thing of Wally's.

– Whose fault is that, Bertha snaps virtuously. All smothered in scarves fit to suffocate!

– Dust gives me hayfever, but.

– Hayfever on the knee! Imaginitis is what you're suffering from Olive. You won't get sympathy out of me, that's for sure. Even so she remembers her own hayfever when she first hung up a hundred naphthalene rings to protect her knitted rooms from moth. One thing leads to another. She also remembers this morning: the race against time, dawn already threatening and the job to be finished before she could leave, balanced on a kitchen chair with her big sewing scissors snipping the threads, the pungent white discs clicking and rolling about the floor, then herself sweeping them outside in the dirt, every sherrick of naphthalene cleared out and clothes moths flocking in for the long-awaited banquet. What do they know about suffering, the Olives of this world, emptyheaded geese? Steaming cups pass round hand to hand, some so shaky the tea spills staining the china. They are used to each other, so they sit quiet, mainly thinking their own thoughts.

(Blades clashing to spark fire, the entire village ablaze, the coat of gold plate sliced apart, the stench of burning fat and split entrails, victims screaming death in the face, houses throwing up flames that can be seen by hiding peasants miles away. The looters dragging heavy treasures through the brilliant flickering shadows. Dead men yell challenges to the marauders who make off for their next victory, while one life-slave of the household, left standing, ignored as a worthless lump of furniture, gazes out at the sacred indifferent river for a sign, witness to the murder of children who could one day grow into avengers.) Mr McTaggart stands, old (useless rag of a man hot with the insult but aware he must not move, that no one suspects his head is his master's treasury rich with stories, the knowledge of survival and law. Smoke hanging in his hair, his skull packed with a catalogue of peril, an encyclopedia of disillusion. They have gone. He moves, sandals crackling through the shards of broken gods, cherishing in him the most precious instrument: humour, to be warmed back to life at another time. He has been trained in the trade of inscribing characters, so using the stones of the fallen house he carves the first symbols. Patiently he begins the rest of his life, recording what he knows, not for rewards or freedom, nor even for posterity, no one can now read the language he learnt from his masters. He records it as an offering of thanks for what he has known, sensing only some remote scholar touching the chipped stone, reverently poring over his script decyphering for the first time in three thousand years the name of the conquerors in a chronicle that opens with a witty tribute to divine justice, a servant singing with the voice of masters) shakes his head to get the memory clear, Mr McTaggart has nodded off, dropping his cup and saucer. He takes a good clean lungful of smoke from the fire and roams through the memory of his orderly maze, his garden, his celestial model. There will have to be a new garden at London, the circles marked out all over again, and plants fetched over from the old when he has the ground prepared.

– Remember them two jumping off a Lovers' Leap, one sentimentalist mumbles through a pat of biscuit crumbs. Well I was the kid who found them. It's not far, the drop from up there, you know.

– Far enough, Miss McAloon observes. To get themselves killed.

Flies cluster to kiss the wet lip-marks on cups.

– We once had a migration, drones a voice. Across a big wide valley it was. Though I don't know where, don't ask me. We sat down to eat some striped kind of meat.

They believe. Vague recollections stirring among actual memories.

– Yes, a valley, says one cautiously.

– There was thousands of us that time, the voice adds more positively. We sat down like this only there was thousands of us.

Ants now join the invasion of flies, big amber ants and midget black ones, tearing along in lines, their two-way traffic communicating from time to time.

– I wonder how the gold diggers are going, says Billy watching the ants.

– The diggers, Ian McTaggart relays the remark to his deaf wife.

– They'll have begun the killing, Violet yaps back from the cab of the Bedford where she's munching lettuce. There'll be murders common as breakfast from now on.

– Whitey's is dead, her husband agrees. Leaving my garden.

– But nobody's going to get us, Bertha McAloon declares. All they'll get is a heap of moth-eaten wool.

– Good on you grandma, Bill laughs at her admiringly so that she grumbles:

– Just you get my Irish up and I'll sort you out too, now that I've got to live where I can smell you. And she strokes her moustache.

– Is there any back-ups with the tea Bertha?

– How should I know? Ask them who dished it out. Nothing to do with me.

– Keep the fire going for the next lot Wally.

– They'll be in a proper sweat.

– Hope the christ it don't rain tonight.

– It'd be the first shower you've had since churchgoing went out if it does!

The laughter evokes a babble of concerned birdcries from the mountain. And the first volunteers for the new band of walkers begin stretching and straightening themselves, refreshed, businesslike, and heading for the track, testing their thighs and pumping their lungs, picking up their feet for the championship.

Four

No one sleeps in the industrial cities. Confidence is shattered; money being in ruins. People buy anything at any price. Gold is declared the sole currency for international trade, speculators pushing its price past a thousand dollars an ounce within hours of trading, only to find their dollars mean nothing when they've got them. Public credit collapses. Paper notes are virtually worthless, the bankcard system discredited. Optimists buy up dead money believing the slump to be temporary. Interest rates soar to 12½% per day. The United Nations Organization closes its doors while the experts rewrite classical economics. The free interplay of selfish interests which is capitalism, so the revised theory goes, paradoxically produces a desirable social result provided wealth is predominantly more apparent than actual. And the Law of Diminishing Returns is made to embrace a rider that when labour is concentrated on land yielding pure gold rather than crops, the ignorant swine who dig it unbalance the delicate mechanism of sophisticated argument. In other words, the law no longer operates. Growth economics are at an end.

Small communities of drop-outs living in home-made shanties worshipping the forests and hoping to be visited by the wisdom of the Aborigines are hailed as visionaries of a future with maximum health and minimum worry. As far as politicians are concerned, their idea of a pioneer is the president of a South American republic declaring all his citizens bankrupt and calling in every last peso of the nation's wealth. We are hamstrung by courtesy. Computers in Johannesburg at mining corporation offices roll out thousands of sheets of analysis to answer the question how to get a year's output of Rand gold from the ground in a week.

Children in a primary school near Renmark, SA, set a class assignment on alternatives to the disaster of a gold glut, encouraged by their teacher, devise the biggest walkathon in modern education, with the proceeds raised for each kilometre walked buying food and drink for the journey: the youngsters leave the school gates on the first day of the six hundred kilometre hike to Whitey's Fall. The holy land of stable commerce is to be reclaimed without bloodshed by the faith of children. No sooner has the ABC News broadcast this item than a boy called Nicholas, a precocious ten-year-old, fires all the youth of Melbourne with the ideal of a cycle crusade and leads them out of the city through Preston and Coburg and along the Hume Highway, pedalling for Albury and the border of New South Wales, filled with the triumph of superior tactics, calculating that they would arrive weeks ahead of the South Australians. Children from all kinds of homes come wheeling their machines, mounting, coasting and racing. They sing popular songs, also *Advance Australia Fair* because everybody knows it. And when the road passes a school, Nicholas calls the children out, he preaches to them, winning hundreds for the cause. Children to rule the world. Boys and girls without bicycles steal them rather than miss the excitement. Past the pea farm belt, out beyond the dairy cattle among the sheep they cycle, thousands of children alight with an ideal, pursued by hordes of adults, guardians and parasites, the parents begging them from car windows to come home, the business people selling them sweets and pornography or interviewing them for their opinions on Euro-communism, quantum mechanics, and the future of God. Onward past paddocks stifled in a purple blanket of Paterson's curse, through orchards and vineyards, ambulances parked along the way staffed by doctors specializing in heat exhaustion and sunstroke, plus psychiatrists of the fanatical order, pedalling ceremonially through cheering countrytowns, waving at white-faced children imprisoned behind their own bedroom windows, Nicholas and his following of youngsters pump along, thighs and shoulders sprouting muscles big as a man's, minds empty of ideas to make room for the cuckoo of self-importance. At Wagga-Wagga the Anglican and Roman Catholic bishops vie in medieval splendour to bless them while the supporting teams of clergy bellow their bit-parts on the assumption that to be heard is a step towards paradise. The mayor of Gundagai is host for a convention of employers and academics who have volunteered to break up the crusade by offering individuals a short-term servitude to curb all this unseemly hysteria, plus a long term contract on their working lives. Now hundreds of children collapse each hour. The hospitals and secondhand bicycle shops are crammed to overflowing. At Canberra the Governor-General assures them he too was once a cyclist of no mean skill. They are met by a humourless Prime Minister who reminds them of their headmasters and whose eyes are so hard and close together it makes you pity his nose. As they reach the Great Dividing Range, coal companies kidnap them in coaches, drive them away as strike-breakers to work in the mines for a pittance with the opportunity to slave the idealist poison out of their systems, to purge them in the blinding dark shafts for sixteen hours a day plus two round meals provided on the job and a free visit from the Sisters of Mercy on the first of each month.

The Renmark children turn back, disenchanted.

Five

At the negligible cost of lameness and exhaustion, the Whitey's Fall walkers have caught up with the picnic. They stretch their bones on the grass, grateful for the offer of a ride the remainder of the way. Uncle is still attending to Vivien's education. We breathe the green of trees, he says. Did you know that? And wherever we go we spread trails of food for the little fellas, there's bits of us fall off like a scab, a drop a blood maybe, speck a dandruff, all food for somethin, and then there's ants we tread on and we never know, left for somethin else to eat and keep goin. We're givin the whole while and takin the whole while. He blows on his tea watching the circles flow out to the side. If God was to stop the world this moment, he says, He'd see my part in it, He'd see the justice of me belongin here. And He'd see your part in it too Vivi. Uncle draws the skin off his creamy tea, sucking it noisily into his mouth. He inclines his good ear towards her in case she has anything to say, but she hasn't.

Vivien listens. She has found what she needs. Her longing is for Billy, that powerful young man with his dark lashes, his clumsy energetic manner, his perpetual failure to understand, to have him follow her about, sit when she sits, stand when she chooses to stand, wait to see what he must do next. She relishes Aunty's famous dictum: The old days? what old days? I don't remember a thing, what do the old days matter when there's today to live? These ugly wrecks, the darlings, she thinks. They don't mind walking out of their places. They're enjoying it. Vivien makes a decision. She goes to the cliff edge and pitches her umbrella over the precipice, watching the silly past flap helpless. The grannies laugh among their hairy moles, toothless grins waggling in her direction.

Well you're right, Uncle tells her as she sits beside him again. You can't own anythin, not even your body. Most you can do is strike up an acquaintance. I had an acquaintance with me house, overgrown as the bugger got across the years. With a switch of tone he asks her pointblank – Are you plannin on stayin?

– You mean, if Bill and I have children?

– We don't want the young ones to go, he explains. Just pray for a girl and don't be ashamed like Felissy was.

They ruminate on this, birds darting about their heads and the plants bursting with woody perfumes. Vivien, plagued by a problem nagging to be solved, finds the moment is spoilt for her. Then Uncle launches into another of his favourite theories.

– A course we eat the mountain, us people. Think of the vegies; we grow them in soil here don't we? And soil's the mountain I suppose? So you see. The same for the milk we get from our cows and that-there. And the beasts we slaughter. What's a lump of beef in Whitey's but a cut off a the mountain?

He is interrupted by a shadow. Mrs Angela Collins the horse lady, her head cocked, one hand on hip, the other wielding a whip with which she slaps her high boots. A transistor radio hanging from her shoulder speaks.

– Uncle, says Angela Collins interrupting the broadcast. I reckon I ought to be able to trust you with my milkcart. Her shadow slaps its shadow boot.

– Angie my dear, he replies pertly. I wouldn't dare set me muddy feet so much as on the running-board a your flash outfit.

– ... brought to us direct by satellite from the BBC, says the transistor.

– Well you got her then, the lady declares. Here's the whip, but you just touch one of them beauties with it and I'll lay about you, you sinner, no worries. Just let them hear it, they'll go.

– Do you reckon I'm too feeble to walk then, Uncle shouts angrily, sensing a favour. The transistor plays a fanfare.

– Yes I do and that's a fact. The point is there's four people sittin in the back sending me mad with their chatter. But how can I get away? They're my aunties. And what if some hamfist drives her for me, steers her into a ditch and tips them out sideways?

– You mean, Uncle's face changes, instantly deceived. You mean you want an expert, he exclaims happily.

– Miss Lang, says Mrs Angela Collins in her loftiest manner. I hope you won't think badly of us in this town.

– I'll do it, Uncle proposes. Only to save them pretty geldings a yours.

At this point Mrs Collins's transistor, one among 155 million round the world, begins to talk about Whitey's Fall, a voice beaming down from a satellite. Uncle goes pale at the sound of it.

– I left Whitey's Fall because that was the old world and I longed for the challenge of the new, says the voice.

– And now here you are in our West Country studios in England, an interviewer marvels in a voice rich with complacent charm. And have you ever been back there Mrs McTaggart?

– No I've stood on my own two feet, replies the voice on the radio.

– Aunt Annie, Vivien gasps. All the old people crowd round the set excitedly.

– What can you tell us about the place as you remember it?

– Perhaps it's a bit rough and ready . . .

– Was there gold to be found on the mountain even then?

– Put it this way: the day the Brinsmeads discovered a reef, I knew it was time to get out.

– You went to serve as a nurse in the Great War, didn't you?

– None of your business.

– She's back, cries Uncle recognizing the mortal wound in his heart as joy.

– Geologists, the imperturbable interviewer continues, today

480

confirmed that the mountain is almost solid gold. I believe you still own some property there. How much do you think it is worth now, Mrs McTaggart?

– Not a cracker more than it was sixty years ago.

– I'm sure the listeners will appreciate your modesty. You're ninety years old, Mrs McTaggart, tell us about the past.

– You listen to me, young man. This is Aunt Annie speaking. I've no patience with the past, not in any shape or form. You take my word it's finished and gone. If you waste your life worrying about the past you'll never have time to live the present. And now I'm speaking to my kin back home. Can you hear? Get out of there if you've got any sense. Do you hear me Arthur? Don't be afraid to change your mind, it's only too late when you're dead. I'm sending you my love. Bless you, and stick up for yourselves. My thoughts are with you.

– How can I tell her? moans Uncle when the voices on the radio change and a couple of Keynesian dons drone statistics to prove the eternal verities of tinkering.

Miss Brinsmead fell in love with me, Vivien understands at last. And I am to re-open her shop at London. Could I be the one to keep this past now? Is that it? She is daunted by the prospect of having to match Miss Brinsmead's practicality.

Bertha McAloon, mortified at hearing her deadly enemy made famous, decides to show off her floating again and recapture the admiration of this ignorant rabble of in-laws. But though she lies down the usual way and thinks pretty hard of success, nothing happens and she has to get up pretending she was only trying out a bit of yoga.

Motors rumble into life, gasp as they're cranked, fire off like machineguns. They warm up. The Bedford sways ahead on to the track the boys cleared when they were making their way down from their fossicking trip. The motorcycle follows, snare-drumming among the stones, then the tractors and buggies, the carts, the flat-top, the two drays. And finally the steam plough, having built a sufficient head of steam, jerks into life, exotic as an Arabian bazaar with chains clittering round the galah cage and a giggling old lady swaddled up in the passenger seat.

The Chinese acrobats produce ten-foot silk scarves from their sleeves, swirl them, floating shapes, illusions of solidity, they perform hallucinations writing messages of hope on the sky with the brilliant fabric, blue on blue. They jump through the loops they appear to have made, they create winter of the world, they are playing with frozen cloud, the sun itself glows from a prison of ice, sharp air catches at the spectators' lungs, crystal rocks underfoot and the creek arrested, snow casts its ermine of blue shadows on the clearing, the bush crackles with frost and individual crows sound harsh answering echoes, *kyrie* and response. Now they are laughing Chinese laughter, highpitched and wholehearted so that the ice evaporates from round the sun, Rupert Ping the priest of warmth, and the mountain flutters humid with parrot feathers. The journey home to London begins again amid applause and the energy of renewed spirits. This time the locals will accept a joss-house among them, if there has to be one.

Vivien, with her hair growing, is walking between Miss Bertha McAloon and Mrs Angela Collins whose transistor is now silent as it swings from her shoulder. Since setting off in the dust-wake of the vehicles, these two ladies haven't left her an opportunity of saying anything, their shrill non-stop voices loud with the excitement of antagonism. They drive the livestock before them, dogs barking and cats dodging (tails up) at their heels. Mrs Collins and Vivien are striding along in step, liking each other. But Miss McAloon as usual is a pilgrim in the desert, a lone figure on that monotonous crust of earth. A tree sweeps up and away past her, a malignant eye darting into hers, the wind becoming a hail of insects or a thicket of thorns, the ghosts of two unwanted women haunting her, hanging on like shadows, now pushing her along, now dragging her back.

– There must be something in that stuffed cow, is what I say. I know you don't agree Miss McAloon but how can it be explained otherwise? It sticks in the brain that cow does. I never saw anything like it. And Rupert Ping showing it off, you'd think he was proud of it.

482

– I reckon it's all a lot of hooey, that's what. And you're behaving like a silly rabbit Angie for taking notice. Look at him: damn primped up little chink in his sonky rig. The thought of him messing with a dead animal and practising his black arts makes me puke. And you lot go in with your eyes popping, so he gets what he wants. Like a kid that bloke is, always angling for attention and never getting enough. Look at him now with his hoop-la.

Vivien thinks his tumbling performance marvellous, but has no chance to put in a word for him.

– I don't know that you've got much call to go looking down your nose at others Miss McAloon, I really don't. You never knew Alice did you Miss Lang? Well Alice was a personality in Whitey's Fall, she wasn't just an ordinary cow. We all knew Alice. And you'd have swore she knew us.

– Fair gives me the pip to hear talk like that, Miss McAloon announces with scorn (without a blemish of guilt remembering, in the knitted bedroom of her own house, a knitted picture of the south paddock with Alice prominent in the foreground).

– Didn't look like Alice any longer, Mrs Collins goes on determined to take no notice, being an independent woman of forty-eight as she is, one of the young people of the district. Alice all the same, and up there to be laughed at, it didn't seem natural.

– It wasn't natural you chicken. The damn cow was dead. And what was it stood on a hoist for?

– That's what I was asking when you interrupted, love.

– Don't love me. Not till you can tell me what's gone on with that dead brat of Felicia's. You can't have a twelve-year-old kid come out of a pumpkin is what I say. It's our town, our reputation. There's more than meets the eye.

– I'd give a packet for the truth myself I don't mind telling you. Though I thought you'd know, being the one who always knows everything. That Miss Brinsmead, although she was such a friend of Mum's and I oughtn't to speak ill of the dead, she used to frighten me when I was a girl. I swear she could read your mind. But you couldn't read hers, no way, not a soul had an inkling that child was in the house.

– I can't tell what you call right and wrong, Miss Bertha McAloon observes virtuously. But I know what I know.

Vivien wonders at the consequences if she'd offered to adopt Fido, why not, when she saw him peep out from under the blind the day Mrs Ping died. And of course she must have guessed he was in hiding, you never saw him around. The thought might have crossed her mind, she thinks it now. A thought she has always known.

– Friend of Bessie's though she was, I don't know that she was anything so special I do declare, declares Miss McAloon.

– And she threw herself on him as if she wanted to eat him, dead as he was.

– Poor little mongrel.

– His uncle standing there like a stuffed I-don't-know-what.

– To my way of thinking she must have brought the child home with her last time she came back from those foreign places.

– He might have been adopted, Vivien suggests to their surprise.

– Might of, Miss McAloon agrees.

– But still he'd have had to be in the place close on a year without anyone knowing.

– I wouldn't be too sure there wasn't nobody knew about that kid Angela, I wouldn't be too sure at all if I was you.

– Well there's people wise after the event as always, love. You can't expect anything else. Always is. Isn't that a fact Miss Lang? Yes, you see. There's no knowing what's in the human heart. Like Heathcliff turning tender.

– Who's this Heathcliff then? Have you been setting your cap down in Yalgoona again? You should be ashamed.

– Yalgoona! You've got to be joking. It's just Mr Brinsmead's book I've been reading at last.

Miss McAloon rounds on her, impressed and deceived.

– You never let on you were a book reader, she says. You never let on Angela.

– Well I have my moments, the other lady offers modestly, speaking past the obstruction of Vivien's dreaming head, but refuses to be drawn further.

Vivien is remembering the sea, the dramatic crunch of waves, foam kicking up, water rushing back off sand, beaches jewelled with shells, and a storm coming over, staining waves dark grey and driving a scatter of seabirds before it, salt and seaweed pungent in the air and a faint sniff of iodine, the fresh tide washing out rockpools where she'd find stiff porcupine shapes of sea urchins, fleshy anemones, striped limpets and periwinkles, sunshine dancing a moment before the shadow, the lightning and the first plickering of raindrops in water. And then jellyfish floating inshore like a dead army.

– Them Brinsmeads! Such particular people they wouldn't poke a pig with a stick, and that bloody great mansion they were building, all full of nothing, dust this thick on the floors and hardly a stick of furniture, rooms as big as a barn with the rolls of fluff wandering about in the draught. I was up there many a time, them being neighbours of my father. And old Brinsmead committing suicide. Now what did he do that for when his son gave him a lump of gold? There's a question never been answered to my satisfaction. And not likely to be now. What I say is look at the grandfather, that's where the clue is, I agree with you Angela.

– I don't hold with suicide myself Miss McAloon though I'm not religious. Always seemed to me that life was give to us for something, else why have we got it? Come on Grandpa Buddall, get a shift on, if you must walk up front you got to keep the pace going. Look out for the ladies! Can't have no slackers up front.

– I damn near think I ought to give you a taste a the back a me hand you young piece, Grandpa Buddall curses her already vexed with fatigue and the dumps. Don't know what this world's coming to. Bertha you got no business letting your girls go misbehaving like that.

– She's not one of mine Grandpa I'm thankful to say. She's a McTaggart girl this one. Married Bernie Collins when he was alive, poor young fellow getting killed by a falling tree, you know. And I was there to see, such a dreadful thing. A fallen tree'll always remind me. No she's a McTaggart.

– Well I can't sort em all out, he grumbles badtemperedly, hands pushing on his thighs to help him along.

Mrs Collins, who doesn't intend trying to understand, side-steps him and stamps her long boots in the dust to annoy him.

– And who's that? he shouts, being left behind, pointing at Vivien.

– Mata Hari! Angela Collins laughs. God help whoever he chooses for a neighbour when we get there, she adds cheerfully.

– Your grandfather, Miss McAloon warns Vivien, was best man at his wedding as I recall. O glory, what a wedding it was to be sure, with the lilies brought down off the mountain and a real horseshoe on the weddingcake.

Vivien glances back at the old man, suddenly curious to recognize this distant connection. She finds him hobbling after them, a fierce glint in his eye and a rejoinder evidently on the tip of his tongue. He looks at me, she thinks, as a stranger, he doesn't remember me helping him during the battle when he hurt his shoulder.

– Be damned if she isn't a dead ringer for Annie Lang, he grumbles threateningly.

– There's always a chance, Angela Collins is saying. A chance the kid wasn't Miss Brinsmead's really. But if it wasn't hers then whose was it?

– Now you're asking!

– Would it be far, Vivien ventures to ask, from here to where we're going?

This sort of question gives away that you are not listening, that your mind is somewhere more urgent.

– Everything's far, Miss Bertha McAloon complains. When you're my age. I'm not used to walking, she explains being cross with herself for failing to show off her floating a second time, her voice developing those mincing tones that so infuriated Uncle. Young Peter gives me a ride in his Land Rover as a rule but he went off to Yalgoona last night about his own business. If you ask me he doesn't know his mind. I think he's in a dither, like a lot of strong men, weak in the head, he is. Now why didn't any of his kids stop in Whitey's? He had a whole regiment of them. All gone now. Those young ones hung around my place hoping to get things out of me, you'd think I had a will to make. For all their pestering they never got a brass razoo, she shrieks triumphantly. They never did. Painfully she remembers her own cadging brother, her younger brother Kel, gone mad and now dead, the only one to go to the Real War and come back, though he came back with stories no one would believe like the winter soldiers frozen to the ground where they slept, stories that made you laugh they were so far-fetched, poor Kel. Though a liar he was, after all, dead.

– I hope Uncle doesn't rein them beauties in too sharp, Mrs Angie Collins worries out loud. They got lovely soft mouths them chestnuts of mine.

– Him! Uncle's ex-wife snorts poisonously. If they're got four legs and no feelings he'll understand them. It's people that's beyond him.

Vivien feels guilty not sticking up for darling Uncle. But she knows the live injury flows between her and Miss McAloon, that her Great-aunt Annie stood in the way of their marriage being happy. There's nothing she can possibly say. Even Angela Collins in her high boots is too courteous to change the subject. With no way out, they must walk together, communicating unspoken hurts. But Miss McAloon is not built for tact.

– That Lang woman's an aunty of yours, is she? she snaps with the Irish showing.

– Aunt Annie? Yes she is.

– Well she did me an injury once you know.

– I know.

– I declare to Jesus I'll never forgive her.

– It's a long time now, says Angela Collins.

– I'll never forgive I shouldn't wonder.

– She lives in England.

– Serves her right too.

– I love her, says Vivien eventually, short of breath.

– Humh! the old lady tosses her head in the air decisively. Their shoes turn on the loose stones. The forest stretches away down to the right in a vast sea of susurrating leaves, glinting and tumbling in sunlight. One thing I will say, says Miss Bertha McAloon exercising the prerogative of her seniority, for a judgment is expected of her. One thing I will say is I got a lot of time for loyalty. Then she adds with venomous relish – Only God help some people for the ones they got to be loyal to. When there's only Aunty Jezebel there's not much future for them.

The future, the future, Miss Brinsmead tells Vivien. If one means anything by the future then it already *is* . . . as I explained to that wretched man in his felt-padded library (oh, when was it?), we don't use the word future if we want to be understood. No. We call it hope. And hope *is*. Or alternatively fear. And fear *is*.

Vivien closes her eyes, she has begun to see the shape of the mountain, a gorgeous silhouette of purples and ambers. She has the unaccountable impression that if she wished, she could move it about and even begin to affect its shape. Then she hears Lance groaning as the Bedford jolted his broken leg; groans hovering at that spot for months to return to the pain where they belong.

– Marvellous how this track's being kept open by some cove, Mrs Angela Collins says. See all the slashing. That's new that is.

Six

So strong is tradition that miners' vigilante groups convene to guard the gold dug. But here at Whitey's Fall they will never have anything to do, because each prospector gets what he came for. As long as he can wield a pickaxe he can go home with a nugget. Strangers pour out with their loot almost as fast as other strangers pour in. A well-known firm operating tourist coaches is accepting two-day return bookings, leaving Sydney at dawn and driving to the roadblock at Yalgoona, then a stimulating guided hike for thirty-seven miles to the goldfields, an overnight camp with the comradeship of thousands, an hour after breakfast to extract your fortune from the bountiful mountain, a return hike of thirty-seven miles (downhill) with a backpack supplied for carrying your personal nugget out, then a fast ride home to the city.

There is no singing on the field now. It is not like it was before. Everybody works soberly at deciding the size of nugget suited to his or her desires; neither too big to carry out, nor too small to provide for a lifetime of indolence. There is little sense of locality once the pirated bulldozers clear a huge swathe of bush, people swarm over the area, pick a spot each at random and, without so much as goodday to their neighbours, claim what they dig out and leave while the next arrival takes over.

489

Into this half-world of clinks and grunts come furtive visitors with familiar surnames. Renegade Whitey's Fallers return, hoping not to meet their relatives and to make a quick getaway with no call on the emotions. They are led by the young generation under the command of Lance Lang, a weightlifter in boarding-school uniform, striped blazer and straw boater, losing his sense of direction without a mirror, a nagging young woman in tow, and bad breath. Maggot Buddall also appears, beginning by pocketing somebody else's gold till he realizes morality is thrust upon him by the prodigality of the supply. There is no future for the pickpocket when you only have to bend down for as much wealth as you could wish. The McTaggart twins arrive in drag straight from The Sky's The Limit Night Club where they work as hostesses. There wasn't time to change, their athletic male bodies stretching the flimsy fabrics, their wolves' eyes among the Elizabeth Arden eyelashes, they teeter about on high heels heaving two-hundred pound boulders aside.

– So we did find the Golden Fleece, Maggot says (glancing over his shoulder expecting a posse of police led by a stool-pigeon). When we ran out of juice and stopped here at the cutting, the truck must have been standing on solid gold if only we'd known. I thought it felt smooth. He laughs with delight at how they were tricked and reviews his brief criminal career, solid as a wall between Maggot then and Maggot now, too cheerful by nature to succumb to the cannibal Regret.

– Bloody Tony singing'd put anyone off their stroke, Lance rages.

– Jeez I'd like to see Billy, says Maggot sensing that he is demeaned by being one of this grovelling multitude.

The big schoolboy is too scornful to bother answering. He pulls off his blazer, wrapping it round a massive nugget, heaving it on his back and tying it by the sleeves around his muscular neck, then trudges away, permanently lame from that leg injury, toward his parents' house for a temporary stop-over and perhaps the use of a tractor to get him across country to an unblocked road.

– Look out mate, Maggot calls after him. You'll break your back. He joins Peter and Dave at their campfire for a billycan

490

of tea while they display their collection: a dozen eggs of gold, pure and clean, which they explain are gifts for special people.

– And what about yourselves? he asks.

They look blank. Why should they need gold?

– We found what we wanted in the city, Pete confesses being a particular friend of Maggot's.

– Shit, Maggot swears, recognizing the truth. What's a man here for? I can't come back. This stuff's nothing more than a fucking trap.

The horror of submission to respectability is suddenly clear.

– Here son, says Maggot accosting a crying child. Take this into captivity with you. Tell your mum a dirty old man gave it to you in return for a look at his dick. He thrusts his gold into the boy's hands.

The twins begin singing harmoniously as they used to:

When first I left old Ireland's shore, the yarns that we were told
Of how the folks in far Australia could pick up lumps of gold!
How gold-dust lay in all the streets and miner's right was free
'Hurrah,' I told my family, 'that's the very place for me.'

The sound, so simple and human, haunts the goldfield. They clap their hands in time and the bitter tradition pours from cherry-gloss lips, blonde wigs bobbing and fire in their mountainfolk eyes.

With my swag all on my shoulder, black billy in my hand,
I'll travel the bushes of Australia like a trueborn Irishman.

Felicia Brinsmead strolls up accompanied by a man in a white sheet.

– Boys, she says giving them her number one expression. This is Mr Julius Caesar. Julius, these are the boys.

– You, suggests Caesar seeing through their disguises as no one else has. Are lusting for danger, is it not?

– Pass the rum, bawls Maggot. More than anything I hate the truth.

491

The twins sing along:

For many years I wandered round to each new field about
And made and spent full many a pound till alluvial petered out.
And then for any job of work I was prepared to try,
But now I've found the tucker-track I'll stop here till I die.

Felicia and her escort walk sedately through the fire towards the waterfall and straight over the cliff.

Caesar's successor in Rome faces the knives of his colonels. The Stazione Termini fills with troop-trains, Ospedaletti and Finale Ligure, those tranquil Riviera villages, witness the arrival of a submarine fleet. The cautious Swiss block off the Simplon tunnel. Russian tanks chew the roads of Bulgaria (such as they are), Czechoslovakia, East Germany, Hungary and Poland, lining up along their western borders, the world's biggest ringside, to watch the European Economic Community tear itself and its neighbours apart. And sure enough, no sooner are they settled than the RAF swoops in for an intimidating show of force over the Alps, the Black Forest seethes with German underground armies surfacing, the French nuclear deterrent gets a final spit and polish, the Belgians and Dutch open a war of words, and Spain invades Gibraltar. The Austrians blockade all milk supplies to Liechtenstein, while Denmark and Sweden negotiate a pact against Norway. The insult of bullets flies both ways across the Irish border. The directors of the trans-national corporations stir the ambrosial air of their Olympus to decide where the first neutron bombs should fall, who and how many ought to die. Sipping at a health-promoting brew of rosehips they consider their verdict. But history is happening too fast for them. Their syndicates are already wreckage being picked over by middle men. Not one person will obey them when they do decide. And power passes for the first time into the hands of the elected governments, a disaster nobody could have foreseen.

From the ashes of authority the peoples' spirit rises. Even those with a liberal education recognize liberty when it happens.

Peasants, savage from ignorance and the struggle to survive, no longer accept as fate the cumulative burden of superstition. Workers who have been debased by their bargain-price labour and employers debased by exploiting them escape their roles. Thanks to Uncle's disclosures about Whitey's Fall, they mingle, walking their own streets freely all round the continent of Europe, also in parts of Asia and Africa, in Australia and the two Americas. The cracked husks of the world are flowering hope.

Seven

The Bedford noses down through the scrub, wattles whipping the screen, leaves brushing up underneath the chassis. In the cab the aged McTaggarts excitedly argue about the exact whereabouts of the track which is now completely overgrown. One of the horses whinnies while the orchestra of motors, wheels, traces, chains and voices has begun to seem hopelessly out of place, wallowing, sinking in the bush. Little wallabies and black goannas tear off among the trees, while high above the caravan a pterodactyl hangs interestedly eyeing the scatter of possible victims.

Suddenly it's all over, they arrive at London, place of terrible memories, to accept their past again as physical fact. The Bedford swings on to a broad flat, the Reo puttering gravely behind, Uncle on the driver's seat of the immaculate milkcart shouting I thought you was gettin us bushed for a while there Billo, the geldings duck their heads to the juicy grass, the steam plough jingling and swaying, passengers totter out, life easing painfully along their limbs again, goods and food supplies are stacked neatly to one side, the galah gives a couple of hallelujahs, and Uncle directs the setting up of camp with tarpaulins being slung over ridgepoles and pegs hammered into the soil, the firearms are stowed in a tent. Vivien is to be put in charge of the food

494

from Brinsmeads', but until she arrives a fly is pitched over the top of the dray. An encampment takes shape on the abandoned racetrack while rivals decide which lots to claim in the old streets according to family rights. There are people reminding themselves of the view, people exclaiming at this and that memory, people wandering among the foundations naming who used to live there, people on their way up to the dam across the creek checking out the water supply, people kicking turf from doorsteps, places of remembered cruelty, years of greed raising the ghosts of violent times and shaking the shafts of a rotted sulky. Those who had been children when they left remember it as a haunted ghost-town where plums and apricots grew mysteriously in the tangled scrub. Mary Buddall discovers the oldest inhabitant, Mrs Nell McAloon, accidentally left where they packed her, high on top of a wagon, her balding head birdlike and waggling, mad Nell the loony with her toothless mouth in an ecstatic grin, feeling herself a young woman again, waving a royal claw; while propped back to back with her sits her son and heir the oldest mongoloid boy in the world. Mary calls four men to lift the baggage down. Mrs McAloon emits whoops and whoos as the wind goes up her skirt.

– Viv'll be here before long son, Uncle chuckles as he observes Bill looking back down the ridge to where the walkers should soon be toiling up. Poor bugger's got himself fallen in love, he explains to Mercy Ping who vanishes at the thought. He'll find out!

And it is true, Bill has been thinking about Vivien all this time, not just about the warmth of her bed and being sure she's managing alright, but hoping the old folks like her, seeing her in his mind's eye strolling up the track swinging a switch at the rump of a lazy cow, shouting hoy to Mrs Collins's goat. Billy thinks. He thinks of her, or when not exactly thinking of her he suspects he ought to be, or rather that he owes it to her and can't help thinking of her, and hopes this is what she'll want, at least that she won't mind. He recalls the day he caught Uncle prowling in her house, his own jealousy pathetic. Had he forgotten the A.L. commemorated in a browning paint heart on a doomed building where so recently some of the population failed to accept the inevitable, killed by the timbers they had set in place to their own design?

– I wonder if Maggot and the boys are back? says Billy.

– The School of Arts, Uncle explains, was the only public building in Whitey's when you come to think of it. The only one they'd a had a right to paint up. No bastard'll be doin my place that's for sure.

– Except when you die.

– I'll last longer than that house a mine, don't you worry. I made the bugger, he jokes and you can see he's younger already with black hairs in his eyebrows again and he leans less on his sticks. Oy, how about you marryin that nitwit from Yalgoona, Billo, in memory of yer father.

– You've got to be joking. She can take her pick of millionaires now.

– You listen to me young fella, I'm yer grandfather an if I can't tell you yer business I don't know who can. Don't matter if Vivi's older than you, she's worth more than all the sheilas in Yalgoona. You treat er right and you won't regret it. Or else by christ I shall have to come and thump yus in the head. I'm not past it yet, you know.

– I'll thump you back, you bloody old stickybeak, Billy laughs. He laughs at anything now. The dazzling leaves dance round him, the mountain air tosses brightly across his face, he laughs at his ugly strong wise grandfather, laughs at his concerned expression, at the comical sight of all these great-aunts and great-uncles who won't die, who won't even lie down and do as they're told, laughs at their plodding concentration as they disentangle ropes and set up tent poles, as they shuffle about lugging boxes and baskets, laughs at the joyful panorama where rivers glitter far in the distance and the dense sea of treetops washes down against the shore of calm pastures. Even the flight of parrots rocketing among the branches carries echoes of a meaning you can understand. He laughs with love at his grandfather, head at a deafman's angle, smelling of sweat, horses, stale piss.

– Bill me boy I can tell what your trouble is. You're sufferin from an advanced case of youth, that's what.

Billy admits his own stupidity, trying to blow up the Golden Fleece alone and at night like a criminal, on the say-so of a jealous madman's secret.

Brinsmeads knew, the parrots are squawking.

Billy accepts them, calmly living out their lives with the power to bring down governments.

– That's the graveyard you was tellin me about isn't it? Uncle points with his elbow.

– Yes your dad Albert Swan died 1894.

– We used to picnic on them graves every year on All Souls' Day. Don't ask me why, but it seemed a good enough custom at the time. When I was your age, Uncle reverted to a previous subject. By jesus I gave them all a headache.

– You wouldn't be able to remember that far, would you?

Uncle's retort is interrupted by his hound Bertha barking a way up the back. People collect in a huddle beside the steam plough, then a deputation comes this way hastily.

– What's hatching do yer think?

So the neighbours gather round Uncle as their natural leader. Poor Ian McTaggart is left behind, a figurehead of his generation, sitting helpless on the grass arguing gently with his crippled wife, already on the lookout for a site to recommence his labour, a place for the new garden of circles, to be the last obsolete garden, and asking when Tony will come home to begin the work of carting the plants which can be moved. An event is unquestionably brewing; another group forms by the ammunition tent. Come and look at this, people are saying. Somebody's here before us. Yes, incredibly as you draw close you hear them say the place is inhabited. The Swans and others are drifting towards the waterhole, hearing how a Collins and a Buddall went to check out the water supply when the dog started barking and they noticed at the edge of the scrub these two trees growing in amongst each other, woven together by creepers, a tent of leaves. They are hearing the story with curiosity, alarm, disbelief, already arguing that it is impossible though they haven't seen for themselves yet, that Kel is dead and none of the new prospectors would have come this way. They reach the spot and sure enough find a tent of living leaves outside which is a steel toolbox and a heap of small bones swarming with ants.

Bill Swan stands among his forebears, alone. The feeling comes over him that he can be the ground under his own feet, he can experience his weight, quite heavy on his two heels, also the weight of his trunk bearing on his pelvis. Alone, he no longer finds the world a place of laughter, he grows cold thinking of Vivien with her burden of hopes, climbing towards this new disaster. He can feel his neck carrying his head and the head heavy with a new turmoil. He should have guessed! His arms hang weights from his shoulders. He opens and clenches the hand in his pocket so the lumps of muscle can be felt rising along his forearm. This is no comfort. He is weak with the knowledge of that one punch, Tony's first and only blow against him. There is a puzzle here he is not able to solve. Bill is not afraid, exactly, but the glittering summer of a few moments ago has darkened. He glances up at the mountain pulsing with life of its own. And assembles his courage.

– That's Tony's toolbox for sure, he says.

– Are yus in there Tony boy? calls Uncle in a strangely courteous voice. The dog wags her tail.

– Yes, replies Nobody.

– It's us mate, says Uncle. Us come to live here.

– We been worried about you Tony, Olive McAloon croons. Come on out.

A gentle singing issues from the leaf tent.

The citizens face one another, assessing what they dread this might signify. Billy freezes in a pool of loneliness exercising the muscles of his arm, ready for anything.

– Are yer comin out to say goodday to yer grandpa and us, Uncle asks eventually (listening to the song, that voice, hearing something in it he recognizes). His tone is even more careful when he repeats his invitation.

498

At the bottom of the leaf wall a hole opens and a shaggy fair head pokes out. Tony wriggles on the ground till he's clear. He stands up, smiling. He knows them of course. He thinks he is still Tony. But they see immediately that he is Nobody. His face works at holding the smile, painfully extreme. Long blond hairs sleek silkily down his body. And his face smiles also at Billy. Yes he recognizes Billy especially. Billy smiles shyly in return feeling a mug. They are no longer friends. They smile as intimate strangers and not with the same feelings. A wind whispers into the mountainside. Grasshoppers are busy communicating. The old people stand in the sunshine looking at the boy they knew who has grown up to be Nobody and must be respected. Yes age is, finally, irrelevant. To say he is young would not make sense. To say he is nineteen would make no sense at all.

– Winnin form, Uncle comments. We thought we'd let yous know we're here to settle.

The black snake that has been curled beside him in the warmth glides out to enquire into the disturbance.

They all stare at Nobody as they back away, and this becomes a notable moment. Nobody is still smiling at them. He knows them, he knows. But they must explain him, placate him for the water they need.

Our forest, Uncle will say. With its bellbirds and lizards, well that's the forest has got inside Tony's skull. Inside Tony is a forest a cockatoos that he's listenin to and flowers that he's touchin and smellin. He was lookin for this, lookin and lookin, Uncle will say. He was feelin lost all them years, but now he's found it, if you ask me, and singin like that he's singin to us out from among his trees. He's a long way off, that's my feelin, singin in the distance. And all of us is outside his forest of birds and animals, that's why he don't speak. What's the point a speakin? He couldn't be understood, so he has to think about that and it makes him a bit queer if you're not used to it. But I'd say this forest is in all of us, do you know that? It's just an idea I been tossin about. For us, we hear it faint-like, now and again and only when we're not tryin. But it's there. He hears it the whole time.

Olive McAloon rescues a forgotten experience, yes she was a child taken to church by her mother and seeing her first Christmas crib, the doll figures, wisemen, coming so far and all to see an ordinary baby, and having to be content with that. She was nervous and angry at the painted faces looking so unblinkingly. She felt a feeling then, and she remembers it now.

They move back: they will begin the work of water-carrying and pitching tents in a moderated mood, thinking about him with his toolbox outside. Yes it's good to know what's happened to the young fellow.

The crisis over, Nobody crawls into his place among the vines, warm again, a great responsibility resting in his heart. So this is what he has been waiting for. They have come to him and they will stay. He has established his place, the respect due to him, his freedom to do what he can do. The snake coils in its nest.

Billy thinks of Vivien again, Vivien and himself in Brinsmeads' shop clearing the goods off the shelves, the dead cat glaring at them from an open box of eucalyptus lollies, the shop whispering *miserable, miserable,* and as they left with the last load for the dray, the double-doors clashing to behind them batting at a mob of ghosts rushing to follow. HABERDASHERY BOOTS & SHOES (on one door), PROVISIONS PATENT MEDICINES (on the other) trembling with gold, mocking them because they are the new storekeepers, the living generation of Rememberers. Being together now won't be the same as it was. He sees something trivial in love, small warm and ridiculous, something that reminds him astonishingly of his own mother and father. Were they in love? he asks himself with wonder and disillusion. In a flash Billy realizes how his mother engineered that eternal game of euchre, that she lost by skill so brilliant he never saw it, lost for the sake of love. And his father, yes, his father cut down the tallow-wood also for love of, admit it, Bill himself How this was, he cannot yet figure out. Yet he knows it. And as Vivien approaches along the track of smashed scrub calling Get up there! hup! hoy! to the bewildered livestock he hopes this will be their kind of love, except that he has enough of his grandfather in him to laugh more at life, and Vivien's way will be differer from his mother's.

– You could trust her to meddle where she wasn't wanted, declares Miss Bertha McAloon referring to the late Felicia Brinsmead. She was into everything except the bath, that one.

Rose Swan, a mouse no longer, manages the Collins bull on a short halter.

– Git the hell along with you, screeches Miss McAloon routing a heifer from among the wattles.

Billy watches his grandmother and hears the admiring jokes people make at the expense of her short temper. He is filled with pity for the strong-willed. Vivien comes toward him with that loping walk. They stand together but he does not claim the liberty of kissing her, or possessing her in public. And instead of joking about the trek, provoking her to compete as usual, he says something he has just learnt.

– Are you tired love?

– She'd better not be, Uncle interrupts. Because we're goin to need the store opened as soon as the gear's unpacked. Look lively Eggie, time to set up the new pub, mate, the booze has come down to you from Jasper at last.

– Shove off Uncle, Billy suggests. He takes Vivien's hand and tells her about Tony.

– I have something terrible to tell you, she confesses. It happened between him and me. I can't stay. I could never live where Tony is now.

– Perhaps I know and he knows, Billy says to give her strength as he walks her slowly towards the waterhole, he in the light, she in the darkness, towards the tent of creepers where the wild man lives with his experience, strolling away from the comfort of everybody else, and on their own mission.

But then you see them stop to whisper, long entreaties and tender offerings coming out with such a rush her whole body flows towards him and her hair gets mixed with this, the dark among the dark. You watch him curve his hand to her belly, so that everyone can tell he is proud, feeling the new life stir. Their heads are in the sunlight, which also pours steadily on the mountain. They live on the food of that land and it's hard to tell them among the flowering trees.

– Miss Brinsmead and I shopped everywhere, Sebastian confides to the speechless Nobody in the secrecy of the leaf tent, to see if a better society could be bought for us with the Fleece. But we never found one.